To: Carla & Ro[...]

March 20 2023

M. S. Sanger

Thank you!

A.K.A

Sue Vogelsanger

GONE

M. S. SANGER

GONE by M. S. SANGER

Copyright © 2022 by M. S. Sanger

Book cover and interior designed by Ellie Searl, Publishista®

ISBN: 9781732880924

Lone Cypress Press
Marble Hill, MO

This book is dedicated to all my family and friends.

ACKNOWLEDGMENTS

I WOULD LIKE TO THANK my family and friends who have encouraged and cheered me on in the process of publishing this book. Especially, I thank Barb Bailey and Aaron Horrell for their beautiful interpretation of the crystal dish for the cover art. Thank you to Don Greenwood for his special drawing, and to Ellie Searl for her excellent cover and extensive formatting work. Lastly, thanks to Marcie Upchurch for her assistance in pulling it all together.

CHAPTER ONE

Saturday, May 10, 2003.

BRANDA A. CARSON WAS DOING morning stretching exercises before getting out of bed when she noticed the smallest toe on her left foot was gone. She lived alone in a one-bedroom one-bath apartment. **"Jumpin' George !!!!"** she yelled. **"I'm dreaming!!!"**

Sitting up, grabbing her foot, looking more closely proved she wasn't. There was no bleeding, no scarring, pain, tingling, or other evidence of anything traumatic enough to cause the phenomenon. It was as though there had never been any toe. A piece of her had simply disappeared!

Letting go of her foot as if it was a snake, she fought looking, unable to completely stop. Nor did she want to touch it again. She sat still for a moment, afraid moving would trigger more disappearance. She really didn't know what to do. She felt adrenaline rushing with fright-flight panic close on its heels but heard a bird chirping outside her partly open window like it was any normal day.

Barely realizing it, she instinctively reached over to a nearby small bedside upholstered chair, picking up her treasured foot-tall doll, Betty, from its usual resting place. Betty had been a childhood gift from her parents who by scrimping and saving had bought it for her one Christmas.

Branda had done her best to keep the lovely washable light blonde hair and removable pink organdy dress in good shape over the years. During times of stress or loneliness, she often privately talked to the doll because it reminded her of her parent's love. She knew some people would find that odd behavior for a grown woman, but it comforted her; much like people talking to pet dogs and cats. Plus, she had learned over the years not to always care too much about what others thought or said.

Shocked, gasping for a good breath, she said to Betty's consoling form, cradled in her arms, "I know being a waitress for 18 years has been hard on my feet, but . . .. This is almost silly. A toe of all things."

Although her voice's sound with its slight tinge of southern accent was comforting, she stopped talking. Continuing to sit on the bed she shivered,feeling a fear related chilliness nudging away warmth in the sunlit room.

Part of her wanted to start running out the door screaming for help, at least call 911, or friends. But her particular balance of the usual amount of human strengths and weaknesses stopped her. Her scales tipped her more toward being an extraordinarily private, strong-minded, person who always tried helping herself first.

"As Mother used to tell me. 'The best helping hands you'll ever have are right at the end of your own arms,'" she said, continuing her monologue to help bolster her spirits, chasing off chill and panic. She liked quoting sayings.

"Besides, if word leaked out about something this bizarre, it would jar loose every publicity seeking nutcase in the business. But I know this isn't only weird, it is something beyond serious." A semblance of calmness was creeping in while she was trying to breathe deeply.

She had once dreamed of becoming a nurse; maybe even a doctor. Lack of money and other factors prevented realization. She enjoyed reading material not only related to the medical field but also about many other subjects.

Friends often told her she should rent a room at the library since she spent a lot of time there. They didn't know the library was giving her the college education she desired but couldn't afford after graduating high school a month after she turned 18. There were other reasons she couldn't attend. Even now, it was sometimes hard to shut out those awful memories. Life had already slammed her around enough to teach her hard lessons.

Staring again at emptiness where her toe had been, she said, "In all of my 38 years I have never heard of or read about anything like this. But something caused it. There has to be a reason."

Taking positive action when faced with an obstacle was another of her strengths. Though still stunned and floundering, she managed to come up with ideas.

"I'll go to the library and see if I can find a book about this. If not, I'll try the clinic doctors or the emergency room over at St. John's Mercy. Or my primary care doctor if he's in today. Since doctors are not supposed to tell anybody else what goes on between them and a patient, maybe publicity would not be a problem."

Deep down she knew there would no doubt be a leak from some source.

"This is just the kind of stuff you read about in tabloids."

Although not the hysterical type, she was feeling fluttery beginnings of a butterfly flock in her stomach.

Plans involving action brought more ease. They also helped quiet a couple of her flip side qualities; feelings of vulnerability and inferiority.

"I'll have a lot of hours to read since it's my weekend off."

For the past 11 years, she had been working in the Neiman-Marcus Zodiac restaurant at Plaza Frontenac on South Lindbergh Blvd. in St. Louis, Missouri. She thoroughly enjoyed working there; especially since her 45-year-old boss and restaurant manager, Sean Truebridge, was such a fair-minded, kind person. For nine years before that, she had been a waitress in various other restaurants; mostly in southeastern Missouri.

After placing Betty back on the bedside chair and closing the window, Branda showered in the bathroom located just across the hall from the bedroom. Afterwards, back in the bedroom, she stood naked in front of her full-length three-way mirror, slowly turning, studying complete views of her slender five foot five well-shaped body weighing 115 pounds.

"Looks like all other parts are still here," she said, trying to sound brave.

She had splurged on buying this mirror because she knew how important it was in her job to look her best from all angles.

Her image also reflected her dark brown eyes, full lips, smooth light tan skin, and shoulder length light blonde hair. The straight style enhanced its silkiness. People often thought she dyed it since she had a smidgen of Cherokee Native American blood in her thanks to an ancestor named Light Moon. Not so. It was God given. Having met a blue eyed blond man once who was half Mexican, half Apache, she knew there was more to the subject than she knew about. Someday, she wanted to read more about genetics. She had also been told by a Cherokee medicine man his people preferred to be called Native Americans. He said when Christopher Columbus landed his boat in America and saw the people he thought he had landed in India so called them Indians. Not so. They were Native to America . . . therefore Native Americans.

Finally, slightly smiling at the mirror, she saw what people called a very pretty face plus her nice even teeth.

"At least they're still with me."

If it had been a magic mirror, it could have also reflected some personality facets; her sense of humor for one thing. For others, that people considered her to be a very nice thoughtful woman, but one who could also show a spunky temper and detested unfairness. Her sense of humor was double edged. Mostly she used it to spread joy to people, but sometimes it also served as a cover up for disturbing emotions.

She was still trying not to look at her disfigurement very much. Sometimes she succeeded.

"I may be imagining it but I think my balance is off a little bit too," she muttered while she began dressing. She had kept talking to Betty since that helped keep the butterfly gathering under control. The whole thing was taking on a surreal quality.

"This simply cannot be true."

Usually she liked wearing sandals on her days off, but today she selected a pair of red socks and tan loafers to go with her blue jeans and red Cardinal baseball team T-shirt. The combined feel of clean body and clothes lifted her spirits somewhat. Since the city was sporting springtime weather in the upper 70's, she didn't need a jacket.

After leaving her second floor apartment on Rue de la Banc just off Olive St. Road in suburban Creve Coeur, she got into her four-year-old blue Saturn, heading south for the library located near her workplace. The surrounding profusion of dogwood and redbud trees in bloom with bright yellow forsythia bushes showing off here and there cheered her.

An aroma of spring blossoms added another pleasant dimension.

Putting in a tape of Mexican music, which she loved whether played good or bad, she sat back listening to the song spiced with intermittent grita type yells and sounds plus the background bass thump-thump of the gitaron. It was such happy music. They could also play songs sad enough to make bronze statues bawl.

She had learned to like the music when periodically living down in the Rio Grande Valley in McAllen, Texas located a few miles from the border across from Reynosa, Mexico. Her parents would sometimes go down there to pick Valley citrus fruit.

The music and physical activity were somewhat easing but her mind was still spinning.

"I wish Kreis' was open this early," she said aloud. "I need to eat even though I don't feel like it."

Kreis', a short distance north of Plaza Frontenac on South Lindbergh Blvd., served, among other foods, the absolute benchmark for prime rib.

"Not that I want anything like that for breakfast. Boy, do I have a bad case of brain chatter," she said, realizing her thoughts and words were tumbling like clothes in a dryer. "Besides, they are only open for dinner."

"Maybe I could grab a quick bite at Schneithorst's," another good place also close by in the other direction. "Or I can go back home and scramble some eggs."

Entering the library, Annie, one of the librarians, greeted her. "Hi, Branda. What'll it be today? Something in A or Z?"

"Oh, I'm not sure. Think I'll just sort of browse." What else could she say. She sure wasn't going to broadcast part of her foot disappeared overnight.

After chatting briefly with Annie about weather and the Cardinal baseball team, Branda headed for the computerized index to see if there were any medical books about disappearing flesh. Her search turned up nothing. She noticed lots of goofy titles; none of whose subjects seemed of any use to her.

"Maybe I should get a Ripley's Believe It or Not book," she thought.

Later, she would search the Internet on her home computer that was dinosaur age but still worked okay for her needs. It had been a hand me down from a friend who had upgraded and Branda appreciated the gift. She still preferred reading books for information. Internet searching often drove her bats with its frequent dead ends.

She wound up checking out five books covering subjects about feet, flesh eating bacteria, and supernatural phenomenon with medical overtones.

Annie exclaimed, "Good grief, that's quite an assortment."

"Oh they just sort of caught my eye," Branda said, snatching them up as soon as they were ready. Heading for the door, she glanced back at Annie, saying, in what she hoped was a normal voice, "See you next trip." The butterflies were growing. Home seemed 1,500 miles away.

Knowing that eating keeps up strength, she scrambled two eggs and fixed a piece of whole wheat toast in the small kitchen adjacent to the larger combination dining area and living room. She skipped her daily vitamin dosage. "They wouldn't mix too well with my flock of flutter butters," she said, using another childhood term, like jumpin' George, her paternal grandpa had taught her. She felt like she was operating on automatic pilot.

After putting on her soft clothes, as she called her nightgown and robe, she propped up in bed, spending the rest of the day reading and napping.

By twilight, she had not found the slightest clue. More and more she dreaded the sight of her foot; trying hard not to look at it. She was grateful there seemed to be no other symptoms of illness. Fear of it happening again kept her from sleeping deeply during the night.

Making herself look the next morning, she was thankful there were no new changes. While dressing to go to her Southern Baptist church, she realized she was able to keep her eyes averted more and more.

"Should I mention this to Reverend Cummings, Betty? No . . . he's in to souls, not toes." Managing a faint smile at her small witticism, she added, "Maybe later."

She had forgotten but the church service reminded her. It was Mother's Day. Afterwards, in the car going home she cried bitterly. Not only for the loss of her mother last year, as well as her father, but for the loss of her own babies years ago.

Reading more the rest of the day turned up no clues. Searching the Internet on the computer in her bedroom was a dead end although there was some strange stuff on there.

"SHC . . . Spontaneous Human Combustion . . . whoever dreamed that one up?!!! Lots of pros and cons about folks bursting into flames for no apparent reason. Imagine that, Betty." She chuckled over the theory about people who drank a lot of alcohol were more likely to wind up SHC victims.

"Half the folks I know would have turned into cinders years ago. The stuff about static electricity makes more sense. Oh well, who can say. As I well know there are lots of mysterious unexplainable things going on in this world."

Magic Acts were the only things that turned up when she typed Disappearing Flesh into the Search box.

Getting ready for work the next morning, she thought the toe next to where the missing one had been looked odd.

"Oh, Lord," she prayed. "Please let me be dreaming this time!" A closer look showed it to be normal . . . or was it? "One time it looks okay . . . then again, it looks different. I am just imagining things now. Get dressed woman, get to work, and keep your mouth shut."

She was grateful to have her sturdy, comfortable work shoes. They not only covered her foot, but also helped correct the feeling she was a tiny bit unbalanced when she walked.

"Funny how one little missing toe can make a slight difference. I'm probably imagining that, don't you think, Betty?" Feeling a sudden sting of tears, she added. "Oh quit messing around and get to the clinic right after work." Her attempts at maintaining privacy and showing bravery were fast giving way to being scared to death.

"I've got to hang on until after work. I don't want anyone there to know."

But she should have known Sean would notice something was wrong the minute he saw her. He was probably more observant than most since he had once been a paramedic. Even her friends and coworkers, Mary Ann and Linda, asked if she was feeling okay.

"Just a sleepless night," she told them, hurrying off to take an order. "Talk to you later."

Sean was not put off so easily. "When you take your break please come to my office," he said, wearing a worried face instead of his usual happy one.

She did as he asked.

"Okay, Branda, what gives?" Sean asked. "You look like your world has ended."

Taking one look at Sean's kind nice looking face, she burst into tears; her vulnerable side breaking through the wall of strain she had been under. He walked over, taking her in his arms, comforting her. His lean, muscular, six foot two inch frame a safe haven.

Finally drying her eyes, she said, "Good grief! I had no idea of doing this."

"Branda, please tell me what is wrong. This isn't like you," he said, releasing her slightly.

Like a dam bursting, she flooded him with facts. When he asked to see her foot, she removed her shoe showing him. Even through her stocking he could see the problem as he knelt to look.

Without a word, Sean got up, went to his desk phone, and began dialing. After reaching an office and requesting to speak to Dr. Andrews, he waited for an answer. He nervously ran the fingers on his other hand through his conservatively cut straight black hair.

"Who are you calling?" asked Branda.

"A doctor friend of mine."

"But, Sean."

"But noth . . . hello Mitch, I have a friend I would like for you to see immediately if possible," pausing while the doctor evidently asked a question.

"No, I can't tell you that, "Sean answered. "It will be better if she shows you and tells you all about it. I doubt if you have ever had a case like this, but I hope you have so you'll know what to do."

Following another pause, after which he hung up the phone, Sean turned to Branda. "He'll see you at 2:30 this afternoon. I'll take you there."

"But, it's 1:30 now. I can drive myself if you tell me where the office is. What kind of doctor is he? How did you get me in so fast? What will I tell the other waitresses? My customers? I would like to keep this weird problem a secret as much as possible." She was babbling. In one way she wasn't ready for this. In another, she was greatly relieved.

"He's a doctor of Internal Medicine. I got you in so fast because Dr. Mitchell Andrews and I have been friends since first grade. Surely you've heard me mention him. He was best man at my wedding 25 years ago. His wife, Helen, who was then his fiancee' was my Cynthia's maid of honor. He is godfather to one of our twins, Erin. Helen was godmother to Sharon, the other one. He knows

I wouldn't call him asking a favor unless it is extremely important," Sean explained.

"Is he the one who moved to Dallas to practice shortly after his graduation?"

"That's right. But we have always kept in close touch. He only moved back here after his wife died a year and a half ago."

"I don't remember ever meeting him at any of your parties."

"He became a recluse and didn't want to be around crowds of people anymore; at least socially. As for the other girls, I fully understand your need for privacy but they'll want to know something. I suggest you go tell them some of it without elaborating and have them tell your customers. You have a foot problem not yet diagnosed that might affect your work . . . and your driving."

"I can still drive," Branda assured him. "I drove to work today."

"We'll see what Mitch has to say. Meanwhile, leave your car here in the underground parking lot. I'll alert Security it may be there a few days."

"But my neighbors will wonder why it's not parked in my space at the apartment."

"Tell them what you tell Mary Ann, Linda, and everybody else." Following a pause, he added, "By the way, Mitch has never completely gotten over losing his wife to brain cancer. Although basically a man with a lot of inner strength, he has lots of hang-ups over this. They were very much in love. He is angry with himself for not being able to cure her or find someone who could even though it was a no-win situation. I've heard that anger often shows up in his bedside manner which has been described as a real son of a you know what."

"Oh great jumpin' George!" she exclaimed. "Just what I need. My ex-husband is one of those."

Sean left momentarily to make arrangements for someone to cover for the two of them. He was not the kind of manager to leave remaining employees shorthanded.

She went to tell Mary Ann, Linda, and the other girls what Sean had advised her to say. They sympathized with her and said if she needed them to please call.

"Bless their hearts. They would pass out if they knew what is really going on. I wish I knew what is really going on. Let's hope this traumatized doctor does. I will just have to keep remembering one of my favorite prayers, Lord help me to remember nothing is going to happen to me today that You and I together can't handle."

Chapter Two

Following Sean's three staccato signaling raps on a hallway door marked Private, the door opened a crack then widened.

"Sean, good to see you," the doctor said, escorting Sean and Branda into his office.

"Same here, Mitch."

Hanging back, Branda watched as they bear-hugged each other like men do who have a special bond with each other. Since both were the same height and build, were tan, and had the kind of straight coal black hair showing bluish tints, they could have passed for brothers.

But after parting, the doctor turning to look at her more fully as Sean introduced them, she saw that was where resemblance ended. Sean's eyes were brown and gentle. The doctor's were darker brown, nearly black; hard looking, piercing right to her soul. Lines from suffering showing on his face. His lips looked like they could change from kissable to cruel in a heartbeat. A slight scar on his upper lip near the left end, and extending at an angle for a half-inch up toward his cheekbone made him look somewhat sinister.

She couldn't say why exactly, but instinctively she disliked him even though her soft caring side felt kinship and sympathy for him and his loss. For one thing, she sensed an arrogance about him that reminded her of Connor Carson, her ex-husband. Also, he was handsome like Connor; something she had learned to almost consider a flaw.

In later years she had realized heart and soul mattered more than looks. She couldn't pinpoint other reasons. But it was more than perhaps being brainwashed by what Sean had told her about the doctor's bedside manner.

While the men were talking about what was going on in their lives, she silently mused, "Truthfully, I can count on one hand the amount of men I like and trust, and I'm not real sure about a couple of them. But I know one thing for sure. I never want to have anything to do with any man ever again. One trip on the marriage merry-go-round was enough for me."

A couple of times she noticed the doctor glancing at her.

Continuing her musings, she added, "If it wasn't for Sean, I would run right out of here."

But feeling a loyalty and obligation to Sean, she would not let him down no matter what. Even though he knew about her past, he had not judged her. He helped her regain a lot of self-esteem she had lost years ago. Not even changes in modern attitudes about what she had done had ever completely erased the shame she still sometimes felt. She realized attitude changes were around in her day, especially in large cities, but not where she grew up. Sean had been the most help by explaining she was a victim; not any other name she had been called. And he was totally sympathetic about the tragedy she had suffered. He was her friend as well as a fine boss. His wife, Cynthia, had also been a big help to her and was also her good friend. She also loved Sean and Cynthia's five children who had no knowledge of her story. They called her Aunt Branda. The twins, Erin and Sharon, were 24, living in San Jose, California since college graduation and running their own restaurant called The Third Place. Paul, 22, Steven, 20, and Jim, 19 were away attending various colleges. Most of their summers were spent in California helping their sisters at the restaurant. They spent about two weeks in St. Louis.

"And now," she thought, "Sean has taken time and made an effort to arrange this appointment trying to help me once again. If I reject the doctor's help, I will, in a way, be rejecting Sean. And I simply must remember Sean and Dr. Andrews are extremely close friends. Maybe my health insurance won't cover his costs and that will let me out gracefully."

As Sean headed out a door leading to the waiting room, Dr. Andrews came toward her.

"Follow me," he said, brusquely, flicking a cool look over her as if taking measure. "Hurry along now. I have other patients waiting."

She got the feeling there was something about her that bothered him and he wished she would go away. He was all business now, hardly looking at her.

Upon reaching an examination room, he asked, sternly. "Now just what is this emergency?"

By then, the two were standing fairly close staring at each other much like battle foes.

From out of the blue, scents of his aftershave and overall maleness triggered sexual emotions in her she had long kept buried deep as an Egyptian mummy. Connor had caused her to hate the sex act but she still had normal urges and sex dreams sometimes. At heart, she was even a romantic. When the doctor abruptly stepped back, she wondered if he was having similar reactions to her.

"Get a grip woman," she thought. "None of that nonsense. He probably took a step back because you had some dumb look on your face." The moment passed.

Despite being temporarily rattled, Branda was certainly beginning to see what Sean meant about the bedside manner. Since she was Sean's friend, she had hoped the doctor would go a bit easier with her. Maybe he was. Maybe he could be worse. She would not let Sean know. Totally out of character, Branda had an urge to shock Dr. Mitchell Andrews and put a dent in his arrogance; not caring whether his overbearing manner was real or a cover up for some other emotion.

"Part of my foot has disappeared," she said, curtly.

"What do you mean . . . disappeared?" he mimicked, emphasizing the last word. "Body parts don't just disappear," again emphasizing the final word.

"Well one of mine has," she almost yelled; indignant, thinking someone ought to report this guy to the AMA.

Giving her another one of those cold looks, he said, "Calm down and let me look. Sit up on the examining table."

She got the idea he thought she was wasting Sean's time and his.

Removing her shoe, she fought a strong urge to throw it at him.

Looking at her foot a moment, then examining it more closely, he said. "Take off the pantyhose." Pausing, he added, "I'll step outside. Open the door when you're ready."

She did as directed then sat back up on the examining table.

She watched as he stared more intently at her foot then absentmindedly, as if in slow motion, pulled a nearby stool closer to her and sat.

Taking her foot in his hands, examining it from all possible angles, he asked, "What in the hell happened here? Were you born this way? Are you sure you're not into self-mutilation?"

"Do you see any scars? I'd think you of all people would know it would take one jumpin' George of a plastic surgeon to perform any surgery like this . . . much less a lay person hacking around."

"One jumpin' what!!?"

"Oh never mind. I'm telling you I woke up Saturday morning and that part of my foot was gone. Now have you, or have you not, ever seen or heard about anything like this?"

She noticed he was turning pale.

"No!! Never!!! This can't be happening!!!!" he came close to shouting, letting go of her foot and quickly walking out of the room.

Thinking she heard him mutter, "Wait here," before closing the door, she continued sitting on the examining table.

"What can't be happening?" she wondered. "It sounded like he was referring to something else."

In a few moments there was a knock on the door and a nurse came in carrying a hospital gown. Instinctively, Branda crossed her legs at the ankles hoping to hide her disfigurement.

"Hello, Mrs. Carson," the nurse said. "The doctor will be back in a few minutes. Please completely disrobe and put on this gown." She started to leave.

"Just a moment," said Branda. "Would you please tell a gentleman in the waiting room named Sean Truebridge that he doesn't have to wait for me. I can take a taxi."

"Will do," said the nurse, heading for the door.

Thirty minutes passed before Dr. Andrews came back.

"Nurse Malone gave Sean your message. He says to tell you he will wait; not to worry."

Some, but not all, of his edginess was gone. She could tell he was apparently trying to holster his verbal six-guns.

"At least for the moment," thought Branda. "I wonder what or who changed him?" She would try following suit.

After checking her vital signs and reflexes he told her to get dressed; he would be right back.

"Are my vital signs and reflexes normal?" she asked, before he could get completely out of the room."

"Yes," he answered, somewhat sternly, his dark eyes giving her another one of those soul-probing glances as he was leaving.

As she dressed she wondered why his behavior bothered her so much. It was reasonable for him to still have problems connected with the death of his wife. She certainly had her share of lingering complexes.

"But why do we keep lighting up like 4th of July sparklers around each other? Oh well, I have other more serious things to worry about."

She tried not to think about how she had to steel herself against letting his touch affect her during the routine examination. A couple of times she thought she detected a slight hesitation on his part about touching her.

"This is crazy," she thought. "Thank goodness he suggested I see my own gynecologist and have mammogram and Pap smear results faxed back to here."

Hearing a knock on the door a few minutes later, she said, "Come in."

Dr. Andrews entered, saying as he came in, "Since we don't have a file on you, I need to ask you some questions. Let's free up this room and go back to my office."

"What about your other patients? I'm taking up a lot of your time."

"I've already made arrangements with the other doctors here to cover for me. I'll do the same for them sometime." Seeing her look of concern, he added, "I didn't tell them anything about your peculiar condition. I told them I have an emergency situation."

"Thank you."

Walking down the corridor toward his office, she asked, "Will you be having tests run or confer with other doctors? I would like for this to be kept as secret as possible."

"I understand about the secrecy part, but I really doubt if that will be possible later on. I will do my best though." With some former edginess to his voice, he added, "And of course, I will be ordering tests done and have conferences with other doctors. That will involve a lot of people. In fact, I've asked Nurse Malone to come to my office and get samples for blood panel testing; also a urine sample. You may use my office bathroom for that. Either we can get a stool sample some other time or your OBGyn doctor can do that if you prefer when you go for your Pap smear and pelvic exam."

Branda guessed she had insulted his medical savvy by asking about tests and conferences. "I'll wait until I go for the Pap smear and pelvic exam."

She sensed there was a big battle going on inside him between his s.o.b. side and a nicer one.

"He reminds me of a teeter-totter going up and down between the two sides," she thought. "And at the slightest provocation. This man needs help as much as I do."

And he sure could trigger an unusual unpleasant side of her that made her dislike him more. He made her lose her usual calm mental balance.

After reaching the office, he motioned for her to sit on the leather couch. He sat in a nearby matching chair, rested a clipboard on his thighs, and began asking questions.

"Full name?"

"Branda Anderson Carson."

"That's an unusual first name."

"My dad wanted to call me Brenda. Mother liked the name Brandi so they sort of combined the two."

"I see."

She wasn't sure he did.

"Your age? And no lies. It could be important."

She bristled. "I'm not a liar. My parents raised me better than that. I'm 38. Birth date May 19, 1965. You can check records at the Southeast Missouri Hospital in Cape Girardeau, Missouri if you don't believe me."

"I just may have to check those records. Not to check on your truthfulness, but in case I might find something in those records explaining what has happened to you. Although, as I indicated before, I have never ever heard anything anywhere about this puzzling condition. Also, have your primary care physician send me copies of your medical file. I will have to confer with him." Seemingly to ease the tension, he asked, "Was Cape Girardeau your home?"

"No. I grew up in Morley, a small town 21 miles south of there; population under 1,000. I did move to the Cape later," she answered, using the colloquialism the Cape.

"Do you have any siblings? I mean brothers or sisters?"

"I know what the word means. I had one brother. He died of spinal meningitis two years before I was born. My parents died last year in a car accident."

After gleaning all of the information he could about childhood diseases, allergies, family member medical history, health and exercise regimens, plus other basics, he said, "I find nothing that even remotely explains your problem. You are basically a very healthy woman. And I find it interesting about your Cherokee heritage from your mother's side. I can tell you are rightfully proud of that."

"Yes, I am," she said.

"By the way, how does your allergic reaction to Aloe Vera affect you? It's not a common one."

"Wherever it's applied turns red, burns, and itches."

"I see. I have a few more questions then we'll call it a day."

"Fine."

A knock on the door interrupted.

"Yes?" he asked.

"It's Nurse Malone."

"Come in please," he said.

"Hello again Mrs. Carson. I'm Karen Malone. I'm here for the samples."

The nurse left after her job was done then the doctor continued his questioning.

"Were you ever married? If so, for how long?

"Why is that important?" She felt a bit faint, not liking the direction his questions were headed.

"The more I know about you, physically, mentally, and emotionally, the better chance I and other doctors have of finding something out about this odd phenomenon."

She could tell he was working hard at being kinder.

"Yes, I was married once. For two years. We're divorced."

"Any unusual reason why it was so brief?"

"Yes," she said quietly. "Connor was physically and verbally abusive plus neither of us could handle the deaths of our twin baby sons, Josh and Jason. They were only 11 months old. They died two days apart. They're buried in the New Lorimier Cemetery at the Cape." Tears were stinging her eyes. She dabbed at them with a tissue.

"I'm sorry to have to ask this. I know it's hard, but what caused their deaths?"

"A viral respiratory infection."

"I'm able to sympathize with you because I lost my wife to brain cancer a year and a half ago."

"I'm sorry for your loss too," she said, somewhat surprised he mentioned it. She thought it best not to let him know Sean had already told her.

Continuing, he asked, "Are you still in touch with your ex-husband? I may need to talk to him."

"No way. He deserted me a few months after the babies died. I will say, although he was unfaithful during a lot of our marriage, after the twins were born he really did try for awhile to be a good father and husband. We were just too young. I have no idea where he is . . . and don't care. Anderson is my maiden name. I kept his name of Carson for the sake of legalities where the babies were concerned."

"How old were you two?"

"I was 18 when we married. He was 20."

"Is there more to this story? Is there even something more about this part of your life that caused, and is still causing, you a great amount of stress? Stress reactions, even delayed and suppressed, can sometimes bring about strange reactions in people."

"Yes, there's more," she said, thinking what difference does it make if he knows. Part of her cared what he thought of her, part of her didn't. Being a doctor, he can't tell anybody. Besides, she was feeling tired, warm, and a bit light-headed. She really just wanted to go home and get in her bed. "It's the classic cliché story. Connor seduced me the summer after I graduated high school. I got pregnant that first and only time I let him get near me until after we had to get married. Connor wanted me to have an abortion but I would never agree to that. I had just had my 18th birthday the month before graduation."

Dr. Andrews said, "Although in today's world, that is not considered as earth shaking an event as it used to be, I imagine in a small town like Morley it would have been."

"You have no idea!" Branda exclaimed. "I not only brought shame to myself and Connor, but to my parents, his parents and other family members, friends, and the whole town. The majority of people in Morley were, and are, law-abiding, God-fearing folks with a strict moral code. The rest of the world would do well to copy some of their philosophy. However, some believed even the little babies were tainted, but I never thought that. They were too innocent."

"I agree. How long had you known Connor?"

"Just a couple of months. He had come down from St. Louis to visit a widowed aunt in Morley during the summer. He was to paint her house and lend help in other ways. I'm not sure he did too much. Later I thought maybe his parents just wanted him out of their hair for awhile. I had never met anybody like him before. He was like a handsome blonde god, drove a red Cadillac convertible, and had money because his folks were pretty well off. He was majoring in journalism at Missouri University in Columbia. It was like having a movie star in town and he knew it. Conceited as jumpin' George."

"What are those words you use?"

"It's something grandpa taught me as a kid. They're sort of substitute cuss words since my family didn't believe in cussing."

"I see. Go on."

She actually saw a smile play across his mouth.

"I was flattered he took a shine to me. Dad and Mom kept warning me about a boy like Connor, but I didn't listen. After our shotgun wedding, Connor and I moved to Cape Girardeau to escape gossip. My parents kept on loving me but his parents had little to do with us until the babies came. They did adore them as much as mine did. Now my parents are dead and his parents blame me somehow for the deaths of Josh and Jason which is nonsense. They also accused me of seducing Connor. I'm feeling very tired and a bit woozy. May we stop for now?"

"Of course. I'm sorry," he said as he busied himself gathering up his notes and taking them over to his desk.

Hearing a gasping sound, he quickly turned around and saw she had gone white. In horror, she was staring at her left foot. Moving closer, he looked.

Through her pale cream-colored stockings they could see her remaining four toes were glowing, changing from pale yellow to light green then to red. As they stared transfixed, the affected toes slowly disappeared leaving a faint acrid odor drifting in the air. The rest of her foot never changed color. Her stocking hung limp where her toes had been.

Dr. Andrews was so stunned he barely caught her as she fainted, slumping forward, nearly falling to the floor. He gently moved her back on the couch easing her whole body onto it.

"My God. I'm not sure I can deal with this no matter what Sean says."

After quickly checking Branda's vital signs using equipment he kept in his office, he determined they were all right for the fainted state she was in. However, the ear thermometer registered two degrees which he thought was odd. Her foot felt unusually warm.

Going to his desk, he spoke to his nurse, Karen Malone, on the intercom asking her to please have Sean come to his office. "And please find a blanket to send along with him."

After a few moments, he checked Branda's vital signs again. All were back to more normal readings. There was no temperature and her foot was no longer unusually warm.

"Damnedest thing I ever saw," he thought as he stepped into the small bathroom to wash his hands. "I wonder if whatever this is is contagious?"

Going to the office closet he took out his sports coat and spread it over Branda, covering her foot. He wanted to keep her warm in case she might be going into shock. Looking at her more closely to see if her breathing was okay, he thought, "My lord, she looks so . . . vulnerable."

Stray strands of hair were covering part of her face. Gently, he moved them back into place.

He didn't know she was beginning to regain consciousness but wanted to just lie there quietly for a moment. She wasn't ready to face the world yet. The touch of his hand had unnerved her a bit but his sports coat, being more inanimate, was having a calming effect; like being in the arms of a loved one. She didn't like one bit, nor understand, some of her reactions to this man.

As Sean walked in, and the two men started talking, she decided to remain still a little longer.

Seeing Branda lying on the couch, Sean asked, "What's wrong?" He handed Mitch the blanket nurse Malone had given him.

"She had another attack or whatever you can call it. The other four toes on that foot have disappeared." He lifted his coat off of Branda, tossing it across a nearby chair.

Before replacing it with the blanket, Sean saw the affected foot.

"Oh dear God. Did you see it happen?"

"Yes, we both did. That's when she fainted. I almost wish I could have. Sean, it was the most bizarre thing I have ever seen." After a slight hesitation, he continued, "Sean, I simply cannot go through with this. Although I must admit, as a doctor, this strange occurrence intrigues me."

"You promised you would try. Remember our talk while you left her waiting in the examining room?"

"Yes, and I'm sorry to let you down. Because she is your friend, I thought maybe I could handle this for your sake. I even tried improving my bedside manner around her; not always too successfully I might add. But this is looking more and more like the same road I traveled with Helen and you know I swore I would never go there again as long as I live. Not being able to save her, or find someone who could, left scars that may never heal. Sean, you know how very deeply I loved Helen. Branda would be better off with another doctor.

"I don't think so, Mitch. Like I suggested to you before, you would definitely be the best person to supervise her treatment and I really feel she would be good therapy for you too. Be realistic, Mitch. You know there's not a doctor in the world that can save each and every patient. Besides, you really have no idea if she is terminal or not."

"My head tells me all that, Sean, but as I've told you, my emotions have caused me to flatly refuse to treat any patients that are even remotely in danger of dying. I simply cannot handle that yet. Perhaps in time. And you know my colleagues have been more than patient with me. They understand and support me. They make sure I only have to take care of patients who have more than a fighting chance. Branda's case has unknown factors. Why, I don't even know whether or not she is contagious." After a moment's hesitation, he added, "Besides there is a sweetness about her that would make my job even tougher. I hate the thought of ever seeing her hurt anymore." Confidentiality between doctor and patient prevented him from letting Sean know he knew Branda's story although he knew Sean could probably figure out that he did. "I'm beginning to see why you and Cynthia like her so much. She sure can get riled up too," he added.

"What about the Hippocratic oath you took?" Sean asked.

Mitch laughed sarcastically, and said, "Sean, there have been so many watered down versions of the classical original one, some doctors now call it the 'Hypocritical Oath.' But, of course, I honor the basic principles despite my personal limitations."

"I'll make a deal with you Mitch," Sean said.

"What kind of deal?"

"You keep on treating her until you positively know she hasn't a chance, God forbid. If that happens, I'll understand if you turn her case over to another doctor. Agreed?"

"But I can't just abandon her. That isn't ethical. Nor would it be fair to her. I would rather bow out now."

"We can work out something," Sean offered.

After some hesitation, Mitch said, "If we can, then I'll agree."

"Okay," Sean continued. "If you find yourself unable to continue, I will insist on getting another doctor for her. She must have the best possible treatment. From the way you feel, I don't think you would be the best man for the job at that point."

"I fully agree. Meanwhile, Sean, I will do my very best. You're right. I need to get on with my life." The agreement, with its possible loophole, also made him feel less trapped in a situation that he still may not be ready to handle emotionally. That helped.

Sean said, "And Mitch, you know I'll be giving you my support all the way."

"I know, Sean. Thanks."

After shaking hands on their agreement they began making plans.

As Branda had listened to the conversation, she came close to fainting again. The thought of possibly dying from this strange ailment had not solidly crossed her mind until now. Surely there was a cure somewhere. She wasn't ready to give up at this point. And now that she better understood where Dr. Andrews was really coming from, she would try being more tolerant no matter how much he sometimes irritated her.

"Complexes like his have to be extremely tough on a doctor; especially on a man like him who appears to have a good deal of basic strength of character," she thought. "I must find out about my health insurance. If it's no good here, that will let Dr. Andrews off the hook as well as me. I'll give them a couple more minutes then I want to get out of here."

But the next words Dr. Andrews spoke galvanized her into instant action. He was saying, "The only immediate solutions I see are to either move her to St. John's and put her in isolation, move her to my house, or I move into her apartment. I want to be with her 24/7 until I see where this thing is going. I'll make arrangements to have the other doctors take over my practice for the time being. I'll tell them I'm needed to supervise an unusual case indefinitely and that's no lie." He added, "Although I will no doubt need their help later on."

Sitting bolt upright, startling Sean and the doctor, Branda spoke. "The jumpin' George you will do any of the things you mentioned."

"How long have you been awake?" Sean asked, looking worried.

"Just long enough to hear those three wacky plans, none of which is going to happen." She decided a white lie was in order at this point. She did not want either of them to know all she had overheard. That would serve no purpose.

"Mitch isn't sure yet if you are contagious," Sean said. "He is just trying to come up with some protective safety measures until more tests are done."

"I need to keep you under close surveillance for many reasons," the doctor said. "For instance, who knows if or when another attack will come and if it does, what will be affected. I don't think it is wise for you to be alone now. And I believe I'm the best person to stay with you at this point."

Branda said, "Maybe so, but I'm afraid someone in the hospital would leak the story about what is happening to me. And I don't want a situation where we are living together in your place or mine because that will start the kind of talk I hate."

"Then we'll get married."

It was a toss-up over who looked the most startled, Sean or Branda.

"My word," mumbled Sean.

"In a pig's eye," Branda said. "I swore I would never ever marry again or have anything to do with men again . . . romantically speaking, that is. My ex-husband cured me for life."

"Believe me this is just an emergency measure on my part," said Dr. Andrews, emphatically. "It would only be for the sake of your safety, my convenience, and your need for keeping up proper appearances. We can divorce later."

"Not even for all of those reasons. I have a cell phone I can use to call you or Sean for help; even 911 as a last resort since that would end my privacy about this. That's enough safety for me, thank you. I don't need a man around for that."

Dr. Andrews asked, "And what if you faint again and are unable to call?"

"I'll call when I come to."

"I'm sorry to bring this up, but what if the worse case scenario happens and some part or parts of you disappear that are necessary for using a phone? Or you can't reach me or Sean?"

"Mitch!" Sean exclaimed.

"I'm sorry. But she needs to fully realize the seriousness."

The last few remarks blew some of the steam out of Branda's arguments. "I'll give it some thought. Meanwhile, may I go home now?"

"Yes," said Sean, "but to my home, for tonight anyway. "Cynthia will need to know about this sooner or later. Since she is a registered nurse, she won't be as easily shocked as a lay person might be."

"But what if I am contagious. Sean, you may have already been exposed, for which I would be terribly sorry; for you too, Dr. Andrews, but Cynthia hasn't?

"Good point, Branda," Sean admitted.

"Oh for heaven's sake," Dr. Andrews interjected. "Branda, I completely understand your need for keeping your reputation spotless, but this situation is more serious than that at the moment. And we'll deal with contagion if and when we have too. I have another suggestion."

"Now what," Branda said. "I'm really not feeling too well."

"Sean, if you wouldn't mind, would you come spend a few nights at my house?" Mitch asked. "Then Branda could come too since you'd be there at night as acting chaperone, not that it will be necessary as we all know. You could explain to Cynthia since, as you mentioned, she will need to know about Branda's condition sooner or later."

"I'd be glad to," Sean answered.

Looking at Branda, Mitch added, "My house is not very close to any neighbors, and the ones that are there are use to my odd hours, comings and goings as a doctor. They are not nosy. That will also give you time to think over my marriage proposal. If we're married, we can move to your place where I think you would feel more comfortable in your own surroundings. You feel okay about having Sean as chaperone at my house, don't you?"

"Yes, absolutely." Branda answered. "But it might seem odd to anyone who found out I'm there with two men. However, I'll go along with your suggestion if it's okay with Sean and Cynthia. I do need time to think." She mainly just wanted to go somewhere and be quiet; preferably home, but that seemed out of the question at this point. She was feeling really tired, somewhat warm and weak.

She remained seated on the couch while Dr. Andrews went off to make arrangements with his staff.

When Sean called Cynthia, she heard him explaining what was going on. He made arrangements for Cynthia to pack a bag for him and leave it on their front porch for him to pick up later. He also asked her to pack some clothes for Branda until one of them could get to Branda's apartment and get her own clothing and other necessary items. Sean had stopped talking and was listening to what Cynthia had to say.

Branda leaned back, resting with her eyes closed until Dr. Andrews came back. Sean was just hanging up as the doctor walked in. The two stood talking with their backs to her.

As she started putting on her shoes, the two smallest toes on her right foot began glowing. She moaned, "Oh no, oh no."

Sean and Dr. Andrews turned around. They watched the colors change from pale yellow to light green to red and the toes fade away. That part of her hose softly collapsed. The faint acrid odor arose.

"Dear God," exclaimed Sean.

Dr. Andrews sat down beside her ready to catch her if she fainted. He quickly checked her vitals that were in the normal range except for the two degrees of temperature. Again, her foot felt unusually warm. He put an arm around her for support. Instinctively seeking comfort, Branda leaned against him and said, "Let's go home, Dr. Andrews, please let's go home."

"To my house?"

"Anywhere. I just want to rest."

"And we'll get married as soon as we can arrange it?"

"Yes."

CHAPTER THREE

WRAPPING BRANDA IN THE LIGht weight cream colored blanket he had used to cover her in his office, Dr. Andrews picked her up and carried her out to his car; a 2001 black four-door Grand Marquis. Nestling against him was restful; his strong arms comforting. She was so weary and unnerved, her dislike for him was dimming.

Walking, he said, "After what we've all been through this afternoon and having Sean for a mutual friend, I think it's time you stopped calling me Dr. Andrews. How about Mitch?"

Looking up to his face, she saw his mouth curving into a faint smile. "He really is trying to be nice but I know how he can switch in a second; just like Connor," she mused. Aloud, she said, "All right. Why not."

She was too tired to think about it. So much had happened so quickly it was as if time was being shrink-wrapped.

Sean handed Branda her purse and shoes he had carried. He helped Mitch get her settled, sitting up in the roomy back seat, then said, "There has been a change in plans."

"What?" asked Mitch, standing by the back car door he had not yet closed.

"All of us are going to my house after all. Cynthia insists. She says a woman's touch could come in handy here."

"She could be right," Mitch said. "But what about possible contagion?"

"That doesn't worry her. As you know that green-eyed red head can be feisty and stubborn even if she isn't any bigger than a minute. She said to remind you she is a registered nurse."

"I know. That could definitely be a plus now and later on too."

Branda spoke up, "But I don't want to put her in jeopardy. And isn't she still working part time at St. John's?"

"She figured you would worry about that but says not to," Sean said. "As for the job, she says she will work something out if necessary. And she definitely wants Doctor Mitch on hand at our house."

"Maybe that is a better plan," Branda said, leaning over to put on her shoes so she could try walking later plus not shock Cynthia. She could hardly bear looking herself.

"Then it's settled," said Mitch. "Sean can you follow me home so I can get some clothes and other things to take to your house? It won't take me long. I don't want to leave Branda alone in the car." The two lived fairly close to each other in the St. Louis suburb of Ladue.

"Fine. I'll call Cynthia on the cell phone and let her know what's up. She also said earlier, she wants to plan a nice wedding for you at our house with just the four of us in attendance. We will stand up for you. What kind of official do you want to perform the ceremony?"

"She shouldn't go to any trouble under the circumstances," Branda offered.

"She understands fully, but still wants to make it nice. Besides, she loves planning weddings, parties, and that sort of thing."

"There's no harm I suppose," said Branda. Turning to Mitch, she asked, "Do you have a preference about what sort of official marries us?"

"No. Do you?"

"I like the Baptist preacher where I attend church, but under the circumstances, I think a judge or justice of the peace would be fine. I really don't want to alert anybody I know about my condition unless I absolutely have to."

"Anyone is fine with me," said Mitch. "Tomorrow we had better start getting preliminary work done. You know, blood tests, license. All that sort of thing. That is, if you feel up to it." Pausing for a moment, he added, "And as soon as possible I want to get started arranging for other types of tests and consultations."

"All right."

Later that night she got her first taste of what it would be like to be married to Mitch and have him around all the time; especially in her bedroom.

After their arrival in front of Sean's house, Branda insisted on getting out of the car by herself, standing alone, and walking. Mitch gave his okay. She did surprisingly well though limped a bit.

Cynthia had greeted her warmly, hugging her, making her feel wanted and welcome. All of them chatted for a while discussing the various issues.

Finally Cynthia broke in, "That's enough for now. You men go fix a drink for yourselves while I get Branda settled in the downstairs bedroom."

"Thanks, Cynthia," said Branda as the two women headed off. "I am tired."

"I've already laid out some nightclothes for you; also some clothing you can wear tomorrow. It all belongs to Erin who is more your size than I am. She left some things here when she moved. Then, if you feel up to it, we can go get your things tomorrow before you and Mitch go take care of the marriage paperwork. Are you hungry?"

"No. I just need to rest," Branda said.

"Fine. I'll check on you when dinner is ready to see if you want a bite then. If you need me before just call on that intercom on the nightstand."

"Thanks."

"Is there anything I can do to help you get ready for bed?"

"No thanks." She wasn't quite ready for Cynthia to see her disfigurement.

"Oh Branda, I am so sorry about all of this," said Cynthia. "You know you can stay here as long as you want."

"I know, but Mitch thinks it best to move to my place after we're married; familiar surroundings and all that."

"How do you feel about it?"

"I agree, I think. It's hard to decide now."

"You can always come back here if that doesn't work out."

"I know and thanks. Oh, Cynthia, I am so scared."

The two hugged and cried for a moment before Cynthia left to go join the men for a drink. She would have been glad to bring one to Branda, but she knew Branda did not drink liquor.

When Cynthia came in later to see if Branda wanted something to eat, Branda was sound asleep. After checking with Mitch, it was decided to let her sleep.

The minute Branda awakened she sensed someone was in the room. With a night-light to see by she stayed still, carefully looking through just barely opened eyes. Mitch was lying on a nearby couch watching her. He was still fully clothed except for his shoes.

"The nerve of him," she thought. "He knows I would not agree with him doing this. I'll just pretend to be asleep and maybe he'll leave."

He didn't.

Closing her eyes all the way, she could still feel his gaze that made her uncomfortable. Trying to seem natural, she slowly moved turning her back toward him. While turning, she was also able to pull the sheet up to cover herself better.

"Well, that's silly," she mused. "He's a doctor used to seeing bodies."

She hated the way her disfigured feet felt against the soft cotton sheets. She quietly cried before falling asleep again.

At first light, she was awakened by a hand brushing strands of hair away from her face. She had turned back over during the night. Again, through barely opened eyes, she looked. This time Mitch was in a chair he had pulled up by her bedside and was intently watching her with those dark piercing eyes. He was just moving his hand away from her face.

Eyes wide open now, she asked, "What are you doing here, Mitch? You know I don't think this is proper." She sat up in bed pulling the sheet to hide some of the upper part of her body that was showing a bit from the top of her nightgown. She noticed his darting glance before she managed to fully cover herself.

Abruptly, Mitch stood up and said, "Dammit, Branda, I'm your doctor, not your lover. I don't want to upset you, but you must put some of those puritanical notions aside under the circumstances. Besides, we're going to be married in a few days so what does it matter?"

"Jumpin' George. That line is so old it has twenty mile long whiskers."

"Sean and Cynthia understand the situation. Why can't you? This is absolutely ridiculous!"

"I guess my old hang-ups just won't let go."

"Work on it," he said rather curtly, then continuing, "Branda, we have a lot of work ahead of us. Let's not let personal problems get in the way."

Realizing he was including his own hang-ups without saying so, Branda said, "I'll try." She could not say anything without letting him know what Sean had told her plus what she had overheard.

Mitch added, "The only thing you need to keep in mind is I am a doctor who is going to do his best to help you."

"Thank you, Mitch. Have you ever had any case faintly resembling this one?" Branda asked, trying to ease the tension.

"No, and one of the first things I want to do is check with the Board of Health to see if any other such cases have been reported. I also want to do some research on my own. I have quite an extensive library in my house." After a pause, he added. "I must admit this problem is most intriguing."

Branda said, "I tried finding information about the condition in some library books this past weekend."

"And?"

"Nothing even came close. I did find that phenomenon SHC interesting though."

"I've never quite believed in that although there have allegedly been documented cases. So you're a reader?"

"My friends think almost obsessively so."

"Any particular subject?"

"No. Although I do like reading medical information."

"Good. Then you can help me with doing reading research."

"You mean you'd trust a dumb little ol' country gal like me to do that?"

"Now where in hell did you get the idea I thought about you like that?"

"I just naturally thought a big city feller like you would think so."

She was pretty sure Mitch was about to really give her a verbal shot when he noticed the faint smile on her mouth ending in eye twinkle.

When she knew he had caught on, she laughed and said, "My friends also think I have a sense of humor."

"They're right. Although how you can use it during this crisis, I have no idea. You really are a strong person."

"I've had to be. But I also fail a lot."

"Don't we all?" Steering clear of the subject he asked, "Would you like to shower first?"

"No, you go ahead. I'll take a cat nap." This intimacy made her nervous.

After breakfast, the four sat discussing plans; especially regarding when and how much to tell Branda's friends. She had not kept in touch with aunts, uncles, cousins, etc. since they still had not fully forgiven her "sin."

Finally, it was decided Branda would contact those she thought ought to be told something and at least tell them part of the truth.

Branda, even with her overly strict conscience, understood the need for secrecy about her condition. Also, her need for privacy prevailed over a guilty conscience from telling a few white lies. If and when the full truth came out later, she knew friends would understand.

The marriage part would be trickiest to explain. Her friends, Mary Ann and Linda, knew she disliked men and had only rarely double dated with one or both of them . . . always in protest. People seemed to think it their duty to fix her up with dates. She had never told them the whole story about her past life; only that she had been married once to an abusive husband and lost twin sons.

Branda said, "I will phone Mary Ann and Linda at their homes this evening after they get off work. They can tell customers and other workers later. I'll tell Annie, the librarian, when I return the books I checked out . . . hopefully today. If I call my friends Mathilda and Carol at my apartment house as soon as possible, they can spread the word although I really don't know that many people there. Everyone sticks to themselves pretty much. Actually, Carol is the apartment manager. Oh, I must not forget Rev. Cummings. I may think of others later. Right now my head feels like it's full of fuzz balls."

Mitch said, "Maybe you should rehearse what you are going to say."

"Good idea," Branda agreed. "Basically, I apparently have some extremely rare fast growing form of cancer affecting only my feet so far. Thinking it was something I could cure myself I did not seek medical help until yesterday. I noticed it several days ago. You, and other doctors, are going to try an experimental medication that will more than likely make me feel very ill for a time. You and other doctors believe normal forms of treatment would not work quickly enough at this point. I won't feel like having visitors."

"Also," she continued. "In case there is a possibility this condition is not cancer but something else that might be contagious, you are putting me under a two week quarantine in my apartment while more blood panel tests are being run."

"That won't work," said Mitch. "If you are under quarantine, you can't leave your apartment for tests."

"This is getting complicated," Branda said. "Isn't there some way you could supposedly arrange for a technician to come to my place and take blood samples?"

"For the sake of appearances, I suppose that could be arranged, unusual as it is. Now, what about the marriage part?" Mitch asked.

"I suppose the truth, the whole truth, and nothing but the truth is the best spin on that. This is such an unusual case, you want to monitor me 24/7. Since I am such a prude I won't let you do that in my home or yours. And I refuse to go to a hospital and be put in isolation unless I have to. So you proposed marriage to get rid of the living together obstacle. It is strictly a marriage of convenience. We'll divorce later. You are taking a leave of absence in case this is contagious. You have been the person most exposed by touching affected parts. How does all that sound?"

"Just fine," Mitch said. "Just tell them the ceremony will be at Sean's and Cynthia's house but we are still looking for an official who agrees to the conditions. Actually, I am going to call a friend of mine this morning who is a judge." Pausing, he added, "You can tell them how much you would like to have them at the ceremony but under the circumstances I forbid it for health reasons." Smiling, he continued, "Tell them I may make the judge and the rest of us wear masks."

Sean broke in. "I guess I had also better take a two week leave of absence since technically I have also been exposed. My assistant can cover for me. Mitch, what about the short time Branda was at work yesterday? Could the other girls and Branda's customers she waited on have been contaminated?"

"I really don't think this is contagious," Mitch said. "We're just being cautious. When you call them, tell them not to worry, Sean. Tell them it would probably take direct contact with affected parts. Besides, if it's cancer they don't have to worry. If they do notice any unusual symptoms, have them call my office. I will check there daily by phone. Stress we are just being extra cautious since this is such a rare condition."

Cynthia broke in. "Well, that seems to cover most all the bases. Do I need to take a leave too from my job just for appearances sake if nothing else?"

"That might be a good idea," Mitch agreed.

The rest of the morning was spent with Sean and Mitch making necessary phone calls while Cynthia took Branda to her apartment to get some of her own clothing. That included a wedding outfit of sorts; a knee-length, pale yellow, plainly cut silk dress with shoes dyed to match. She had worn it one time, to a customer's wedding. It showed off her figure beautifully. The shoe heels were medium height.

After putting the load of clothing inside Cynthia's car, they returned for some other items including Betty and the books she was going to take to the library on their way back to Cynthia's house. She probably brought more than necessary but wasn't sure how long it would be before the wedding and she could move back to her apartment.

Under the circumstances, she was glad they had not run into anyone at the apartment. She didn't want anybody to think later on she had exposed them to possible hidden dangers. This had been a good time to come to the apartment since most tenants were at work. Later on she would call Mathilda and Carol and explain the quarantine and marriage.

Cynthia took the library books in to Annie and explained the situation. She stressed the fact Dr. Andrews was being overly cautious about possible contagion but advised Annie about calling his office if she noticed anything unusual.

Cynthia suggested Branda's returned books be wiped off with disinfectant. Annie sent her sympathies back out to Branda and waved to her from the doorway. Branda would try to call her later.

After returning to Sean and Cynthia's house she greeted Sean and Mitch.

"Hey boys," Cynthia said. "How about helping unload the car while Branda gets a snooze?"

After her nap, Branda called Annie, Mathilda, and Carol.

When she came out of the bedroom the others could tell she had been crying. Mitch reached her first. "What is it, Branda? Do you feel another attack coming on?"

"No. After I explained my situation to Carol the apartment manager, she said I was not to come back to the apartment under any circumstances until the quarantine was over; maybe not even then until the diagnosis is firm. She doesn't even want me to bring my car back over there and park it."

"Well, damn her for upsetting you" said Mitch.

"Stupid woman," added Sean.

"Never mind what I think," Cynthia chimed in.

Branda continued, "Oh I can see her viewpoint since she is responsible for the safety of other tenants. Her attitude just came as a shock since she wasn't very pleasant about it. I thought she was a friend."

Sean said, "As a salesman pal of mine once said, 'First, think of what they're selling.'"

"At least Mathilda was okay about it," Branda said.

Mitch asked, "Then would you consider giving up your apartment and moving into my house after the wedding?"

"Yes, I think that would be best," Branda agreed. "And it would be more convenient for you to be nearer to your home library and for other reasons that would no doubt be helpful to you."

"Thank you for understanding, Branda," Mitch said. "And if you like, we will move your car to my garage. There's plenty of room."

"That is fine with me," Branda said.

Mitch continued, "Now, what is that Carol's phone number? I am going to call her right now and make arrangements to cancel your lease and move your possessions out of there as soon as possible. Then she can fumigate or do whatever the hell she wants to do. We can store your things in my basement. There is a door in the basement that opens to the outside the movers can use. I'll be sure to lock it afterwards."

He was a man of his word.

"Now, Branda," he asked after making the phone call. "Do you feel up to going to town and starting the paperwork and other things it will take for us to get married as soon as possible?"

"Yes."

"I have already talked to a friend of mine who is a judge and he is quite willing to marry us. I told him the truth about your condition plus the version we told others. He's the sort of person who likes to know all there is to know about anything. I thought it best. I hope you don't mind."

"No, of course not. I trust your judgment. But what's the catch?" asked Branda. "Will he make all of us wear surgical masks or is his name saint something or other?"

Sean, Mitch, and Cynthia chuckled at her attempt at humor in a sad setting. It made her feel better to hear their laughter.

"Judge Steve Limson will not require masks nor is he a saint. Actually, his hobby is skydiving so he is not the timid type," Mitch explained.

On the way downtown, Branda asked Mitch, "What will your family think about all this?"

"My parents died years ago and Helen and I had no children. She was allegedly barren and although we talked about adopting, we never did anything about it. Then it was too late."

He grew quiet and introspective. They finished the trip in silence except for him telling her the results of her blood panel and urine sample were in the normal range.

After accomplishing their goals and returning to the Truebridge's house, Branda went off to take another nap before dinner. Her overall energy level was much lower than normal. Mitch joined Sean and Cynthia for a drink in the family room.

When she awakened, Branda called Mary Ann, Linda, and Reverend Cummings.

All were most sympathetic and ask her to call them if they could do anything. The Reverend understood about Mitch wanting his friend to marry them. He said he would pray for her and have the congregation add their prayers too for her recovery.

After dinner, she watched some TV with the others then went to bed. She wondered if Mitch would stay in her bedroom all night. He did.

She was glad of it when she awakened about 4 a.m. to see a familiar glow on her right foot. She called to him on the couch. Coming to her immediately, holding her sitting side by side on the bed, they watched the large toe on her right foot. It proceeded through the usual color changes from pale yellow, to light green to red then disappeared leaving the acrid odor in the air. A checkup of her using equipment he had in his nearby black bag proved to be as usual.

She didn't faint this time but held tightly to Mitch for a long time, sitting up, crying softly. Later on, they told Sean and Cynthia about her new loss. They were most sympathetic.

They were married at noon three days later. Cynthia cried. Sean kissed the bride. Mitch told her he liked her dress. She admired his dark blue suit. She was glad the judge understood the circumstances and didn't ask the groom to kiss the bride. That would have been very awkward for both of them. Mitch did surprise her with a lovely diamond wedding ring. Each had brief flashbacks to their other weddings, other people.

Towards the end of the luncheon that followed, Mitch noticed Branda was beginning to look pale and tired. Everyone ate a piece of wedding cake and drank a champagne toast except Branda. She had ginger ale. The toast theme was aimed towards a complete healing for Branda.

After thanking the judge for performing the ceremony and Sean and Cynthia for all of their hospitality, including the wedding, Mitch took Branda to his home.

CHAPTER FOUR

AFTER PARKING HIS CAR IN the garage, Mitch asked Branda, "Will you be all right here for a moment while I open the garage side door and the one leading off the garden area into the master bedroom? That's the shortest way to carry you in."

"Of course, Mitch. But I can walk."

"Grooms always carry their brides over the threshold . . . two in our case," he said in a lighthearted way.

Branda guessed he was trying to ease any tension she might be feeling. Maybe he was feeling some too. He was right. She was a bit nervous and appreciated his intent.

"Besides," Mitch continued. "I know you must be tired and that you often feel unbalanced and uncomfortable when you walk."

"I can't argue with those reasons. But why straight to the bedroom? What are your intentions, kind sir?" she asked, also in a humorous way to keep the moment light.

Pretending to twirl a non-existent mustache and adding a villainous leer, he answered, "My intentions are most sinister in nature, Fair Maiden. I want you to take a nap while I unload the car." His scar added to the look.

She had to laugh at his uncharacteristic repartee. She was learning there was more to this man than she had first thought. And he was right. Taking a nap sounded like a good thing to do.

Returning shortly he began carrying her out of the garage into and through one of the loveliest garden spots she had ever seen; mostly in books and magazines. The wide, smooth, marble pathway he walked along was pale silver gray with intermittent swirling pale pink tinges.

"Oh, Mitch!" she exclaimed. "The pink part looks like clouds. I want to sit out here someday soon and take it all in."

"Absolutely, just what the doctor orders," he said. "And now my beauty, we are about to enter the master bedroom."

She gasped as he stepped over that threshold. "Two jumpin' Georges, I never saw such a huge bedroom."

"When you're up to it, I'll give you a tour of the house," he said, placing her on a custom-built king size bed, removing her shoes, then covering her with a quilt that had been folded across the end. "Oh, I forgot. Maybe you would rather take off that lovely dress and hang it up now . . . or use the bathroom. Both closet and bath are over there," he said, pointing toward a wall.

"No, but thanks for asking. I'll hang up the dress later. I'll have to have it cleaned anyway since I spilled a few drops of ginger ale on it. And I don't need the bathroom. Right now, that snooze you mentioned sounds like the best idea."

"In that case, Branda, I'm going to start unloading the car if you think you'll be all right for a while."

"I'll be fine." Managing a slight grin, she added. "Tell my car hello."

When they had pulled into the three-car garage attached to his sprawling one-story ranch house, she noticed it was parked there. She guessed he or Sean had transferred it from the Neiman garage since she had given Sean the keys Monday before going to Mitch's office.

Knowing Mitch had expedited getting her furniture moved to his basement the day before, she added, "Maybe I can visit my other belongings sometime soon."

"Of course, Branda. Whenever you want to."

Earlier, Sean had privately explained to her how Mitch usually managed to get things done quickly, like getting her apartment lease canceled and her furniture moved.

"He comes from an extremely wealthy family and inherited all of the money since he is an only child. He isn't particularly spoiled by the money since he grew up with it, but uses it if necessary to get things done faster than usual. Would you like to know how much Mitch is worth?"

"No, Sean. I don't want to know unless he decides to tell me sometime. I don't even want him knowing I learned this much. It seems like the least thing can set him off. He might get some idea I am a gold digger."

"Well, I can assure him you definitely are not," Sean said.

"Thanks, my friend. I just don't know how I can ever pay him back. Maybe my health insurance will cover some of this."

"Don't worry about that now, Branda."

"It's hard not to, Sean."

Dozing, sometimes hearing Mitch coming and going from the garage, Branda was aware he often stopped to check on her. She knew he was tired too and wished she could help him but he had turned down her offer to do so.

She was awakened by gentle nudging on her arm as he stood by the bed.

"Branda, you have been asleep for quite awhile. It's 7 o'clock. If you're hungry I can fix you something to eat. I ate a ham sandwich and some mushroom soup a couple of hours ago."

"Thank you, Mitch. That would taste good. Where's your kitchen? I can come out there to eat."

"No, you just stay put. I'll bring them to you. I want you to rest all you can today and through Tuesday at least. We'll be starting the testing and consultations as quickly as possible. You'll need all of your strength."

"All right. If you don't mind then, I think I'll wash my face and put on my soft clothes."

"Your what?"

"My nightgown and robe."

He chuckled softly. "I like the way you say things . . . different than most."

"You mean countrified?"

"No. Just different . . . and pleasant; especially with your slight southern accent. Besides, there is nothing wrong with being from the country."

"I agree."

Both smiled.

"Mitch, who chose the dark apricot and navy color combination for the bedspread and drapes in here?"

"I did."

"Looks great with the light beige carpeting." Turning slightly to look at the fairly large picture window behind the headboard, she added, "I really like the way the drapes and ivory colored sheers are designed to cover most of the wall. The closed sheers look so lovely now; especially with the light from the nightstand lamps adding their glow to the warm feel of the room."

"Thank you very much, Branda." Smiling, he added. "You have a poetic soul. And I'll close the drapes later. We're very private here so you don't need to worry about a peeping Tom. Plus, those sheers dim the view. Right now you need to eat."

"Thanks for the compliment. And how do you close and open all of that? There's so much material."

"There are switches on that nightstand on the other side of the bed. Depending on which ones are pushed, the drapes and sheers close or open together or separately."

"Well, how about that!" she exclaimed.

He left and she got up to hang her good dress in what turned out to be a cedar-lined walk-in closet nearly as large as her apartment bedroom. Mitch had already put her other hanging clothes in there. There were also drawers, cabinets, shelves, plus shoe and tie racks along the end wall.

"Jumpin' George. You could roller skate in here," she said. "Or, as my dad would have said, 'you could sure store a lot of corn in here.'"

The yellow silk and her other clothing looked strange to her among Mitch's. His wardrobe consisted mostly of casual and sports wear, several suits, two tuxedos, some dress slacks, and assorted shirts. There was still room left for additions.

"More and more I feel like I'm in some science fiction Star Wars movie," she muttered.

Having found her yellow wedding shoes on the floor by the bed, she placed them on the closet shoe rack.

"They stand out like pewter dollars in a water puddle," she said, removing pieces of tissue stuffed in the toes.

Even though they only had medium high heels, she still had used tissues to make them comfortable enough to wear for the ceremony. In fact, she had learned to normally wear flat-heeled footwear and put tissue in them to fill up the gaps left by her missing toes. In some way, that helped her feel more balanced.

After finding her four suitcases he had placed in a corner of the bedroom, she got out what she needed for the night plus her laundry sack. She would fully unpack later after Mitch told her where to put her things and she felt more like doing the job.

Seeing her pink fake-fur house shoes, she put them on. The flat soles were just hard enough to give adequate support and were a welcome relief, even without tissues.

Although there was no pain connected with her problem, she noticed the imbalance was causing her to limp more and feel overall discomfort.

"Oh, there you are, Betty!" she exclaimed upon seeing her doll resting on a small pillow on top of one of the suitcases. "I guess Mitch put you here," grinning at the thought as she moved Betty to a chair near the bed.

During one of their conversations, Branda had told Mitch the history and significance of Betty. He had not laughed at her which she appreciated.

The unusually large, fully carpeted, bathroom in which she changed clothes was decorated with a lot of pale cream-colored marble with flecks of darker cream and light tan. This included the frosted-glass enclosed Roman tub complete with Jacuzzi jets and the double-sink area that was along an opposite end wall. A large marble-lined shower, surrounded by the same glass type, was slotted between the tub enclosure and walled off area containing the commode.

"I'm surprised the potty isn't marble," she humorously mused. "Or the floor. This plush creamy colored carpeting is too beautiful to walk on even with bare feet. But it sure feels great even to mine. And I imagine it has some treatment protecting it within an inch of its life." She had removed her house shoes and pantyhose upon first seeing the light colored carpeting.

She was overwhelmed and thoroughly enjoyed performing all of her nighttime rituals in such surroundings.

Three fairly good-sized, uncurtained, rectangular windows were placed high along the wall above the tub ending a bit before the start of the sink area below. A lower, smaller, traditional type window was in that remaining wall space. "I'll bet when the sun shines in here in the daytime, it is gorgeous." She was trying not to catch a glimpse of her disfigurement in the full-length mirrored panel on one bathroom wall near the entrance door. Seeing her problem reflected in a mirror always made it seem twice as bad. She busied herself taking off her slip and undergarments and putting them in her laundry sack.

Afterwards, she put on her pretty, short-sleeved, pink cotton nightgown with the long-sleeved matching robe. Both were ankle-length. Then she put on her house shoes, deciding they were clean enough to wear on this carpet.

She knew her attire wasn't exactly bride-like except perhaps for the somewhat low-cut gown top.

"But then I'm not exactly a bride," she mused, finally taking a look in the mirror.

For a moment she dwelled on thinking about taking her tub bath in the morning, soaking a good long while, then rinsing in clean water until she was squeaky clean. Showers didn't appeal to her nearly as much.

When he returned with her food on a tray, she was under the covers but sitting up leaning against the pillow. She had made sure her robe fully covered her. After placing the tray in front of her, he sat on the edge of the bed nibbling on some cookies while she ate as they chatted.

"This tastes good, Mitch. Thank you."

"You're welcome. I see you found your suitcases," he said.

"Yes. And Betty."

Both smiled.

Branda continued, "And thank you for hanging up my clothes in that huge closet. I hope that's okay with you for them to be there."

"You're welcome and absolutely. It's our closet now you know."

"Thanks, Mitch."

"If you need more hanging space, there is a bit in that amoire over there against the wall where the entertainment center is. And that big dresser over in the corner near the hallway is empty if you need to put things out of your suitcases into the drawers. Mine is the one on the other side of the garden entrance door. If you need more space, we can find some. Just let me know. Is that a deal?"

"A deal. Thanks again Mitch for making me feel at home plus for all you have done and are still doing. I know you have quite a lot on your mind."

Patting her arm, he said, "You are most welcome." Then he asked, "Would you like for me to empty your suitcases and put things away or would you rather do it yourself when you feel up to it? I probably wouldn't do it right."

"You're right, Mitch," Branda said, "That's what is known as a 'woman thang.'"

They laughed.

Continuing, Mitch said, "One of the first things I want to do is get some sort of small intercom device each of us can carry. In case you need help and I'm in another part of the house, I want you to be able to contact me immediately. Or if I need to check up on you, I want to be able to do so."

"That sounds like a good idea," Branda agreed. Pausing, she added, "You look like you could fall down. All of this has been hard on you too. You're worn out aren't you?"

"To be honest. Yes. It has been rather like being in a whirlwind."

"As they use to say back home, you probably feel like 'I'm so far behind, I think I'm up front.'"

He laughed again. "That about covers it." Yawning, he added, "Before I collapse, I'm going to turn in too."

"Where? I don't see a couch in here."

"I believe that ring on your finger and the license on top of my dresser means we are legally married and can share a bed," he said with just a hint of the old edginess in his tone.

"And I thought we were married in name only," she said, also with a slight edge to her voice.

"You're right, Branda," he said more calmly, as if remembering what she had been through in her past, and was going through now. "But I have no ulterior motives. I'm just bone tired and the other available bedroom is too full of stuff to sleep in. One of the other four bedrooms was divided and converted to serve other purposes. I use the last one for a study. That couch at Sean's was okay short term, but I need my own bed now. Besides, if you recall, this marital arrangement is so I can watch you closely 24/7."

"I'm sorry. I should have realized you haven't had a decent sleep for several nights. Besides, this bed is so large five people could sleep in it and never touch each other."

"I had it made after I came back from Dallas because I like to be able to stretch and sprawl."

She wondered if this was his way of telling her he had never slept with Helen in this bed.

He added, "Small beds give me claustrophobia."

"Sean's couch must have driven you bats."

"I managed. Besides I really didn't do much sleeping on it."

She smiled at his last remark, watching as he removed the tray, taking it back to the kitchen. When he returned and went to put on his soft clothes she took off her robe, laying it on the nearby chair where she had placed Betty, and slid under the cover. It still made her nervous to think about him being in the same bed. If she had more energy she would find some other place to sleep.

Later, neither of them remembered exactly when their lovemaking began. When Mitch had turned out all but the night-light, he had laid down as far from her as he could comfortably get without falling off the bed. She was already sound asleep and he followed suit in a blink.

At first it seemed like a dream since neither was awake. In their sometimes restless sleep they had ended up in the bed's center as dawn began spreading light throughout the room. He had forgotten to close the drapes. With bodies lying side by side they instinctively turned toward each other to fulfill the age-old craving of humans and other creatures to comfort each other by touching. They remained quietly embraced for a time.

In a while, still half-asleep, their lips touched briefly. As if sipping nectar, they did not rush to a full kiss. They kept on romantically, softly, and briefly exploring parts of each other's lips; sometimes with mouths closed, sometimes slightly opened, touching a moment, backing away, then touching another part, savoring the moments. They never ruined this special time with a for sex only kiss in the modern way where people disgustingly appear to be trying to swallow each other.

Still as if in a dream but more awake, Branda felt Mitch's hand come underneath her gown. She moaned softly as he began stroking her skin and felt her own hand moving across the smoothness of his back underneath his loose pajama top. He had slipped out of the other half, moving closer until she felt his nakedness. When he began feeling her skin her body briefly stiffened, arching toward him as waves of desire and passion calmed, weakened, then fired her. She felt like she was melting. Their kisses became more passionate; lovemaking more intense.

Hearing his heavy breathing and her cries of passion, she became aware she was raking her fingers none too gently down his naked back. She stopped. They remained fused to one another, awake now, but too weakened by complete satisfaction to move right away. Each looked deeply into the other's eyes not knowing what to say or do. His dark, dark eyes had a troubled look.

Finally moving out of her, Mitch spoke first. "I'm so sorry Branda. So sorry. You know I had no intention of doing that."

"I know, Mitch, I know. I didn't either. It just happened . . . like a dream. We're two lonely people with hungers that have been denied too long. At least mine have."

"Mine too." After a slight pause, he added, "That was truly beautiful no matter why it happened. And I don't think it was all just for the sex."

Feeling herself blush, Branda said, "I agree on both counts. But Mitch, we barely know each other."

"Well I think we know each other better now."

Both smiled, though knowing some of their old hang-ups still lurked in the background.

Still feeling drowsy from satisfaction, they held each other and slept for over an hour.

When they awakened, Mitch reached to smooth her hair and said, "You're amazing."

"What do you mean?"

"With the way you feel about men and marriage I would have thought you would be raging mad about this happening. It goes against all of your principles."

"I don't quite understand it either. Maybe I can sort it out later. I read somewhere the heart has reasons that reason itself knows nothing about. You're amazing too, Mitch."

"How so?"

"I figured your deep love for Helen and how you feel about not being able to save her would keep you away from any intimate relationship."

Raising up on one elbow, looking down at her, he asked, "How did you know about that?"

"Oh jumpin' George! I slipped up."

"What do you mean?"

"I may as well admit it. I had awakened from my fainting spell that day in your office and overheard all you and Sean spoke about."

"Everything?"

"Yes, but it doesn't matter. I understand. At least I think I do. I'm trying," Branda said.

"Why didn't you tell us?"

"It would have served no purpose and I knew you preferred keeping everything a secret."

"I do . . . or, I did. But, well," he hesitated, then continued, "since we're definitely married now perhaps we should have a talk and share our feelings more."

"You're right. That sounds like a good idea," Branda agreed.

"I also think we should get cleaned up first," Mitch suggested.

"That also sounds like a good idea. And I'll take care of the bed. Where do you keep your linens? And where's the laundry room?"

"That's right. All you've seen is the bedroom," Mitch said.

"Well, it certainly turned out to be an exciting place."

Laughing, they instinctively hugged, kissed, and ended up making love again; wide awake and totally naked this time, enjoying every sky-rocketing orgasmic moment.

Afterwards, they slept again in each other's arms. Upon awakening both decided it really was time to get up, bathe, and go eat.

"I'm starved. What time is it?" Mitch asked.

"Me too and Now," Branda answered.

"What do you mean, Now?"

"I read somewhere that's how Native Americans tell time . . . or at least some tribes. The time is always Now."

"You come up with some interesting facts, Mrs. Andrews."

A bit startled, she said, "That's right. I really am a Mrs."

"You certainly are," he said, reaching for a quick kiss.

"I guess that hadn't really sunk in although it certainly should have," Branda said, kissing him back. Then glancing at a wall clock, she told him it was ten thirty.

Mitch sent her off to bathe while he started the laundry. He had turned down her offer to help, because he didn't want her exerting herself anymore than necessary; although the lovemaking had not seemed to bother her.

Later, opening the bathroom door a crack and hearing the tub water running, he loudly asked, "Branda, is it okay if I come in to shave and shower or would you rather be alone? I can use one of the other bathrooms but all of my stuff is in here."

"Come on in, Mitch. The water's fine," she added gaily.

"Don't tempt me, woman."

With that, Branda cracked open the sliding tub door, peeked out and winked coyly at him. She was sitting up surrounded by bubbles.

"Oh, lord, Branda. I mean it. Don't tempt me."

"I'm sorry, Mitch. I guess we had better behave," she said, smiling at him and starting to close the door.

Before she could finish, Mitch reached in and gave her a kiss. She was laughing and splashing water at him as he finished closing the door.

"Enough for now, you beautiful female. Not that I don't want to, but I think we had better take a rest."

"I know, Mitch. Of course you're right. It's just that I've never enjoyed sex before and you're so good at it. And I'm learning that you can also be fun. I've never seen that in a man before."

He opened the door again and said, seriously. "Thanks Branda. I'm also enjoying being with you. I'm learning things from you too."

"What?"

"How to get some enjoyment out of life again."

"Why, thank you, Mitch."

"You're welcome."

She could hear him singing in the shower as she got out of the tub, dried off, and went back to the bedroom to dress. After putting on a pair of pale blue slacks and a white cotton blouse she decided to lie down and rest a moment.

She must have dozed off. The next thing she heard was, "Branda, are you all right?"

Looking up at Mitch standing by the bed with a towel wrapped around his waist, she said, "Oh yes, Mitch. I'm sorry. I guess I am more tired than I thought."

"You need food, woman. Wait here until I throw on some clothes and I'll go cook breakfast."

She liked watching his tall, lean, muscular, half-naked body move toward the closet.

"But remember Branda," she warned herself. "Be careful. He has that flip-flop personality."

They ate in the large sun-filled kitchen decorated in varying blue tones and tan Spanish tile flooring. She noticed there was a lot of countertop space, an island, and a large walk-in pantry. A glass-paneled door angled in a corner provided a view of the unusually large garden patio area. They sat at the rectangular cherry-wood table placed near the wall in common with the living room.

She thoroughly enjoyed the scrambled eggs with melted extra sharp cheddar cheese in them, crisp bacon, that turned out to be ordered from Esicar's Smokehouse in Cape Girardeau, freshly squeezed orange juice, and buttered whole wheat toast slathered with seedless black raspberry jam. Cups of hot black coffee had topped off the meal.

"If you get tired of being a doctor, you could be a chef," Branda said.

"Thank you but breakfast is about all I can cook."

"Well, it is delicious. By the way, how come you know about Esicar's?"

"My folks knew about them and I just continue to order from there."

"Did you know Elvis use to also order his bacon from there?"

"No. Can't say as I did."

"It use to sort of bother the Esicar's because Elvis reportedly liked his bacon nearly burned. The Esicar men preferred it to be cooked otherwise to retain its high quality."

After they ate and cleaned up the dishes, Mitch was ready to give her an inside tour of the rambling four-bedroom ranch house. Being hungry before, she had not taken time to seriously look as they headed from their bedroom to the kitchen. They had come down the long hallway, turned right to come through the spacious foyer that merged into the open ended living room that was off to the right. The main entrance double doors were to the left. Then they continued ahead toward the also open ended dining room. Part way through the dining room they turned right to go through the kitchen doorway.

"We'll start in here," Mitch said, sliding apart two heavy pocket doors separating kitchen and den.

The first things Branda noticed were bookshelves going from floor to ceiling. The largest, along an end wall to her right, also had an entertainment center built into the middle section. A smaller one partially covered a side-wall. A fireplace and doorway to the mudroom leading to the garage were also on this wall.

"Looks like an annex to the St. Louis County Library!" she exclaimed. "And what a great looking stereo setup as well as all of that other mysterious looking electronic equipment."

"Dad and Mom loved good music. I do too. By turning the right controls, music can be piped to or turned off in any room in the house. If Dad wanted to read in here, Mom would switch music to the living room or somewhere she wanted to listen."

"Wonderful. But say if we wanted to hear it in the bedroom, would we have to come clear back in here to turn it off?"

"No. There are controls for doing that too. Some are in our bedroom on the same control panel as the drapes."

"Jumpin' George and then some."

A larger than usual half-bath was on one part of the common wall with the kitchen along with a closet used to store extra CD's, DVD's, old records, audio and video tapes and photo albums. The bath was closest to the kitchen doorway.

The fairly large picture window on the other end wall offered a view of the lovely maple, dogwood, red bud, and pin oak trees spread among a large parklike area. Forsythia and other blooming bushes were interspersed. This whole area was on the other side of the driveway that led from a curve in front of the house around to the back ending in the large paved area at the garage entrance.

"I'm surprised there isn't a window looking out over the patio garden area," Branda said.

"Actually, Dad and Mom had a big debate about that. Dad won that one," Mitch explained. "He said he liked to come in here to read, be quiet, and not be distracted by what was going on in the garden area that he loved. That's also why he had those pocket doors put in between here and the kitchen. Said he didn't want rattling of pots and pans disturbing him when he was trying to read Shakespeare."

"What about the picture window on this other wall?"

"He said that was a quieter scene."

"Couldn't he have just pulled the drapes if the window was on the garden side?"

"That was Mom's argument too. But Dad said he wanted the entertainment center and some bookshelves over there."

Grinning, Branda said, "They sound like a genuine long-time married couple."

"They were for sure," Mitch said, adding his grin to hers. "I miss them."

"I know the feeling. I miss mine too. Could we come back in here later for our talk?"

"Yes, of course."

Groupings of comfortable chairs, two couches with coffee tables in front of them on opposite ends of the room added to the general warmth of the den. Earth tone colors predominated among furniture coverings, accessories and drapes. Those colors, along with the same plush light beige carpeting seen throughout the house, honey-toned wall paneling and the fireplace, rounded out the cozy atmosphere.

Adding some further explanations, Mitch said, "Besides having a door leading to the garage, the mudroom also has a side door opening to the patio, garden, and swimming pool areas. That room is very helpful in bad weather for leaving wet or dirty clothing, and messy shoes. There are knob hangers along available wall space and a tile floor like the kitchen."

He opened the door so she could see for herself.

"Well that's a great idea," she said, stepping into the room for a moment.

"Sometimes swimmers like to use that as a changing room after a dip in the pool," Mitch said.

"Where's the pool?" Branda asked. "I didn't notice it when you carried me in."

"Out in the patio garden area. It's been covered up all winter which is probably why you didn't notice it. We'll uncover it and get it into working order if you like when the weather warms up."

"Which it can certainly do in St. Louis in the summer." Branda said.

"Amen."

"And yes, I would like to be able to swim in it. Thank you."

"You're welcome, Branda."

Coming back into the den, Branda noticed two doors on the other part of the kitchen common wall.

"Where do those lead?" she asked.

Stepping toward the one nearest the window, Mitch said, "This opens to the basement stairway." He opened it so she could see then closed it.

Opening the one closest to the kitchen doorway, he said, "And this is the elevator that goes to the basement. It can also serve as a dumbwaiter."

"Well, jumpin' George. An elevator!!! And it's so roomy. I never saw any house with its own elevator."

"Would you like to ride it down and take a look at your furniture?"

"I sure would," she said.

He showed her how to work the controls.

Upon reaching bottom, she said, "That is wonderful." Leaning to look more closely at the wood paneling on the elevator walls, she asked, "What kind of wood is this? It is so beautiful."

"Rosewood."

"It is so lovely."

She was shocked when she saw her furniture, computer, lamps, tables, and such placed in a nearby open area.

"Why Mitch. How thoughtful."

He had the workmen arrange everything as it was back in Branda's apartment.

Mitch explained, "I thought it would be better to do this than have it just piled here and there; maybe somehow make you feel more at home and have your own space if you need it from time to time. I also had two separate phones lines installed; one for your computer, one for your private phone."

She cried a bit, hugged and kissed him. "No one has been that kind to me in ages; not since my folks. I'll have to bring Betty down here to see," she said, trying to lighten the mood.

She was also surprised at the rest of the basement that was underneath the entire house. The spacious recreation room had a full bar, lots of tables and chairs plus some comfortable looking couches. There were bookshelves, dart boards, a couple of pin ball machines, a juke box, poker table, separate stereo system, plus a closet full of games. She was sure there was much she was missing. There was too much to see at one time.

Two furnished small apartments were underneath the house bedroom area. They had living rooms, kitchens, dining rooms, full baths, and fairly large bedrooms. Some of the areas were carpeted. There was even a centrally located laundry room.

"This basement is like having another whole house," said Branda. "Why the apartments?"

"For the privacy of guests," he said. "If you like, we can empty one of the apartments and put your things in there."

"Oh my no, Mitch. Everything is fine the way it is . . . unless my stuff is in the way and you would like to change it."

"It's not in the way in the least. If you change your mind, let me know," he said.

"Okay," she said, adding jokingly, "I'm surprised there isn't a bowling alley down here."

"Actually, Dad wanted one but mom vetoed that big time. Said she didn't want that racket in her house no matter how much he said the sound could be muffled."

He showed her the extra wide door leading to the outside. It was located just before the garage started and had a door with bars on the outer part. Dead bolt locks were on both inner and outer door. Coming back upstairs and continuing their tour, they reversed their former route. The formal dining room was elegant with its wide-panel white wainscoting all round and a lovely floral patterned wallpaper above. A coffer ceiling with a gorgeous crystal chandelier hanging from the center added to the scene. The flame mahogany table seated twelve. Champagne colored silk drapes hanging in swags framed the beveled leaded glass window along the end wall.

Before going left into the living room, Mitch took her to the front double doorway to give her two keys and explain about the burglar alarm system. He showed her which key opened every door in the house and the one that only worked the barred basement door.

"Dad and Mom wanted to keep it simple," he explained.

Putting them in her slacks pocket, she said, "Thanks, Mitch. I will put them somewhere safer soon. I'm very good about not losing keys and things like that."

"I'm sure you are," he said. "Now, besides here at the front door, there are alarm pads at the doors from the garden to the master bedroom, mudroom to the den, and the basement."

He gave her the code and had her work the combination several times until she felt comfortable about it all.

"Boy, I hope I don't set that thing off sometime."

"Me too. It's an armed response system."

After giving her a few more explanations about the system, they started their tour again.

The open-ended living room was decorated in monochromatic white tones ending in a whisper of light tan. Book shelves lined most of one wall, fine art was displayed on the other. Touches of color in pale sandstone, dark brown, and palomino golden were used in throw pillows and other accessories. A picture window framed the garden area at the far end. Pale ivory silk drapes hung in tailored folds that could be pulled closed. Comfortable easy chairs, a couch, occasional tables, and a white grand piano added to the inviting look of the room.

"Mitch, whoever designed and decorated this house certainly knew what they were doing."

"Well, actually, Mom and Dad did. Most of their furniture and decorations are still here. They had the house custom built to their specifications."

"I can see why you wouldn't want to change a thing. I know I wouldn't." Treading on thin conversational ice, she asked, "Did you and Helen ever live here?"

"Would that matter?"

"No. I just wondered."

"We only lived here a short time after my parents died. Helen and I had an apartment near the St. Louis University medical school campus while I was still in school there. Then shortly after I graduated, Helen wanted to move to Texas to be near her folks," Mitch explained.

"Who took care of this lovely place?" Branda asked.

"A girl cousin of mine rented the house and kept it up . . . beautifully, I might add."

"Where did she go after you came back home?"

"She married and moved to Ireland with her new husband. He is Irish. She is happy as a clam."

"That's great," said Branda.

Continuing toward the long hallway just past the living room, then turning left and walking down it, she noticed a lot of light colored wooden cabinets on the left side.

"These are extra closets," Mitch explained, opening doors. "The ones farther down have shelves for linens and other types of storage. There are other storage cabinets out in the garage and downstairs."

"As they say, you can never have too many closets or storage areas," said Branda. Continuing, she asked, "Why is this hallway so much wider than most?"

"Both Dad and Mom thought if either one of them ever ended up in a walker or wheelchair, they wanted space to move around in."

"They really did think of everything," Branda said. "I guess that's why all of the doorways in this house are extra wide. I noticed that. Did either of them ever need a walker or wheelchair?"

"Mom used both for a short time when she broke a leg, but thank God neither of them needed either aid permanently. And you are very observant," said Mitch, moving on. "The other three bedrooms, which are larger than those in most houses, are here on the right side," he explained. But Mom divided the middle bedroom. She made one part into an exercise room and the other into the laundry room. Each room has its own entrance from the hallway."

"The laundry room?" Branda asked, amazed.

"Yes. Mom won that debate. She said why haul laundry all over the house when most of it winds up right back here in the bedrooms and linen closet."

"Well, by golly. I think she had a point. May I see it?" asked Branda.

She couldn't believe her eyes. "Why this is wonderful.," Branda exclaimed. "Besides the washer and dryer, there is a big table for folding clothes, an ironing board all set up with a rod for hanging clothing that has been ironed, a television, a comfortable chair and foot stool, a couch and coffee table, plus that window to let in natural light. I never saw anything like this."

Mitch was laughing. "I think you like this room best."

"No, not necessarily," Branda said. "It's just that I never would have thought of doing this. And the wallpaper pattern is so pretty . . . light and airy looking. Your Mom was one smart woman."

"I like to think so."

Going back one door he showed her the exercise room which also impressed her; especially the Nordictrack. It was the equipment with which she was most familiar.

"In bad weather, I use to work out on the one in our apartment exercise room," she explained.

Walking forward again along the hall and reaching the door closest to their bedroom, Mitch said, "Now remember, I told you about this cluttered bedroom."

When he opened the door she saw what he meant.

"Jumpin' George, Mitch. What happened here? There's hardly room to move."

"Well, anytime I didn't know where to put something, this is where it landed. This use to be dad's combination study and office. Maybe I'll get it straightened out some day."

"We'll work on it together," she said, smiling at him.

He smiled back and headed on toward their bedroom.

"How about that other bedroom back down by the exercise room?" Branda asked.

"It was my bedroom when I was growing up here . . . and later. Now it's my study and sort of . . . well . . . "

"I understand," Branda broke in, assuming it was also a cluttered mess.

"I hope so," said Mitch.

Maybe it was her imagination, but she thought he was acting secretive about that room. Much later, she found out she was right.

"Anyway, Mitch," Branda continued. "I love the overall feel of this house. It's warm and comforting; I suspect like your parents were."

"You're right," Mitch said.

"And the beautiful various sized Persian rugs placed here and there on the carpeting certainly adds to the luxurious atmosphere," Branda continued.

"You sound like a decorator yourself, Branda," Mitch said, adding a smile.

She laughed. "I've always been interested in that field."

"And many others I have an idea," Mitch said.

"What makes you say that?" Branda asked.

"I know you like to read, and I've noticed you take a keen interest in things."

"Some people might think I'm just nosy," she said.

"To me those are signs of intelligence."

"Why thank you, Mitch," she said, feeling a bit shy from his compliment. "By the way, how do you keep this big house so clean?" Branda asked, steering the conversation away from her.

"I have the same cleaning people we've had for years. They come once a week, on Wednesdays, and I try to do my share in between."

"Do they know you're married now?"

"Yes, but not about all of the circumstances. We'll deal with that problem when and if we have to."

"Who takes care of the big yard?" she asked.

"Some men we've also had for years," he answered. "They usually come on Wednesdays too."

Having finished their indoor tour, Mitch carried a tray holding a thermal coffeepot and two cups into the den. He placed the tray on a low rectangular table in front of a big dark brown overstuffed couch. They sat on the couch, turning slightly to face each other, and sipped from the cups Mitch had filled. Suddenly a sunbeam flared through the window in back of them making a rainbow of colors on a small lidded crystal dish on the table.

"Is that Waterford crystal?" asked Branda.

"Yes," Mitch answered.

Branda commented, "I have read about that special crystal, but this is the first time I've personally met a piece. It's beautiful."

For a moment she continued admiring the play of colors on the dish.

Then on a more serious note she said, "Mitch, I realize our first lovemaking session was a surprise and the second so spontaneous you didn't have time to use some sort of precaution to keep me from getting pregnant. When we go to town to get the intercom you mentioned and some groceries, could you please also get some condoms? With my condition I don't think getting pregnant is a good idea. Or, like most men, do you already have some in the house or somewhere else handy?"

"What the hell for?" He was getting mad. "I don't sleep around. I have too much respect for the memory of Helen to do that!!! What about you? Most women pop down birth control pills like they were peanuts."

Branda was stunned at his outburst.

"No sir!!!" she exclaimed. "I don't sleep around either . . . "

Mitch got up and stomped out of the room before she could say anything else. Tears stung her eyes.

"Oh when will I ever learn," she thought. "A man is a man is a man." She sat for a time watching sunbeams make rainbows on the crystal dish then took the cups and coffee pot to the kitchen to wash them. She suspected Mitch had headed for the room he hadn't shown her. She was glad she hadn't fully unpacked her suitcases.

"I guess I had better take Betty and get out of here," she said out loud. "This isn't going to work. Not with his short temper. But I really don't know where to go. Oh jumpin' George!"

CHAPTER FIVE

N OT KNOWING QUITE WHAT TO do, Branda decided to go to the basement.

"I can sit on my own bed and think things out," she mused. "I wish I had Betty with me, but I don't dare try to go get her."

She took the elevator down and ended up stretching out on her bed.

"I don't know whether to stay with Sean and Cynthia until I can rent another apartment, or what," she thought. "I hate to impose on anyone."

As thoughts whirled round and round in her head, she finally fell asleep. The phone ringing over on the bar awakened her briefly. When it stopped, she drifted back to sleep.

The next sound she heard was Mitch's gruff voice, "So there you are. I've been looking all over the house and garden for you. But I should have known you would be here with your things. You scared me."

"Scared you?"

"Yes," he said, in a kinder tone. "Branda, I am sorry. I don't know what got into me flying off the handle like that. Forgive me?"

"I don't know, Mitch. Not knowing when that temper of yours is going to flare makes me edgy. It reminds me too much of Connor. And I think I cause you to have too many flashbacks to Helen. I guess we both have a knack for waking up each other's demons. Maybe I should go somewhere else but, quite honestly, I don't know where at this point."

"I don't blame you for wanting to, but could you think about it?" Mitch asked. "I'll try harder to control myself. Damn I hate being like this. But you really should consider the importance of our staying together for your health reasons if nothing else."

"I know, Mitch. I know. Maybe when we get those intercoms, I could stay down here."

"We'll think about that later. Right now, why don't we finish our talk then go run our errands; pick up any items you need and get the portable intercoms. There's already a built in intercom system in the house but it needs some repair which is scheduled for Wednesday."

"Can we take my yellow dress to the cleaners?"

"Certainly. Did you hear the phone ringing a bit ago?" Mitch asked.

"Yes. Vaguely. I was pretty sleepy."

"That was Sean and Cynthia. They ask if they could come over about six and bring some salad and other food plus steaks for barbecuing. I told them yes. I hope you don't mind. I can call them back if you do."

"No, of course I don't mind," Branda said.

"Do you want to talk here or go back up to the den?"

"Here. I like being among my things."

"I can understand that. But first I would like to check your vital signs."

"With what?"

Reaching over to a nearby chair, he picked up a black bag he had brought down with him. He put it on the bed.

"Oh," she said. "But why now?"

"I should have started before since you came to live here, but . . . . . . well . . . let's just say I've been distracted which is not a good thing for a doctor to be. I apologize for that too."

"Were you carrying that bag around the whole time you were looking for me?"

"Yes."

"Why?"

"I was afraid you might have fainted or fallen and I wanted to be ready to check you," he answered.

She had to steel herself against the feelings his touch aroused in her, but she managed. She sensed he might be having similar problems.

"Your blood pressure and other signs are all normal and no temperature," he said, putting equipment back inside the black bag."

"That's good," she said. Putting her hand on his arm and looking into his eyes, she added, "Mitch I forgive you for the flare up. As for the doctoring part, I have a feeling you have been watching me very closely."

"Thanks Branda on both counts. Actually, from time to time when you were asleep I have taken your pulse, listened carefully to your breathing, and otherwise watched for possible other signs of problems. But from now on, my black bag is going to be close at hand."

"Thanks. But I've never felt neglected in the least. And Mitch, without meaning to I guess I say and do the wrong things that set you off. I'm sorry for that," said Branda.

"You don't do anything wrong. I am just still way too touchy," he said.

"I guess all of this is just too new for us," Branda said. "Our memories have left us with a lot of ragged edges. But I have had more time to come to terms with mine. You're relatively new at it. We're like two pieces of raw meat being eaten by our starved emotions."

"Ye gods, but you definitely have a different way of describing things. Or did you read that somewhere?" Mitch asked.

"Not that I remember. Anyway, we seem to send each other to a child ego level pretty easily."

"Now that's straight out of "Born to Win" written years ago by those two women doctors in California," said Mitch

"Yep. You're right on that. Wonderful book on human behavioral patterns and relationships."

"Well, I'll be damned!" Mitch exclaimed.

"Why?"

"That's one of my favorite books. It should be required reading for every human on earth. Branda, you are a constant surprise."

"A good one, I hope."

"Most definitely," he said, reaching to gently take her face in his hands. "Could we try working things out? At least we won't be lonely people anymore."

"You have a point there," said Branda, still feeling cautious. "Let's move over to my couch to talk. I think we'll be more comfortable."

"Is that the only reason?" asked Mitch.

"No."

Both smiled knowingly.

After they were seated, Mitch took her hands in his, and said, "Branda, if you have gotten pregnant, I would be very happy."

"So would I, but what if . . . ?"

"I know what you're going to say. We'll just have to take this a day at a time and deal accordingly with whatever happens. I know I don't want you to even think about having an abortion."

"I would never do that anyway," she said. "To me that is murder from what I have read and studied."

"I agree."

"Mitch, do you think it is possible we could be falling in love . . . or just in need?"

"Maybe it's a little bit of both," Mitch suggested.

"Of course, everybody's heard of love at first sight, but I certainly don't think that is true in our case."

"What makes you say that?" he asked.

"Well I don't want to hurt your feelings again, Mitch, but to be perfectly honest I really did not like you at all the day we met. I got the idea from your reactions that the feeling was mutual."

"You are half right," he said.

"How so?"

"When I first saw you there was something about you that reminded me of Helen. Not in looks, but in some spiritual way. That made me feel like you were an intruder to my memory of her and I resented that."

"Is that why you acted so . . . well . . . mean?"

"I guess that was part of it. As you know, I do that to cover up other emotions."

"What was the other part?" she asked.

"I was also attracted to you physically and to that sweet vulnerable quality you have. That made me feel like I was betraying Helen even more in some way. You're the first woman I have looked at twice since her death. You hit me right between the eyes for sure and I was in no way prepared."

"Well, I'll be," Branda said. "I thought you just generally disliked me as a person."

"In one way I guess I did because you turned my protected little world upside down."

"And now?"

"From what happened a while ago, you know I am still mixed up sometimes and have a long way to go. But I have learned to respect you a great deal and find you fascinating as well as extremely beautiful."

She blushed, and said, "Why thank you, Mitch. I have the same feelings for you . . . only you're handsome rather than beautiful."

"Thank you, too," he said.

Continuing, Branda said, "I think my original feelings of dislike for you came from the fact you seemed so arrogant and are so handsome you reminded me too much of Connor. As you know, he is someone I really don't like being reminded of. But I must admit, you stirred up some sexual physical parts of me that I thought had long since been buried; not that I haven't had sex dreams and romantic notions since my divorce."

"Is that why you acted sort of riled up in the examination room?" Mitch asked.

"Yes, and the scent of your aftershave and overall maleness hit me like a sledgehammer all of a sudden. I was fighting against that plus you for causing it. And, by the way, didn't you have some sort of response like that too? Is that why you stepped back away from me rather abruptly?"

"Yes," Mitch admitted.

"After you saw my foot, is the reason you ran out of the examining room so fast was because the thought crossed your mind I might be terminal and you could not deal with that?"

"Again, yes," said Mitch.

"How do you feel about that now?"

"As you overheard, Sean says I need to work harder on getting rid of that phobia. He's right of course. As a doctor, I know full well cures are not always possible no matter how badly we want them. I need to internalize that fact. I think you are helping me do that somehow."

"I hope I can help," said Branda. "Did you realize that when you were giving me my routine examination I had to steel myself to keep from responding to your touch?"

"No. I was too busy trying to keep my own emotions under control."

"Well, jumpin' George. My instincts were right. I thought I noticed you hesitating."

"As I've mentioned, you're very perceptive, Branda," said Mitch.

"How about that time last week when I was falling out of my gown top and trying to cover up?"

"Branda, the sight of that lovely body bothered me then, before then, covered or uncovered, and probably will forever. Your beautiful silky blond hair, gorgeous eyes and face, those lovely long legs . . . well, your entire body is fantastic. But, as I mentioned, I'm learning there is a lot more to you than your physical beauty. You know if I ever acted strangely, it's because I still felt like I was betraying Helen. But, as I've said, I'm working on that."

"I understand," said Branda, "And thanks for the nice compliments. By the way, you are helping me too."

"How?"

"For one thing, by taking care of me in such a special way throughout this ordeal. And for making me feel like a complete woman again . . . not that the road is smooth . . . but at least it's a start. I'm sure I'll think of other reasons as time goes on."

"Thanks Branda. You've made me feel like a man again."

"Mitch, there's something else I need to say to clear away some more of my emotional cobwebs."

"Go ahead. That's why we're having this talk."

"This will sound trite, but I never knew making love could be the way it is with you. Your gentleness and caring is heaven to me. With Connor it was hell. Just sex, and painful sex at that; often abusive. He just used me with no love involved, real or otherwise, although he pretended to love me. I managed to fend him off for a long time but he was persistent. After the initial pain of losing my virginity, the first time wasn't so bad since he was being gentle while succeeding in seducing me. After that I wouldn't let him do it anymore. He was furious. I stopped seeing him. I won't go into details of what it was like after we had to marry, but a couple of times I had to go to an emergency room for treatment. I became so afraid of losing the babies I would not let Connor near me. He managed to rape me twice during that time. The last time I bled so badly he had to take me to the hospital. That scared him and he let me alone after that."

"My God, I'm more amazed than ever that you let me near you even though we were both more asleep than awake the first time," Mitch said.

"Even with all the trauma I went through, I am still a romantic at heart and evidently have a very healthy sex drive; one that has been repressed way too long. I thought I was just having a dream that first time with you. By the time I knew it was real, I was too far gone to care. You must think I am what is known as a wanton hussy."

"No way. You are only human, like me, and some drives are nearly impossible to resist under some circumstances, especially when they have been repressed a long time."

"Repression sure wasn't easy all those years I was alone but my strict upbringing helped me. That's what hurt my feelings when you said what you did earlier about me probably popping birth control pills like peanuts since most women do."

"That was a stupid remark I made."

"That's ok. We all do that from time to time."

"What about the second time we made love?" she asked.

"Same deal about drives, circumstances, and repression; plus the second time we welcomed the expected pleasure. And deep down you knew both times it was okay because we are married. You felt morally free to do it."

"You're one smart doctor," said Branda.

"I'm not sure sometimes. I only know I try to be a good one." Hesitating a moment, he asked, "Branda, have you ever read about something called transference?"

"I think so," she answered. "Isn't that where patients think they are in love with their doctor, dentist, psychoanalyst, or other type of caregiver because of the help they are being given? It's a transfer of feelings thing."

"That pretty well sums it up," said Mitch.

"Do you think I might be doing that?" she asked.

"I don't know."

"Time will tell," said Branda. "Mitch, did our lovemaking cause any guilt feelings to surface regarding Helen?"

"Certainly not at the time. But I did have some twinges later on."

"Regrets?"

"None."

"Maybe that's progress," said Branda.

"Let's hold that thought. And now, I think we had better go run our errands. I want to get home in time for you to rest before Sean and Cynthia come over."

He drove to an area where he was sure no one would know him, took her dress to a cleaners and picked up two small two-way radios in an electronics store. Next he went to a Dierberg's grocery store to get milk and other items. Since he didn't have to stay long in any store, she waited in the locked car, wearing a head scarf and sunglasses as a disguise just in case.

On the way back home, Mitch said, "Branda, while I was in the store I also got some condoms. If you want me to I will use them from now on."

"Maybe that would be best under the circumstances. Otherwise, I would say no because I think having your baby would be an honor."

"You're something else, Branda."

"Do you mind wearing them, Mitch?"

"Well, let's put it this way. Making love with one on is sort of like taking a shower with your socks on."

"How would you know that?" Branda asked. "Forgive me for mentioning it but since Helen was barren I wouldn't have thought you needed them."

"We didn't know she was for a long time and we weren't ready for a family right away."

"I see." Noticing some other sacks, she said, "Looks like you did a bit of shopping."

"Oh, just some odds and ends. Bread, milk . . . that sort of thing."

Upon reaching home, she offered to help him put away the sack contents.

"Thanks, but I'd rather you went to get a nap."

"I am kind of tired. So adios for now mi amigo."

"Adios, me amor."

They laughed at their swerve toward Spanish.

"By the way, Mitch, where is the barbecue grill?"

"Out on the patio. It's built in. If the evening air was a bit warmer we could eat out there. Maybe next time. We'll eat in the kitchen unless you want to try out the dining room," he said.

"The kitchen is just fine with me." Hesitating a moment, she asked, "Do you think Sean and Cynthia will know by looking at us that we've made love?"

"I wouldn't be at all surprised. Now go take your nap."

The two couples had an enjoyable evening and even got Branda to take a sip or two of Merlot with her filet mignon.

With a twinkle in his eye, Sean said, "I think there's some changes going on here."

Cynthia smiled knowingly, and said, "Some very nice ones I'm thinking."

Branda blushed and Mitch acted a bit shy. Both knew their lovemaking had been detected. People always seemed to be able to spot the familiarity lovemaking left with a couple.

After the meal, the men shooed the women out of the kitchen offering to do all the clean up chores. Branda suspected Mitch was behind the offer thinking she might not feel up to the work.

After the women were seated in the den, Branda said, "I have a favor to ask. I want to buy Mitch a gold wedding band. I don't think he's in to wearing diamond jewelry."

"You're right," Cynthia agreed.

"Is there a way you could get one for me without him knowing it? I'll pay you back of course."

"I'll do better than that. I have a jeweler friend. He'll let me bring a selection so you can choose. I'll call you and let you know when," said Cynthia.

"Thanks a lot," said Branda. "Did he wear one before?"

"Yes."

"What kind? I sure wouldn't want to get anything to remind him of the other one."

"It was white gold with some yellow gold design work. Kind of fancy. That was Helen's taste. Is there anything else Sean or I can do for you or Mitch?"

"I have a feeling he needs to go grocery shopping. Maybe you could sit with me someday soon while he does. We haven't had time to think about things like that yet."

The minute the words were out of her mouth, she realized how they must have sounded. Sure enough, Cynthia couldn't contain a good old-fashioned belly laugh.

"Oh jumpin' George," Branda said, feeling embarrassed. "You know what I mean."

Cynthia reached to give her a hug and said, "Of course I know, honey, but . . . well, your choice of words tickled my funny bone for sure. And Branda, Sean and I are very happy for you both."

Branda hugged her back, saying, "Thanks, Cynthia. I just hope his hang-up ghosts don't seriously haunt us. Or my ghosts either, for that matter."

"I think you'll work through them all."

In a while, Sean was calling to Cynthia. "Come on woman. It's time for us to go home and leave these newlyweds alone." They were still grinning from ear to ear as they left to go to their own home.

After making sure both double doors were locked, setting the alarm, and turning out the foyer light, Mitch turned to Branda, "Do you still want to sleep downstairs?"

"No."

With that, Mitch swooped her up into his arms and carried her toward their bedroom. Sensor night lights in the foyer and along the hallway blinked on showing them the way.

Mitch kissed her ear, lightly touching it with his figertips, then whispered, "Do you want protection tonight ?"

"No. I want you to enjoy yourself to the fullest."

Stripping naked they climbed into bed, holding each other tightly, kissing passionately, heading for ecstasy.

Suddenly, Branda stopped and cried out. "I feel so weak, Mitch. So warm and weak."

She fainted as he sat up and watched the remaining two middle toes on her right foot glow then turn from pale yellow to light green to red and disappear. Afterwards, the acrid odor came.

Grabbing the black bag he now kept close by, Mitch checked her vital signs. As usual they were normal for the fainted state she was in and she had two degrees of temperature. Her foot felt warm. Covering her with the sheet, he put on a robe, watching her all the time.

She regained consciousness as he was checking her again a few minutes later. Everything was back to more normal ranges including her temperature. Her foot had also cooled.

"What happened, Mitch?" she asked. "Did . . . ?"

Interrupting, he said, "I'm afraid so, Branda."

"Oh no!" she exclaimed, lifting the sheet to briefly look. "Hold me tight and don't let me go, Mitch."

After helping her into a nightgown and putting on his pajamas, Mitch held her closely, gently caressing her silky blonde hair. She quietly wept, finally falling asleep. He fought to push away his growing fears.

CHAPTER SIX

MITCH WOKE UP AT 9 A.M. when he felt her body stirring beside him. "How are you feeling?" he asked.

"All right. The sleep helped," she answered. Noticing his sad expression, she asked, "How about you?"

"I'm okay."

Both sensed haunting negative shadows hovering around them.

Branda was first to try and lighten the mood. "I'm hungry. How about I go cook us some breakfast after we bathe?"

"How about we cook it together . . . that is if you feel up to it."

"Listen, if I held up twice, almost three times, yesterday through our glorious lovemaking, I can certainly manage to scramble an egg."

Mitch had to laugh. She joined in, trying hard not to look down at her latest disfigurement. He reached to kiss her. For a moment she thought he was going to make love to her. But he stopped.

Looking and pointing toward her feet, she asked, "Are these the reason you don't want to make love now?"

"Oh no, Branda," he said, reaching down to hold them. "No, you sweet woman!" Moving back, looking her in the eyes, he added, "Well, it was supposed to be a surprise, but I guess I had better tell you."

"What?"

"Sean and Cynthia are coming over at noon and we're having a party"

"A party? What for?"

"Happy Birthday, Branda!"

"Oh for Pete's sake. I had forgotten all about that."

"Pete's sake? What happened to jumpin' George?"

They laughed.

"Let's not mention my latest loss," said Branda. "It might dampen the party spirit for Sean and Cynthia."

"Good heavens, but you are thoughtful," said Mitch. "I've never known anyone quite like you."

Privately, she was thinking. "I could scream I am so unnerved and scared, but that's best kept to myself. As my Aunt Mayme used to tell me, 'Showing out doesn't solve anything.'"

Showing out was her aunt's term for behaving badly and causing a scene.

Continuing with her private thoughts, "I can cry later when I'm in the tub with the water running to drown out the sound. Sometimes Mitch can get upset enough about my problem."

Aloud, she asked, "Should I act surprised?"

"No. I'll just tell them I let it slip," he said.

She was genuinely able to forget her troubles during the party that began in the kitchen with all of them chatting.

Sean, Cynthia, and Mitch had put in a lot of effort to make it a success. The two friends had brought lobster and filet mignons for grilling plus a great Caesar salad and fresh asparagus they knew she loved. Cynthia had also prepared her famous twice-baked potatoes made with cream and butter. Whipping the filling for stuffing back into the potato skin halves until almost fluffy, she lightly tucked strips of extra-sharp cheddar cheese into the filling tops. She added bits of butter over the cheese, all of which melted during re-heating. Sour cream was on the side since she knew Branda did not care for it. They had also brought her favorite Haagen-Daz butter pecan ice cream.

"And just look at that beautifully decorated cake with my name on it and the delicious looking snacks and pretty party favors." Branda exclaimed. "Thank you for only putting a few candles on the cake. But all of you know I'm 39 today."

Cynthia smiled and said, "Now you're a member of the 39 Forever Club like the rest of us. And Mitch shopped for the snacks and favors. He could not figure out how to get the other things bought and into the house when the party was in the surprise mode."

"I'm sorry, Cynthia," said Mitch. "It just slipped out."

"And they say women can't keep a secret," Cynthia said in a kidding way.

"But I did get the snacks and favors secretly," said Mitch, defensively.

"How did you do that?" Branda asked.

"Yesterday afternoon during our errand run while you waited in the car. I found them when I went into Dierberg's to get the milk and stuff. That's why I didn't want you helping me unload the sacks."

"Why you sly person you," Branda said, reaching up to give him a kiss.

"Also, Branda," Cynthia said, "Mitch insisted on buying all of the food for the party even though we wanted to do our share."

"You did enough by going to get it and doing the food preparation," said Mitch.

"At least he let us furnish the wine, champagne, and ginger ale."

"Well I really and truly thank all of you," said Branda.

All agreed blowing the surprise element was not really a big deal.

While the men went outside to prepare the grill, Cynthia showed Branda the wedding ring assortment she had brought. Branda chose a plain gold band 1/8 of an inch wide with a minute decorative grooved edging. Hurrying as best she could, she went to the bedroom to write a check to repay Cynthia and put the box with the ring inside in her nightstand drawer.

Back in the kitchen, Branda said, "I'll surprise him with the ring later on."

"Maybe in bed tonight?" asked Cynthia, grinning mischievously.

Branda blushed and grinned back.

Using a more serious tone, Cynthia asked, "Branda, is everything okay between you and Mitch? I feel a tension in the air this afternoon. Sometimes I'm rather psychic you know. Is something wrong?"

Branda was saved from having to answer when they heard the men coming back into the den.

As they came into the kitchen, Mitch was saying, "Ladies since this is such a special occasion, we are going to eat in the dining room. Sean and I will even help set the table."

Having been family friends for years, Sean and Cynthia knew where to find table linens, good china and silverware. Mitch helped.

Since they would not let the "birthday girl" help, Branda sat nearby watching in amazement as the flame mahogany table was transformed into a picture perfect look reminiscent of settings seen in upscale decorating magazines. Gleaming silverware, sparkling crystal, cream colored Lenox china, and tall pale rose colored tapers in silver candleholders transformed the room.

"Good heavens!" exclaimed Branda. "And that white tablecloth is gorgeous. The whole setting looks like something out of a movie. Thank you so much."

Mitch explained, "That Irish linen tablecloth belonged to my maternal grandmother."

"What a treasure!" said Branda.

While continuing to look at the lovely setting, her glance moved to the top of one of the sideboards across the room. She noticed some beautifully wrapped presents. There were two sideboards along that outer wall with a large china cabinet centered between. All pieces matched the table.

After the delicious meal was eaten and dishes were removed, but before cake and ice cream were served, the presents were brought to the table for Branda to open.

Mitch handed her two large boxes and one smaller one from Sean and Cynthia. The first one she opened contained a Dupioni silk pants suit in a beautiful shade of golden tan.

"This is too pretty to wear . . . but I will," she said, laughing happily.

The next box held an ivory colored crepe de chine blouse that would go well with the pants suit or look nice worn separately with the pants. Gold costume jewelry to accessorize her new outfit was in the smaller box.

"This is too much, just too much," Branda said, getting up to go hug the couple then sitting back down to the right of her husband seated at the head of the table.

When she opened the two beautifully wrapped small boxes from Mitch she could not believe her eyes. The first contained a diamond bracelet; the second, a matching diamond barrette.

"These are so lovely, Mitch. Thank you very, very much," she said. She was almost speechless.

"You are very welcome," said Mitch, reaching to put the bracelet on her wrist. Then standing up and coming around to her, he took the barrette out of the box and put it in her hair.

Kissing the top of her head, he said, "There now. That makes your beautiful hair look even more lovely."

Reaching up to pull his face toward hers, she kissed him for a longer than necessary moment before letting him go.

Tears stung her eyes. Sean and Cynthia admired the diamond jewelry for a moment then went off to get the dessert and serve it. Branda blew out all of the candles with one puff.

"What did you wish?" asked Cynthia.

"I can't tell or it won't come true. But I will say I wish this day would never end. It's just perfect. Thank you again."

Although Branda drank ginger ale with her dinner instead of joining the others with wine, she did have some sips of champagne afterwards during the toasts to her happiness. Turning to Mitch, she asked, "How did your presents get here? I don't think they were in the sacks from Dierberg's."

"Oh I have my ways, woman. I have my ways."

She suspected, correctly so, that Sean and Cynthia had a hand in helping him.

While the other three did clean up work, they had Branda sit at the kitchen table. She sat at one end so she could see and talk to them. By turning her head she could also see the garden patio through the corner angled glass-paneled door.

Afterwards, they all went into the living room to have some hazelnut-flavored coffee.

Deciding to surprise the others, Branda excused herself on the pretense of going to the den bathroom and went off to try on her new pants suit, blouse, and accessories. She was able to pick up the presents in the dining room without anyone seeing her.

Looking at herself in the full-length bathroom mirror on one wall, she said, "What beautiful clothes. I'm not sure about wearing this gold jewelry with the diamonds. I'll ask Cynthia." She decided her leather, cream colored, flat shoes looked all right.

Upon entering the living room, she thought Mitch was going to drop his coffee cup. Sean and Cynthia looked at her in awe.

Nearly in unison, all said, "Branda you look beautiful."

"Thank you. If I do it's because of these lovely clothes and jewelry."

Mitch put his cup down, rose, and slowly walked toward her. "Yes, the outfit is truly wonderful, but you make it look even better."

Sean and Cynthia agreed.

"You're more gorgeous than those models we hire at Neiman-Marcus," said Sean.

"By far," agreed Cynthia.

Mitch could not take his eyes off of her. "I should have gotten you a tiara. You look like a queen."

"Stop it, Mitch. You're making me blush."

"That also becomes you," he said, reaching to give her a kiss. Taking her by a hand, he led her back to sit beside him on a couch. "We wondered why you didn't go to the closer guest bath at this end of the hallway. Now we know. Thank you."

"Cynthia, does the gold and diamond jewelry go together or would just one or the other be better?" Branda asked.

Laughing, Cynthia answered, "Honey, diamonds like those go with any color of anything, anytime, anywhere."

Mitch went to turn on some slow romantic music, piped it into the living room, and asked Branda to dance. Hesitating at first, she lost her fear of not being able to do it well when she felt Mitch's strong arm come around her, the other holding her hand.

"Don't worry," he whispered in her ear. "I won't let you fall." Turning to Sean and Cynthia, he added, "Come on you two. Let's see some of those fancy ballroom steps that let you win that contest years ago."

"There's too much furniture to knock over in here," Sean said.

"Or you've just forgotten how," teased Mitch.

"Stand back and watch," Sean warned.

With that he and Cynthia went into a routine that was dazzling and beautiful despite the rather restricted space. Mitch and Branda applauded at the end.

Finally, all agreed they had eaten way too much and were sleepy. It was after six when Sean and Cynthia left. Mitch and Branda danced a while longer then sat on the couch listening to the music. They fell asleep.

Much later, they awakened, decided to have a bite of leftovers and get ready for bed.

Mitch switched the music to play in their bedroom. Since he had learned Branda especially liked romantic Spanish guitar music, he had added some of that to the mix.

Branda had hung up her new clothing and put away the gold jewelry but decided to leave the diamonds on a while longer.

She came out of the closet heading for the bath wearing only undies, jewelry and her pink fake-fur house shoes. She saw Mitch sitting on the edge of the bed he had turned down.

He chuckled and said teasingly, "I like your costume. It shows off those lovely long legs among other things."

She had to laugh too. Seeing he was still dressed in his black trousers and white dress shirt that was now partially unbuttoned, she asked, "Aren't you going to bed?"

"Yes, but first I want you to take these with you and put on what's inside." Reaching under a pillow, he pulled out two beautifully wrapped boxes, one smaller than the other.

"Mitch, what on earth? You have given me too much already."

Getting up to take the presents to her, he said, "These are for me too. And before you ask, yes, Cynthia and Sean helped me out after I phoned them Sunday morning while you were bathing. They had two or three sets in their car Sunday night when they came for dinner. I sneaked out and picked this one."

When she came back into the bedroom he was sitting on the edge of the bed again.

"I knew you would look like that," he said.

"Like what?"

"A bride. Stand there a moment and let my eyes drink you in."

"Oh, Mitch I never saw anything as lovely as this long Chantilly lace peignoir and matching nightgown. Is the gown supposed to be this form fitting?"

"I certainly hoped so," he said, smiling, getting up to go to her.

"And the satin slippers feel so comfortable. Thank you again and again."

"You're most welcome. And I thank you for the beautiful sight of you," he added, taking her face in his hands and kissing her. "I'm glad you left on the diamonds. They add a special touch."

"But I can't sleep in them. I'm afraid something will break."

"If it does, I'll get you new ones. Live a little. Wear them to bed."

"All right. I will. They make me feel a bit wicked with this nightgown on."

"Good. Now stand still. I want to get some pictures of you."

"Do you have any film left? You took a lot at the party and afterwards in my new pants suit."

"I saved some for this special occasion."

"You are something else, Dr. Mitchell Andrews," she said as he took pictures.

"Something good, or something bad?"

"Like all people, probably a little of both."

"Well, I know one thing," he said, finally putting down the camera.

"What's that?" she asked.

"I want you to come here Branda and undress me."

She had already noticed he was aroused. After she slowly unbuttoned the rest of his shirt, kissing his chest then his mouth as she did, she slipped the shirt off, letting it fall on the floor. She remembered telling him once that a man in a white dress shirt left partly open turned her on. She wondered if he had recalled that. She hadn't told him a man in black pants tight across the front also got to her.

Moving closer to the bed as they kissed again and again, he began taking off her peignoir as she unzipped his trousers, letting them slide to the floor. By the time they were in bed, he was naked but had left her gown on.

"I just want to look at you for a moment longer with that gorgeous body showing through that lace."

But when he began touching her body and kissing her, she could stand it no longer.

"Please undress me."

Kissing her lace covered body one more time, he reached down and slowly began pulling the gown up and off.

As usual, their lovemaking was special and satisfying. Erotically exhausted, they slept in each other's arms until morning light, covered only with a sheet.

When she awakened at daybreak, she pondered the fact neither of them had ever said, "I love you" to each other even in the heat of passion. In fact, they rarely said anything at all except for the occasional comment he made about how beautiful she was. She would tell him he was handsome.

"Strange," she thought, mentally talking to Betty. "I suppose he can't let go of Helen, and I'm still too leery of men. I told Connor I loved him. He was the first man and the last I said that to. Now I know that was just infatuation and I swore I would never fall into that trap again. I'm confused and certainly never dreamed of having sex with a man I barely know. Truthfully, I know it's too early to be thinking about us loving each other. My feelings about Mitch are all mixed up. One of them almost seems maternal. He's still hurting so much it makes me want to take care of him like I would a child. Other feelings are most definitely not maternal. Oh well, at least we're married and can enjoy each other. I do things instinctively with Mitch that Connor could not even force me to do. I let him do things to me I never dreamed I would allow because his lovemaking is never profane. He makes me glad I waited all of those years, hard as it was to do sometimes. Not that I ever dated that much or met anyone who made me forget how much I basically dislike men."

Leaning over to kiss his scar, she whispered, "I hope I can at least make you happy, Mitch." He didn't stir.

Since they had forgotten again to close the drapes, she was able to lie there watching his slow breathing, looking at his sexy body and handsome face with wayward strands of black hair falling over his forehead. Raising her arms to stretch, she saw her diamond bracelet shimmering in a sunbeam.

"Oh, jumpin' George!" she thought. "I forgot all about giving him the wedding ring."

Reaching over and getting the ring from the drawer, she slipped it onto his third finger, left hand as he slept.

The movement roused him. "What are you doing?"

"With this ring, I thee wed," she said, holding up his hand so he could see the gold band.

Sitting up quickly, he said, "What on earth?"

"I had Cynthia bring some yesterday and I selected this one. Do you like it? If not, you can pick another."

After looking from her to the ring and back a few times he grabbed her, kissed her, and said, "You really are something else. It's perfect. Thank you, Branda. That is very thoughtful."

"You're welcome. I meant to give it to you last night but you . . . well . . . you rather distracted me. By the way, do you think we are turning into sex fiends? And you must wonder if I have always been an easy woman since I certainly have been with you. It's like my sex dam has broken."

Laughing softly at her humor, he said, "No I don't think we're sex fiends. I think we're just hungry for love and sex is part of that. And no I don't think you were ever an easy woman as you call it. I think . . . well, I don't know what I think but I know deep down you were never that." Giving her a quick kiss, he added, teasingly, "But I sure am glad you are now." Patting her on the rump, he added, "Much as I would enjoy making love to you right now, we've got to get up and get going."

She wondered for a second about his use of the words hungry for love, then said, "Oh Mitch," tears welling in her eyes. Looking toward her feet, she asked, "Are you sure these aren't the reason you don't want to make love?"

"Come here," he said, as he began kissing her slowly and thoroughly.

She wasn't sure but she thought she had seen a somber look shadow his eyes. When he abruptly stopped kissing her and quickly sat up on the side of the bed, she knew something was very wrong.

"What is it, Mitch?" she asked.

Not even glancing back at her, he answered, "Nothing. We just have a lot to do today and had better get started. Remember this is the day we start some tests."

"I thought the first one with my gynecologist, Dr. Cline, wasn't until 1:30 this afternoon and the mammogram at 2:30."

"Yes, but I want you to be completely rested and ready. Besides, I have a lot to do before we go."

"Oh, I see," she said, but she didn't. She wondered if giving him the wedding ring had somehow upset him. He seemed totally distracted by something.

"You go on and get cleaned up while I go work out in the exercise room," he said. "I'll shower after we have breakfast."

Having said that, Mitch got up, put on a sweat suit, went into the bathroom for a minute, then headed for the hallway.

Stopping for a moment, he called back to her, "Don't forget to carry your two-way radio with you."

She noticed his was clipped to his waistband.

"I won't forget," she said.

Branda sat for a minute trying to figure out what had happened. She was so sure he was ready to make love.

"Maybe he's just tired," she thought. "After all we have been more than rather active."

Putting on her peignoir and slippers, she went to the chest of drawers to get her underwear and socks then to the closet to get a pair of jeans and sweatshirt to wear until time to get dressed for her appointments. She went into the bathroom and laid the clothing on one end of the marble vanity top. Never having been prone to do much crying before in her life since her divorce, she briefly wondered why she felt more and more like doing it lately.

"Perhaps it's connected in some way to this illness," she thought.

Feeling suddenly hungry, she decided to go to the kitchen and get a banana to hold her over until breakfast. She picked up her two-way radio she had put on the vanity top with her clothes and put it in her peignoir pocket.

Going down the hallway, noticing the exercise room door was closed, she decided not to bother Mitch. As she neared the study door, she saw it was slightly open.

"Maybe he needed to do some office work first or check on some appointments," she thought.

But at the sound of his agitated voice, she opened the door preparing to ask him what was wrong? The words never came out.

She stood frozen at the sight of the room's contents and of Mitch sitting on a dark brown leather couch facing forward giving her a view of his left side and profile.

He was holding a framed picture saying, "Oh Helen. Part of me still loves you so and always will. I'm sorry I have betrayed you. I'm so mixed up and feel so guilty. Branda is such a sweet person and very beautiful like you but in a different way. You would like her I know. I need to let go of you, Helen. Please help me. I'm . . .."

Becoming aware of Branda's presence, he stopped, turning his head to look at her.

"What the hell are you doing here?" he asked, gruffly. "You're supposed to be taking a bath."

Ignoring the question and comment, she exclaimed, "So this is why you never wanted me to see this room? It's more of a shrine to Helen than it is your study." Broadly gesturing to include all of the room, she continued, "I'll be damned," using a word she had never said before in her life.

Taking a few more steps into the room, she took a good look at the various pictures of Helen placed on every available spot and covering a lot of wall space. One huge one was a formal wedding portrait in color of her and Mitch. A spacious wall niche contained three medium size red votive glasses with lighted candles in each. Our Lady of Guadalupe was painted on the back wall. Framed pictures of Helen hung just outside the niche on either side; one in her wedding dress, the other of Mitch kissing the bride.

She did notice the room also contained traditional furniture found in a study plus a great many bookshelves filled to the brim.

Putting down the picture, Mitch got up and came toward Branda. "Dammit it to hell, Branda. At least let me explain."

"Explain what? That you still love Helen. And quit using cuss words all the time."

"You may be my legal wife, Branda, but you are not my legal boss. I'll cuss anytime I feel like it."

She fought back tears. "Well, at least that's honest."

As Mitch reached to hold her, Branda jerked away. "Oh no you don't. Now I know all you want from me is sex. You can't have sex or make love, or whatever you want to call it, with any of these pictures," she said, moving her arms to include the many images of Helen. "So tag . . . I'm it. Well, think again Dr. Andrews. I need you for medical reasons . . . at least until I can make other arrangements, but I won't be sleeping in your bed anymore. I'll move to the basement with my own things."

She started to turn and leave but Mitch took her by the arms and held on.

"Oh no you don't. Not until I've had my say."

"Well this ought to be good since I'm standing knee deep in a room full of evidence contrary to any excuses you might think up."

"I thought you understood about my hang ups," Mitch said.

"I thought I did too, but now I realize they go beyond hang ups. They're hang ons . . . forever. I'm not sure I can deal with that."

"Why not?" he asked. "You're not in love with me. At least you've never said so."

"I've never heard those words roll off your tongue either," Branda countered. "So I guess we're not in love. We're in heat. We don't make love. We make sex. Well go take a cold shower, doc. The fun's over."

"Branda, if you had waited a moment, you would have heard the rest of what I was getting ready to say. I was . . ."

Pulling away from him, she turned and left, giving him no time to finish. Pausing in the hallway, she called back, "You stay home with Helen. I'm sure you were getting ready to tell her again how much you still love her. I'll drive myself to the appointments this afternoon."

He yelled after her, "But I need to tell you . . ."

As she kept walking, she yelled back, "There's nothing you could tell me that I want to hear."

He slammed the door shut so hard, she thought it would jar loose from its hinges.

"Like I've always said," she muttered. "A man is a man is a man. Remember that."

She wondered about her reactions to a dead woman.

"That's not like me. I just hate feeling like a sex object again in my life."

CHAPTER SEVEN

GRABBING ONE OF HER SUITCASES out of a hallway storage cabinet, Branda headed for the bedroom and bath, hurriedly packing necessary clothing and items. The suitcase was slated to be put in a garage cabinet but hadn't made it there yet. She put the diamond bracelet and barrette on his pillow.

"Payoff jewelry," she muttered. "Makes me feel like a whore."

She came close to leaving her wedding ring but decided she needed that.

"Since some people know we're married it might look strange for me not to wear it. I wonder if he is still wearing the one I gave him? I'll have to remember to look."

Also taking a few clothes from the closet, she headed for the basement elevator.

Upon reaching the foyer, she remembered she had forgotten Betty. Putting down the suitcase and clothing, she went back to get her. Even though she was running on adrenaline and feeling little else, her feet were beginning to bother her.

She prayed Mitch would not come out of his study. She was in no mood to listen to him.

While looking for a basement closet in which to hang her clothes, she discovered a darkroom. She remembered Mitch saying both he and his father were camera buffs and preferred developing their own film. She had noticed some of their beautiful work hung throughout the house; mostly landscapes.

After getting settled, she felt hungry again. She found small cans of tomato juice, cheese and some kind of fancy crackers in the bar refrigerator.

"This will have to do for now," she said to Betty, now propped in her former apartment chair. "I'll leave early and stop at a fast food drive-in to get something else. Hopefully, no one will recognize me." Continuing her thoughts, she added, "Since I'm going to my own gynecologist's office over on Ballas Road, I know where that is. I wonder if Mitch has told him about my condition? Betty, be glad you never have to have a pelvic exam, Pap smear, or mammogram."

She had a vague recollection that a woman wasn't supposed to have sex or do any internal cleansing 24 hours before getting a Pap smear or pelvic exam.

"Well, I'll just have to hope for the best because I am going to clean up no matter what Mitch advised. I'll mention this to Dr. Cline and see what he has to say. From what Mitch said, doctors sometimes have different opinions on the subject. If Dr. Cline wants me to reschedule I will."

Although the downstairs bathroom she had chosen in one of the apartments wasn't as spacious as the one upstairs, it was still roomy and beautifully decorated in cream colored marble. The carpeting was a pale sage green. She had hung her clothes in a closet in that apartment but used her own chest of drawers for other things.

After enjoying a fairly long soaking bath, she dressed, double-checked to make sure she had her house keys, money, cell phone, and two-way radio then went upstairs to the garage. Her car would not start.

"Dead battery from sitting too long I guess," she thought. "I'll call a taxi and just have to hope I'm not contagious."

Continuing her reverie as she went back downstairs, "Somehow I don't think I am or Mitch would not have scheduled these appointments. As much as possible, I think he is trying to be cautious. He thinks it's urgent to start tests and says doctors and others in the health field are constantly dealing with contagion of one sort or another. But my ailment is such an unknown. Anyway, it has already been 11 days since my first episode. Mitch told me when he called the Board of Health the other day, they had no reported similar cases. He said after giving them a description, they acted like he was nuts."

Not wanting to run the risk of hearing his voice, she did not activate her two-way radio.

"If I need to call him, I will. But I think I will soon be out of range to send or receive although Mitch said he bought the most powerful one in the store. I think it's good for five miles. If I run into trouble I'll use my cell phone. I must remember to charge the radio and phone when I get back here."

She arranged for the taxi to pick her up at the basement door. The driver might think that odd but she didn't care. She didn't want to go back upstairs and maybe run into Mitch. Making sure she worked the alarm correctly, unlocked then locked the door, she waited in the soft spring air.

"My but it feels good to be outside."

As the taxi drove away, she was sure she saw the study room draperies move.

"Well, Doctor Andrews. You just sit there and visit with Helen," she thought.

She asked the driver to stop at a nearby Steak n' Shake; one that still offered curb service. She wanted to get something for him too, but he said he wasn't hungry.

Since it was nearly 11 a.m. she ordered a double steakburger, french fries, and chocolate malted milk to go. She knew of a quiet outdoor patio area adjacent to the medical complex where some fairly comfortable chairs and nice tables were available.

"I'll eat there and read the book I brought," she thought.

The sight of security guards patrolling near the somewhat isolated spot made her feel safe. She ate, dozed, and read until her 1:30 p.m. appointment time neared.

As she started walking toward the medical office building, Mitch appeared seemingly out of nowhere. He was carrying his black bag.

"Well, jumpin' George. What are you doing here?" she asked angrily. Glancing at his left hand, she saw he was still wearing the wedding ring she had given him.

"You didn't honestly think I was going to let you go off alone did you?" he asked with that old familiar edge in his voice.

"I certainly hoped so."

"Don't you know that, as your doctor, I could not allow that; especially with your condition being such an unknown. I may be a lousy husband, but I'm trying to be a good doctor. Branda, there's something you should know before going to Dr. Cline's."

Ignoring his last words she said, "Well you're fired as soon as I can make other arrangements. And we can divorce too."

"As you wish," he said.

"I'll get out of your house as soon as I can."

"Don't be hasty, Branda. Where would you go?"

"I don't know. I'll think of something."

"You're welcome to stay downstairs as long as you want. I won't bother you."

"You bet your life you won't! I'll think about staying there . . . for the time being at least. How did you find me on that patio?"

"The minute you left, I started having you followed. As the taxi drove past the study window I jotted down the company name and license number. I would have followed you myself, but I was afraid you would spot my car. You have been under constant surveillance shortly after you left the house. And didn't you notice those security guards patrolling that patio area?"

"Yes. I thought that was normal."

"It is, but they were also watching you to make sure you were all right. We were in constant contact by walkie-talkie. I told them you are not feeling well."

"I can't say I like the thought of being spied on."

"Well, I'm sorry, Branda. But knowing your medical problem plus our being married, I could not in good conscience let you just go out wandering around by yourself." After pausing a moment, he added. "Besides, I genuinely do not want anything to happen to you. And what if another episode occurred in the taxi or sitting by yourself on the patio?"

"I could have dealt with that somehow."

"Well you could not have called me on your two-way radio since you didn't have it on. I tried calling you before I thought you might be out of the five-mile range. I . . . "

Butting in, she said, "You're right about that. But I could have turned it on. Also, I do have my cell phone and could have called yours or the home phone if I needed to and at least left a message on the answering machine. I'm not totally brain dead. You seem to forget I have been living on my own and taking care of myself for a good many years."

"But you weren't so ill during that time."

Their eyes met and held the glance for a moment. She was glad they were nearing Dr. Cline's office. She knew he kept trying to tell her something, but she wasn't in the mood to listen fearing it had something to do with the scene in the study.

"Mitch," she said, "I do have a couple of medical questions for you."

"All right."

"If I'm correct about one of them, I may have to reschedule the pelvic exam and Pap smear test. I seem to recall a woman isn't supposed to have sex or douche 24 hours beforehand. Of course I still remember your advice about douching in general although I still prefer to do so."

"That's what I have been trying to tell you now and was trying to tell you before you stormed out of the study. I had hoped to tell you before you left the house, and again when I tried calling you on the two-way radio. I should have told you this morning when we woke up but I was distracted by other thoughts. In fact, I should never even have made love to you last night but I was so caught up in the party fun and the sight of you in that lace nightgown, I simply did not think clearly. As a doctor, I can't believe I did that although I knew we could reschedule. I'm sorry. Rest assured nothing like that will happen again. I knew you would have to cancel today and get another appointment. Also, some doctors prefer 48 hours or longer regarding sex and douching since the latter can wash out signs of abnormal cells or an infectious condition. Some doctors don't want patients taking tub baths a day or so before. And a woman should schedule an appointment so a smear can be taken approximately 12 to 14 days after the first day of her last menstrual period and never during time of active bleeding."

"Well, that's that. I'll have to reschedule. Not because of a period problem but the other two."

"I'll take care of changing your appointment for you. I'll tell them you aren't feeling well which is no lie. Then we can go to that next wing and check on maybe getting your mammogram over with earlier."

"Well okay. Thanks, Mitch," she said, grudgingly.

"No problem. And what is your other question?"

"Do you really think I might be contagious? I worried about that taxi driver and maybe transmitting any germs through money to him and the waitress at the drive-in. But from what you said about the Board of Health Department people, I really don't think I am."

"I don't either after this length of time. It is just a precautionary move." Pausing, he added, "And I think if it can be transmitted by close direct touch, I am the one who might come up with symptoms sooner than anyone else."

She did her best to ignore his inference.

Changing the subject, she asked, "Did you find the diamond jewelry?"

"Yes. It's in the wall safe. Don't you want it anymore?"

"No. Makes me feel like a whore."

"Well if that isn't the silliest damn thing I ever heard!" he said, dark eyes flashing with anger. "I would never think of you like that."

He left her sitting on a small chair in the corridor outside Dr. Cline's office while he went inside to change her appointment.

Coming back out a few minutes later in a calmer mood, he said, "You're to come back Friday the 23rd at 10 a.m. In case you are wondering, Richard . . . Dr. Cline does know about your condition but not about our original marriage arrangement that seems to have changed in one important area. I felt I had to tell him in case he feared contagion and didn't want to examine you. His nurse knows too since she has to be in the room with him during the exams."

"I can understand that. I guess that has to be. What did they think?" she asked, letting his reference to their lovemaking slide by.

"They aren't particularly afraid but will take extra precautions to prevent any possible spread of germs or whatever is causing this. Of course neither has ever heard of such a thing happening and are as personally concerned for you as I am."

Branda let that last remark slide by as he continued.

"As a doctor and nurse, they are also as interested in the case as I am. The mammogram technician and doctor also know. They are not worried and will keep the secret. So far, no one really believes you are contagious. I told them about the Board of Health report. Anyway, during your visit to my office that's why it was necessary for you to sign that certain form. It allows me to release information to other doctors. Remember?"

"Yes, I do. And I trust your judgment."

"Thank you. By the way, when we go for any appointments anywhere, we will enter by a private office door if possible."

"Why?"

"Just another precaution. You don't need to be near people in waiting rooms in case they are ill and carrying germs, and it's better if you don't unknowingly subject them to anything."

"I see. Like Typhoid Mary?"

"Well I wouldn't put it that strongly."

"Do the doctors in your office know, or your staff?"

"Yes, I decided it was only fair to let them know too since I will be checking with them about a lot of things; especially about any of your friends calling to report similar symptoms."

"I can see where that was a good idea. We'll just have to hope for the best where privacy is concerned."

"That's right," said Mitch. "Frankly, Branda, I am having to deal with this on a sort of fly by the seat of my pants approach since it is such an unknown situation."

"I understand," she said.

Their fingers touched briefly as he handed her the appointment card. She tried not to feel any reaction but wasn't entirely successful. "Blast his jumpin' George hide," she thought. "Why does this man affect me so? I wonder if he felt anything?"

"I'll call the mammogram office now," Mitch was saying, taking a piece of paper out of his shirt pocket. He had jotted down the number before leaving home just in case he needed it. After a brief conversation on his cell phone, he told Branda, "They can take you right away since there was a cancellation. By the way, this test result, and all others from now on will be faxed to our house."

"I thought they were to go to your office?"

"After thinking it over, I decided there would be more privacy and one less burden on my staff if they were sent to my home office."

"I didn't know you had a home office," she said, beginning to walk toward the next wing.

"Branda, I thought you understood the study is also my home office."

"I didn't know you had a fax machine in there," she said, somewhat sarcastically.

"Yes, there's quite a bit more in there than you saw," he said, also with an edge to his voice. "If you would just listen . . . "

"No! I don't want to listen. I'm tired and want to get the mammogram over with and get home and rest."

"Maybe when you feel better we could talk things out," he said.

"I can't think of a thing you could say to change my mind. I saw what I saw and heard what I heard!"

Neither spoke as they continued walking. Branda was limping more than usual from all of the day's activities. Mitch reached to hold her arm as support, but she pulled away.

"I'm fine," she said, gruffly.

Coming back into a private office after the mammogram, she asked Mitch if they could sit a moment before walking to the car.

"Certainly," he said. "And when you are ready, I'll go pull it around to the front of the building."

Walking slowly toward the elevator, Mitch asked, "Pretty rough exam isn't it? I imagine you women wish men had to undergo something similar with a sensitive part of our anatomy."

"You've got that right," she said. "Although I really would not wish that exam on anybody . . . not even a man."

As mad, tired, and sore as she was, and as leery as he was of her present angry mood, they both managed a slight smile. She waited on a bench outside while he went to get the car. When he came around to help her in, she let him.

"If you feel up to it, Branda, we'll stop and pick up your dress at the cleaners and I'll get a few groceries for us."

"That's fine."

"Is there anything special you are hungry for?" he asked.

"No, but thank you for asking."

By the time he got back to the car from picking up her cleaning, she was sound asleep. He roused her before going into Dierberg's to shop to let her know where he would be.

He also asked her to get her two-way radio out of her purse and activate it as his was.

"Okay, Mitch," she said. Still drowsy, she found her two-way radio and did as he asked. As soon as he left, she fell back asleep.

She awakened as he was carrying her from the car into the house. He had first propped open the garage and mudroom doors leading to the den and was heading for the elevator.

"Oh, for heaven's sake, Mitch," she said, gruffly. "Put me down. I can walk." She didn't like being in his arms because of the disturbing feelings he caused.

"You sure are a stubborn woman," he said, also gruffly. Holding her body was disturbing him too. Then adding more calmly, "You seem so tired I didn't want to awaken you." He put her down.

Neither spoke again until reaching the basement.

"Are you sure you want to stay down here, Branda?" Mitch asked.

"One-hundred per cent certain," she said. "Now, if you'll excuse me, I am going to get in my soft clothes and take a long nap. If I can help with fixing dinner, call me."

"I'll grill the steaks I bought if that's okay," he said. "If I need some help though with the salad and other things, I'll let you know."

"Fine."

"Please keep your two-way radio on in case you need me."

"All right."

He lingered a moment. "I'll go unload the car now," he said. "After that I would like to check your vital signs. As I said you seem very tired. Too tired. That worries me."

"You can just forget that!" she exclaimed. "I've had enough doctoring for one day."

"Oh, all right," he said, turning angrily and leaving by the stairway, taking them two steps at a time.

After getting comfortable, Branda stretched out ready for sleep. Before dozing off, she said to Betty, "What a mess I'm in. When I feel more like it I must take some time to think and sort things out. My thoughts are all jumbled."

Mitch called her on the two-way radio when he had dinner ready.

"Don't bother getting dressed. It's okay to eat in your soft clothes. Also bring your cell phone. Since we'll be together for a time, this will be a good opportunity to recharge our two-way radios and cell phones."

Hurriedly, she put on some jeans and a lightweight sweatshirt with no bra underneath. She was still sore. For one thing, she thought leaving on her nightgown and robe might create too intimate a mood.

When he saw her, he said, "As I mentioned, you didn't need to change."

"My mama and daddy always said only lazy people eat in their nightclothes."

"Whatever makes you comfortable," he said, taking their two-way radios and cell phones, hooking them up for recharging.

Aside from complimenting him on the meal he had prepared, and a few other casual remarks each made, they ate in silence. Tension between them was thick enough to cut with their steak knives.

Finally, during dessert and coffee, Mitch said, "Branda, don't you think we should have one of our talks and try ironing out our problems?"

"I'll see, Mitch. I'm not always a fast thinker. I have to ponder things sometimes before coming up with answers and solutions. You have thrown me for a loop . . . or, perhaps it's only my ego that has been stomped on . . . but I need some time. Too much has happened too fast. After all, we've only known each other nine days."

"In some ways, Branda, I feel like I've known you forever."

"And I think your Merlot is talking."

"Oh good grief, Branda. I had one glass of wine. It might not hurt if you had a glass or two now and then."

"No thanks."

After helping him with the dishes, which she was surprised he let her do, she said, "I'm going back downstairs now, watch Jeopardy, and whatever else looks interesting."

After unhooking her two-way radio and cell phone, she took them and headed for the elevator.

"Are you sure you don't want to talk now?" Mitch asked.

Stopping a moment, she answered, "No. I have to think about some things before I do."

"How long will that be?"

"I don't know. Probably tomorrow."

"Remember, tomorrow is when the cleaning and yard crews come plus the intercom repairman."

"Oh, jumpin' George. I had forgotten that," she said. "What time do they arrive?"

"The cleaning crew usually gets here about 9:30 a.m., the yard men about 10 a.m., and the other guy is scheduled for 1 p.m. The cleaners are here most of the day, the yardmen for about four hours depending on what needs to be done. I have no idea how long the intercom man will need to be here. Later on when the weather gets warm, a pool man will come too."

Pausing a moment, she said, "Mitch I would not want to embarrass you in front of any of them so I will get up early. I'll remove all evidence of my living downstairs."

"I would appreciate that very much, Branda. They are looking forward to meeting you."

"No problem. I'll act like the dutiful wife."

"I wish it wouldn't be an act," he said.

She ignored his remark, asking, "How many cleaners are there?"

"Four. Two women, Ella and Jane and two men, Pete and Joe."

"And the yard crew?" she asked.

"Also four. Jim, Al, Bob, and Norman. The intercom repairman's name is Arthur."

"What will you tell them all after I leave?" she asked.

"I'll figure that out later," he said. "Hopefully, I won't have to."

"Don't count on it. And now, good night. I'll leave my two-way radio on," she said, again heading for the elevator.

"Damn but you're a stubborn woman," he said.

"You said that before and quit cussing at me."

"I'm not cussing at you. I'm just cussing," he said, angrily. "This is stupid."

"Go take a cold shower. That will cool down more than your temper," she said.

Afterwards, in bed, she wondered what made her say such a silly hateful thing.

"I remember reading frustration breeds aggression," she said to Betty. "I guess that's what is going on with Mitch and me now . . . snarling at each other . . . me especially."

While watching Jeopardy, she heard the phone ring. Shortly afterwards, Mitch contacted her on the two-way radio.

"Yes?" she asked.

"Did you hear the phone ring?"

"Yes."

"That was Sean and Cynthia. They are going to their Lake of the Ozarks cabin tomorrow afternoon and come back Sunday unless we need them here. They thought they would take advantage of their time off from work. They want us to go with them. I told them that wasn't a good idea since tomorrow is a busy one and I really don't want to get that far from our hospitals. But if you would like to go, we can work out something. I told them I would call them back."

"No I don't want to go for the reasons you mentioned plus one you didn't. But please thank them for me. I'll give them a call when they get back."

"I understand," he said in a quieter tone than usual. Continuing, he added, "They also said a lot of your friends have been calling them to see how you are. They all said to tell you hello and hope you are doing well."

"Who, for instance?"

"Mary Ann, Linda, Mathilda, Rev. Cummings, Annie. They want to come see you as soon as it is okay; or at least call you. Cynthia and Sean said they would certainly let them know. Even some of your customers send their regards."

"How nice. Please tell Cynthia and Sean to thank everyone and that I send hellos back to them. Mitch, I have wanted to call them because I miss them very much but under the circumstances of what they believe I decided to wait until my quarantine is over."

"That's probably a good idea, and I'll have Sean and Cynthia relay your message. Branda, I have a favor to ask you."

"What?"

"Would it disturb you if I came down and used the dark room tonight? I've gotten behind on developing some of my film."

"Mitch, this is your house. Of course that would be all right. Thanks for letting me know."

"You're welcome. I don't know exactly when I'll be there. If you are asleep and wake up and see that red light on over the door, you'll know I'm in there working."

"Okay. I won't open the door."

"Thanks."

She wondered if he would bother developing the roll he shot last night during and after the birthday party.

Thoughts whirling around in her head like a dust storm choked off sleep.

"If I leave, where will I go? If I get worse, who will take care of me? It wouldn't be fair to impose on Sean and Cynthia or any of my other friends."

Turning toward Betty, she asked, "Why am I so upset about Helen's pictures? If I'm jealous, why? Is it the woman scorned thing? How can that be since my marriage is really in name only . . . not for love? Or, am I falling in love with Mitch? Am I enjoying sex so much after all those years of repression, I don't want to give it up but I hate the idea of being used just for that? Oh, that's silly. We didn't even plan to have sex. It just happened. Why am I so drawn to Mitch besides sexually? I do know underneath all of his problems, he is the most decent, thoughtful man I've ever known . . . besides my dad, of course. What, Betty, What?"

The doll's blank glass-button eyes continued staring back as Branda fell into a fitful sleep while some other thought kept niggling at her.

She didn't hear Mitch come downstairs, come over to check on her, then go to the darkroom. Nor did she know when he left much later on, stopping again at her bedside to make sure she was all right and her alarm clock was set. It was, for 8 a.m. He was carrying a large manila envelope full of developed pictures.

Towards dawn Branda had a strange dream. One so real she was sure she was awake. Her mother and father were standing at the foot of her bed. Each was holding one of her sons. All were smiling and were the same ages as the last time she saw them. Since Branda always dreamed in color, the scene was especially vivid.

It sounded like her mother was saying, "Don't worry, Branda. Everything will be fine and one day we'll all be together again."

Branda awakened, sat up, reaching to touch them as they withdrew into a disappearing silvery mist.

Suddenly feeling warm and weak, she sat watching a small part of her left foot where the two smallest toes used to be attached. It glowed, went through the usual color sequence, disappeared, then gave off the acrid odor.

Trying not to cry out or in any way alert Mitch via the two-way radio, she clamped her hand over her mouth. She decided not to tell him anything about it since the day would be a busy one with other people around.

Reaching to turn off the alarm on her combination clock, radio, and calendar, she muffled a gasp. The sight of the calendar date jarred her memory.

"Betty, now I know what the thought is that has been nagging at me! With all the excitement in my recent life I haven't been paying attention. I don't know for sure since my periods have always been so erratic, but I have a feeling I'm pregnant."

CHAPTER EIGHT

"**B**ETTY, I MUST BE THE most fertile woman on earth," said Branda. "I got pregnant the first time Connor touched me, and maybe now with Mitch, sometime during the three times. Oh dear Lord, if this is Your will I'll accept it, but You had better be ready to give me lots of strength. You must think I am one strong person."

She didn't know whether to laugh or cry. The thought of having another baby to hold and love filled her with joy. The possibility of not living long enough to see it grow up brought tears to her eyes.

"Maybe I'm just starting menopause. Or maybe it's the upheaval in my life from my sickness, getting married to a man I barely know, having sex again after all these years, or . . . Oh Betty, there could be a lot of different reasons. Well I know one thing. I'm not going to mention this to Mitch until I am as sure as possible. I've heard some girls talking about these new home pregnancy tests that can practically let you know as soon as you get out of bed after having sex."

Checking her watch after bathing and dressing, she saw she would have time to boot up her computer and make a quick search on the Internet for such information.

"Thank goodness Mitch was kind enough to have these two separate phone lines put in even before I came to his house; one for the computer, and one for my bedside phone. He said he figured I might like that kind of privacy at times. Little did he know how handy this would be."

She found one test that might possibly let a woman know as early as six days after she conceives.

"That's for me," she said, looking toward Betty's unblinking eyes. "When I get a chance, I'll check into some of those others mentioned that need more time. Now, just how am I going to get to a drug store on my own to get that test? If I can get it today, I can take the test Saturday and know. Maybe even Friday, but I'll play it safe and wait the extra day."

A plan formed in her mind as she turned off her computer and removed traces of living downstairs. She did leave the few clothes she had put in the apartment closet and did not remove anything from her chest of drawers.

"The cleaning crew surely won't be looking in the closet."

By the time she finished, her plan was in place. With so many people around today she would ask Mitch, or one of the workmen, to jump start her car so she could drive around a bit and charge the battery. Mitch would not be likely to make a scene or object with others around. She would be sure to leave her two-way radio open and would let him know that. She hated being sneaky but decided it was the only solution.

"And if I remember correctly, Betty, there is a drugstore nearby with a drive-thru window people use to drop off and pick up prescriptions. I can use that saying I have a sore foot that makes walking uncomfortable and it would be nice if they could serve me from that window. If they won't . . . well, I'll just have to find some place that will. I won't take the chance of going inside and jeopardizing anyone or picking up any stray germs myself. I suppose saying I have a sore foot is stretching the truth a bit, but under the circumstances I don't think I will burn in hell for saying so. Anyway, both of them do bother me at times."

Mitch's voice coming in over the two-way radio broke into her thoughts. "Branda, breakfast is ready."

"Thanks, I was just getting ready to come upstairs. Everything is shipshape down here. You can come check for yourself if you care to."

"That won't be necessary."

Looking toward her as she came into the kitchen carrying her purse, he exclaimed, "Branda, what on earth has happened to you? You're as pale as a ghost."

"I am? Maybe it's because I saw four of them in a dream I had at dawn," she said, trying to steer him away from her looks.

While putting on her makeup, she had noticed she didn't look up to par. She thought perhaps it was caused from the combination of the dream, losing another body part, and wondering if she was carrying Mitch's child. "Any one of those things would make a person fade a shade or two," she thought.

"That sounds more like a nightmare," Mitch was saying.

"No, it was okay after the initial shock. At first it was so real I didn't know I was dreaming."

"Who was in the dream?"

"My parents and twin sons. Mother was holding Josh. Dad had Jason. When I reached out to touch all of them they disappeared."

"Did they say anything?"

"Yes. Mother told me not to worry, that everything would be fine and one day we will all be together again. Since I dream in color, it was all very vivid."

"I can see where that would be upsetting to you," said Mitch, reaching to hold her in his arms and comfort her.

She drew away.

"Oh, it's still like that, is it?" asked Mitch. "I was hoping we could have our talk."

"Maybe we can later."

"Well at least let me check your vital signs just in case."

"No way! We can do that later too."

"Listen, Branda, as your doctor, I insist," he said sternly.

Reluctantly, she let him, steeling herself against reacting to his touch. Pretending he was just another doctor, she was partially successful until he put his stethoscope on her chest checking her heartbeat. She just had to clamp her jaw tight and hold on. She noticed he began breathing faster too.

"Your blood pressure is down a little, but nothing serious," he reported after finishing.

"That's good. I'm feeling a little better anyway."

Conversation was kept to a minimum during breakfast.

"I hope I didn't disturb you when I came down to use the darkroom," said Mitch.

"No, I didn't hear you at all. Did you get caught up with your work there?"

"Yes. Later today or early tomorrow I would like to show you what I did."

"That would be fine," said Branda. "You must have worked late. You look tired."

"I am somewhat. It was a long night. Would you like to take a walk in the garden while I wash the dishes?"

"I'll be glad to help you."

"No, you go on. The cleaning crew should be here in about 30 minutes."

"By the way, Mitch, how did they get into the house when you were still working in your office?"

"Ella has a key and knows the burglar alarm code. But she doesn't like using the key. She is always afraid of setting off the alarm and having the police arrive with guns drawn. Like a lot of doctors, I always tried taking Wednesdays off which worked out fine for Ella and the others."

"How come the others don't have keys or know the code?"

"They didn't want the responsibility or something. I offered, but they said they preferred to just let Ella handle it all."

"How much do they know now about what is going on with us? I remember earlier you said you preferred not telling them about all of the circumstances unless you had to . . . meaning if I get worse."

"The same things we told Mary Ann and the others. Basically, you may have a rare form of cancer and experimental medication may be tried. You don't feel well enough for a lot of visitors and may be contagious if it isn't cancer. We aren't that sure yet about your ailment. The quarantine is up the 26th. Since you need to be monitored 24/7 and refused to go to a hospital, you agreed to this marriage of convenience idea. I gave them and the yard crew the option of not coming to work until after the 26th, but all said they are not afraid. I told them as much of the truth as I dared since they are my friends. I think the women with their romantic notions secretly hope we fall madly in love and live happily ever after. I also felt it only fair to tell Arthur, the intercom repairman. He is not worried about possible contagion. Says he's around all sorts of people on a daily basis, some of whom are ill and rely on intercom systems more than others."

"I wish you had been as truthful with me about your study."

"Branda. At first I didn't see how it would matter whether you knew about the pictures of Helen or not. Later, after we made love and I thought our feelings for each other might be changing, I wasn't sure how to handle telling you."

Thinking for a moment, Branda said, "I guess I can see your viewpoint on that. When we talk we can explore that further and maybe some other subjects as well."

"Oh, then you are becoming willing to talk."

"Yes, I'm pretty sure I am at least. Maybe this evening after everyone is gone."

"Good. I think we need to clear the air. Truce?" he asked.

"Semi-truce for now," she answered, turning to go to the den and out to the garden while he cleaned up the kitchen. She left her purse in one of the den cabinets.

Branda was outside admiring some of the spring flowers when she thought she heard the front doorbell ring, then voices.

"Since they have been told I am very ill, they might think it strange if I go off in my car. I'll have to think of something to tell them," Branda thought. "I simply have to get that kit."

All of the cleaning crew was coming into the kitchen as she approached, coming from the garden through the den. Mitch introduced everybody.

Ella said, "Dr. Andrews, you didn't tell us how beautiful your wife is."

The rest chimed in agreeing with Ella.

"I'll bet she's smart too," said Jane.

"She definitely is both," Mitch said.

Branda stood blushing, finally managing a heartfelt, "Thank you very, very much."

After exchanging a few more pleasantries, the crew went off to do their chores.

"Mitch," said Branda. "I think I will go back out to the garden and rest on one of those chaise lounges. They certainly are larger and more comfortable than most. I imagine you had them custom built."

"Mom and Dad did. I'll join you for a while if you don't mind. Then I have some test appointments to check on plus do some other scheduling for you."

"Where? In your study?"

"Yes, Branda. That is primarily my home office. What's wrong with you? I never knew you to show such a sarcastic streak," he said, with a hint of the old edginess in his voice.

Hesitating a moment, she said, "I don't know, Mitch. I really don't know. I haven't figured it out yet. And I'm sorry. By the way, do all those people that work for you call you Dr. Andrews?"

"Yes," he said. "I've known them for years and told them to call me Mitch, but they are of the old school and won't do it. It's a sign of respect for them to call me doctor."

"That's kind of nice. I didn't really think you were the kind of person who would insist they call you by your title."

Silently, they walked to the garden. She stretched out on a chaise lounge and dozed. He sat in a nearby chair reading a medical book he had picked up in the den.

When she awakened a while later, he was not there.

Ella and Jane were walking toward her. Jane was saying, "The doctor said if you were awake to tell you he had to go inside to do some work. We just came out here on our break like we always do weather permitting, but we can go somewhere else if you would rather be alone."

"Oh no. Please stay," said Branda. "Mitch tells me you two have worked for his family for a long time."

"Yes, for the past 22 years. We were just out of high school when we started. Both 18 years old. Pete and Joe have worked here for about 15 years," said Ella. "Wonderful family, the Andrews."

"Dr. Andrews is just like his folks. Nice as can be," Jane said. "The cousin that lived here for awhile is really a good person too."

Figuring they were hesitant about mentioning Helen, Branda broke the ice. "It was such a shame about Mitch's wife, Helen. From what I hear, they were very much in love."

"Oh my yes," said Ella. "Like two peas in a pod. I imagine you know he's had an awful time getting over her death? I've never seen a man grieve so."

"Yes, he's told me."

"I think in the long run you will be very good for him, and maybe he will be for you too," said Jane.

"We sure wish the two of you all the happiness you can find in this old world," Ella said. "We also hope you recover from your serious illness."

"Thank you very much. Mitch and other doctors will do all they can. Actually, I'm feeling pretty good today. I may take a short drive later just to get out in this nice spring air."

"You'll enjoy that, I'm sure," said Ella.

After discussing the beauty of the surrounding garden flowers, the weather, and the Cardinal baseball team, Ella finally said, "Well, we'd better get back to work. This house is easy to keep if you stay on top of it."

"I enjoyed our chat," said Branda, as the two got up to go back inside.

Looking at her watch, she realized the intercom repairman was not scheduled to arrive for about an hour. "I think my best bet to get out of here is when he shows up and I can get him to jump start my car," she thought. "I'll have to tell Mitch but not until the last minute so he won't have time to put up much of a fuss; especially in front of the guy. Anyway, if Mitch is like most men, he will feel duty bound to follow the man around to see what he is doing and ask if he can help."

She went back into the den, found a Smithsonian magazine and sat reading for awhile, periodically glancing at sunlit-made rainbows on the Waterford dish she admired. Using the den phone, she called Sean and Cynthia wishing them a good trip and hoped they had a wonderful time. They were just getting ready to leave for their Ozarks cabin. Finally, she went to the kitchen to eat a ham sandwich and drink a glass of milk.

At 12:45, after getting her purse out of the cabinet, she walked out to the front porch. Its large light tan squares of Spanish tile covered a medium-size floor area outside the double front doors, expanding into spaciousness over toward the dining room side of the house. The tiles complimented the light cream stuccoed exterior walls. She waited, sitting on a roomy, cushioned, dark tan wicker chair in the large area. From this vantage point, she would be able to see the repairman the minute he drove up.

When she saw the truck coming into the driveway, she called Mitch on the two-way radio.

"Yes," he answered. "Are you okay?"

"Yes, Mitch. Can you come out front? I need to discuss something with you."

"Where out front?"

"On the porch."

As Mitch walked out of the door, Pete and Joe from the cleaning crew came around the outside corner of the study, coming over to greet him.

"Hi, Dr. Andrews," they said.

"Hi Pete, Joe," said Mitch.

Joe continued, "We're getting ready to wash the outside of your study windows like we've done all the others. Some of the spring showers left them spotted."

"Good idea. Thanks," Mitch said.

Seeing the group, the yardmen came to join them. Branda walked over to where all were standing.

"Hello again, Pete and Joe," she said.

"Hello Miz Andrews," they said in tandem.

Mitch introduced her to Jim, Al, Bob, and Norman who stood chatting with her and the others.

Arthur joined the group, smiling politely as Mitch introduced her.

"Howdy ma'am," he said.

"Hello, Arthur. Beautiful day, isn't it?"

"Yes, ma'am, it sure is."

"Arthur, if it's okay with my husband, I wonder if you could do me a small favor before you start on the intercom?"

"I'll do my best," said Arthur.

Turning toward Mitch, she asked, "Would it be all right if Arthur gave my car a jump-start? I would like to just drive it around the neighborhood a little bit . . . to recharge the battery and also see how 'Ol Betsy is running these days."

She could tell Mitch was doing his utmost to control himself.

"No need to bother Arthur," he said. "I can do that for you with my car."

"I just thought Arthur might have better equipment in his truck; maybe stronger jumper cables."

"In a way, she's got a point there, Dr. Andrews. I'm sure yours would work just fine, but my truck probably has more extra juice to spare than your car. You wouldn't want to risk running down your own battery in case you need your car for some medical emergency."

"Good point, Mitch," said Branda, hoping he wouldn't start cussing. "I know you would be glad to go with me but I thought perhaps you might be needed here to help check out the intercom as Arthur repairs it."

"That would be a help during part of the work, Dr. Andrews," Arthur said. "Since you're pretty savvy about these things, I could use you to explain what is happening as I fix the system and we talk to each other from the various rooms."

"And I'll be back before you know it," Branda said. Before Mitch could say another word, she added, "Arthur, if you'll drive your truck down to the garage area, we'll walk and meet you."

"You're both welcome to ride in my truck."

"Thanks," Mitch said. "But we need the exercise."

Branda knew she was in for it as she told Pete, Joe, and the yardmen goodbye, leaving them to go complete their chores. Arthur drove his truck slowly past the couple.

After drawing away from anyone's earshot, Mitch said, "Just what in the hell do you think you're doing, Branda? You know I don't approve of this maneuver."

"Mitch, I just need to get away for a bit and think. Besides, my car does need to be driven before it falls apart completely."

"But what if something happens to you?"

"I have my two-way radio open, my cell phone open, and I am not going to drive across the Mississippi River to Illinois. I just need a little space for maybe half an hour."

"Well, I don't like it, but I didn't want to make a scene. And I think you were counting on that, weren't you? I never thought of you as being devious."

"I'm really not. I'm just feeling sort of desperate," she explained. "Please try to understand, Mitch."

Nearing the garage where Arthur was waiting, Mitch said, "We'll talk about this later. You be sure to leave your two-way radio on. I'll be nervous as a whore in church until you get back."

"What a thing to say," Branda said, coming close to laughing out loud at his remark.

"Branda, did you have any lunch? I got busy and forgot to fix any for you," he said, a bit more calmly. "I'm sorry."

"Not a problem. Yes. I had a ham sandwich and a glass of milk. I would have fixed something for you but didn't know where you were exactly and I needed to be ready to go."

"That's all right. I'll grab a bite after you leave. Please be careful, Branda."

"I will."

"I don't like this. I don't like it at all," Mitch was saying, mostly under his breath.

She gave a sigh of relief once her car was started and she was on her way. She knew Mitch was ready to bust wide open he was so mad at her.

"I just hope he doesn't show out in front of anybody at his house. Since they have no idea why he should be upset, I think he'll be okay. He sure isn't used to being crossed. Sometimes he can behave like a spoiled rich kid. I wonder what he'd say if he knew he might be a spoiled rich kid father?" She smiled at the thought.

Turning on her favorite Mexican radio station, she enjoyed the trip to the drugstore she had in mind up on Olive Street Road.

"It's nice being in my car again."

As she approached the pharmacy drive-thru window, she decided to get two of the tests; one to try Friday, the other for Saturday.

"I'll have to turn off this two-way radio so Mitch can't hear me ordering them. I'll just have to tell him a white lie and say I accidentally turned it off. I can't believe how sneaky I can be but I think this situation justifies it."

Since there was no hitch in getting the tests at the window, after paying for them and stuffing them into her large purse, she was soon on her way back home. She turned the two-way radio back on.

Checking her watch, she saw she had estimated her trip about right. "By the time I get back, it will be about 30 minutes," she thought. "I'll call Mitch and tell him I am headed back. That should make him feel better." It did.

"Thanks, Branda for letting me know," he said, with a slight edge to his voice. "Was there something wrong with your two-way radio? I didn't hear any sounds for a short time . . . like your Mexican music. I was about to call you on your cell phone."

"I'm sorry, Mitch. I accidentally turned it off and didn't realize it until I stopped hearing you and Arthur talking." Before he could say anything else, she said, "See you soon," and turned the volume louder on the radio so she couldn't hear him anymore; only the thump-thump of the gitaron more clearly.

Rolling into the driveway, she saw Mitch standing in front of the house signaling for her to stop.

"Oh jumpin' George," she said out loud, turning off the radio music. "What now? He still looks mad. Thank goodness my purse is large enough to hide the test kits."

Stopping, rolling down the passenger window, she leaned over calling out, "What's up?"

Walking to the car, opening the door and getting in, he said, "This," handing her a garage door opener. "It's a spare. If you insist on flying off into the wild blue yonder again you'll need it."

"Thanks, but I didn't go flying off anywhere."

"You could have fooled me. And be more careful about that two-way radio switch. Now drive on down to the garage and park. I need to get back inside in case Arthur needs me again," he said in a grouchy tone.

"You can get out now," she said, sounding equally grumpy. "I believe I am capable of parking a car inside a garage, or do you think I'm one of those women drivers that hasn't got a brain in her head?"

"I really don't know what to think about you anymore. Now drive on. I want to make sure you can handle that last turn without knocking off the edge of the garage."

She wanted to cry but didn't, knowing if he was like most men he would say something like, "That's right. Turn on the waterworks."

Instead, peeling rubber, Branda sped down the driveway pushing the door opener button as she went, praying no one inside or outside was watching. Slowing down to pull into the garage, she parked expertly and asked, "How was that?"

"Stupid. Just plain stupid and silly. I don't know what the hell has gotten into you, but I think you'd better go take a nap and sleep it off," he said, getting out of the car, slamming the door and stomping into the house.

She soon followed, stopping in the den long enough to squeeze her purse back inside the cabinet that held photo albums, videos and the like. She would rather have taken it downstairs, but didn't want to run the risk of any workers seeing her.

"I wonder where everyone is?" she thought. "I sure hope none of them saw that dumb NASCAR maneuver I just made going down the driveway."

Evidently no one inside had since she ran into all of them in one place or another as she made her way back to the bedroom to take a nap. At least no one said anything about it. She really was too tired to care much at this point. She had not noticed any of the yardmen close by outside either.

Nearing the bedroom, she saw Ella coming along the hallway.

"Are you finished in the bedroom?" she asked.

"Yes ma'am."

"If not, that's okay. I was just going to take a nap. My little outing wore me out a bit more than I thought it would. I haven't driven my car for several days."

"You go right on and get some rest. The doctor told us you required a lot. We're pretty well finished with this end of the house."

"Thank you," said Branda. "Where is Dr. Andrews?"

"Downstairs with Arthur. I think they have found the problem and solved it. They have checked out the upstairs rooms and are checking downstairs now. Evidently there wasn't much wrong."

"That's good," said Branda. "If I don't see you or the rest before you leave, thank you for doing such a good job keeping this large house so nice. Please tell the others too."

"Why thank you, Mrs. Andrews. I will be sure to let the others know."

She wished Ella and the others would call her Branda, but something told her they wouldn't; just like they always called Mitch Dr. Andrews. Reaching the bedroom, she closed the door, laid down on top of the bedspread pulling the quilt at the end to partially cover her. She soon fell asleep despite the many disturbing thoughts chattering at her. The ones that had bothered her most related to her recent behavior.

"I'm acting like a nagging shrew and not being fair to Mitch at all. I keep forgetting this is a marriage of convenience, not for love. Or is it becoming that? I don't know what is wrong with me." Her last trailing thought was, "I wish I could cuss. I wonder if that would help?"

She awakened sensing someone was in the room with her. Opening her eyes, she saw it was Mitch sitting on the bed's edge looking at her. He didn't look so mad anymore.

"What are you doing here?" she asked. "Have all the workers gone?"

"Just checking on you. I am your doctor you know . . . plus a concerned husband . . . whether you care to believe that or not. And, yes, the workers have gone. It's 5 o'clock."

" Good heavens, I'm turning into a real sleepyhead."

"You must need to be."

"Maybe so, but I don't need to also be so bitchy. I'm sorry, Mitch."

"That's all right. There has to be a reason. That isn't like you," said Mitch. "When you feel up to it I would like to talk."

"I would too. Maybe after dinner?"

"That's fine. Would you like to eat here or go out and get something at Steak n' Shake? I imagine you do get cabin fever being in the house most of the time. We can use curb service like you did before."

"Great. But do you like their food?"

"I'm from St. Louis, remember? Just about everybody here either chooses them or White Castle. I'm a Steak n' Shake man myself although I do stray to the other side occasionally."

After enjoying dinner sitting in his car then returning home, Mitch said, "Branda, I have a surprise for you." Taking her by the hand, he led her toward the study.

For a split second she held back, but decided to stop acting foolish about a roomful of pictures.

"Now close your eyes," said Mitch. "And don't open them until I tell you."

"Okay," she said, closing her eyes, allowing him to lead her into the room.

"Now open," Mitch said.

She gasped at what she saw. There were no more pictures of Helen in the room; only ones of her he had taken at the birthday party and some of his parents. There were a few of him as a young boy and man. She was also surprised to see three taken during their own wedding ceremony at Sean and Cynthia's house.

"I didn't know anyone took pictures there," she said, pointing toward them.

"Cynthia managed it," he said. "Now I'm glad she did."

"Me too."

She didn't see the ones of her in the filmy nightgown.

"Where are the sexy ones you took of me after the party?"

Opening a desk file drawer, he pulled out a folder. "These are for my eyes only," he said. "And yours, if you want to see them."

"I do." After looking at them, she added, "Why, Mitch, these are truly beautiful; not like cheesecake pictures at all. And all of the others of me on the wall are more like art than pictures."

"I had a truly beautiful model."

"Thank you, but you made me look better than I really do I'm a thinkin.'"

"And I don't think any camera could do you justice."

Reaching to take her in his arms and kiss her, she drew away. "Oh, Mitch. Please don't be offended. It's just that you turn me on so fast, I have no will power. And I don't want to have to keep changing appointments at Dr. Cline's office. Remember, I have one Friday morning?"

"Yes, I remember, damn it. Just looking at you and being near you turns me on like a mercury switch. But, you're right. We'd better behave."

"I'm glad you feel that way, because I plan to keep sleeping downstairs until at least Saturday night."

"What!!!!" he exclaimed. "I want you back in our bed."

"Mitch, I just could not handle that right now. If I can't take a kiss in here, I know I wouldn't last two seconds in bed with you."

"But why until Saturday?"

"Because, as I recall, sometimes I stay a bit sore after whose procedures."

"Of course. I'm being thoughtless and selfish. I'm sorry."

Changing the subject, she asked, "Mitch, when did you do all of this rearranging?"

"Last night after I developed the pictures."

"Jumpin' George, you must be exhausted . . . physically and emotionally. That could not have been easy for you. You must have been up most of the night."

"It was a bit hard but I managed. And I was up most of the night," he said.

"And then here I go all day pushing your buttons. No wonder you were so grumpy with me."

"Well, that's over. Now, do we want to talk now or wait until tomorrow after we've had a good night's sleep . . . not that I slept very well even for a short time with you not beside me . . . and probably won't again?"

"I didn't sleep too well either and don't expect to the next few nights," she said. "And I agree it might be best to postpone our talk."

She started to tell him about her latest foot episode, but decided it would make him worry too much about her being alone downstairs.

"Maybe I'll tell him tomorrow. I'll see," she thought.

He escorted her to the basement, waiting by the elevator as she stopped to pick up her purse from the den cabinet.

"Tomorrow I'll show you how the house intercom works," he said. "It's easy. And please be sure to keep your two-way radio open all night."

"I will. Thanks, Mitch . . . for everything."

"You're welcome. Until tomorrow, Branda."

Turning he went back up, taking the stairs two at a time.

Betty's unblinking eyes stared at her.

"Oh, damn," said Branda, using that word for the second time in her life. "Why does this man affect me so much?"

CHAPTER NINE

SLEEP CAME QUICKLY TO BRANDA and stayed until 4 a.m. Awakening slowly, she sensed a presence near her. Thinking it might be the dream vision of her parents and sons returning, she kept her eyes closed, waiting for them to appear. When nothing happened, she opened her eyes looking toward Betty.

She had to stifle a laugh. There sat Mitch sound asleep in Betty's chair with the doll lying across his lap. He had on pajamas, robe, and house shoes. With only Branda's angel night-light shining in the area's dimness, it was easy for her to imagine what Mitch would actually look like holding a real baby.

"Poor Mitch," she mused. "He is so exhausted. Why is he down here sitting up? Do I really worry him that much? But in what way . . . as a wife he may be beginning to love, a sex object, a patient, or some of each?"

As she was getting up to awaken him and tell him to go back to his comfortable bed, she must have made some noise because he woke up.

Leaning forward, still holding onto Betty, he asked, "Are you okay, Branda?"

"Yes. I'm fine. But you look beat. What are you doing here?" she asked, moving to sit on the edge of the bed.

"I couldn't sleep for worrying about you down here alone." Hesitating a moment, he added, "And our bed is too big without you in it."

"But you need your rest. Especially if you're going to put up with the likes of me," she added, slightly laughing.

"Well, actually," he said. "I tried sleeping in one of the apartment beds for awhile, but I still felt too far away from you. I keep thinking maybe your two-way radio might not be working right, or you have fainted, or something else might prevent you from getting my attention if you needed to."

"Jumpin' George, Mitch! You really are a concerned doctor aren't you?"

"I'm more than that, Branda. I'm also a lonesome husband without you beside me. I miss you. I know this is no hour to start our talk, but before we try getting back to sleep I do want to tell you one very important thing so you can be thinking about it."

"Okay, Mitch, but first I want to ask if you got upset Tuesday morning and left me rather abruptly because I gave you the wedding ring?"

"Yes, Branda. The ring, plus the lovemaking, suddenly brought on those feelings I get about betraying Helen. As you know, I thoroughly enjoy making love to you and your giving me this ring overwhelmed me. I felt guilty but I don't anymore. Maybe I will again, but I think the worst is over. I treasure this ring. It makes me feel whole and complete again. Thank you from the bottom of my heart. I was going to tell you all of this later during our talk. I'm sorry for hurting your feelings. Forgive me?"

"Of course, Mitch. I'm glad you told me all of this," she said, reaching to hold his hand. "And what is it you wanted to tell me before I interrupted just now?"

"Just that if you had waited until I finished all I was going to say when you walked into the study day before yesterday, you would have heard me say I'm falling in love with you."

"Really, Mitch?" she asked, surprised and happy at hearing his words. "Really?"

"Really . . . and truly."

"All I heard was you felt like you were betraying Helen, were all mixed up, and felt guilty about being with me."

"I also said you are a sweet person, very beautiful like Helen but in a different way and I know she would like you. I was telling her I needed to let go of her more and needed her help. I think I meant not only her help, if she could, but also God's or anyone else's."

"You also said part of you would always love her, but honestly and truthfully Mitch I can understand that."

"That's true, Branda. And I'm glad you can understand. Helen died the day of our 23rd wedding anniversary. That's almost a quarter of a century . . . a long time. I can't just erase all of those memories. We were married on June 5th."

"Oh Mitch, how sad. On your wedding anniversary," she said, holding his hands tighter. "Oh how very, very sad."

"Yes. It was. And you know the other parts of the story. But I have to get on with my life. I can see that more and more clearly now with you around me." Hesitating a moment, he asked, "Branda, is there any chance you could fall in love with me?"

"Yes, of course, Mitch. I think I am already doing that although I fight against it. I don't want to get hurt again. I want peace, not another upsetting episode in my life like I had with Connor. I guess I am being overly cautious. And you and I have only known each other going on 11 days. Falling in love in that short a time is sort of ridiculous when you think about it."

"Stranger things have happened in this old world," said Mitch.

"I guess so, Mitch. Let me try and explain why I think I reacted so angrily when I walked into the study and saw you talking to Helen's picture."

"The hell hath no fury like a woman scorned thing perhaps?"

"I thought that too at first, but later I realized I would have had to feel loved in the first place to think I was being scorned."

"And you didn't feel loved at all?" Mitch asked.

"I really had not taken time to sort out my feelings very well. But, after all, neither of us had ever said we loved each other . . . even during lovemaking. Frankly, for one thing, I think it was so nice having sex again; especially good sex with a gentle man like you, I just wasn't seriously thinking about love at that point. My sex-starved body was happy for just getting fed after so many years. But I guess deep down I also romantically hoped both of us would develop a true love for each other someday."

"So why did you get into what I thought was the hell hath no fury part so quickly?"

"As I told you, I suddenly felt like I was just a sex object for you like I was with Connor. What bothered me and hurt my feelings more is you sounded like you had no intentions of ever even remotely trying to fall in love with me. Sometimes I wasn't sure if you even liked me. I felt betrayed and used."

"In "Born to Win" language, I put you on a child ego level."

"Yes, I guess that's what happened. I just felt cheap . . . something I never wanted to feel again in my lifetime."

"I'm really very, very sorry Branda for having made you feel that way. We do have a lot of demons to fight against don't we?"

"Yes, but I think we'll work it all out if we try."

"I do too. Do you want to try?" asked Mitch.

After gazing in the dim light at him holding Betty and looking so serious, she said, "Yes, Mitch. I do. If and when our past ghosts pop up to bother us, we'll help each other get through it. Now why don't you go back upstairs to your bed, or the apartment one down here? You need to rest too. I think I can go back to sleep now."

"Me too. Are you sure you'll call me if anything goes wrong with you? And I agree about helping each other through any bad times."

Giving his hands an extra squeeze, she said, "Yes, Mitch. I promise to call you if I need to. And by the way, Mitch, I don't happen to think you are a lousy husband as you said yesterday when we were over at the medical complex patio. You are really one of the kindest men I've ever met."

"Thank you, Branda."

"You're welcome."

She was still leery about telling him of her last foot episode because she knew he would sleep on the floor by her bed if he knew about that; not wanting to leave her alone a minute as she slept.

"Could I at least kiss you on the cheek?" he asked, releasing her hands and putting Betty back on the chair.

"Of course."

After the oh so light kiss, he reluctantly went off to the apartment bedroom double checking their two-way radio connections as he went. They worked fine.

Branda slept until 9 a.m. Wondering about Mitch, she went to check. He was still asleep, his breath coming and going in a slow measured rhythm.

"He really must be tired," she mused, looking at his handsome face a moment, then leaving to enter the bathroom she had been using in that same apartment. She noticed his shaving things in there too.

"Oh, dear. It's a good thing I didn't put those pregnancy kits in here in a drawer like I came close to doing. He just might have found them. Well, I can't move out of here now or he would wonder why. We're both too used to being in a bathroom at the same time now. I'll have to think of some other place to test myself for the first time tomorrow morning."

After bathing and getting dressed, Branda left a note on the pillow beside the still sleeping Mitch.

"Good morning sleepyhead number two," she wrote. "I'll be upstairs getting breakfast started."

Debating on how to sign the note, she finally wrote, "Love, Branda."

"After all," she mused. "I have a feeling I am headed in that direction despite my worries about doing so."

Before going upstairs, she took the test kits out of her purse putting them in her chest of drawers underneath her underwear.

Not wanting any possible elevator noises to awaken Mitch, she decided to use the stairway.

After making coffee and doing as much as possible toward breakfast preparation, she went into the den to wait. Taking a banana and a cup of coffee with her to hold her over, she sat reading a medical journal. She almost dozed off while also periodically looking at tiny intermittent rainbows on her favorite Waterford dish.

She was so engrossed reading an account about Spontaneous Human Combustion (SHC) in the journal, she didn't hear Mitch until he spoke from the open basement doorway.

"Good grief, Branda. Why didn't you wake me up? It's 10:30."

"Because dear doctor, you needed the sleep. Come on in the kitchen. Coffee is ready and it won't take a jiffy to fix the rest."

"But I haven't showered or shaved yet."

"Not a problem. You still look mighty handsome to me. You must be starved."

"Yes, as a matter of fact, I am," he admitted.

Still groggy, he sat watching her prepare bacon, eggs, toast, and the trimmings.

After they finished eating, making mostly small talk throughout the meal, Mitch asked, "After I clean up, would you like to have our chat?"

"That would be fine with me," said Branda. "I'll clean up the kitchen while you do your thing."

"Are you sure you feel like it?" he asked.

"Yes. As a matter of fact it felt good to cook for you. Maybe I can take over fixing some of the lunches and dinners too. I'm a pretty good cook."

"I'll bet you are. We'll play that by ear . . . depending on how you feel at the time."

"Okay," she said.

"Where would you like to talk?" he asked.

"I really like sitting on that one couch in the den," she said. "I seem to have a special affinity for it and that room . . . or maybe it's that dish."

"Fine with me. But first, I would like to show you some more in and about the study."

"Okay. I'll wait in the den for you. I'm reading about SHC in one of your medical journals."

"As I may have mentioned, I tend to look at that alleged phenomenon like I do UFO's."

"It's interesting reading nevertheless."

After Mitch returned, they headed for the study. On the way, Branda said, "Mitch, at the risk of upsetting you, I need to tell you something. I didn't tell you before because so many people were going to be around yesterday I didn't want to give you anything else to deal with."

"What is it?" he asked.

"I lost another part of my left foot Wednesday at dawn."

"WHAT?!!!" he yelled. "What part? And you didn't tell me? Branda, don't you ever, ever do that again no matter what is going on. Do you understand me? Did you have your two-way radio turned off?"

"No the radio was on. I just managed to stifle any sounds that would have tipped you off. And I promise not to ever keep such information from you again no matter what. I knew you would be mad."

"Yes. Mad. Because you scare me doing something like that. And I also can't be a good doctor to you unless I know what is going on."

"I'm sorry," she said.

Upon reaching the study, he said, "Now sit down on the couch and show me your foot."

After examining it thoroughly, he asked, "Did it go through the same procedure as always . . . you felt warm and weak, there was a glow, the same color changes, disappearance, and acrid odor?"

"Exactly the same."

"Okay, tomorrow after your tests if you feel up to it, and from now on, we start reading more medical books and journals, researching the Internet, and so on. I also have more tests scheduled for you that we'll discuss tomorrow. We're going to go into a higher gear now trying to find out what is going on with you. But I don't want to overwhelm you either. I think I have paced things so you won't get more exhausted than necessary."

"Thank you, Mitch. And again, I'm sorry for not telling you about my foot and also for acting so bitchy yesterday and part of the day before."

"Is the bitchy part one of your woman thangs as you say?" he asked, smiling slightly.

"Could be," she answered, smiling back. "But you know it got started in this room as we talked about earlier downstairs."

"I remember."

For a split second she considered telling him of her suspicions about being pregnant since she had just agreed not to ever withhold pertinent information from him again.

"But," she thought. "Pregnancy isn't exactly in the same category as this strange ailment I have. I really don't want to get his hopes up and then have it turn out to be false. I really don't see how he could be angry with me about that. I'll wait. This really is a woman thang."

Breaking into her thoughts, she heard Mitch saying, "Branda, I would like to show you more about this room than you saw before."

"All right. I've already noticed it is a lot larger than I realized."

Moving around, he pointed out pictures of his parents, himself as a baby, young boy, young man, and adult.

"Were those here the other day?"

"Yes, they have been here for years."

"I really did have on my blinders, didn't I?"

"Understandably so," Mitch assured her.

She admired the floor to ceiling bookshelves right angled in the corner at the house's front. There was another one on the opposite wall where a large, long table filled the rest of the wall space. Since formerly, this was Mitch's bedroom there was also a large full bath and spacious closet.

A large, beautiful, black walnut desk was in the center of the room. The usual computer setup was on top and in cabinet and drawer spaces below. A dark brown leather chair was in front. It matched the couch where she had seen him sitting talking to Helen's picture.

Mitch showed her his appointment books and other paraphernalia.

"This is where I schedule your appointments, communicate with other doctors and facilities by phone or email, and generally do what needs to be done regarding you. Later on, we'll go over your appointment and test list. If there is something you want to change, we can do it from here."

"When did you set this up?"

"I began some preliminary work the first day you came to my office and have continued. Remember all of those questions I asked you? I transferred that information to this home computer. And I got a lot done when we were staying at Sean and Cynthia's prior to getting married. At odd times, like when you were napping, I would come over here and work."

"Well, I'll be. Why didn't you tell me?"

"I thought perhaps it might be upsetting to you to know how very concerned I am about your condition. Now, after getting to know you better, I believe you are quite capable of handling it."

"What makes you think that? You know how weak I can be at times."

"Because I know now you are basically a very strong person."

"I try." Changing the subject, she asked, "Mitch, why is that wall niche in here with the painting of Our Lady of Guadalupe inside?"

"That was mom's idea after I moved out. She always admired Our Lady of Guadalupe, had the niche built, and hired an artist to paint the picture. She kept candles burning for various reasons . . . mostly as a way of showing her reverence for God. I do too."

"I get the feeling your family was Roman Catholic."

"You're right."

"But I haven't seen you going to church . . . even when you had a chance while we were staying at Sean and Cynthia's."

"I'm afraid I'm not much of a church goer; especially since Helen died."

"Don't you believe in God anymore?"

"Yes, of course. I just was mad at Him for awhile. But now I have begun thinking about going to Mass again one of these days."

"You mean when you can get someone to sit with me while you go . . . or have me go with you when I am no longer considered contagious?"

"Something like that. Would you go with me, Branda? I know you are a Southern Baptist and from what I understand, they don't take too kindly to our religion."

"We'll see. I think I sometimes have a broader viewpoint than some others although I am pretty straitlaced according to your way of thinking."

"Nothing wrong with your way," he said. "Now I want to show you how the house intercom works."

Following that demonstration and making certain she understood it well enough to work it in the dark if necessary, he asked if she had any questions.

"Not about the intercom system. But I would like to know what you did with all of Helen's pictures."

"Follow me," he said, leading her out and down the hall toward the other bedroom.

"Oh, Mitch," she said, as he started opening the door. "Don't tell me you put them in with all this clut . . ."

She stopped as the door swung wide. The room was totally cleaned up. Only bedroom furniture remained.

"How on earth did this happen?" she asked. "And when?"

"Ella, Jane, Pete, and Joe did it yesterday. Didn't you see them hauling stuff out of here?"

"No. To be honest, I was too wrapped up in my own little excursion to notice much of anything else. Where did they put it all?"

"Here and there . . . in downstairs and garage storage cabinets . . . wherever they could find a place."

"And Helen's pictures? I neglected to ask you yesterday. Please don't tell me you put them in the garage. They don't belong out there."

"No, they are boxed up and put in one of the downstairs bedroom closets."

"Mitch, I really don't mind the pictures. It was just seeing you talking to one of her that got to me . . . which I realize now was nothing but a smack to my silly ego. Please put them back in the study."

"All of them?" he asked.

"Yes, if you want to."

"No," he said. "Perhaps I'll bring a few back up to my study . . . ones you help me select. Or maybe I'll just leave all of them where they are. I'll think about that. But thank you, Branda."

"You're welcome. If you decide later to bring some back to the study, the selection is yours to make, Mitch." She added, "Maybe you could find a special spot for the rest somewhere downstairs . . . perhaps in one of the apartment bedrooms."

"I'll see," he said.

"Whatever you choose to do is fine with me. I understand more clearly now where you are coming from."

"Branda?" Mitch asked. "Do you have some pictures of your sons and parents you would like to hang in the study?"

"Thank you. I'll think about that. It still makes me very sad to see their faces in the pictures I have."

"How about some of friends or other relatives?"

"I'll think about that too," she said.

Actually, her mind was busier with thoughts about how this bedroom would be an ideal place for a nursery.

"But," she mused. "What if things don't work out between Mitch and me? I still have my cautious side and he still has his strong memories. I'll just take it a day at a time."

Mitch broke into her thoughts, "Should we go to the den now?"

"That would be fine."

"I'm not hungry since we had such a late breakfast. Are you?"

"No."

"Maybe later we can go to Steak n' Shake or some other drive-in place for lunch."

"That's a good idea," said Branda.

After settling down on the den couch, Mitch asked, "The first thing I need to know is if you were serious about firing me and getting another doctor."

"I was at the time I said it, but not now. I'm pretty certain I have a better perspective on our relationship now. At least I hope so and am trying."

"That's good to hear," he said, smiling slightly. "I've never been fired before. That shook me up a bit although I thought you were saying it just because you were angry."

"I'm sorry, Mitch. But one thing still bothers me."

"What?"

"I'm not sure you're under my HMO umbrella which means I can't pay you anything. And I'm sure all of this is going to be very expensive."

"Branda, believe me that would not be a problem. But since Sean told me you were worried about that, I checked it out. The other doctors in my office and I are most assuredly under your HMO umbrella."

"Well. That's a relief. I kept meaning to check but just haven't seemed to find the time. Even so, I doubt if my health insurance will pay it all."

Mitch laughed right out loud.

"What's so funny about that, Mitch?" she asked.

Taking her face in his hands and giving her a quick kiss before she could do anything about it, he said, "I think it's time you knew about the family fortune. Branda I'm a billionaire."

"WHAT? Jumpin' George several times!!! Nobody has that much money except people with names like Getty and Rockefeller."

"Dad and Mom made the fortune in real estate, oil, blue chip stocks, shipping and other wise investments. With help from advisors, I keep it going."

"I don't know what to say, Mitch. That flabbergasts me to say the least. How many people know about it?"

"Sean, Cynthia, and people who have a need to know. Dad and Mom never broadcast the information and neither do I. Of course, there are ways people can find it out if they want to. Anyway, you stop worrying about your doctor bills."

"No, Mitch. I want to pay what I can, or rather, what my HMO will pay. That's only fair. I won't have it any other way."

"Thank you. That is very nice of you, but they may cancel your insurance when they find out we're married and you don't really need it."

"Well, that's a different story then. But I hope you know I am not the gold digger type nor would I ever tell anyone about the fortune."

"Yes, Branda. I had already figured that out. That's another reason I told you about the money."

"Thanks for having faith in me."

"You're welcome. And just so you know, Branda. I added an amendment to my will. In case I die before you, the bulk of the fortune will go to you; the rest to some favorite people like Sean and Cynthia and their children, plus to favorite charities of mine, Dad's and Mom's."

"Oh, Mitch. Please don't talk like that; about your dying. Besides, I wouldn't even know what to do with that kind of money."

"You would learn. And there are advisors my family has had for years plus new ones coming up through the ranks. They would help you. I'll introduce you one day soon."

"Why are you telling me all of this?"

"Because, as they say in the business world, you have a need to know."

"Because of my medical condition?"

"Yes. That, plus other reasons. The main one being, I love you more each day."

"Oh thank you, Mitch. I think I'm headed in the same direction too. But, let's be realistic. It's much more likely that I will die before you."

He quickly took her in his arms and held her tightly before she could stop him.

"Not if I can help it, Branda," he said. "Not if I can help it."

She hugged him back, remaining silent, knowing full well it was all in God's hands.

Slowly letting go of each other, Mitch, asked, "Are we into a full truce now?"

"Yes, I think so. I really do think so; except for maybe the occasional lover's spat."

"Is there anything else you would like to talk about?" he asked.

"Yes. What happens to that will if our relationship doesn't work out for some reason and we end up getting a divorce as originally planned?"

"I don't think we'll divorce, Branda. But if we do, God forbid, my lawyers and advisors know to reverse the will back to its former state; with the exception of a sizable settlement for you. Any other questions?"

"After all you have just told me, nothing that won't wa . . . Oh Mitch. I . . ."

"What, Branda, what?"

She had fainted, slumping toward him.

Holding onto her with one arm he quickly reached down with his other hand and removed her loafers and white anklets. Getting her into a lying position, he sat watching a piece of her right foot glow; the part where her two smallest toes used to be attached. The pale yellow, light green, red sequence began, followed by the usual disappearance and acrid odor.

Grabbing his now ever-present black bag, he checked her. Her signs were as usual including the two degrees of temperature. Her foot felt very warm.

Carrying her back to their bed and putting her down on it, he removed the two-way radio clipped to the waistband of her slacks then placed the quilt over her. Since they kept their radios in off position when they were together, he opened both before dashing back to the den to retrieve his bag and her shoes and socks. Before going, he made certain her breathing pattern was normal. It was. When he came back, he switched the radios off again. They were also careful about keeping them and their cell phones charged.

A follow-up check of her showed the usual aftermath readings and the foot was cool.

Sitting in a nearby chair, he grew drowsy watching her sleep and went to stretch out beside her. He was still not completely rested from being up most of Tuesday night.

He only hoped if she woke up before him, she would realize he wasn't there trying to seduce her.

Waking an hour later, she was surprised to see where she was and to see Mitch sleeping. She managed to get up and get to the bathroom and back before he stirred.

"He always seems to sense when I am moving about," she thought. "Maybe that's a habit with doctors."

"You okay, Branda?" he asked.

"I guess so," she answered, trying as usual to hide how scared she was and her deepening fears about her ailment. "I'm hungry now. Are you?"

"Yes. Where do you want to go or would you rather I fix something here?"

"Let's go to Steak n' Shake. I like their chocolate malted milk."

As they drove along, Mitch asked, "Branda would you like for me to get another car?"

"Why? This one is extremely nice."

"I bought it because it was comfortable for Helen to ride in after she became very ill. I thought maybe you would like to pick out a different one."

"Not unless you want me to," she said. "I have no more qualms about any of your former ties with Helen. That's all resolved."

"You sure?"

"Yes. I think I know the score now."

"Thank you, Branda.

"You're welcome."

"Branda, I meant to ask you earlier when we were talking in the study. Did you ever get a chance to call your primary physician and ask him to send me your records?"

"No, Mitch I haven't done that. But I will."

"Who is he?"

"My HMO chose Dr. John William. And I also go to his colleague, Dr. Stephen Francis. I like them both equally."

"Oh, I know them. Fine men. Tell you what. Why don't I make an appointment and we'll go together so I can explain the situation in full. Then you can sign a release form so their office staff can send me copies of your medical records."

"That would be great. Thanks. That might make the HMO folks more agreeable to helping me pay my way."

"We'll see," said Mitch. "I will also need to have you sign another release form for me to be able to share information with all other doctors I deem necessary. Nurse Malone called to say some newer version has just come out. The one you signed for Dr. Cline and the mammogram group is still valid though."

"Not a problem. Tell anybody you have to. I meant to ask you if the Truebridge boys and girls know about my condition? I know they call home a lot and usually ask about me. They even call me Aunt Branda. I know Sean and Cynthia agreed not to call them though; to just wait for them to do so."

"At last report, the kids had not called yet," said Mitch. "But when they do, and with your permission, they will be told the whole truth. Those youngsters have the right stuff and can handle it."

"I think in the long run, that would be wisest."

"I'll be sure to tell Sean and Cynthia when they get home Sunday . . . or before if they call. I don't think their kids will call them at the Ozark cabin. They're old enough to realize that is sort of a honeymoon spot for their parents."

"One more thing, Mitch," said Branda. "I have always wondered how you got that facial scar?"

"Sean did it."

"What!!! I don't believe that. Not intentionally anyway," she said.

Mitch chuckled and said, "You're right. It was not intentional at all. It happened when we were about eleven years old riding our sleds down Art Hill in the snow. We were never really sure exactly what happened, but suddenly Sean's sled got out of control behind mine, slammed into mine and knocked me off. Before we stopped completely the front tip of one of his sled runners hit my face. Our dads had driven us to the park and were watching us as they chatted on a bench. They rushed me over to Barnes Hospital on Kingshighway where I got stitched up. Sean felt terrible about it but it was an accident; nobody's fault. I was so impressed with the doctors and nurses and the whole hospital atmosphere, I decided then and there I wanted to become a doctor."

"Well, I for one, am certainly glad you did."

After eating in the car then driving home, Mitch asked, "Branda, do you still want to sleep downstairs tonight?"

"No I don't, but since our chemistry seems to jump from simmer to boil-over when we're very close to each other, I think it is best under the circumstances."

"I suppose so. I sure do miss you in my bed though."

"I'm lonesome too. Will you be downstairs again in the apartment?"

"Yes . . . and don't forget to leave your radio open. If you get hungry later on, wake me up."

"Okay," she said. "But I think that late lunch or whatever you want to call it will last me through the night."

After getting into their soft clothes, Mitch sat in the chair by Branda's bed. He handed Betty to Branda. She propped up in her bed and she and Mitch watched television until they grew sleepy. He went off to his apartment bed, she stretched out after looking at her newest loss for a moment which sent shivers down her spine, put Betty back in her chair and switched off the lamp.

In the dim room, Betty's unblinking eyes stared at her.

"Oh Betty," said Branda. "I wonder what morning will bring?"

During a short dream, she could have sworn the doll was smiling at her.

CHAPTER TEN

SOUND SLEEP ELUDED HER BECAUSE she was apprehensive about being able to take the pregnancy test in complete privacy. Although the commode area where she needed to be to take the test was a small separate room with a door, if Mitch was anywhere near that would make her even more nervous than she already was. Finally, she slept well.

Just as she was beginning to awaken, the dream vision was coming. Only this time, it was only her mother and she wasn't holding Josh or Jason. She was smiling and holding the most beautiful newborn baby girl Branda had ever seen. Her eyes were dark like Mitch's, her hair blonde like Branda's.

Her mother was saying, "Here's Michele." The baby smiled and held out her tiny arms. As Branda reached to take her, the alarm clock went off and the vision disappeared into the silvery mist as before. As it was leaving, she saw a faint image of her father approaching.

"Michele, our little girl," she called, still half asleep.

Mitch's voice on the two-way radio brought her through the other half.

"Hey, sleepyhead. Wake up. You're mumbling in your sleep. Turn off your alarm and come upstairs for breakfast. I'll wait until you get here to finish fixing it."

Still a bit groggy, she said, "Okay, Mitch. Just give me a few minutes. I'll be up after I go to the bathroom."

Hoping that would keep him from coming downstairs for any reason, she grabbed one of the test kits out of her underwear drawer and headed for the bathroom.

"I must remember not to make any suspicious noises since our two-way radios are on," she thought. "But if I turn mine off, he will be down here like a shot. Hopefully, that sound I'm hearing coming over his is bacon frying and will cover minor noises from me; like unwrapping the box."

After completing the test, she wanted to shout for joy, cry for happiness, or do something to celebrate. She tested positive.

"Oh thank you, God," she silently prayed, shedding a few tears in spite of herself. "If I am going to die from my ailment, please let me live long enough to have this baby and be with her . . . or him . . . at least for a time."

Continuing her thoughts, she added, "I guess Betty is the only one I can tell right now. I wonder if . . . oh that's silly, no one dreams of exactly the baby they might be having. Maybe this test is a false alarm. I'm probably just starting the change or there's some other reason. I'll see what tomorrow's test results are."

After listening to Mitch's sounds upstairs she took a chance, went to the bathroom sink, and thoroughly rinsed off the test stick. After putting everything back in the container box, she put the whole thing inside the drugstore's plastic sack, washed the sink with plenty of soap and hot water, and went to shove the sack back into the same drawer.

"I'll have to find a time to put that sack into the trash compactor upstairs after I take the other test. I think there's one down here but there's nothing in it now and I'd rather leave it that way. I'll wait."

Mitch was calling, "Branda, are you okay? Come on up. Breakfast is almost ready."

"I'm on my way." Turning to Betty, she very quietly added, stifling a giggle, "I guess I could say we're on our way."

"Are you saying something, Branda?" Mitch asked. "I didn't quite catch it."

"Nothing, Mitch. Just some girl talk with Betty."

On the way up in the elevator, she thought how glad she was she had found time to call a couple of gynecologist's offices at random on her downstairs phone. She wanted to verify that it was all right to have a Pap smear if she suspected she might be pregnant. It had been a long time since she had had to think about such things and she could not remember all of the facts. Both office nurses assured her there was no problem with having the test. They indicated that included the pelvic exam too.

After eating and cleaning up, the couple headed for Dr. Cline's office in her car.

"I thought it might be wise to charge the battery," said Mitch. "Do you mind my driving it?"

"No, not at all. But aren't you afraid I'll go hot-rodding again if you charge the battery?" she asked, laughing.

"No. I would hope that was your first and last performance," he said, also laughing. Continuing, he asked, "Did you enjoy your shower this morning, Branda?"

"It was okay but I still prefer soaking in a tub. But I'm glad you reminded me about taking the shower since effects of a tub bath can interfere with test results." She was also remembering that tub baths were not allowed for pregnant women, if at all possible.

"Anyway, you sounded like you were enjoying yourself since you were singing your head off," Mitch said.

"If you can call what I do singing."

"You sounded fine to me and quite happy," he said. "Any special reason?"

"I was just counting my blessings . . . a thing I do quite often."

"I see," he said. "Are you sure you feel all right? You seem different somehow."

"Oh, it's just such a beautiful spring day and we're not mad at each other anymore. That makes me happy."

"Me too," he said. "By the way, do you want me to go in with you during the examination or wait in Richard's office?"

"To tell you the truth, Mitch. I am always very embarrassed during this procedure. I think maybe it would be worse for me if you were in there even though you're a doctor. Don't ask me why. It's just how I feel about it. It's bad enough having his nurse, Sandi Wade, in there because it's a law or something. I feel like a sideshow."

"Not a problem," said Mitch. "Since it will be near lunch time after this appointment, would you like to have lunch out somewhere . . . maybe a picnic in Forest Park."

"That would be great, but I'm still in quarantine."

"Oh, I think we can get around that by finding a secluded spot. What are you hungry for, Branda? You name it and I'll get it."

"Actually, I'm hungry for Mexican food. But maybe you don't like it."

"Oh yes I do. Remember, I lived in Texas for a long time," he said.

"I only know of one or two places here that have it anywhere near what I like. I usually just make my own like I learned in Reynosa, Mexico at the U.S. Bar across the river from McAllen, Texas."

"I've been there. How do you like your Mexican food?"

"Not spicy and absolutely no sour cream near it. Hot, spicy foods make my throat close up. Oh, and only masa . . . corn tortillas, white preferably but yellow will do in a pinch."

"I agree except for the spicy. I do like that but can always get some hot salsa on the side and add to my food," he said. "How about guacamole? Do you like that?"

"Is the sun round and hot? Oh yes, if it's made right."

"Which is how, Senora Andrews?"

"Just well mashed avocados, minced tomato and onion, a dash of salt and pepper, some olive oil and fresh lime juice to taste."

"That sounds like the real McCoy to me too."

"Now just where do you intend to get this lunch?" she asked.

"You leave that to me, ma'am," he said, as they pulled into the medical complex parking lot.

She debated on whether or not to tell Dr. Cline about her suspected pregnancy but decided against it.

"He'll know soon enough if I am," she thought. "Plus, I don't know how the doctor patient confidentiality deal fits in when there is another doctor involved . . . even if one is my husband. Best I wait."

In the examining room, she had a chance to ask Dr. Cline his opinion on douching.

He essentially told her the same thing Mitch had said, but there could be extenuating circumstances she could check with him about. He suggested she not overdo it, if done at all, and to stay away from harsh chemicals. And if she should become pregnant or even suspect she was, she should stop immediately and not get in any water that was too hot; especially in a tub bath, hot tub, or swimming pool. He also advised showers over tub baths. She was glad he said swimming and walking or other low-impact exercising was okay to do if pregnant and no special risks were involved. He mentioned that after a baby is born, it usually takes the mother six weeks to heal and she should not have sex or douche, and to still stay away from hot water as she did during pregnancy. Most of that information, and other things he mentioned, sounded familiar to her. She had either heard it from Mitch, read about it, or remembered from years before.

After the exam was over and she was dressed, Dr. Cline escorted her to his office where Mitch was waiting.

He said, "Mitch, everything appears to be normal. Hopefully, we'll have the lab reports in a few days including the one from the stool sample. I requested a rush order on all of them, but you never know how that will turn out. I'll send all reports to your home as you requested; either by fax, email, attachments, snail mail, or perhaps phone you in some cases."

"Thanks, Richard," said Mitch.

"But I have the mammogram results for you now. I asked to get that faster than usual too. Everything checks out fine. Nothing suspicious at all," said Dr. Cline, handing Mitch copies of the report papers.

"Thanks," said Mitch.

"Yes. Thank you Dr. Cline," said Branda.

"You're welcome. How are you doing otherwise, Branda?"

"I've had some more problems."

"I'm terribly sorry to hear that," said Dr. Cline. "Any idea yet what the cause is?"

"Not yet," said Branda. "But Mitch is doing everything he can to find out and plans to do more."

"If I can be of any help, Mitch, please let me know," said Dr. Cline.

"Just keep your eyes and ears open for anything that sounds like information on the subject."

"I certainly will."

"Thanks again," said Mitch and Branda in unison.

"You're welcome," said Dr. Cline.

On the way back to the car, Mitch asked, "How did it go? Are you all right?"

"It went as usual, and I feel as well as can be expected as you doctors often say," she said, giving him a slight smile to let him know she was really okay.

"Would you rather skip lunch out and go home? I can fix something there. Then you can take a nap if you like."

"No, I would enjoy eating out. I can rest later. Where are we going?"

"You'll see. It's not too far. I phoned ahead for the take out order while I was waiting for you but I can cancel if you need me too."

She sat quietly, enjoying the outing and seeing the beautiful spring scenery St. Louis was showing off.

"I must have dozed," she said, waking up as the car was stopping. She looked at where they were. "Oh Mitch. This is one of the places I was talking about . . . The Casa de Palmas."

"You wait here while I go get our picnic order," he said.

After reaching the park and finding a secluded table with benches, they sat enjoying their meal. Skittery squirrels were running around underneath and up and down giant oaks. An occasional rabbit hopped about before bounding away to somewhere he or she considered important. Chirping birds provided a musical background to the idyllic scene.

"Oh, Mitch. This is so pleasant. Let's do this again sometime . . . often."

"All right. We will."

She helped him clean up the table and he disposed of the used plates and containers in a nearby trash barrel.

By the time they reached home and were pulling into the garage, she was sleepy again.

"I'm like a puppy. Get my tummy full, and I need a nap."

"Me too. Where shall we nap . . . your place or mine?"

"Mitch, I'm sorry. Why don't I stay in my place and you go to yours? Hopefully, I will feel more like moving back upstairs by tomorrow night."

"I understand, Branda. I'm being selfish. I just like having you near me."

"Believe me, this is hard for me too, Mitch."

After giving her a quick kiss on the cheek, turning on and checking their two-way radios, he started walking toward the apartment bedroom.

Calling back as he went, he said, "If I wake up before you I will probably go to the study and start reading or searching the Internet for information."

"Okay. I'll find you," she said.

She slept three dream-free hours.

Taking the elevator, she stopped in the den to pick up the medical book she had been reading, and walked on to the study. Mitch was sitting in front of the computer reading a webpage.

Hearing her come in, he turned, asking, "How did you sleep?"

"Fine. How about you?"

"Very well."

The two spent the next hour and a half reading; Mitch finally switching off the computer and getting a book. He sat in one of the easy chairs that had a footstool. She sat on the couch. Neither found even the remotest information pertaining to her condition.

Branda broke the companionable silence. "Mitch, could this possibly be some mutant form of leprosy?"

"I don't think so. Why do you ask?"

"No particular reason except it's sort of a wasting away disease too. Maybe we could try the cure for it."

"I'll add that possibility to my computer list of possible causes and do some further checking. If you're through reading for a moment, I'll add it now and show you what I have done."

When his work came onto the screen he added leprosy, its cure, possible side effects, and other information in medical terminology she didn't understand. The list was in alphabetical order. She was amazed at what he had done even if she didn't know a lot of the words. She noticed he had entered Spontaneous Human Combustion which surprised her. He had already told her he thought that was in a hoax category.

"I really haven't found much to put on here . . . yet," he said. "Hopefully, as we read we will find more."

After punching more keys, he said, "Here's a list of your upcoming appointments and related test subjects. If you have any questions or want to change anything, let me know."

She saw appointments scattered over the next few months. They covered an alphabetical range of subjects and/or testing that included acupressure, acupuncture, allergies, alternative medical practices, American Indian remedies, blood panel (monthly), bone marrow, CAT Scan, DNA, grafting, herbal remedies, hypnosis, immune system, mineral baths, MRI, oriental and other worldwide cultural medical practices, plastic surgery, static electricity, stress, vitamin/mineral therapy, and Yoga.

"Jumpin' George. That will keep us busy."

"And we'll continue adding to the list if we find other information. Is there anything you want to change?"

"Not that I can see. I guess we'd better just take all of this a day at a time," she said.

"Good idea. What say we stop for now, go fix a bite to eat and take it out to the garden? Later tonight, or sometime soon, I have something else to show you in here.

"Okay, but I can't imagine what else you have in here. And eating in the garden sounds like a fine idea. A sandwich will do for me since I ate that big lunch."

"Me too. Ham? Or roast beef or . . . what?"

"Roast beef on whole wheat bread with lettuce, mayo, and tomato sounds good. It may get dark before we finish."

"If it does, I'll switch on the lights out there," he said.

Mitch had turned on some classical music selections that made their time sitting at a poolside table even more enjoyable.

"Mitch, what is that enclosed area with the door over there; the one with that trellis of roses all around?"

He laughed out loud before answering. "That's a room Mom and Dad used to go off to and make love; mostly at night after I was asleep when I was very young . . . or so I guessed later on. They had a one-way monitor setup so they could hear me but I couldn't hear them. They had that same setup all over the house during that time of my life."

"Mitch! When you got older, did you understand about the room?"

"I didn't know for years. I just thought they liked to go there to read and listen quietly to music; which they did sometimes alone or together. It was one of those please don't disturb us when we're here places . . . unless it's an emergency. As a teenager I suspected the room's purpose which, of course, at that age embarrassed me. As I grew older, I just thought it was romantic. I never told them I knew. I thought they needed to keep their little special secret."

"That was thoughtful," said Branda. "Have you ever . . ."

"No, Branda. I know what you're going to ask. I never used that room . . . even during the time when Helen and I were here. It was special for Mom and Dad."

Changing the subject, she asked, "I've noticed there are a lot of beautiful flowers out here but no plants or flowers inside other than silk arrangements. Any special reason?"

"Yes. Mom and Dad used to travel a lot and didn't want to have to get someone in to water plants while they were gone; especially on extended tours. Whenever they wanted bouquets inside, they just came out here and gathered whatever they needed."

"Well, that makes sense. If it's okay, maybe I'll start bringing some in. I love flowers."

"Me too. Good idea," he said. "Is there anything else you would like to change or do?"

"Not really, except for the swimming pool and hot tub. How soon do you think we could get them in working order?" she asked.

"Since some of the days are getting warmer and both pool and hot tub are heated too, I suppose anytime. I'll call Johnny soon and have him come over and get them in shape."

She thought, "If I really am pregnant, the heated part will have to be toned down."

"Do you have a bikini?" he asked.

"Yes. Why?"

"I may go call him right now," he said, chuckling and giving her a wicked grin.

She laughed too, blushing at his insinuation. "But I've never worn it. It was sort of a fun gift from Mary Ann and Linda one year for my birthday.

They knew I would be too strait laced to wear it in public; even at the apartment pool. I wear a one-piece with an attached skirt. Seriously, Mitch, swimming would be good for both of us. I miss going for my long walks and doing other exercises although I'm going to try out some of your exercise equipment someday soon. I'll bet there's some things you miss too even though you work out once in a while in your exercise room."

"Yes, besides what I do in there I also like to walk, swim, ride horses, and play golf, among other things," he said.

"Well, you could still play golf. I could ride around with you in the cart and sit there while you play your game of pasture pool."

"Pasture pool!" he exclaimed. "Woman, don't ever let anybody at the Ladue Country Club hear you call it that. I'd be drummed out of the membership," he said, laughing.

She laughed too.

"But you know," he added. "That is a good idea. The fresh air would do us both good. Also, I've thought about going sightseeing right here in St. Louis once in a while, and maybe taking some short trips."

"That does sound like fun. Thanks, Mitch."

"You're welcome," he said, getting up to turn on the lights in the garden area.

Sometimes what was happening to her body overwhelmed her, making her flush hot all over and having what actor's call flop-sweat. Tears would well up inside to the point of bursting out. More and more, negative fears were winning the battle with her normal positive outlook.

"I have to hang on for Mitch and now maybe our baby," she mused. "I think Mitch is also worried more than he lets on since he is checking my vital signs much more often."

Breaking into her thoughts, Mitch said, "Would you like to go inside now?"

"That would be fine. It is getting slightly chilly out here."

"If you aren't too tired I would like to show you something in the study that I mentioned earlier. You need to know about it," said Mitch.

"All right," she said, wondering what it could be.

Mitch carried their tray of dishes back inside, stopping in the den long enough to show her which wall switch would turn off the garden lights.

After finishing kitchen chores, they headed for the study. Sensor lights helped show them the way.

Before Mitch turned on the room's lights, she noticed the red votive glasses were aglow from lighted candles; Our Lady sweetly smiling.

Lightly touching Branda's left arm, Mitch guided her over to the large table placed against the far wall. After moving some magazines and books to one end that had been scattered across its surface, he stood close to the table's edge.

"Watch," he said. "This is my main computer network system used for conducting other types of business besides that from my doctor's office."

"I don't see . . . Oh my!" she exclaimed as the table top slid into hiding and more computer apparatus than she had ever seen in her life rose up, locking in place. "How did you do that?"

"By pressing this button underneath the table," he said, showing it to her. "And by pushing other buttons I can lower a world map and other pertinent maps and graphics that are hidden in the ceiling-level decorative molding you also see all around the room." He did so to demonstrate.

"My word," said Branda. "This is like something out of a James Bond movie. But what do you need all of this for when you have a perfectly good computer over on the regular desk?"

"As I said, this is for other types of business. I keep the two operations separate because this one is extremely private . . . almost secret you might say. No one knows about it but my lawyers, advisors, Sean, Cynthia, and me . . . and now you because you are my wife, in my will, and I know I can trust you completely as I do the others. Dad and Mom knew because they set it up a long time ago; at first with equipment current at the time. But when computers came in, they switched."

"Why, Mitch. I'm flattered but it is also quite a responsibility for me to know about it. Also, you have only known me for a few days. How can you be so sure about me?"

"For one thing, Sean and Cynthia have told me what a good and honest person you are and I have seen that for myself."

"But you know how mad I can get at times."

"Yes, but as I've said before. That is really not your basic nature. Your anger is usually very justified. And I don't think you would betray my trust in you no matter how angry you would get. You're that sort of person."

"You're right. I would never reveal this secret no matter what. But I must say your faith in me is overwhelming. I'm flabbergasted."

"I want you to also understand my medical computer system is also extremely private. Any information about you and your condition that is stored here stays here. I am the only one who can access it here or in my office . . . unless some hacker gets lucky which I doubt. I'll show you how though if you would like."

"No, Mitch. No. I see no need. If I do later, I'll let you know. I probably wouldn't understand the medical system any better than I will be able to understand the other one. You've done enough by just letting me know about all of these operations. I still can't believe it."

"I'm not worried about you knowing and I don't want you to be," he said. "And I have a feeling if you put your mind to it, you could understand all of this information and anything else you decided to learn."

"Thanks for the compliment but I still can't get it through my head why you want me to know."

"Besides the ones I have mentioned, another reason is because I love you and I don't want any secrets between us."

"I thought you were only at the stage of falling in love with me," she said.

"I seem to be going faster and faster. I'm beginning to treasure each day with you . . . the minutes, hours . . . each moment."

"Oh, Mitch," she said. "I think I may be too although the ghosts of the past are still holding me back."

"I'll make them go away yet."

"Please do, Mitch. Please do."

He took her in his arms, kissing her long and sweetly. She held onto him, returning his kiss until she felt passion swiftly rising in them. With great effort, she stopped.

"Oh Mitch, I am so sorry. I am just not up to doing anything about this tonight. Forgive me."

His voice husky with passion, he said, "Of course, Branda. I'm sorry for even tempting you with my kiss. We'll have other nights."

"Oh I hope so, I hope so. And days too." Moving away from him, she added, "If you don't mind, I think I'll go get in my nightgown and watch some television or read in bed. I know it's a bit early."

"I understand," said Mitch. "You've had a busy day. I'll do a bit more reading up here before coming down."

After opening their two-way radios and checking them, they parted.

She fell asleep watching TV and never knew when Mitch came down to turn it off. He stood a moment looking at her as a doctor checking a patient, and as a husband admiring his wife who was smiling sweetly as she slept.

Had he known what she was dreaming, he could have also looked upon her as a possible mother. She was cuddling a baby girl named Michele.

Chapter Eleven

About five a.m. Branda began screaming. "No! No! Stop it Connor! No! Stop it! Oh, please, Connor. No more. Please don't hurt me anymore." She was weeping.

Mitch came running.

"Branda wake up," he called gently but firmly. "You're having a nightmare."

He was afraid if he tried touching or holding her writhing body she might mistake him for Connor and continue struggling.

"Branda, please wake up. It's me, Mitch. You're dreaming. Everything is all right."

Finally coming awake and seeing Mitch, she reached to hold him.

"I haven't had that nightmare in a long, long time. Oh Mitch it was awful. Just like it use to be sometimes. He was trying to . . ."

"Shhhh," he interrupted, lying down to hold her closely, stroking her hair, comforting her. "Shhhh now. It's all right."

He wiped away her tears with one hand, saying soothing words, quietly waiting until she stopped shaking.

"Oh Mitch. I feel so safe in your arms. Thank you."

"You're welcome. Would you like to try undergoing hypnotherapy to see if that would erase that bad dream forever? I know just the man I would trust to do it."

"I'll certainly give that some thought. Meanwhile, that theory about the sense of touch being healing is helping me a lot right now," she said, snuggling closer.

After a time, when she grew calm, he asked, "Is there anything I can get you or do for you? Are you thirsty or hungry?"

"Maybe a glass of milk would taste good and help steady my nerves."

"How about some toast or a sweet roll? I'll fix you a full breakfast if you like."

"I don't think I could eat that much right now. Some buttered whole wheat toast with that good seedless raspberry jelly on it would taste good."

"How about orange juice and coffee?" he asked.

"No coffee. Just orange juice."

"If you're sure you're okay now, I'll run upstairs and fix it and bring it back down. Breakfast in bed for my lady," he said, trying to lighten the mood.

"Or I can go up there."

"No, you stay put," he said. "Branda, I know even though you don't complain, walking is often difficult for you. I notice you limping at times."

"Yes, sometimes it bothers me more than others; mostly when I've been standing too long. So okay, I'll stay put; except I do need to use the bathroom."

After he was out of sight, she got the test-kit sack and headed for the bathroom.

"I was beginning to wonder how I was going to take this second test too first thing of a morning as suggested," she thought. "This works out just fine. I just wish I didn't feel so sneaky."

Again, the test was positive. "Heaven be praised," she thought, tears of happiness filling her eyes. "Thank you dear God. Please let it be true, and if it is, let me live long enough to have this baby and love it as long as I am able."

Wanting to get the sack into the drawer before Mitch came back down, she skipped the cleansing routine she had done before and just made sure the second test strip was stored inside the box it came in.

"I'll do all that other later when he's not around then take the sack upstairs to the trash compactor." After washing her hands, she headed back to her bed.

"Now how and when am I going to tell Mitch he may become a father?" she mused. "I would like to do it in a romantic atmosphere or should I just tell him since he has been surprising me with things lately like the money and James Bond table, I'm pretty sure I have a surprise for him too. Or out in the garden. Or . . ."

She stopped in her tracks when she saw Mitch sitting up in her bed propped against the pillows holding Betty on his lap. The breakfast tray was beside them.

Patting the area on the other side of the tray, he said, smiling, "Come join us."

Surprised he had returned so quickly, she stood mute looking at the scene reminding her of father and child. The likely prophetic sight totally erased her ideas of how and when to tell him her suspected news.

Noticing she was frozen to the spot, Mitch sat up straighter and asked, "Branda, are you all right?"

As if in a dream, she heard herself saying, "Oh Mitch, I think I'm better than all right. I think I'm pregnant."

"What?!!!!! Oh Branda!!!! Really? Really and truly?" he asked, smiling from ear to ear as he sat up even straighter, still holding on to Betty. "What makes you think so?" Now he was frozen to his spot.

"For one thing, my woman's intuition," she said, moving closer to the bed. "For another, this," she added, taking out test stick two and showing him.

After a quick look, he got out of bed so fast he knocked over the breakfast tray spilling its contents on sheets, spread, and pillows. Betty escaped the spill since he was still holding her. Putting the doll down on a dry place at the end of the bed, he reached for Branda who had hurriedly put the test stick back inside the box then dropped sack and all on the floor. Betty's unblinking eyes watched as the two embraced and kissed.

Slightly releasing her, Mitch's speech dam broke. "Branda, you have made me the happiest man in the world with this news that I do believe is true. What made you suspect you might be pregnant? Why didn't you tell me? How did you get the test kit? Did you tell Richard Cline?Should we call Sean and Cynthia? We've got to get this information on the computer upstairs, determine the due date, choose a name. Do you want a boy or girl? Do you want to know beforehand? What . . . ?"

"Whoa, Mitch. Whoa," said Branda, laughing. "You're going to strip a gear if you don't slow down." Giving him a hug, she added, "I'm also extremely happy about this. I thought I might be pregnant when I was two days late with my period. I've always been like clockwork with very few exceptions. With all of the new excitement in my life I had actually lost track of my period schedule but it finally dawned on me I was late. I didn't want to say anything to you until I took the tests."

"Tests . . . plural?" he broke in to ask.

"Yes, after doing the math, I thought results could possibly show up on Friday; if not then, on Saturday. I did some Internet research and chose the kind of test that is supposed to predict very early. After the positive one yesterday morning, I had a hard time not telling you. A couple of times during the day I almost did. I didn't mention anything to Dr. Cline either. I did ask him some questions though as you suggested and he told me a lot of things . . . mostly what you had already told me. He likes to give his patients lots of information. He even gave me advice in case I ever got pregnant or suspected I was . . . all about water temperature, showers instead of tub baths, exercise, healing time after a baby is born, sex, and on and on. And remember on Wednesday when I insisted on taking that little jaunt in my car?"

"I certainly do. I was furious."

"I know you were and I felt bad about that, but that's when I went to get the test kits. I went through one of those drive-through windows at some pharmacy over on Olive Street Road."

"Well, I'll be dam . . . oops . . . darned . . . oh jumpin' George, I shouldn't cuss around the baby," he said, patting Branda's belly. "A woman who can keep a secret. I knew I was right about you being able to do that," he said, laughing.

Still loosely embraced, Branda said, "I guess those test-strips are right. Your reaction to seeing the one I used this morning makes me believe they are."

"Yes they can be a fairly accurate indicator if all of the conditions are right and directions are followed correctly; which I'm sure you did. But to be very honest, there is a measure of controversy about them since so many variable factors are involved in detecting pregnancy early. Sometimes claims made by some test strip manufacturers can be misleading. We will definitely want to get a blood pregnancy test done since that is much more accurate. That can usually be done seven to 12 days or a bit longer from possible conception and is more reliable. I'll call Richard Cline later on and set up an appointment."

"What early bodily changes occur so tests can show a doctor a woman is pregnant?" Branda asked. "For some reason, I've never read anything about that. The other time, I missed two periods and had my doctor examine me. I was too embarrassed to go sooner and kept hoping I was skipping for some other reason."

"Basically, detection has to do with something called HCG which is an abbreviation for Human Chorionic Gonadotropin. That is produced by developing placenta beginning the day an embryo implants in the uterine wall. It can show up in both urine and blood."

"It was too early for Dr. Cline to tell from the pelvic exam he gave me Friday isn't it?"

"Yes. Normally, you would have to be about eight weeks into the pregnancy for that exam to show up anything."

"Is it possible that I may just be starting menopause?

"Possible but not probable."

"Could I be late for other reasons? I have not only wondered about the change but other things as well such as this strange ailment I have."

"Again, possible but not probable," he said. "You're basically a very healthy woman. Yes, Branda. For some reason, I feel in my bones you are carrying our baby. Maybe that's my man's intuition." After taking her face in his hands and tenderly kissing her a long moment, he added, "I realize now I love you very much. I think I started loving you the moment I first saw you."

"Oh, Mitch. I love you too and I think I also began falling for you that first day. Both of us sure fought against it though for our separate reasons. I also believe I really am carrying our child," she said, looking deeply into those dark, dark eyes, reaching to give him a lingering kiss.

Afterwards, she asked, "Do you want a boy or girl?"

"It does not matter one bit. How about you?"

"It doesn't matter to me either. I just want it to be healthy and strong," she said.

"Do you want to know beforehand what it is?" he asked.

"No. Do you?"

"No. I like the old fashioned ways whenever possible."

"And I would prefer not having any type of test that might remotely bother or harm the baby unless, for some reason, it becomes necessary," said Branda.

"That's fine with me too," he said. "Do you want to call Sean and Cynthia and tell them now or wait until they come home tomorrow?"

"Whatever you want to do. I can tell you're bustin' to tell somebody."

"In one way I am," he said. "In another, I would just like to share this only with you at least for today and tonight."

"I feel the same way, Mitch. Or do you think we should wait until I have that blood pregnancy test just so we're absolutely sure?"

"Whatever you think best. But I'm sure now. For several days I've noticed something was different about you but I couldn't put my finger on it. Now I know," he said, kissing her tenderly.

"Cynthia is so psychic she'll probably guess anyway. Let's just see what happens."

"Okay," he said.

"And now, Papa, I had better start cleaning up this mess," she said, glancing toward the bed as she leaned over to pick up the dropped sack.

"No, ma'am. I made the mess. I'll clean it up. But first I want to take a picture of it. I'll go get a camera I have down here in the darkroom. And I want to see those test strips again."

"Mitch, why on earth would you want to take a picture of spilled milk, orange juice, toast and raspberry jelly?"

"Someday I want to show our baby how much I reacted in happiness when I learned he or she was on the way. I'm going to start a collection of such things today," he explained before leaving to go get his camera.

By the time he returned, she had gotten out both test kit boxes from the sack, opened them, and was getting ready to put Betty back into her chair.

"I want Betty in the picture too," he called out. "And the test strips."

"Mitch. You're something else. Why would you want a doll and test strips for pregnancy in a picture?"

"Because they are part of the beginning scene."

"I must tell you I washed off the first test strip but didn't have time to do the second because I was trying to get back in here before you came down. My intentions are to put them both back in their boxes after I wash off today's and put them in the trash compactor. Or do you want to bronze them?" she said, laughing.

"I guess that would be carrying it a bit too far," he admitted, also laughing. "I'll just get a picture of the one that still shows evidence."

"Jumpin' George, Mitch. You're too funny . . . and sweet . . . and I love you. You'll have this child spoiled rotten."

"That's where you're wrong. I've seen too many of that type of kid lately. I fully intend to let this child know how much it is loved but I also believe discipline done the right way is another way of showing love."

"I totally agree with that."

She watched as he took out the test strips and examined them without touching the actual test area. As he looked at the second one, he smiled broadly, and said, "Yep, if that isn't a true positive, I'll eat my stethoscope." He snapped three pictures of them from different angles before putting everything back in the sack.

"And now, Branda," he continued. "If you would, please take this sack and stand over where you were when you came in and told me you thought you were pregnant."

"Okay. You should have been a movie director."

They both laughed, as he snapped the picture.

"If you like, Branda, why don't you go take a shower. Remember what Dr. Cline said, and I agree, tub baths are not recommended for pregnant ladies. There are built in seats in all of the house showers so you can at least sit down. Grip bars are there too just like they are with the bathtubs. I'll finish taking pictures and clean up this mess. I'm going to use the laundry down here if you don't mind. Are there any special instructions I need about washing your sheets, spread, etc."

"No, there's no special instructions. You seem to know your way around a washing machine. Oh Mitch, why don't you let me help you?"

"No way. Now git," he said, leaning down, lightly kissing her belly, then giving it a pat.

Ruffling his hair and lightly kissing the top of his head, she said, "Mitch, thanks again for everything. I really do appreciate all you do for me."

"You are most welcome," he said. "Oh, before I forget, I called Johnny and he will be here Monday at 1 p.m. to get the pool and hot tub going. I'll ask him to keep the temperature lower than usual so you can go in. I won't tell him why; just you like it that way. We'll be back in plenty of time from Dr. Cline's. I have to be here to unlock the garden gate for Johnny."

When she came back later, he already had the bed stripped, laundry going, and Betty was back in her chair.

"I'll watch the laundry, Mitch, if you want to go get your shower now."

"Okay. Since I wrecked your bed, why don't you rest in the one I've been sleeping in while I do that?"

"I'm really not tired. I guess I'm too excited. But I'll find a book to read and sit in there waiting for you."

"Good. Then after we have a nice breakfast, I'll start moving us back upstairs. At least I hope you're ready to move back to our bedroom."

Coming closer to hug and kiss him, she said, "Yes, Mitch. I'm ready. And I'll help you load the elevator and get our stuff back upstairs."

"Oh no you won't. You're going to take it easy from now on," he said.

"Now Mitch. Some exercise will be good for me. You know that. Don't try to make me an invalid. Remember, I am basically healthy. And I'm not about to do anything that would jeopardize our baby."

"I know that. Okay. You can take Betty back upstairs," he said, smiling.

After eating and checking laundry between hauling loads of clothes and things back upstairs in the elevator, both were ready to rest. It had been a long busy morning. Since she had insisted on helping, Mitch had given in and allowed her to carry some other light items besides Betty. One thing she took was the sack of test strips, placing them inside two other plastic bags, and putting all of it in the upstairs compactor.

She told Mitch, "If I didn't consider it unsanitary to keep them, I might have. But I guess it's silly to feel sentimental about something like that."

"Not at all, Branda. I had a twinge or two myself about getting rid of them."

"Mitch, there's something I want to tell you about the day I got those strips and you couldn't get me on the two-way radio."

"What?" he asked.

"Well, to be honest, I had switched it off when I went through the drive-thru window to ask for the test kits because I didn't want you to overhear the conversation I was having with the pharmacist. I felt so sneaky but felt it was the best thing to do in order to keep my secret. I didn't want to get your hopes up for no reason. I switched it back on afterwards, as you know, since I called you. Forgive me?"

"I imagine you were pretty nervous about having to do all that in secret. Bless your heart," he said, giving her a hug and kiss. "Of course I forgive you. You really didn't do anything wrong you know."

Sitting in the kitchen having a glass of orange juice, Mitch asked, "How about we have a dinner party next week and invite everybody we need to since you are no longer considered contagious as of Monday?"

"Great idea. Maybe Cynthia will help me get everything ready for it."

"We'll all help," said Mitch. "I'm thinking we could invite your friends, my lawyers, advisors, medical people, Judge Limson, the cleaning and yard crews, as well as everybody's spouses, and . . . well just everybody that already knows your true story or needs to know now. I'll make a speech about it all. No young children or teenagers though. Older grown up ones are okay though don't you think?"

"Yes. But won't telling the truth about me to those who don't know put a damper on the party?" she asked.

"I thought of that, but, if all goes well, we will have some exceptionally good news to tell them. That should offset the other. And being in a group should help them accept the down side more easily. I guess I'm thinking it would be better psychologically that way," said Mitch.

"I see your point. And knowing my friends, they will be able to take everything pretty much in stride and I'm sure yours will too. Actually, I guess it's as good a way as any to get this information to them. It will be easier on us too since we can do it all at once instead of in bits and pieces. Good idea. Let's do it. How about next Saturday night; say 6 p.m. If the weather is nice, we can barbecue, if not, we'll do a buffet dinner since there's probably too many for a sit-down one."

"Perfect. I'll start calling my bunch later today, if you'll call yours," Mitch said.

"Done."

Finally, Branda stretched out on their bed, pulling up the quilt.

"My but it feels good to be back up here with you," she said to Mitch who was sitting on the edge of his side of the bed.

He was getting ready to call Dr. Cline's office and make an appointment for the blood pregnancy test.

Turning toward her afterwards, he said, "You're scheduled for 10 a.m. Monday, May 26," he said. "It's Memorial Day, and the day we set for your contagious period to be over. If I believed in omens, I say those are good ones."

Counting on her fingers, Branda said, "That will be eight days from the last time we made love."

"That should work out okay," said Mitch, stretching out beside her. "I'll put that information on the computer as soon as I rest a bit. If that first test isn't positive, we'll have it redone a few days later. I just know you are pregnant."

She fell asleep so quickly, Mitch wondered if she had fainted. Double-checking to make sure she had not, he also nodded off, smiling at the thought of the baby.

When he awakened, it was noon and Branda was gone. Raising himself up on one elbow, he saw a note pinned to her pillow.

"Hi Sleepyhead. I woke up starving. I'm in the kitchen. Call me when you wake up and I'll fix you something too. Love, Branda."

He called her but there was no answer. As he ran toward the kitchen carrying his black bag, he kept calling. Still no answer.

He found her lying on the carpet at the entrance to the living room. She had fainted and when he checked her feet he saw another piece of her left foot was gone; another small portion from where the last section had disappeared. It still felt slightly warm and the acrid odor slightly lingered in the air. The results of his vital signs check were the same as usual. He made sure he put her socks and shoes back on since she had become more and more self-conscious about having her feet uncovered.

Cradling her head in his lap, he called gently, "Branda, wake up. Wake up, Branda."

She did not respond.

He leaned over, kissing her several times, stroking her hair, calling her name.

"Oh God," he prayed. "Please don't let anything happen to her. Please don't."

At last her eyes fluttered open. "What happened? Oh Mitch. You're here. Thank God. I was just walking along and suddenly went down. Is another piece gone? It happened so fast I don't remember getting that warning of feeling warm and weak."

Before he could stop her, she looked down at her feet, removed her socks and loafers and saw what had happened.

Reaching to cover her feet again, she said, "Oh, Mitch. If this is my fate and has to happen, I just wish it would stop long enough for me to have our child and enjoy him or her for a long while."

"There. There, Branda," he said, holding and comforting her until she felt like getting up. "Are you still hungry or would you rather go back to bed? Or I could bring you something to eat in bed."

"I think I would like to sit on my favorite couch in the den. May I eat in there?"

"Of course. What would you like?"

"Some milk and a sandwich of some kind. Something easy for you to fix."

"Leave it to me. I'll leave the sliding door open so I can see you and hear you if you call out."

After getting her settled, he rechecked her. The aftermath readings were the same as usual and her foot was cool.

He quickly brought her some milk and a small dish of carrot and celery sticks.

"Munch on that until I get back. Would you like for me to turn on TV?"

"No. I'll just sit here looking at the Waterford dish and read a book."

When he returned a while later, he put down a tray set for two on the coffee table in front of the couch where she was sitting.

"My gosh, Mitch. This looks like a feast. Are those filet mignons you have there?"

"Yep. I cooked them on the stove grill."

"And a baked potato, green salad, and green beans. I still say you could be a chef."

"You haven't tasted it yet."

She did and declared everything to be just what the doctor ordered.

"I thought maybe you needed a more balanced meal than you have probably been having lately," he said.

"No doubt you are right. Maybe I keeled over because I was so hungry."

"The thought crossed my mind."

"Well, I certainly am beginning to feel much, much stronger," she said, before taking more mouthfuls. "One of these days, I am going to cook a major meal for you."

"It will be delicious I know."

"What is your favorite meal?" She asked. "I don't even know."

"Rump roast cooked with carrots, potatoes, onions, a little garlic, wine, and brewed coffee . . . all in one pot. Then make gravy at the end."

"Well I'll be. I didn't know city people knew about putting about half a cup or so of brewed coffee in with roasts and some other cuts of beef."

"Actually, Mom learned that from a lady she met down in New Madrid one time at some special garden club meeting. Do you know how to cook that meal?"

"Learned it at my mother's knee. And somewhere in my belongings I have her good old heavy roasting pot."

"I'll do the lifting of that, Mrs. Andrews."

"That's a deal."

She did feel a lot better after eating his delicious meal.

"Do you feel up to calling the party people?" he asked. "If not, we can wait."

"I feel a lot better, Mitch, thanks to you. Yes, I would like to call my group. That will take my mind off of what happened this morning in my nightmare and this afternoon with my foot. I can go back downstairs and call on my phone."

"You don't have to go down there. With all that's been going on, I guess I neglected to tell you about the separate phones and phone lines in my study used for different things; two for company business, one for medical, and one is a private line. There is also a phone connected to the regular house line. Each computer has it own line."

"I wondered why there were so many phones in the study," she said.

"Now you know. If you like, we can move your computer and phone up to the study."

"Thanks, but they're fine where they are. I don't use them that much and I kind of like my space as they say."

"I thought you might. Anyway, you can sit on our bed and call your list of friends . . . or would you rather use the private study phone and I'll go sit on the bed?"

"I'll take the bed. Then if I get sleepy I can take a nap."

"Good idea. Are you sure you're up to doing this now?" he asked.

"Yes, it will be a change of pace and good to chat with Mary Ann, Linda, and the rest. Do you think Rev. Cummings will want to come since I know you'll be serving wine and liquor?" she asked.

"I suggest you tell him and let him make up his own mind. He just might surprise you."

"Okay. You're on."

After cleaning up the dishes, they walked down the hallway toward the bedroom. Mitch left her to go into his study to start making his list and phoning the people. Branda went on to their bedroom.

Later, after completing their calls, Mitch came to the bedroom.

"Whew . . . that was more of a deal than I thought it would be," he said. "Everybody wanted to talk a long time and they are delighted to come. Good grief, it's nearly five o' clock. How did you do?"

"The same. Everybody wanted to talk too and they are excited about coming. But I got the job done."

"Then I guess we're all set. Tomorrow we'll do some menu planning and so forth."

"Okay."

"Branda, what do you think about making that ex-cluttered bedroom into a nursery?"

"I think that is a great idea. But we won't know whether to decorate it in pink or blue until the baby comes."

"How about a neutral creamy yellow?" he asked.

"We'll think about that. Mitch, I know it is awfully early, but this has been an unusually busy day. Would you mind if I put on my soft clothes and got in bed to read or watch TV?"

"Not at all but aren't you getting hungry? It's been a while since we had lunch."

"And what a great one it was. And so much. How about you? Are you hungry?" she asked.

"Maybe just a sandwich would do. Tell you what. Why don't I fix us a snack and we eat out in the garden. Or are you too tired to sit out there for a bit?"

"No. That would be nice," she said.

"Go put on your soft clothes while I fix the food, and I'll meet you out there shortly."

"Will do. But can't I help you?"

"Thanks but not this time. I'll put you on KP another day."

As they ate, they enjoyed looking at the flowers surrounding them in the garden, listening to the birds sing, and thinking up baby names.

She had never told him about her dream of her mother holding a baby named Michele. Maybe it was time now.

"This is so peaceful and restful," said Branda.

"That it is."

"Mitch, what do you think of the name Michele if it's a girl?"

Leaning forward, he said. "That's it! That's perfect. Our daughter's name."

"What about a middle name?" she asked.

"We'll think about that. Maybe after our mothers. Mine's name was Anne. And yours?"

"Marie."

"Michele Anne Marie Andrews. I like it. Or the other way around. Michele Marie Anne Andrews. How about you, Branda?"

"Yes, I like it too . . . the first way better, even if it is a lot of name for a little girl."

"She will grow. Or would you rather use your name in some way?"

"No. It doesn't fit in right," said Branda.

Then she told him about the dream.

"Well, I'll be dam . . . oops. Well I'll just be. Wouldn't that be something if it's true?"

"What if it's a boy? We would name him Mitchell after you, of course. Maybe use our father's names in some way. Mine's was Thomas."

"Mark was my father's. Mitchell Thomas Mark Andrews or Mitchell Mark Thomas Andrews."

"As Scarlett O'Hara would have said, we'll 'think about that tomorrow,'" said Branda.

"Right," said Mitch. "The sun is beginning to set. Let's go over by that bed of yellow roses and watch it. We can see better from there."

Standing there holding hands, they watched blazing colors of deep apricot, blue gray, and gold mix, intermingle, and change hues until they trailed away. As last bits of color burst across the horizon, Mitch turned to Branda, taking her in his arms.

Their long lingering kiss ended with him picking her up and carrying her to their bed.

His exploring hands brought her body quickly to burning passion and she marveled that he was more tender, gentle, and loving with her than ever before. Guessing he was being thoughtful of the baby, she was overwhelmed.

At the same moment, they looked into each other's eyes, and said, "I love you."

After smiling for another moment, they kissed passionately, continuing to give each other pleasure until neither could hold back any longer. As always, cries of passion began sounding in their ears.

Later, after resting in each other's arms for a long time, Mitch stroked her lovely hair and said, "Let's never be separated again, Branda. I was so lonesome without you."

Kissing him sweetly, she said, "I missed you more than words can say. Mitch, I never want to be away from you again."

"Branda, will you please take back the jewelry I gave you for your birthday?"

"Yes, Mitch. And thank you again for such a lovely gift."

They slept until dawn, holding each other closely, completely happy for the first time in many nights.

Neither saw the dream-driven vision hovering over them with Branda's mother holding a baby girl in her arms. As they began disappearing in the silvery mist, Branda's father was approaching in the dimness . . . holding something or someone.

CHAPTER TWELVE

BRANDA WAS GLAD SHE WOKE up first. She loved looking at her handsome husband as he slept. It was eight a.m.

"He looks so peaceful and happy," she mused, reaching to kiss him softly on his cheek. "Thank you God for putting this man in my life. At least I'm hoping and praying it works out."

But, as usual, the minute he sensed she was stirring, he was awake.

"How do you do that?" she asked. "You are sound asleep one minute and wide awake the next. Is that something you learn in medical school?"

"No, that comes from the school of experience," he said, moving closer to quickly kiss her. Afterwards, he continued, "Branda, I know it's supposedly safe for a pregnant woman to have sex, at least as long as it is comfortable for her, but I tried to be very careful last night and not hurt you or the baby in any way."

"You were very gentle and caring, Mitch. I could tell you were trying and I appreciate that a lot. Even if it turns out I'm not pregnant I will still remember your thoughtfulness. Thank you."

"You're welcome. And now, woman of the house, how about we get cleaned up and get some food? I'm hungry as a bear just out of hibernation."

"That sounds great to me."

Looking thoughtful for a moment, he added, "Branda, I know how you like to be clean so maybe from now on I should wear a condom when we make love; unless you are latex sensitive."

"That's very thoughtful of you and something to think about. We'll see. And I'm not latex sensitive."

"Since you had a rather traumatic day yesterday, I really should have let you rest and not made love to you at all last night. But I wanted you so badly and you did seem refreshed after being in the garden awhile," he said.

"Oh, Mitch. The garden was restful for me. And I wanted you too. If you hadn't made the first move, I think I would have."

"Really, Branda?"

"Really, Mitch."

"That makes me feel better," he said.

"And if I feel tired today, I promise to take a nap or two."

"All right. Good idea," said Mitch. "Now let's get showered and go eat."

"And that is also a good idea," said Branda.

While eating breakfast they decided to hang some of Helen's pictures back in the study and some of Branda's twin sons plus her parents and grandparents.

"Then if we feel like it, we can plan the party menu and other details," said Branda. "What time do Sean and Cynthia get back? I know Cynthia enjoys planning parties and things like that. But maybe she wouldn't feel like it after just getting home."

"They weren't exactly sure about their return time but said they would call when they got in," said Mitch.

"If it's not too late and none of us are too tired, maybe they would like to come over for a light supper."

"Fine idea. We'll play that by ear," he said.

"I think we'd better hold off on saying anything about the baby though until tomorrow's test results are in. How do you feel about that?"

"I agree with you," said Mitch. "I'll bet we'll never be able to keep our faces straight though if Cynthia gets one of her psychic hunches."

"We'll play that by ear too," said Branda, smiling, knowing he was right.

"That reminds me, Branda. We may have to reschedule some kinds of tests if they would be intrusive as far as your pregnancy is concerned."

"I understand," she said.

"Tomorrow I'll call your PCP, Dr. John William, and set up an appointment for you. As I mentioned before, while we're there you can sign a form so his office can release copies of your medical records to me and we can also fill him in on what is happening to you. I'll ask that Dr. Francis be included too.

"Thanks, Mitch."

"You're welcome. Now shall we go select pictures to hang in the study?"

"Yes, I guess so," she said.

"Or will it make you too sad to see pictures of your sons and family?" he asked.

"It probably will, but I would still like to hang them in the study. How about you? Are you up to seeing Helen's pictures?"

"I think so. It will make me sad too, but since we'll be doing this together, that will make it easier. Branda, I don't know how you feel about doing this project, but in a way it will bring some closure to me. How about you?"

"I hadn't thought about it doing that, but you're right, Mitch. Since we appear to have a future now, this may help us let go of our individual past painful memories; or at least most of them. Oh, I know my chances of survival aren't good, but let's make the most of whatever time we have."

Mitch took her in his arms, kissing her tenderly for a long moment. Finally releasing her, he said, "I love you more each day."

"And I love you more and more too, Mitch. I thank God for you everyday. Mitch, will it bother you to see pictures of my sons in the study since they were by another man?"

"No, not at all. They were innocent babies. I could never harbor any ill feelings toward them."

"I didn't think so," she said.

"Frankly, I only think of them as being yours."

"How kind of you," she said.

After she located her box of pictures downstairs, Mitch carried them over to a nearby coffee table in the bar area in front of a comfortable couch. She had thought about sitting on her bed to do the sorting but it was still too damp to make up or sit on.

"Please sit by me for moral support, Mitch."

"I'm here," he said.

First she found some medium size wedding pictures of her parents and both sets of grandparents. The poses were stiff, but all had pleasant looks on their faces. Branda had splurged and had the pictures framed in ovals of cherrywood.

"They were fine looking people," said Mitch. "I can see a little bit of all of them in you."

"Thank you."

"You're welcome," he said.

There was another of her mother and father standing beside a Model-T Ford.

"I think that was when they were going on their honeymoon trip which wasn't far since they had little money."

She found three other informal pictures of her parents taken at various ages. In one of them her mother was holding her when she was a baby. In another, her father held her brother, Bill, who died two years before she was born.

"Okay, all of those are the ones I like best," she said. "Now for the boys."

But before she could put the parental pictures aside, Mitch spied one of her sitting on a pony. She looked to be about six years old.

"Oh, Branda, please hang that one. That is you isn't it with your cute little dress and your hair cut in a Dutch Boy bob?"

"Yes. Remember how those traveling photographers use to go around with a pony so the kids would beg to sit on it and have their pictures made than get a short ride?"

"Yes, there's one of me around here somewhere like that."

"Well, that's what this one is. If you like it, we'll hang it."

"Great," he said.

She chose seven of the best poses of Josh and Jason taken at different ages. Five were eight by ten, the other two, 11 by 14. All were in color. There were others, but she especially liked these.

"If these frames aren't suitable for the study, I'll get new ones," she said.

"They are very suitable, Branda," he said, putting an arm around her since he could tell she was near tears. "Choose more if you like."

"No, these favorites will do, but thank you."

"You're welcome," said Mitch. "And, Branda, your sons were very handsome babies. I don't know what Connor looks like, but I see a definite resemblance to you in their faces. They were adorable, just like their mother is."

"Bless you for thinking and saying those things, Mitch," she said, giving him a quick kiss.

"Well, it's the truth. And from what I see in their eyes in their pictures, they look like they had your intelligence."

"A lot of people said that, but I don't think it all came from me if indeed I am intelligent. Connor was spoiled and acted stupid, but he really was basically intelligent. Our folks and other ancestors probably added their brain-power to the mix too. I always heard they were smart people. I know my parents and grandparents had an innate intelligence even if they never had much formal educational opportunity to fully develop it. I like to think Light Moon, my Cherokee ancestor, added something too. From what I have been able to find out she was my great-great-great grandmother and was the wife of a chief. I hope someday to find out more. That's one of those things I was always going to research but never took time to do so. I have learned that practically everybody with Native American blood in them thinks they are a chief's descendant."

While looking through a picture album, she described to Mitch where some of the snapshots had been taken and what age Josh and Jason were at the time. She seemed to be remembering some happy times with her sons. He noticed blank places where pictures had been removed; evidently ones that had included Connor.

But tears spilled when she looked through the twin's baby books. At first there were happy entries regarding names, date of birth February 2, 1984, birth weight, length, eye and hair color, first smiles and laughs, coos, rolling over, crawling, standing while holding on, saying mama and dada, trying out baby foods, first Christmas, visits to grandparents, and so on. Entries ended abruptly during their eleventh month. The final ones were: Josh: died of viral respiratory infection, January 5, 1985. Jason: died of viral respiratory infection, January 7, 1985. Both buried at New Lorimier Cemetery, Cape Girardeau, Missouri.

Mitch reached and gently closed the book, putting it back in the box. He held her quietly until her tears dried, stroking her hair, saying nothing, letting her take her time to mourn once again.

Finally looking at him, she said, softly, "I know Mitch. I know. As they say, 'Don't cry because it's over, smile because it happened.'"

"That is a wonderful thought, Branda. It gives me a new perspective too. Thanks for sharing it. I may have heard it before but had forgotten it if I ever did."

"You're welcome. Now, if you like, let's put my box away, and go make your selections. Are they still in one of the downstairs bedrooms? I'll leave mine here on the coffee table and gather them up later."

On the way to the downstairs apartment bedroom where Helen's pictures were stored, Branda said, "If this will be too hard for you, maybe we should wait."

"I'll be all right since you're with me. But if I do run into a problem, I'll stop and try later."

Mitch pulled out five boxes from the bedroom closet floor.

"How about I pull that easy chair over here so you can sit and watch me?" he asked. "I'll just sit on the floor and go through them. That will be easier than trying to carry them someplace else."

"That's fine with me," Branda answered.

"Good. I pretty well know which ones I may want . . . with your approval. I don't want you being hurt or upset."

"That's very kind of you, Mitch, but I think you should make the decisions. I'll be fine."

"Okay, here we go."

As she sat in the comfortable chair he had pulled close to where he was, she watched as he looked at picture after picture. Whenever she saw sad memory shadows cross his face, crowding his composure, she leaned to rest a comforting hand on his shoulder.

Smiling up at her in acknowledgment, he would say, "Thank you."

Soon she began noticing a pattern. He chose only pictures of Helen when she was younger and none of them as a couple. He did not take any wedding pictures out of the box including the ones she had noticed on either side of the wall niche; the one with him kissing Helen, the other the formal portrait in her beautiful wedding gown.

Nearing the end of his search, he paused a moment to look at an informally posed picture of Helen standing by the car. It looked more recent than the others.

"Oh, Mitch. She looks so lovely in that one. Why don't you take it too?"

"No!" he said firmly, almost shouting.

Taken aback by his reaction, she said, "I'm sorry, Mitch. I must have said the wrong thing."

As he turned to look at her she saw tears in his eyes.

"I really am very sorry, Mitch," reaching to touch his shoulder.

"No, I'm the one that's sorry, Branda. I shouldn't have reacted like that. Forgive me?"

"Of course. That picture must have a special meaning for you."

"It was taken the day we were going to the hospital for tests that resulted in showing she had an incurable cancerous brain tumor."

"Oh dear Lord," said Branda, getting up so she could join him on the floor, putting one arm around him, using the other hand to brush away tears on his cheeks. She gently took the picture out of his hands and put it back in the box.

Continuing, she asked, "Is that why you chose pictures of her when she was younger? They are less of a reminder of the tragedy?"

"Yes, I suppose so. I really had not thought about that. Must be a subconscious thing."

They sat for a long moment holding each other.

Finally, she said, "You know Mitch, for the first time I really had a chance today to look at Helen and see what a lovely woman she was. I don't mean just the fact she had that gorgeous dark hair, green eyes, and marvelous figure, but the camera also captured an inner beauty as well. She was intelligent too, wasn't she?"

"Yes, she was."

"How did you meet her?"

"Sean and Cynthia introduced us. She was a model they had met at a food and culinary cocktail party. After seeing her several times at various other culinary related functions, they got to know her better and became friends. She was from St. Louis too. Finally, Sean and Cynthia had a dinner party and invited Helen and me plus a few other people. They seated us together and the rest is history."

"Love at first sight?"

"Not quite. But I did call her soon after the dinner party to ask for a date. We went together for a year before I asked her to marry me. She accepted even though I was still in college and had not even started medical school. That's why we thought it best not to start a family right away. Later, when we wanted a baby we found out she was barren."

"Yes, I remember you mentioning that. How awful for you both," said Branda.

"It was devastating for both of us. I use to be sorry we didn't go ahead with our plans to adopt. As it turned out, I guess that was for the best."

"I suppose so."

"We did do one thing though that helped not only us but others as well."

"What was that?" asked Branda.

"We started contributing to a local orphanage; first just money, then later, some of our time. I still send money but haven't gone for a visit in ages. I feel badly about that too."

"I imagine it felt strange to go without Helen along," said Branda.

"That's it exactly. You're very perceptive. And those kids adored her. They cried when they learned she was gone. The orphanage staff thought it best to tell them the truth though. Would you like to go with me sometime?" he asked.

"Yes I would but I don't think that is a good idea."

"Why not?" he asked.

"Think about it. They got use to Helen coming, then she stopped. If the worst case scenario happens with me, I think it would be unfair to put them through that circumstance again."

"As usual," said Mitch. "You see right through to the heart of a matter. You're right of course. And you'll be busy with our own child."

"That alone would not stop me. There's always room to include needy children. It's the other unknown factors that stop me. But why don't you start visiting them again?"

"Yes, I would like to do that. Maybe Cynthia will wife sit for me," he said, leaning to kiss her.

"By the way, Mitch. Has Sean always been interested in culinary arts in general and restaurant management in particular?"

"Yes, except for his one-year stint as a paramedic which I imagine you know about. He just wanted to check out doing that but realized it wasn't for him. His parents were excellent cooks; chef quality. Sean grew up in that atmosphere and took to it like a duck to water."

"Is that how he ended up at Neiman-Marcus?"

"Exactly."

"Why didn't he work there as a cook?"

"He did for awhile then decided he liked the management end better," said Mitch.

"I see. How did he and Cynthia meet?"

"At a dance contest. Both loved dancing. Still do. It was their hobby and they kept meeting at various places, including amateur contests. Each had different partners at first. But cupid finally won out."

"So in between doing the tango and fox trot, she pursued her nursing career and he ended up at Neiman-Marcus," said Branda.

"That's right."

"Although I've known them a long time and know most of their life story it's nice hearing a new slant on it from you. Now what say we clean up down here and go hang pictures?"

"Fine with me. Unless you're needing a rest."

"Not now. Maybe later," she said.

"Branda, before we go upstairs, let's talk about what you would like to do with your furniture. It can stay right where it is as far as I'm concerned, but I've been thinking of a plan," said Mitch, while shoving picture boxes back in place along the closet floor.

"What kind of plan?" she asked.

"I'll show you in a minute."

After helping her up and moving the easy chair back to its place, he picked up the box of pictures he had chosen to hang in the study.

Since she felt a bit stiff after sitting on the floor, she lightly held on to his arm to steady herself as they walked back to her bedroom area. Mitch put down his box full of pictures and went to a storage cabinet to find one for hers.

After returning and boxing her pictures, he took her by the hand, leading her over to her mini-apartment area.

"Now, Branda. What I have in mind is to have this whole area remodeled into a regular apartment. It will have to be small, but at least it will be your private space if and when you should ever need it. I hear pregnant woman can get moody."

"Well I hope I don't," she said. "And Mitch. That is a wonderful idea about the apartment. But don't you need this space for other things?"

"Not really. What was there before was mostly just extra furniture we used sometimes for the bar area if there was a big party. It fits just as well where it is; closer to the bar."

"You are too kind, Mitch. Too kind. And thanks. I think I'll give you a big hug," which she proceeded to do. He hugged her back. They began kissing.

As their kisses sparked a magnetism that quickly pulled them toward fiery passion he began moving her toward a couch.

"I wish that bed was dry," she whispered.

"I could carry you back to one of the apartment beds," he whispered back.

"No, the apartment's too far," she said, her breath coming faster and faster.

They had just reached the couch when the telephone on the bar rang.

"Oh, dammit," they both said at the same time.

He was so shocked to hear her cuss, he burst out laughing.

His laughter was so contagious she joined in. "I meant to say jumpin' George," she said.

"Well I don't think those two words fill the bill in this case," he said, chuckling.

"But we should watch our language for the baby's sake," she said, barely able to contain her laughter.

"I know. I believe babies can hear in the womb. But that sounded so funny coming from you," he said, laughing again.

As the phone kept ringing, both began laughing heartily; their funny bones definitely bull's-eye targeted. Not even trying to contain himself as he walked toward the phone Mitch picked up the receiver, trying to stifle his mirth.

"Hello," he said, calm at last. "Oh, Sean, it's you. No. No. You didn't disturb us." Looking toward Branda, sitting up on the couch he continued, smiling broadly. "We were just working on a project and couldn't get to the phone right away. Sorry. Are you and Cynthia home now or just leaving the lake?"

He watched as Branda doubled over laughing, putting a pillow over her mouth to muffle the sound.

Hanging up after a few more minutes of conversation, Mitch came back to Branda who was still sitting up. Tears from laughing so hard were still coming down her cheeks.

"Oh Mitch," she said between gales of laughter. "So now I'm part of a work project am I?"

Reaching to tousle her hair, he said, "Yes and a dam . . . oops . . . doggone pleasurable one at that. I see you put your blouse back on. Does that mean we're not going to continue?"

"Of course we can continue if you like. I'm ready if you are."

"Under the circumstances, I guess we had better postpone our lovemaking until later," Mitch said.

"All that laughing did kind of take the edge off the passion. Maybe that's another way of releasing sexual tension."

"I just don't want to leave you frustrated," said Mitch.

"I'm okay. How about you?

"I'll survive. Anyway. We had better get these pictures upstairs and start hanging them."

"Okay. Now tell me what Sean had to say?"

"They got back home late last night; about midnight. They didn't want to call us at that hour."

"Why last night instead of today as planned?" Branda asked.

"Some official from Neiman-Marcus called Sean yesterday at the lake. Sean had left a number in case anyone needed him. The man suggested Sean be here this evening for an informal business dinner being held at the store's restaurant for some high ranking people from the head office in Dallas. Tomorrow they will hold a regular business meeting."

"I wonder what they want?"

"Something about doing some changes, revisions, and remodeling throughout the store, including the restaurant. They want Sean's input. No mention was made though of doing any personnel changes."

"I guess that means Sean and Cynthia can't come here for dinner," she said.

"Yes. That's what I meant by saying under the circumstances we'd better postpone our lovemaking."

"You mean our work project?" she asked, smiling.

"Oh you are having fun with that aren't you?" he asked, smiling back at her. "I think we now have our own private code name for our lovemaking."

"Good. I like it, Mitch. Makes me feel closer and special to you somehow," she said, looking deeply into his dark eyes.

"Same here," he said, looking at her the same way for a long moment. Continuing, he said, "I had invited Sean and Cynthia to come here tonight then he explained about the company dinner. However, Sean said they could come here for lunch today if that's okay with you. I didn't dare ask you since you were still in the giggle mode."

"Of course, that's fine with me. And I wasn't giggling. I was practically belly laughing. What time are they coming?"

"I told them 12:30 would be good. But if it isn't, I can call them back," said Mitch.

"Fine with me. That gives us a couple of hours to hang the pictures. If we don't get finished, we can do the rest later. What will we serve for lunch?"

"Sean said sandwiches would be fine since all they've done is eat since they got to their cabin. They mainly just want to visit."

Branda and Mitch were getting ready to hang the last few pictures when they heard the front doorbell ringing.

Both went to greet Sean and Cynthia. Except for Mitch and Sean, everybody hugged then kissed each other on the cheek. The two men only did their usual manly bear hug thing.

"It is so good to see you," said Branda. "It seems like you've been gone for ages. You look so rested. You look great. And you're both a shade more tan."

"Yes, we were out in the sun quite a bit because we did a lot of swimming and boating."

"Didn't you wear sunscreen?" asked Mitch.

"Yes, doctor, we did. And wide-brimmed hats too," Sean said, smiling. "But we still managed to get some tan."

"Well, if you're not starving, come see what we're doing in the study," said Mitch. "We were just finishing up."

As they walked toward the study, Branda thought she saw Cynthia looking at her strangely several times.

"Must be my imagination," thought Branda.

But after they got inside the study, she was sure of it. "I wonder if . . ." she began musing when Cynthia's voice broke into her thoughts.

"Well, my goodness gracious, Mitch," Cynthia said.

"Good heavens, Mitch," Sean chimed in. "This is certainly a change. I . . ."

"I know," Mitch interrupted. "Neither of you ever thought I would change the room in this way."

"You can say that again," Cynthia said. "Congratulations, Mitch. This is a positive step forward, don't you think?"

"Yes I do. It's a step forward for Branda too. Until now, she hasn't wanted to look at any pictures of her family, especially of her twins, because it makes her too sad. It still does, but not as much. Right, Branda?"

"Right," she answered. "We seemed to be able to give each other the strength needed to put this room together in this way."

"Wonderful," said Sean. "Was this the work project I interrupted when I called earlier?"

Stifling a laugh, Branda quickly turned to straighten an already straight picture on the wall. Mitch busily shuffled some papers on his desk knowing if either of them looked at the other the next sound heard in the room would be gales of laughter.

"Yep. This is the one," Mitch managed to say.

"Well, I guess two heads really are better than one because you and Branda have certainly done a fine job here," said Sean.

As Branda turned back around, she noticed Cynthia giving her another one of those odd glances. Looking toward Mitch, Branda thought he might be noticing too.

The mystery was solved when Cynthia smiled sweetly and knowingly, then said, "I think there are more than two heads involved here. I think there are three. I sensed it the minute I saw Branda."

"What in the world are you talking about Cynthia?" asked Sean.

"Are you, Branda?" asked Cynthia.

"Is she what?" Sean asked. "Make sense, woman."

Going to stand beside Branda, putting his arm around her waist, Mitch looked at her. He asked the question with his eyes. She nodded yes.

"We'll know next week," he said.

"Know what?" asked Sean. "Will someone please tell me what the hell you're talking about?"

"Don't cuss, Sean. The baby might hear you," said Branda.

"What baby? Wha . . .? Oh my. You mean you're. Oh my. Branda. Mitch. That would be too wonderful for words. Leave it to my psychic wife. You probably wanted to keep it a secret for awhile," Sean said.

"That's okay," said Branda. "We were thinking to wait until Dr. Cline's test results are in. I go tomorrow for a blood pregnancy test. But two other ultra sensitive test strips have already shown positive."

"Let's just keep this between the four of us though for now. Okay?" asked Mitch.

Sean and Cynthia totally agreed.

"Well, I'll just be dam . . . oops . . . well, I'll just be," spluttered Sean.

More hugs, kisses, and a manly bear hug were in order.

Sean and Cynthia helped hang the last few pictures then all went to the kitchen to eat a bite.

They were just finishing doing the cleanup when Branda turned to Mitch.

"Oh no. I'm getting that warning warm weak feeling."

Quickly carrying her into the den and stretching her out on a couch, he called for Sean to bring the black bag from the kitchen. He removed her shoes and socks and checked her vital signs. They were as usual. He saw the left foot was being affected; a small part where her large toe had once been attached. Also as usual, the foot felt unusually warm.

He sat on the floor, watching her and holding her hands.

Before fainting, Branda managed to say, "Oh Cynthia, Sean. I am so sorry. Don't watch."

But the mesmerized couple stood side by side, also holding hands as they watched the piece go through the sequence of passing from glow to pale yellow, to light green, to red, disappear, then give off the acrid odor.

"Dear God," Cynthia quietly said.

"The poor girl," said Sean. He had seen this happen before in Mitch's office and was again absolutely stunned by it.

As Branda was regaining consciousness, she could hear the three talking.

Cynthia was saying, "Mitch, you know Sean and I will do whatever we can to help you two. I'll give up my hospital job completely and become Branda's nurse if you need me."

"We're okay for now," Mitch said. "But thank you from the bottom of my heart and I will certainly keep that in mind."

"That goes for me too Mitch," Sean said. "If I can be of more help here, my assistant manager at the restaurant can take my place."

"Thanks Sean," said Mitch. "You two are the best friends a man ever had. And I know Branda feels the same way about you."

Branda, now fully awake, startled them by saying, "I certainly do, absolutely one-hundred percent."

Cynthia asked, "Branda how are you feeling now? Doesn't that take a lot out of you?"

"Yes, I do feel tired afterwards . . . and frankly, it scares me a lot, especially now."

"Just remember we're here for you, Branda," said Cynthia.

"We certainly are," Sean said.

"I know and I can't possibly thank you enough."

After making sure everything was under control and there was nothing they could do to help, Sean and Cynthia said their good-byes and started to leave. By then, Branda felt well enough to go with Mitch and walk them to the front door although they insisted that was not necessary. She assured them she was headed that way anyway because she was going to the bedroom to nap.

Before letting her go, Mitch quickly rechecked her. Everything was back to normal.

She slept until 4:30. Mitch had left a note on his pillow letting her know he was downstairs making up her bed and doing some planning about the proposed remodeling they had discussed regarding her private apartment. He signed off with "Call me, Love, Mitch."

Reaching for her two-way radio, she called to let him know she was awake.

"I was just finishing. I'll be right up," he said. "May I bring you anything?"

"Just yourself."

After reviewing their handiwork in the study, and eating a light supper out in the garden, they got into their soft clothes and sat in bed watching TV for awhile.

"How are you feeling, Branda?" asked Mitch.

"Fine. That nap helped a lot."

"Is there anything I can get or do for you before we turn in?"

"Yes, Mitch. There is."

"What? Just name it."

"I have another work project for you to complete."

"What?"

"Me."

CHAPTER THIRTEEN

THE NEXT MORNING, HAVING JUST awakened and lying in bed, Mitch said, "Congratulations. This is the day your quarantine is over."

"You mean I don't have to wait until the stroke of midnight?"

"Nope. It's close enough. I now declare it officially over. And how would you like to go out to breakfast?"

"That would be great," said Branda. "Where?"

"Your choice."

"How about Schneithorst's?" she asked.

"Fine with me." Pulling her closer, he added, "Even with wearing protection, I certainly enjoyed our work project last night."

"Same here," she said, snuggling against him. "I have a feeling if we don't get going, we'll be working again."

Laughing, he said, "You're right and we really need to get a move on to get to your appointment on time."

They arrived at Dr. Cline's office building with minutes to spare after having eaten a delicious breakfast. While eating, both realized it was the first time they had been together in a restaurant.

Branda had said, "Somehow, being here like this with you makes me feel more married . . . sort of cozy."

"You come up with the da . . . most unique way of putting things. But I know what you mean. I feel it too."

As they came down the hallway approaching Dr. Cline's office, she noticed Mitch was heading for a door marked Private.

"Mitch, since I'm out of quarantine and have been in a public restaurant, are you still concerned about me being exposed to germs in waiting rooms or might have some unknown ones to spread myself? I know you said earlier you always planned to enter and exit doctor's offices privately if possible."

"Good point about being in a public restaurant. But I think where doctor's offices are concerned we'll just continue using private doors whenever possible. Habit I guess," he said, knocking on the one in front of them.

She secretly guessed correctly he had gotten in that habit when Helen was ill.

Sandi Wade, office nurse, opened the door.

"Good morning, Dr. and Mrs. Andrews. Please follow me."

"Good morning," the couple said in unison.

As they walked along behind the nurse, Mitch asked, "Branda, I almost forgot. Do you want me to come with you or wait in that private office?"

"Come with me."

"Thanks," he said, giving her hand a slight squeeze.

As they waited for Dr. Cline to come to the room they were in, Branda said, "Mitch, I hope this turns out to be the historic day we want it to be."

"I have a feeling it will be," he said, taking her in his arms and kissing her.

The door opened and Dr. Cline walked in, seeing them. "Well now, that's exactly the kind of thing that can end up with you having to have a blood pregnancy test," he said, laughing.

The couple laughed too, feeling somewhat embarrassed at having been caught.

Dr. Cline continued, "I have some good news for you. All of Branda's test results from the Pap smear, pelvic exam, and stool sample are in the normal range. Here's the copies, Mitch."

"Thanks, Richard. And that is good news," said Mitch, taking the brown envelope handed to him.

"Yes, Dr. Cline. Thank you," said Branda.

"You're welcome. Now let me take down some pertinent information and then do what you came here for. And, again, I will request a rush order. I'll give you a call when I hear anything."

"Thank you very much, Dr. Cline," said Branda.

"Yes, thank you, Richard," said Mitch.

"You're welcome."

Mitch said, "Richard, two ultra sensitive test strips Branda tried showed positive results."

"That's good. And we'll be absolutely sure fairly soon I hope," said the doctor.

Afterwards, on the way to the car, Mitch asked, "Would you like to go to your favorite Mexican restaurant for lunch, or are you still full from breakfast?"

"I'm still full. How about you?"

"Me too."

"But I'll take a rain check," she said.

They decided to go home, continue some research reading and wait for Johnny to arrive to get the pool and hot tub ready.

As they drove along, Mitch said, "I'll also call John William and Stephen Francis for an appointment and do some work on updating your computer medical files. I want to keep that up on an ongoing basis as I have been doing."

"More and more I think it might be a good idea for me to learn about how you do that," said Branda. "Then I can be of some help to you."

"Good idea. How about starting today?" he asked.

"All right."

"And someday I want you to start learning the business operations," Mitch said.

"Okay. That kind of scares me but my mom and dad use to tell me a quotation that often gives me courage. 'You can go as far as your mind will take you.'"

"So true. Your parents were wise."

"Yes they were; even without formal education."

"There's a lot of very intelligent people out there who never set foot in a college. You, for instance. On the opposite side of the fence, some of the dumbest people I know often have graduate degrees," said Mitch.

"I know the type. I've heard it said 'they may have lots of book learnin', but don't have a lick of sidewalk sense.'"

"Also true," he said, chuckling at her humor.

As they pulled into the garage, Mitch said, "Let's go to our bedroom through the garden entrance. I want to stop and unlock the gate now for Johnny."

"Okay," said Branda.

After he did so, Branda asked, "By the way, Mitch. Does Johnny know about my condition?"

"Only the story the others were told."

"He'll find out at the party then. Or did you call him?"

"Yes and he happily accepted. He too has been with our family quite awhile," Mitch said. "He's looking forward to meeting you today too."

"Why doesn't he have a key to the gate?"

"He doesn't want one. He's afraid he might lose it. Usually he comes on a Wednesday which was my day off when I was working at the office. I opened the gate then for the yardmen too so they could do whatever needed done in the garden. If I left to go play golf or something, all of them knew how to lock the gate and where to leave the key. But if Ella was here she took care of everything. As I've mentioned, Ella has a house key and knows how to use the burglar alarm although that's not her favorite thing to do."

"I'm surprised the gate doesn't have its own alarm system," Branda said.

"Dad didn't think that was necessary since the wall surrounding the garden is so high and even if someone did manage to get over it, the house alarm would prevent them from entering. Besides, there are very bright sensor lights aimed toward the wall that would trip if anyone tried to climb over. They use to be so sensitive a squirrel would set them off but Dad had that fixed."

"He thought of everything, didn't he?"

"Just about," said Mitch. "Not much escaped him . . . or Mother either. If you ever see those lights go on at night and I'm asleep or in another part of the house, just call 911 immediately."

"Have you ever had to do that?" she asked.

"Dad did a couple of times over the years. I've only had to once a year ago. The first time with Dad it was some drunken burglar thinking he was Superman and could leap tall walls at a single bound. The poor guy ended up in the hospital with two broken legs. The other times it was feisty teenagers trying to beat the system. They lost."

"I'm surprised your dad and mom, or you either for that matter, didn't and don't have guard dogs."

"Dad and Mom thought it would not be fair to have a dog or any animal since they traveled a lot. I had an Irish Setter for awhile, but the poor thing was lonesome with me gone most of the time. I sent it to Ireland with my cousin."

"I didn't see any pictures of it in the study," said Branda.

"Oh, there's some around here someplace. Rusty was his name. He was a very nice dog and I still miss him sometimes."

Having reached their bedroom, they put on jeans and comfortable shirts then went to the study to do some work. Mitch first called Dr. William and made an appointment. It was for Wednesday, May 28, at 11 a.m.

Instead of reading, Branda pulled up a chair, sitting beside Mitch as he started entering data into his computer medical files; first her new appointment, then the information Dr. Cline had given him today. She didn't understand all of the medical jargon but Mitch patiently answered her questions, telling her in layman's terms what some of it meant whenever possible.

"I must say, you understand more about some of this terminology than most people," he said, complimenting her. "That must come from all of the reading you love to do."

"Thanks. I don't know if I ever mentioned it, but I once had dreams of becoming a nurse or even a doctor."

"You would be good in either profession I have a notion."

At 12:45 Mitch shut down the computer. He and Branda went outside to wait for Johnny so Mitch could introduce her.

"This upcoming party should be quite a get together," Branda said.

"From the reactions we got during our phone calls, I think everybody is looking forward to coming. Of course, not all are married, but the ones that are will be bringing spouses but no small children or teenagers, as you and I talked about earlier. I told them it was a party for adults. That was no problem. They know they can bring grown offspring if they like."

"That's nice," said Branda. "Reverend Cummings and Annie are the only ones married in my group. And their children are teenagers that don't think it's cool to go anywhere with their parents anymore so that was no problem.

Mary Ann and Linda are divorced and Mathilda hasn't married. I know other people but these are the only ones that need to know now. Mitch, does Johnny know the first story of my condition?"

"Yes. And he is most sympathetic."

"I hope we don't shock everybody to pieces with the real story. I forgot to ask, even though they already know, did you invite the three doctors and staff from your office?"

"Yes, I thought they would enjoy getting out to a nice party. At least I hope it will be a nice one. I also invited doctors Cline, William, Francis, and Fred Windom the mammogram specialist plus their office people. At least if anybody faints when they hear the news, we'll have immediate medical help available," he said. "Also as I talked about doing earlier, I have invited the business advisors, lawyers, and, of course, Judge Limson."

"Mitch, I think it is very nice, and somewhat unusual, for you to invite such a diverse crowd to the party. Not many people in your position would do that."

"What position? I'm just a very fortunate man to be who and what I am. I have no delusions that I am better than anyone else. In fact, social snobbery irks me no end. I like people for what they are not who."

"You're amazing."

Hearing the gate being opened, Mitch got up to greet Johnny.

After Mitch introduced her and all of them exchanged a few pleasantries, Johnny got to work on the pool and the hot tub. Mitch and Branda went inside to eat a light lunch then went to the study to do some research reading. He also taught her more about the computerized medical files and showed her the custom built combination safe and file where he kept backup CD's and hard copy material.

"You're really being careful," she said.

"Yes. I sure would hate losing any of this medical information, or any other information I have on here. Such as this," he added, quickly clicking on icons and typing in a file name.

Their Saturday night party popped onto the screen with the complete list of people the two of them had invited; plus their older children.

"Jumpin' George!!!" she exclaimed. "There must be one hundred people on there. Where will we put them all?"

"Inside, upstairs, downstairs, and maybe also outside weather permitting," he said. "We'll figure it out."

"Mitch, after seeing that list, how would you feel about having this affair catered?"

"Hey. That's a great idea!" he said. "That would save us a ton of work, fuss, and muss. We'll call Sean and Cynthia and get them to suggest a good one. The four of us can get our heads together and decide about food. I'll give them a call and see if they can come over after awhile, have supper with us, and make plans. We should have done this before but we still have time; especially if we get a caterer."

"The two of them know a lot about the food world that's for sure," Branda said. "And the caterer will no doubt have suggestions. You're right though. We should have been doing this before but I guess our minds have been elsewhere," she said, smiling at him. "I guess I just didn't realize how many people are involved so far. I'll wake up and smell the coffee now though. Wow! This isn't a party. It's a convention!"

The phone rang. Mitch picked up the receiver, listened a moment, then said, "Yes, we've been to see Dr. Cline. He said he would put in a rush order and let us know as soon as possible. Talk about ESP. We were just getting ready to call to see if you can come over for supper and help us plan the Saturday night party. Oh, okay. Then how about tomorrow for lunch? Oh that's right. I had forgotten you both went back to work as of today. How about supper tomorrow night? 6:30? Good. See you then. Meanwhile, can you give us the name of a good caterer we can call in the morning to get the ball rolling? Oh. Okay. I've heard of them. I think Dad and Mom used them on occasion," he said, quickly grabbing a pen and pad, writing down the name. "If they can't, who's your second and third choices? Okay. Thanks," he said, scribbling down more names. "We estimate about a hundred or so people including the four of us. Yes, we just realized we need to get a move on. We've been a bit distracted you might say. Branda is waving her hellos to you. I'll tell her. Thanks. See you tomorrow night."

After hanging up, he told her the couple said hello back. "They said the Dallas bunch is leaving tomorrow about noon."

After showing Branda some more about the computer, he shut it down and said, "Now how about a lesson in business management?"

"If you mean that James Bond operation inside that table, I think we'd better wait on that. My brain has had enough exercise for one day."

"Let me show you how to at least open it up."

"As I remember, you press a button underneath," she said.

"That's true, but there's more to it than that. Not much more, but something you need to know," he said, taking her by the hand, leading her to the table.

Placing her hand on the button he told her to push it. Nothing happened.

"Now hold it and count to ten," he instructed.

She did so and the table opened up.

"Jumpin' George, but this thing seems like it's alive."

"In a way it is," he said. "Alive with information from around the world. Now press that green button on this desk top."

She did so and a world map unwound from inside the ceiling level molding.

"Now push the blue button."

A map of the United States came down beside the other one.

"How many maps are there?" she asked.

"Twenty-four in various sizes. They're all around the room as I mentioned before. If you like, push all the buttons and take a look."

"I think I'll wait until another day. I'm feeling a bit tired. No, don't get nervous. This is just a normal tired. I'll go lie down for a bit."

"Okay. Want me to tuck you in?"

"No I'm a big girl now."

"You sure are," he said, taking her in his arms, giving her a long slow kiss.

Stepping apart at last, laughing softly, she said, "Whoa doctor. Whoa. Why don't you go out and see if the pool is ready. Maybe a dip will cool you off . . . for now."

Giving her a last squeeze, he let go, watching as she left to go to their bedroom for a nap.

After putting the study back in shipshape order, Mitch went out to check on Johnny's progress.

"Hi Dr. Andrews. I'm just finishing up. It's all ready to go. I'll be back Wednesday about 3 p.m. if that's okay to check and make sure everything is working all right. Meanwhile, if you have any trouble, give me a call."

"Thanks, Johnny. See you Wednesday. We have an appointment at 11 a.m. but should be home in plenty of time. If not, Ella and the rest will be here to let you in."

"Thanks Doctor Andrews. You sure have a beautiful wife and she seems real nice. I hope she gets to feeling better."

"Thank you, Johnny."

"You're welcome. Bye now. See you Wednesday . . . and again Saturday. Thanks again for the invitation. My wife, Donna, and I are really looking forward to the party."

"We're looking forward to seeing you then," said Mitch.

After locking the gate, Mitch stayed outside puttering around looking at the pool and hot tub. Everything seemed to be just fine which didn't surprise him. Johnny, about 35 years old, was an excellent workman. Finally he went inside to check on his wife.

She was sleeping peacefully and looked like an angel to him. For a long while, he sat on the side of the bed just looking at her. Betty's blank gaze from her nearby chair joined his.

Evidently, Branda sensed his presence, slowly waking up to smile at him.

"I'm sorry. I didn't mean to wake you up."

"That's okay."

"You know, Branda, that pool and hot tub look very inviting. I'm thinking to take a swim then sit in the tub. Care to join me? I asked Johnny not to get the temperature too hot either place so you could enjoy them too."

"I don't know Mitch; especially about the hot tub. I'll have to check them both to see. But right now, if you don't mind, I feel like another snooze. You go on out though and enjoy yourself."

"Are you sure you don't mind?"

"Not at all. You would no doubt enjoy some exercise and relaxation."

"Okay then. And I'll have my opened two-way radio close by and double check it after I've been underwater to see if you are trying to call me. I won't stay under long."

"Fine. And mine will be open too."

After he had put on his swimming trunks and headed outside, she made sure he was busy swimming before she got up and put on the white bikini she had located among her things a few days ago. After putting on the diamond bracelet and hair barrette, she looked at herself in the full-length bathroom mirror.

"Jumpin' George," she said to her reflected image. "What would Mama say? Or Papa? Well I can't worry about that now. I think surprising Mitch in this getup I told him I had will be worth it."

As she came back out to the bedroom, she glanced toward Betty, and said, "This skimpy outfit is enough to make even you blink. I hope I don't just look silly. My white slippers are bigger than this bikini."

As she entered the garden, heading toward the pool area, she didn't see Mitch at first. Then his head emerged from the water at the deep end just as she came sauntering into view with diamonds shimmering in waning rays of sunlight.

Clinging to the pool's edge, mesmerized by her beauty, he simply stared at her, speechless. She had no idea a man's eyes could roam over her body in admiration as his were doing.

As she continued slowly coming closer to him, they looked deeply into each other's eyes, sending signals with them as lovers have done since time's birth.

"I have never seen a sight as lovely as you walking toward me like some heavenly vision . . . all blonde and white and glittering like some goddess," Mitch said. "There are no words to say what other feelings I'm having . . . besides desire."

As if in slow motion, he used the pool's edge to help lift himself out of the water then stood entranced, watching her move nearer. Still dreamlike, he reached for a beach towel on the chaise lounge close by and began drying off.

"I don't want to get you all wet," he said.

"You are very thoughtful, Mitch," she said, now standing in front of him.

As he reached to put the wet towel back on the chaise lounge and pick up a dry one, he caught a glimpse of Branda's back.

"Oh, lord, you are not real," he said, taking off his wet swim trunks and wrapping the dry towel around his waist, sarong style.

"Oh, yes I am," she said, slightly laughing.

The sweet sound of her laughter brought time and motion back into focus for him.

After kissing passionately, he picked her up, carrying her toward the special garden room only his parents had ever used for making love.

"Oh Mitch. Are you sure?" she asked, in a voice husky from passion.

"Yes. I know they would approve. You are carrying their grandchild."

"But why are you honoring me like this?"

"Because I love you more than I can say."

"I love you the same way," she said.

Having reached the doorway to the room, he asked her to lean and open it since his arms weren't free. The last rays of the sun quickly faded.

Once inside, he put her down on the bed, gazing at her while he switched on a bedside lamp that gave off a soft glow. She was removing the diamond bracelet, putting it beside the lamp.

"Why don't you leave it on?" he asked.

Smiling at him, she said, "I'm afraid it could become a lethal weapon in the heat of battle so to speak. Remember that scratch from the other time when I wore it with my new white lace nightgown?"

"I do. But that was nothing serious," he said, smiling back.

Only early evening stars starting to twinkle through the skylight saw the rest of their lovemaking.

Afterwards, they got underneath the covers and slept for almost three hours, waking up at the same time.

Rolling over to face him, Branda asked, impishly, "How would you like to go skinny dipping? Last one in is a rotten egg. Or is that water too hot or cold for me?"

"It's just right," Mitch said. "Let's go."

Since running was awkward for her to do, he picked her up and carried her to the pool.

"We're both rotten eggs, I guess," he said, trying to make light of the situation.

They both walked into the shallow end of the pool at the same time heading a bit deeper. Their only companions were the dim, low sensor lights spaced along garden pathways, and the bright full moon starting to rise. The two splashed, swam, touched, kissed, dodged, and playfully cavorted, being ever mindful of Branda's possible condition. After a few minutes, they calmed down, went below the water, hugged, and came up kissing, still embraced.

Feeling the heat rising between them again as they stood at her shoulder depth with her back to the wall, Mitch whispered in her ear, "Oh Branda. I can't get enough of you. Do you mind if we . . . ?"

"I want you too," she said, giving him a tender kiss.

Afterwards, Mitch said, "Branda, thank you. That was a new experience for me . . . and a great one I might add."

"And I also agree it was a great new experience. Thank you also," she said.

As they slowly walked hand in hand out of the pool, she added, "I'm beginning to feel chilly now. I'd better go take a shower and get into my soft clothes."

"Would you like to sit for a minute in the hot tub to warm up quickly? Johnny has regulated it to a nice temperature so it won't be harmful to you."

"If you think it's all right; yes, I would like to do that. The pool was certainly nice," said Branda.

"Okay, and I'll get a beach towel to put around your shoulders and some for us to wrap up in when we get out."

She sat in the hot tub just long enough to warm up, then moved to sit on the edge with the towel around her shoulders, her legs dangling in the water. Mitch sat submerged to his chin.

"Mitch, that special room looked so cozy. I'd like to take a better look in the daylight sometime. And I sure didn't realize it had a small full bath in it. That was handy. I was surprised the outside door wasn't locked."

"I sometimes unlock it so Ella can go in there and dust or do whatever needs to be done. I evidently forgot to lock it again after she was here last time. I'm getting forgetful in my old age I guess."

Branda laughed, and said, "You are far from old age. You have just had a lot of distractions lately."

"Nice ones too," he said, leaning over to give her a quick kiss.

"And you do remember important things. Mitch, do you think your parents only used that room for lovemaking, reading and listening to music?" Branda asked. "Somehow I have a feeling there was more to it than that."

"I always had that feeling too," Mitch said. "Like maybe it was a very small replica of some place they had been in their travels; one that had wonderful memories attached."

"I wish I could have known your mom and dad. I think we would have been good friends . . . maybe even closer. I've learned to love them just because of what I've learned from you and because they had you."

"Why thank you, and they definitely would have loved you too. Are you feeling warmer now?"

"Yes. Thanks. But I think I'm about ready for bed. Those last two work projects took my energy level down . . . but in such a pleasant way," she said, smiling at him. "And Mitch, I don't know what to say about your extravagant compliment about seeing me walk toward you."

"It doesn't even begin to cover what I meant," he said.

"I was afraid you might think I looked cheap and tacky."

"Oh no! Oh no! Absolutely not. Far from it. But I'll tell you one thing. I don't ever want any other man to see you in that suit. You're too fantastic in it. It is for my eyes only, just like those pictures I took of you in that white lace nightgown. Okay?"

"You never have to worry about that. I would never wear it in front of or for anybody else. As you said, it's for your eyes only."

"And any woman that saw you in it would scratch your eyes out from jealousy."

"You're making me blush, Mitch."

"You really have no idea how beautiful you are, do you?" he asked. "Someday soon I want to take pictures of you in that bikini."

"All right, but I never consi . . . oh Mitch. I'm getting that feeling I get before . . .

Suddenly she noticed a vision approaching; this time not dream-driven. "Mitch, can you see it? Can you see the vision?"

"No. What are you talking about? But Branda, a piece of your right foot looks like it is trying to glow but isn't . . ." He stopped, looking shocked. "Oh

Branda, I do see it! I do see that vision. Someone is coming inside that silvery cloud."

Both sat mesmerized, watching her foot one second, the vision the next. The piece of her foot glowed but did nothing else. It was more of the small part where her two smallest toes use to be. Then an elderly Indian chief appeared. He was trying to tell them something but the words made no sense.

Over and over he was saying something that sounded like, "Slow fire water. Water slow fire."

After mumbling some more unintelligible words, the vision drifted away in a silvery mist. As it dimmed, they saw Branda's father approaching, holding something or someone. An Indian woman was behind him, smiling.

"Branda. I never saw anything like that in my life. And look at your foot. It hasn't done anything else. It looks all right. Do you suppose the old Indian was trying to tell us water will stop this?"

"Wouldn't that be wonderful, Mitch? I'm afraid to take my foot out of the water, but I'm not only sleepy, I'm hungry. We haven't eaten since lunch."

"Oh, good grief. That's right. Now that you mention it, I'm starving too. Tell you what. Take your foot out and see what happens while we're still sitting here."

"No matter what it does, we need to get some milk or a sandwich or something," she said.

"I agree."

Her foot remained the same after she took it out.

"Amazing," said Mitch. "The water must have aborted the episode."

Even while showering and eating a bite afterwards, her foot stayed all right.

"Mitch, do you think we've found the cure . . . or rather . . . the old Indian chief found it for us or what? I wonder who he is?"

"Time will tell," he said. "Time will tell."

The couple went to bed, holding each other, happy, wondering about the mysterious vision they had seen.

Soon drifting off to sleep, neither saw another one return with the Indian woman standing there smiling at them, holding a papoose cradle board with the opening facing toward her. Something else, only dimly visible, was propped against her legs.

CHAPTER FOURTEEN

W HEN BRANDA AWAKENED, SHE COULD not believe it was almost noon.

"Jumpin' George," she said to Betty since Mitch was not beside her. "I don't ever remember sleeping this late in my life."

She was just starting to read the note Mitch had left on his pillow when his voice came in over the two-way radio. "That you talking to Betty, Miz Rip van Winkle?"

"Yes, tis' herself. Why did you let me sleep so late?"

"Because you needed to. If you recall, yesterday was rather busy you might say. I've been coming in to check on you and you looked so peaceful I didn't see any reason to wake you up. I slept until ten which is late for me. Are you hungry?"

"As a wolf. Where are you?" she asked.

"In the study. I called Angel's Catering and the owners, Chad and Bonnie Adams, will be here tonight for dinner along with Sean and Cynthia. Since you told me it's okay to tell people the truth about you when I think it is necessary, I felt it only fair to tell them in case they would be nervous about being around you tonight and at the party. They told me they aren't worried. Even though this is a rush job for them, they agreed to hire some extra staff and do it; including serving and clean up people. They'll screen their workers and tell the true story to ones they carefully choose. If anyone wants to back out they may. We'll just have to hope they would keep quiet about what they have been told. I'll give everyone a nice bonus. I hope letting that many people in on the truth is still okay with you. They would hear it at the party anyway and might be angry if they had not been told in advance and given a chance to back out. Of course, a lot more people will learn at the party, but at least we know that group."

"Of course it's all right. You know I trust your judgment. We'll just have to hope for the best in all cases. And what will we be feeding Mr. and Mrs. Adams tonight, Dr. A?"

"I thought bologna sandwiches would be good," he said, laughing.

"On rye or whole wheat?" she asked, laughing back.

"Actually, Chad and Bonnie are going to bring some food samples for us to try."

"Well, that's a sneaky way to get out of cooking dinner," said Branda. "Just for that, would you mind fixing me some bacon and eggs for breakfast. I'll be there shortly."

"Just what the doctor ordered," he said. "I already had my breakfast, but I'll enjoy visiting with you while you eat, or maybe I'll have a light lunch . . . a sandwich or sal . . . "

Her loud gasp and the words, "Oh no, oh no," brought him running, black bag in hand.

He found her sitting on the floor by the bed holding her right foot.

"Oh Mitch, look. The small part that was starting to glow underwater last night has disappeared. I didn't realize it until I put my feet on the floor and noticed this right one felt a bit different."

Sitting down beside her, he quickly checked her over. All vital signs were normal. Her foot was not unusually warm and none of the other usual symptoms were present.

"What do you think has happened, Mitch?" she asked. "I was hoping water was the cure like the elderly Indian chief seemed to indicate."

"Apparently, it only delays the process," he said, putting an arm around her to comfort her. "The rest of it must have happened while we were asleep or after I got up and left the room."

"When I have another episode, maybe we can get the part underwater again and then observe it closely afterwards."

"You mean conduct an experiment?" Mitch asked.

"Exactly. We must know what is happening. With the baby coming, we might find a way to have some control over these losses so I can be around to meet our child. Maybe I'll end up having to stay in water or use water compresses."

"Good heavens, Branda !" Mitch exclaimed. "You are a strong woman."

"Not always. Frankly, I'm scared to death most of the time."

"I know you are, sweetheart, but you cover it well," he said.

His use of the word sweetheart made her feel warm and loved. She hugged and kissed him.

"And I know you are scared too," she said.

"Yes I am. I worry about you, don't like having you frightened, and don't even want to think about the possibility of los . . . "

"I know, Mitch. I know. Our fears lie beneath the surface of everything we say and do. But since there's nothing more we can do right now I guess I'd better go wash my face and come eat the breakfast you have cooked, or are cooking. I'm still hungry," she said, trying to lighten the mood.

"You're something else," he said, giving her a final hug and helping her get up before he started back to the kitchen.

"See you in a minute," she said, heading for the bathroom, happy to find out she was still able to walk; with a limp to be sure, but she could manage. She was beginning to wonder about using a cane.

While she ate her breakfast and he had a sandwich, they discussed food possibilities for the party; subject to caterer approval of course.

Both agreed on baked ham, smoked turkey, and roast beef to be carved and served as needed instead of slices drying out on platters.

Branda said, "And I guess the usual assortment of breads, cheese, crudités, nuts, dips, chips, fresh fruit, desserts, and so forth."

"How about shrimp, some king crab legs, and lobster tails with drawn butter?" Mitch asked. "And how about an ice sculpture . . . a dolphin perhaps? And I'll have an open bar set up to serve wine, champagne, liquor, mixers, sodas, fruit juices and anything else we can think of."

"All that you mentioned would be great but would cost a fortune," she answered.

"I have one of those. Remember?"

Laughing, she said, "To tell you the truth Mitch, that really has not quite sunken into my head yet. I just cannot imagine anyone having that kind of money. It doesn't seem real."

"It is, Mrs. A, it is and let's enjoy it. I want this party to be something extra special."

"Well, with all you have in mind, it certainly should be. Now, should we have this inside or outside?"

"I've checked with the weather bureau and it looks like the weather will cooperate with having it outside in the garden area; again subject to caterer approval."

"I hope no one falls in the pool," she said. "Maybe we should have told them to bring their swim suits."

"I thought of that but decided that might turn into too much of a hassle."

"You're right," she said. "And the half-bath out there will come in handy or people can use the one in the den. I imagine you'll lock up the hideaway room."

"The hideaway room? What a great name for it!!! And yes, I think it's best I lock it."

"If anyone asks, we can tell them it's a work room," Branda said.

Laughing loudly, Mitch said, "Oh Branda, that too is a great description. You're something else !!!"

"Mitch, could we have some sort of pretty lights strung out there, and I guess we'll need extra chairs and tables."

"You bet, and you're right about the tables and chairs. There's plenty of room without making it look overcrowded," he said. "And now, young lady, how about you go take your shower while I clean up the dishes? Then maybe we can do some research reading this afternoon."

"Fine with me. But I'll be glad to help you with the clean up. And thank you for a scrumptious breakfast."

"You're welcome. You go on along now, " he said, giving her a quick hug and kiss.

She couldn't tell for sure with the water running in the shower but she thought she heard a phone ringing. She was right.

Just as she was finishing, Mitch burst into the bathroom.

"Branda," he said, breathlessly, sliding the shower door open.

"What on earth, Mitch?"

"Branda, Dr. Cli . . . "

"Did Dr. Cline call?" she exclaimed.

"Yes, but . . ."

"Am I really and truly pregnant?"

Still trying to catch his breath after running from the kitchen where he had answered the phone, Mitch was finally able to say, "He doesn't know."

"What do you mean he doesn't know. What did the test show?" she asked, stepping out of the shower, drying off.

"Nothing. It sort of blew up!"

"What do you mean, it sort of blew up. Blood samples don't blow up . . . do they?"

"I never heard of one doing that but then no one person can know everything," he said, finding her terry cloth robe and helping her slip it on.

"Well what happened, Mitch? What happened?"

"Dr. Cline told me the lab technician running the test said the sample suddenly started glowing, turned pale yellow, went to light green, then red, vanished, and left a strange odor. Then she fainted."

"Oh my God," said Branda, prayerfully. "Oh no. Poor girl. I hope she's all right. What does all this mean I wonder?"

"I have no idea, Branda," Mitch said. "The girl is all right now but her supervisor did give her the rest of the day off. Dr. Cline asked if we could go to the lab, give another sample, and stay there while the test is run. He wants me to observe."

"When does he want us to do this?"

"Right now, if possible. He's going to try and be there too, but couldn't promise."

"I won't be a minute," she said, going off to get dressed.

Mitch phoned Dr. Cline and told him they would be on their way shortly.

Dr. Cline was at the lab when they arrived. He was able to make arrangements with other doctors in his office to take his remaining patients.

As the technician replacement went through the procedures using the new blood sample, the two doctors and Branda watched intently. In fact, the doctors were so engrossed they did not see what Branda noticed was hovering over the test area. Even though Mitch had seen the one vision, he evidently was not tuned in to this one. She was pretty sure neither Dr. Cline nor the lab technician ever would see such a thing.

The elderly Indian chief and Indian woman were closely watching the proceedings.

When the blood sample started faintly glowing, the two Indians began chanting and sprinkling what looked like water onto it. The glowing stopped. No one else in the room gave any indication they had even seen the glow or its halt from sprinkled water. Branda looked up at the Indian couple and smiled her thanks. They smiled back, fading away into the silvery mist.

She noticed Beverly, the lab technician, was having Dr. Cline, then Mitch check the test results after she had done so.

All three were beaming.

Mitch turned to her as the other two looked on.

With tears in his eyes, he hugged her gently, and said, "Looks like we're going to have a baby for sure."

"Oh, Mitch," she said, hugging and kissing him, completely oblivious of the two onlookers who were smiling from ear to ear.

"I'll buy the cigars when the time comes," said Dr. Cline. "Later on, do you want to know if I should buy pink or blue ones?"

"Thanks, Richard," said Mitch. "But Branda and I decided we would rather just let the baby show us when he or she arrives."

Everybody laughed.

"That's fine," said Dr. Cline. "Just fine." Taking some notes out of his jacket pocket, he added, "Now let's see. Based on figures Branda gave me, and allowing for unknown factors that may be involved in this particular case, I calculate the baby should be arriving late January or early February. I never like to give an exact date because there are too many variables involved and parents often get anxious if the child isn't here on the dot."

"We'll be ready whenever Michele or Mitchell makes a debut," Mitch said.

"For sure," said Branda.

"Already named, eh?" Dr. Cline asked.

"Those are the basic ones. There will be some family names added on too," Branda explained.

After Branda and Mitch got back home, they went to the garden and stood for a moment near the rose trellis, holding each other quietly, gently. Finally taking her face in his hands, looking deeply into her eyes, he kissed her sweetly and tenderly. For the first time in her life she felt that special kind of love a man and woman can have for each other in all its splendor.

"You have fulfilled my life more than I ever thought possible," Mitch said, stroking her silken hair. "I love you beyond belief. Thank you from the bottom of my soul. Our baby. Oh Branda, I am so happy."

"Now I know I have been empty all of my life and now I am full and whole. I thank you too from the bottom of my soul. I love you completely," Branda said.

Their usual romantic passion was replaced this moment by a deeper bond; one she had never known before, and although he had come near to it with Helen, it was not like this. The baby was like a drawstring pulling their circle of love stronger and closer together.

Taking his hand, she held it with one of hers over where their baby nestled inside.

"Oh Mitch, I pray everything will be all right. This life you put inside me is so precious."

"We'll do everything possible to make it right," he said, gently patting her abdomen.

Removing his hand, he once again held her in his arms and kissed her tenderly.

Afterwards, they stood quietly embraced enjoying their newly found, heightened, emotional plane.

"I could stand here like this forever," Mitch said. "But I'm thinking you ought to take a rest since we are having company tonight. As I mentioned, yesterday was a bit strenuous for you between the lovemaking and swimming."

"Maybe so, but I certainly enjoyed them," she said. "And, in all honesty, if I had thought I was overdoing anything I would have stopped, or you would have. I know you watch over me very carefully."

"That's true," he said.

"But, you're right, Mitch. I would like to rest before dinner, but first I would like to do some research reading in the study as you mentioned doing earlier. Care to join me?"

"Yes. I did some this morning, but enjoy it more when you are near me. And now that we definitely know you are pregnant, I want to review the proposed test list and see which ones might not be a good idea now. As I mentioned before, I've held off scheduling until we got the results of the blood pregnancy test. Now it's going to be full steam ahead without overwhelming you."

After spending time in the study reading and discussing various theories, Branda finally went off to take her nap. Mitch stayed to check the testing list on his computer and consult with his advisors on business matters. He stopped at 4:30 and went to take a rest beside Branda. He set the alarm for 5:30 just in case. After leaning over to kiss her cheek, he was soon sound asleep too. The alarm awakened them.

"Oh Jumpin' George," Branda said. "I am turning into a Rip Van Winkle."

"That's okay," Mitch said. "You're sleeping for two now."

"I've heard of eating for two, but not sleeping," she said, laughing softly.

"Well, right now I guess we'd better shake a leg for all of us. Company's coming in about an hour."

"I know. What do we need to do to get ready?"

"Since Chad and Bonnie are bringing the food, I guess we'll wait until they get here and tell us what is needed. I suppose plates, knives, forks, spoons, glasses, napkins for a start."

While waiting, Branda and Mitch sat on the living room couch listening to some of her favorite, romantic, Spanish guitar music. With one of his arms around her shoulders, she snuggled close to him. She held his other hand with both of hers, resting them on her abdomen.

"I hope Mitchell or Michele enjoys this kind of music," Branda said.

"I have a feeling he or she will," said Mitch.

"Should we start reading Shakespeare out loud, and some of the other classics?" she asked.

"Well, why not."

Both smiled, continuing to sit quietly and peacefully, enjoying being together listening to the music.

The doorbell broke their reverie. Before they could get the door fully open, Cynthia and Sean were asking, "Well. Have you found out yet? Did Dr. Cline rush it through? Are you?"

"Yes indeed. We surely are," Branda and Mitch said at the same time.

"We found out this afternoon," Branda said. She would tell Sean and Cynthia the rest later.

Teary eyed, all performed their usual hugging rituals with more fervor than usual.

"I just knew you were. Congratulations," said Cynthia.

"The same goes for me," Sean said, giving Mitch an extra bear hug.

"Oh, please do excuse us," Branda said to Chad and Bonnie as she introduced herself. "We just found out today we're going to have a baby."

"How wonderful," Bonnie said, giving her a hug first, then Mitch. "We gathered it was something extra special like that."

"Indeed. Indeed," said Chad, shaking her hand then Mitch's.

Sean and Mitch helped Chad bring in the food from the Angel's Catering panel truck. Branda and Cynthia held open the front doors while Bonnie did the woman thing of telling the men to "be careful and keep the containers right side up."

Sean quipped, "I've never yet seen anything that has to be packed in a car trunk or carried somewhere that can be done just any old way. It has to be placed standing up or carried a certain way; otherwise the world ends."

"I'm glad you've learned that," Cynthia said.

All laughed and headed for the kitchen.

After Bonnie and Chad put out what they had brought, everybody grabbed a plate, filled it, and began enjoying the food. Samples included beef, lamb, veal, pork, baked ham, chicken, turkey, fish, shrimp, lobster, crab legs, an assortment of fruit and green salads, nuts, cheese, dips, breads, chips . . . well, you name it, it was there. Dessert selections were awesome. Branda's favorite was the chocolate Creme Brûlée.

"Jumpin' George," Branda said. "You could feed a small nation with all of this food. And it's all so delicious. Not the usual fare I must say."

"Thank you," said Bonnie and Chad. "That's why we call it Angel's," Bonnie added, with a chuckle. "It's heavenly . . . or so people tell us."

"They're right," said Mitch.

"We do try hard to do a good job," Chad said.

"You succeed very, very well," Branda complimented.

After eating and doing the clean up, the group got down to business. First they checked the garden area for space and flow, then the living room, dining room, den, and basement in case the weather had a sudden change of mind and turned stormy.

Mitch and Branda pretty much stuck with their original food plans with some additions suggested by the caterers, plus Sean and Cynthia. Chad and Bonnie knew an ice carver that could do the dolphin and someone else to string tiny white lights. They would arrange for tables and chairs to be delivered and set up in the garden area the day before the party, along with the long buffet serving table. Branda had suggested using a good grade of paper plates and utensils. Mitch vetoed that.

"I want white linen tablecloths and napkins, glassware, china dinnerware, and nice silverware . . . not real china or silver or course, but something nice."

"But Mitch," Branda said. "That will require a boatload of people to do the clean up."

"That's okay. We'll bring in extra portable electric dishwashers if necessary."

Chad spoke up. "Don't worry. We'll see that everything gets done."

Branda had never in her life seen firsthand what money could do, but she was getting lesson 101 now.

"Okay, Mitch. I'll just sit back, relax, and enjoy the party," she said.

"That's my girl," he said, giving her a quick kiss.

Later, when she overheard Chad and Mitch discussing the fee, she nearly fainted but kept quiet. It was well into five figures, not including the bonuses. She went over to talk to Cynthia and Bonnie who were discussing whether to use white plates or a pastel shade.

"What do you prefer?" asked Bonnie.

"You two know more about that than I do," Branda answered. "But I think yellow is Mitch's favorite color . . . or one of them; a pale creamy yellow.

"That would look elegant for sure," Cynthia said.

"Okay," said Bonnie. "We'll go with that color theme . . . pale creamy yellow and white. What do you think, Sean?"

"That will look beautiful," Sean said.

After Chad and Mitch finished discussing the business end of the affair they walked over to be with the rest of the group. Bonnie explained the proposed color scheme to them.

"Sounds great to me," Mitch said.

"Me too," agreed Chad. "Mitch, Branda, is it okay if we start doing some of the preliminary work here Thursday instead of trying to cram it all in Friday and Saturday?"

Both agreed that was an excellent idea.

"Our cleaning and yard crews will be here tomorrow so the house will be ready for the party . . . especially in case it rains and we have to move indoors," Mitch said.

"Fine," said Bonnie.

While Mitch, Bonnie, Chad, and Sean finished talking about some party-related details, Branda managed to get Cynthia aside. She told her about the problems with the first test and ask her to tell Sean later. She didn't mention the vision hovering over the test, or say anything about any of the other dreams and visions. Maybe later.

"Good heavens, Branda. You're a brave soul," said Cynthia, giving Branda a hug.

Finally, everyone headed for the front door, each person lugging some carrier or container. Mitch made sure Branda's load was very light.

After the guests pulled away in their respective vehicles, everybody waving good bye, Mitch closed and locked the front doors and set the alarm. Branda was yawning.

"That went well, don't you think, sleepyhead?" Mitch asked, smiling at her.

"Yes. I still don't believe the whole thing."

"You will Saturday night, my love, you will. And between now and then, plus at all other times, I want you to get the right amounts of rest and exercise, eat well, and keep on loving me."

"Whatever you say, doctor. Whatever you say."

They walked toward their bedroom, arms around each other's waists.

"Mitch, I can't figure out why my energy level is so much lower than it has ever been. Is it the illness, the pregnancy, or what?"

"It may be a bit of both," he said.

"I'm so glad I have you to take care of me," she said.

"Thank you. I'll do my best."

"I know you will, Mitch. I know you will."

After they were in bed, they lay in each other arms for a long while, talking about the baby, how their lives had changed so drastically in such a short time, and wondered what the future held.

Then slowly and quietly they melted into a lovemaking unlike either had ever experienced before.

"I feel like I am flowing into you body and soul," Branda whispered.

"And I into you."

His gentleness overwhelmed her to the point she felt she could never hold him close enough or get enough of him.

Afterwards, looking deeply into each other's eyes, Mitch said, "I wish I knew the words to tell you how deeply, completely, I love you Branda. For the first time, I fully understand what is meant by two becoming one flesh. Did you feel it too?"

"Oh yes, Mitch. That's what I meant when I said I felt like I was flowing into your body and soul. And I also love you more than I know how to say. You are my very life," she said, reaching to gently kiss him.

Just before drifting toward sleep, Mitch leaned to kiss her abdomen, saying, "Good night little one. Now you know what true love is and how you began."

After tenderly kissing one more time they fell asleep with one of his hands on top of one of hers, both covering the baby.

CHAPTER FIFTEEN

BOTH AWAKENED AT FIRST LIGHT, turning to look as if seeing one another for the first time. Emotions from their special bonding last night were still surrounding them like a whisper-soft, silken cocoon.

Kissing softly, gently, both murmured "I love you" more than once, quietly staying in each other's arms for a long moment.

Finally, Branda spoke, softly, "I suppose we should get moving. The cleaning and lawn crews plus Johnny will be arriving and we do have to be at Dr. William's and Dr. Francis' office at 11."

Stretching lazily, Mitch said, "I know. But this is so much more enjoyable. Now I know what people mean when they say they are floating on cloud nine."

They smiled at each other, kissed again then slowly got up to start the day's rituals.

Since they had decided against telling anyone else about the baby until the party, when Ella and all the rest arrived they just visited for a bit then left for the doctor's appointment.

In the car on the way, Mitch asked, "Would you like to go downtown after this appointment and do a little local sightseeing, maybe have lunch at The Broadway Oyster Bar?"

"Oh yes, I would enjoy that," she answered. "But what about Ella and everybody? Won't they wonder about us?"

"I'll call and let Ella know. She can tell the others."

After exchanging greetings with Dr. William and Dr. Francis, Mitch explained Branda's condition, how she wound up being brought to him by Sean, and a brief outline of proposed testing and procedures.

Both were sympathetic, shocked, had never read or heard of anything like it, and offered to do anything possible to help.

"I'll do some extra research reading to see what I can find out," said Dr. William.

"And I will comb the Internet too," Dr. Francis said.

"Thank you both," said Branda, echoed by Mitch.

"Also," said Mitch, "I am having a special telephone tip line installed in my home office tomorrow so if anyone hears anything that might throw some light on this they can call and talk to me or leave a message. And I'm having it set up so if I'm away for any length of time, I can access it. I'll let you and everyone else know the number at the party Saturday night. I'll have business cards printed with that number and have a stack of them put on each table after I make a speech. And I hope you'll be available for consultation."

Both agreed to be available at any time.

After completing necessary paperwork, getting copies of Branda's medical records, and phoning Ella, the couple left and headed downtown on Highway 40.

Branda had been to The Broadway Oyster Bar a lot but never quite gotten used to the overall eccentric look of the place with its odds and ends decorations. But the delicious food served in the back room made up for that. The first time she had gone there with friends, she put one foot inside the doorway then backed out saying she wasn't going in "that place." Another time she had had her first taste of fresh alligator there and loved it. She hoped it would be on the menu today.

Since it wasn't, she ordered an Oyster Grinder; a lot of fresh, cooked oysters with a good sauce stuffed inside a hefty sized roll.

Mitch ordered shrimp. She asked for water, he had a bottle of Budweiser beer.

Afterwards, they meandered through the underground museum at the Arch. Since both had seen the movie a few times about how that magnificent structure was erected, they skipped that and looked at exhibits. She loved seeing certain optical illusion walls that were slatted in such a way the scenes on them changed as a person walked forward. The stuffed horse also fascinated her as well as the teepee in a replica of an Indian campsite.

"You are enjoying yourself, aren't you?" asked Mitch.

"Yes, each time I come here I always see and learn something new."

"I think I'll send you to St. Louis University so you can get a Ph.D."

"Oh don't tease me, Mitch. You know I'm not smart enough for that."

"Oh but I know you are that intelligent. And if you feel up to taking some classes, we'll go enroll you today."

"You're serious, aren't you?" she asked.

"Yes I am."

"Well, under other circumstances I would take you up on your generous offer, but I think now is not a good time. What if some part started disappearing during a class? That would not be fair to those around me."

"Perhaps not," he said. "But I could hire a tutor to come to the house. What would you like to study?"

"Oh Mitch," she said, throwing her arms around him right there in front of everybody and giving him a kiss. "You are too good to me. Thank you so much, but I think I have my hands full already."

"If you change your mind, let me know."

"I will you sweet man. I will."

"Well since I can't interest you in a doctorate degree today, how about a ride to the top of the Arch?"

"I've done that a couple of times, Mitch, and I'm sure you have too. Unless you really would like to go I would just as soon skip that today," she said.

"That's fine. Are you getting tired?"

Smiling, she said, "No, I'm all right but I think the baby needs a nap."

They got back home just as everyone was getting ready to leave. After a round of good byes they said they were looking forward to seeing everyone Saturday night. Mitch and Branda thanked them for their hard work today as well as other days. They also thanked Johnny for getting the pool and hot tub temperatures just right and for helping clean up the garden and pool area for the party.

Mitch went off to his office to do some work and Branda went to their bedroom to nap. Later, he came to lie down beside her and also fell asleep. Both awakened an hour later.

"Are you hungry?" he asked.

"Not very much. How about you?"

"No, that big lunch pretty well fixed me for the day," he answered. "How about a bowl of soup and a sandwich out by the pool?"

"That sounds nice."

As they ate, the sun started its downward trip going to wake up another part of the planet. Garden sensor lights twinkled on. The two sat in companionable silence watching God's evening light show.

"You know Mitch," Branda said. "I once heard it said that Nature is God's artwork. It certainly seems that way."

"You're right," he agreed.

After cleaning up the dishes and getting into their soft clothes the couple sat in bed watching an old Fred Astaire, Ginger Rogers movie.

"Now that's real dancing. Talent coming out of their ears," said Branda.

"Absolutely!" Mitch agreed.

Snuggled close to each other they did not see the movie's romantic love scenes. By then they had dissolved into another tender, marrow-melting, one of their own. The automatically set television switched itself off.

Still feeling satisfied and dreamy they awakened early the next morning and lay holding each other, kissing gently, whispering love words and phrases. They faded in and out of light slumbers kissing and touching in between.

The ringing phone jolted them wide-awake.

"Oh dam . . . I mean dar . . . I mean nuts!" Mitch exclaimed, fumbling to pick up the phone. "Hello," he said. "Oh. Oh yes. That's all right. Yes. That will be fine. See you then. Good-bye."

"Who on earth was that?" Branda asked. "What time is it?"

"That was the telephone man and it's 7:30 a.m. He'll be here in an hour to put in the special tip line."

"Guess we'd better hop," she said.

"No need for you to hurry."

"I'll go fix breakfast while you shower, or, we can take a shower together," she said, mischievously.

"And that phone man would be standing at the front door ringing the door bell until cat's bark," Mitch said, laughing. "Seriously, why don't you shower in our bath and I'll use one of the others?"

"I can use another one too," she offered.

"Thanks, but it's easier for me to move a few shaving supplies than it would be for you to move all that woman stuff," he said, smiling.

"Well!" she said, with pretend huffiness. "All that woman stuff, eh?" she added, throwing a pillow at him.

He gently tossed one her way, then lightly grabbed her, holding her down on the bed while he kissed her.

"I surrender," she said, mockingly.

Letting go of her, leaning to kiss her belly, he said, "See what kind of woman your mother is? A real fighter. But frankly, she's a better lover than she is a fighter."

They kissed again, then Mitch got up and headed for the bathroom in the nearest bedroom off the hallway while she went to theirs.

They were just finishing breakfast when the doorbell rang. Branda stayed to clean up the dishes while Mitch went off to answer the door.

She was headed to his office when she heard a phone ring. There were so many lines, she was never sure at first which one it was. Maybe Mitch and the man were testing the new line. She waited. There were no more rings.

As she approached the office, which she still thought of as the study, Mitch was coming out the door.

"Oh good," he said. "There you are. That was Chad calling. He wanted to know if he, Bonnie and other catering crew members could come over and start doing some prep work for the party."

"Sure. Chad mentioned that the other day. What time are they coming?"

"In about an hour if that's all right with you. I told them to come on unless I called them right back and told them otherwise."

"I wonder what they plan to do today?"

"I think measure and things like that. Kind of get the lay of the land so to speak . . . inside and outside."

She poked her head inside the office door and spoke to the telephone installer.

"Good morning, ma'am," he said. "I hope I didn't wake you up too early. The office said this was an important installation so I put it first on my list."

"Why thank you. No we were awake," Branda said.

Mitch and Branda stood watching as the man finished his job and tested the phone several times.

Finally handing Mitch a card with the new phone number written on it he stood watching Mitch sign paperwork and said the charge would be on their next phone bill.

Both thanked the man and Mitch walked him to the front door. Branda went to look at the new phone. It was dark red with lots of buttons on it. She hoped Mitch knew how to work it.

When he came back in she asked him, "Do you know how to work that thing?" she asked.

"I think so. He explained it and left a booklet of instructions. We'll learn together."

"Okay."

"Now I'm going to call the printers on the regular house line and order some cards with this new tip line number printed on them. I'll ask them to deliver the cards tomorrow or Saturday morning. I hope they can do a rush job."

While he was busy doing that, she wandered into the living room. She wondered who had been the piano player in the family. Lifting the lid to expose the keyboard, she sat down and lightly began playing one of the few songs she had memorized and still knew; "Smoke Gets In Your Eyes."

The doorbell interrupted her. When she got up, turning around to go answer, she was startled to see Mitch standing in the foyer gazing at her with a strange look on his face.

"Oh, I'm sorry Mitch. I guess I should have asked you first if I could play your piano."

He said nothing, turned and went to open the door.

They welcomed Chad, Bonnie, and five other catering members; Brandi, Bill, Will, Helen, and Jo Anne.

The rest of the morning and a good part of the afternoon was a hubbub of questions among themselves, answers, measuring, discussing, making notes, calling people for information, caterer cell phones ringing, and general confusion . . . inside and outside in the garden patio area.

Mitch and Branda tried to stay out of the way unless needed. Mitch went to his office to read and work. Branda mostly stayed in the den reading. She still couldn't figure out his attitude about her piano playing and didn't think this was the time to bring it up. He had acted like he didn't want to be with her . . . at least not just now.

The caterers asked questions of them only when necessary. Branda was fascinated with their professionalism and listened whenever possible to learn what was going on.

"I'd have a nervous breakdown if I had to do all of this," she mused.

Once she had gone into the kitchen to get a bite to eat. The lady named Brandi was in there.

"We have similar names," Branda said, explaining how her parents had named her.

"That was a nice compromise," said Brandi. "They must have gotten along very well."

"Yes, as a matter of fact, they did."

Branda was glad her illness was not brought into the conversation.

Finally the day wore down along with Mitch, Branda, and the caterers.

As Mitch and Branda were standing at the front door thanking everyone and telling them good bye, Chad said, "All of us will see you tomorrow at 10:30 to oversee workmen, bring more equipment, and finalize plans. We'll be here a good part of the day. The people delivering tables and chairs and setting them up are scheduled to be here at 10:30 too. In the afternoon, light stringing people will be here. Some of us will be back Saturday morning about 11 to do some food prep and take care of other details. The main cooking will be done in our kitchen and transported here. The dolphin ice carver will be here Saturday afternoon; that is if all of those arrangements are all right with you and Branda."

"That's fine," Mitch said.

"Okay," said Branda. "See you then."

After closing the doors, Mitch turned to her and said, "I owe you an explanation."

"About my playing the piano? Something about that disturbed you didn't it?"

"Yes. Let's go sit down in the living room and I'll try to explain. Or would you rather go to your couch in the den?"

"No. The living room is fine. I gather I unknowingly resurrected one of your ghosts?"

"Yes. If the caterers had not been at the door, I may have had to go for a long walk . . . with my phone open, of course."

Walking toward the couch, Branda said, "Again, I'm so sorry, Mitch. I won't play it again."

As they sat down, Mitch took her hands in his and said, "I'll just say it straight out. No one has touched that piano since the day Mother found Dad slumped unconscious over the keyboard. She called for an ambulance but he died of a coronary before they got to the hospital. He had been playing some of her favorite songs while she was in the kitchen fixing dinner. They had the intercom on so she could hear him more clearly. When the music suddenly stopped, and she heard the harsh sound the keys made as he fell on them, she knew something was very wrong."

"Oh Mitch, oh my. You poor thing. No wonder you were so upset with me. Why didn't you tell me before?"

"I really don't know. I should have but, frankly, I don't like to think about it or remember it. I loved my dad . . . and mom . . . so much."

Branda reached to hug him and they sat silently holding each other for a moment.

"I understand," she said. "Did your mom play piano too . . . or do you?"

"Yes, Mom did and I know how to read music but am not much of a musician. By they way, where did you learn to play? You're quite good." Hesitating, he added, "Branda, please feel free to play the piano anytime you feel like it. Really and truly, you've helped me pretty well lay that ghost today. Thank you."

"Thanks, Mitch. Maybe you and I can play duets sometime."

"We'll think about that. And again I ask, where did you learn to play?"

"From a wonderful pianist named Kathleen Phinney. She taught English and other subjects at Morley High School but she had learned music from a German lady in Cape Girardeau. Whenever school kids would seem restless or tired, Miss Kathleen . . . as we all called her . . . would just stop lessons and play piano for us. Sometimes she would play songs for us to sing along with, then at other times she would play classical music so we could learn about that category too. She could play any kind of music and was always willing to share her gift when asked. I took lessons from her all through high school and was allowed to practice either on her piano at home or the one at school. She never charged my folks a dime but they brought her produce or chickens or whatever they could to make up for their lack of money. Miz Kathleen said I was talented and it was a pleasure to teach me. She once had a thirty-minute radio show at KFVS in Cape that was broadcast Saturday mornings from the old Marquette Hotel. She sat inside a glass booth. I got to go a few times to watch her. Her show was called Musical Medleys by Kathleen Phinney."

"She must have been quite an inspiration to you and the other students," Mitch said.

"Definitely."

"By the way, in all the uproar today, did you eat lunch?" Mitch asked.

"I managed to grab a cheese sandwich and a glass of milk. The baby was hungry," she said, smiling. "How about you?"

"I was able to get a ham sandwich and a glass of orange juice."

"I'll bet you're starved," she said.

"Pretty much. Would you be interested in going to Kreis' and have a prime rib dinner?"

"Oh yes."

Mitch called to check on getting a reservation and they were soon on their way.

In the car, he said, "I'm glad you're not one of those people always worrying about her weight, on a goofy diet, or only eating wild hickory nuts."

"I used to then I started paying attention to how my body works and learned to eat accordingly. I just don't think diets work long term, or are healthy, and I think God put all kinds of food on this earth for us to enjoy. I maintain my weight just fine if I generally graze like horses and cows do in the fields. It seems like grazing keeps a person's metabolism burning all the time not just in spurts. When a person eats otherwise the brain may think that person is starving its body and begins to store fat for a rainy day so to speak. Also, there is no strict calorie counting with the grazing method of eating. You just have to be sensible and not eat eleven chocolate candy bars everyday. Besides I've heard and read where sugar is like a poison. I've heard a man named Hippocrates said food is medicine. Some disagree he said that. Anyway I decided to try the grazing method and it works fine for me. I do remain flexible and don't let food control me. I try to control it. Tonight I will thoroughly enjoy the prime rib. The only thing that worries me now is I can't exercise walk like I use to. I guess swimming or some other way will have to do."

After eating world-class prime rib dinners they shared an apple strudel a la mode.

"I'm ready to pop," Branda said.

"Ditto."

"Do you mind if I ask for a doggie bag and take the prime rib bones and leftovers home? I make a very good beef barley soup out of them. What we don't eat right away I can divide into separate portions and freeze."

"Sounds wonderful. Right now, I am just happy the drive home is short. After this busy day and all this food, I am ready to go to bed."

"Same here," she said.

After climbing into bed, they kissed and fell asleep; bodies touching, with one of his hands on one of hers resting over their child.

Neither knew when another small piece of her left foot disappeared; the same area where her two smallest toes use to be.

An Indian vision appeared over them but neither the old chief nor the woman made any effort to stop the procedure. They watched solemnly, hands folded in prayer.

CHAPTER SIXTEEN

BRANDA AWAKENED BEFORE MITCH. AS before, she didn't notice the missing foot part until she stepped on the carpet getting ready to head for the bathroom.

"Oh no, please no," she thought, not wanting to say anything out loud and disturb Mitch. "I'll have to tell him though as I promised I would, won't I Betty?" looking in the doll's direction.

She managed to get to the bathroom and back to the bedside before Mitch woke up.

"I'm sorry Mitch," she said. "I was hoping you could sleep late. I was trying not to disturb you."

"I reached for you and you were gone. That opened my eyes," he said. "Are you staying up or coming back to bed?"

"Both."

"What do you mean, both?" he asked.

"I'm going to sit in bed and show you what must have happened last night and then I am going to get up and get started. Remember? A lot of people will be swarming in here today. It's 7:30 now and the first group is due at 10:30. I want to make that soup and freeze some of it before they get here."

"Good heavens woman," he said, playfully. "Let a man get his eyes open all the way before you hit the chore trail. And what happened last ni . . .? Oh, Branda. Do you mean?" he asked, quickly sitting up.

"Yes."

She showed him the place on her foot. He checked her over and found everything back to normal.

Holding her closely, stroking her hair and kissing her, he said, "I'm so sorry. So sorry."

"Thanks, Mitch. But as you once said, 'we'll take it one day at a time.'"

"Why don't you rest here?" he asked. "I'll serve you breakfast in bed."

"You're sweet, but I really do need to get moving. I'll be all right. It's better if I stay busy and don't have time to think."

"I can understand that."

"I'm going to go start the soup first. It's tastier if it slowly simmers for a long time. I can shower and get dressed while it is cooking. Then after it simmers some more I have to let it cool a bit before putting it into freezer containers or bags."

"You're the cool one," he said. "Most women would be hysterical about having your problem."

"Deep down, I am panic stricken as I've said before. I just try not to 'show out' as my Aunt Mayme use to say. Should I save out some soup for our supper tonight?"

"That would be great," he said, reaching to kiss her before she headed for the kitchen.

By the time their morning round of routines was over, plus the soup making, it was nearly time for the various people to arrive. The "thundering hordes" as Mitch put it, meaning it in a humorous way.

With a night's break in between, the rest of Friday spun its flurry of activity over into Saturday, clear up until party time.

Mitch made sure Branda got plenty of rest before the big event. Both had enjoyed a bowl of her homemade beef and barley soup Friday night. Mitch had two. During the day Saturday he made sure both of them ate well despite the hubbub.

"We'll need our strength for tonight," he said.

"I imagine so," said Branda.

While they were dressing for the party, Mitch read his speech to Branda.

"That's nice," she said.

"Do I need to change anything?" he asked. "And do you think it's still a good idea to give the speech after everybody has been here awhile enjoying themselves but before we eat?"

"I can't think of a thing to change. And yes, I think your time slot is good. As you suggested earlier to me, people will be relaxed after visiting a while, having hors d'oeuvres, and some having a few drinks. Then after your speech, everybody will still have that delicious dinner buffet to look forward to plus the good news about the baby should outweigh the bad. And by the way, you look very handsome tonight. That dark brown sports coat looks great with the light tan trousers and cream colored silk shirt."

"Thanks. I didn't want to wear a tie since we mentioned dress would be casual. I'm not much for wearing ties, period. And you look terrific in that pants suit Sean and Cynthia gave you for your birthday."

"Thanks. I hope you understand I'm wearing their gold jewelry and not your diamonds because I don't want my friends to think I'm trying to put on airs. They probably wouldn't because they're not that kind of people, but I'm more comfortable doing it this way. My beautiful wedding ring will be fine though. I hope so because I'm going to wear it."

"I understand. Besides that diamond bracelet and barrette look much better with that Chantilly lace nightgown or less," he said, grinning at her. "But, seriously, you know I would have bought you a whole new outfit if you wanted it. I will buy you anything you want anytime. I hope you realize that."

"I know, Mitch, and thanks. But under the circumstances, new clothes, or much of anything else, aren't high on my list. Maybe later I'll need some maternity clothes."

"Just say the word," he said, coming to hold and kiss her before they went to do a last minute check on things. "I'm glad you're not one of those women who won't let her man kiss her because she doesn't want her makeup disturbed."

"Makeup can be repaired. I would never turn down a kiss from you."

"Good. Just for that, here's another." Afterwards, he patted her tummy and said, "Okay, little one. Tonight is your first party. I hope you enjoy it. And if you get tired, I hope you let your mother know so she can let you rest."

"Don't worry, Mitch," said Branda. "I'll be careful. And now, let's go see how things are going."

First they checked outside. Mitch had arranged for valet parking. There were signs directing guests to drive their cars to the front entrance. A valet would open their doors and help them out, tag and number their keys, then go park the car along one side of the long driveway. Afterwards, the keys would be hung on a special board by the front door valet station and would be guarded at all times by one of the three security guards Mitch had hired for the evening as an extra precaution.

Guests would be driven in flower decorated golf carts down toward the back gate entrance to the garden patio. Beginning just beyond the garage doors, there was a white canopy trimmed in red. White wrought iron poles supported it. People were to be let out of the carts at the beginning of the canopy and walk on red carpeting to the open gate.

Mitch had made sure the valets would also be served dinner after all of the guests had arrived. Guards would take turns.

"And I'm quite certain all are getting paid quite well," Branda said. "You are so generous, Mitch."

"Well, some of the valet boys are still in college and can use the money," he said. "Since they are handling other people's cars, I won't allow them to drink alcohol while on the job though. Actually, I know the boys' parents so that was part of my screening process. I also personally know the guards who can also use some extra money."

Mitch drove Branda down to the gate in one of the golf carts. When they entered the garden patio, Branda stopped.

"Oh my, Mitch. This is just beautiful. I can well imagine how it will look later when the lights are turned on twinkling away." Looking toward the pool, she exclaimed, "I didn't know you had flowers put in there to float around. Nor did I know you were planning to have the dolphin ice sculpture put on that silvery looking platform and anchored in the middle of the pool."

"I was hoping to surprise you."

"Well, you have. Thank you."

"I thought doing the flowers and dolphin that way added a nice touch," Mitch said. "I had called the ice sculptor earlier and suggested doing this. He said he and his helpers had done it before and would bring the necessary equipment and platform. I invited all of them to the party. The flowers were tossed into the water after the fish was in place."

"You're right. This is definitely a nice touch."

"You'll see the special effects after dark. The lighting people, whom I also invited to stay for the party, worked out the illumination for the dolphin. I explained what I wanted yesterday when they were here stringing lights and they worked out their plan. This afternoon they came to finalize it. They will oversee the operation tonight. The dolphin is highlighted in colors changing periodically from pastel blues and greens to silvery glittery ones."

"Well now I'm more glad than ever I didn't peek earlier. With all the activity going on, I really did not want to get in the way. I can hardly wait to see it all after the sun goes down. Thanks again, Mitch. Now what is this comfortable, padded bar stool from the basement doing here inside by the gate entrance? Is someone going to sit here and pass out name tags?" she asked.

"No. That is for Michele or Mitchell to sit down in when they feel tired. I thought you and I should stand here and greet guests as they arrive. But the baby might not feel up to standing for a long period of time and need a place to rest," he said, leaning to give her a quick hug and kiss. "I thought a regular lower chair might look a bit odd. Check this one out. Since it also has a padded back to support you and a foot rest, it should work okay."

After testing, she declared it to be fine.

"Well, that is kind and thoughtful Dr. Andrews. I'll give you a hug and kiss right back. In fact, I'll give you two; one for me, one for the baby." After doing so, she added, "Seriously, speaking of name tags, I'm glad we decided against them. It is nicer at a party like this for people to introduce themselves and strike up a conversation. The same goes for place cards. Those who know each other will try sitting together anyway. If not, it's good for them to meet new people."

"Righto."

"By the way, Mitch. Do Chad and Bonnie know you invited the valets, guards, lighting and ice carving crews?"

"Oh sure. I made sure of that when I decided to do it a couple of days ago. I guess I forgot to tell you."

"Not important. I know you have been super busy."

"Anyway, it's fine with the caterers," he said. "They said they always allow for no- shows and last minute guests. The bartenders, servers, and so forth will take turns getting a bite to eat after the main guests have eaten."

As the couple walked through the garden inspecting this and that, Branda asked, "Mitch, I know the printers delivered the tip line cards this morning. When will you have them put on the center of each table?"

"I decided it would be best after I make my speech. Otherwise, if people happened to spot them before they would wonder what the heck they are for. Some of the servers are going to put them on the tables after my speech and just before dinner is announced."

The couple started to enter the kitchen through the angled door from the garden patio. Seeing the super busy caterers at work, they stopped.

Bonnie saw them and said, "Come on in."

"No way," Mitch said, laughing. "That would be like walking into a beehive. I just wanted to make sure you're okay and remember about not announcing the buffet dinner being ready until after my speech."

"We're right on schedule, and I have a note posted on our battle plan board so everyone in here will know the score about the timing of your speech and the dinner buffet being ready for the guests' dining pleasure. Chad and I will personally engineer that part plus make sure those cards get put on the tables at the proper time."

"Thank you, Bonnie," Mitch said. "Is there anything you need?"

"No thanks. Everything is in its normal state of chaos at this point . . . which means we're doing fine," said Bonnie.

Branda stood in amazement watching what she gathered was controlled chaos. She managed to say, "Thank all of you for your hard work."

"Our pleasure," said Bonnie.

Other workers smiled at her but never missed a beat in continuing what they were doing.

Branda and Mitch went back outside, then entered the mudroom through the patio door and went on into the den.

Mitch said, "Since it's almost show time I thought you might like to freshen up here, relax, and sit on your couch for a moment before we go take up our post at the gate."

"Good idea. Thanks," she said. "Mitch, would it be all right if Mary Ann, Linda, Mathilda, Reverend Cummings and his wife, Martha, sat with us since they won't know anyone else except Sean and Cynthia who will be at our table too? That will leave one spare chair. If you have other plans, that's okay. They're flexible . . . and not bashful about meeting new people."

"That's fine with me. I know you have missed seeing them."

"Thanks. When they come in I'll show them where we're sitting so they can go stake out their places," she said. "I would also like to take them inside at some point and show them the house."

"Good idea. Oh, that reminds me, Branda. Do you have your new two-way radio clipped to your waistband under that beautiful pants suit jacket or the blouse?"

"Yes, but it's not open since we have been together today," she answered. "I'm certainly glad you had this new customized miniature model made with the vibrator mode included. It's a lot easier to wear."

"I know. That first kind was the smallest I could get at the time. This new one has a ten-mile range instead of five like the other one. Let's leave ours on the vibrator mode tonight so outside noises won't be filtering through."

The two set their "communicators" as Branda often called them.

"Well, I guess we had better go out and get ready to greet our guests. Are you nervous, Branda?" Mitch asked, standing and helping her up too.

"Not really. Not with you at my side."

Mitch took her in his arms, kissed her, and said, "Just remember, even if I get called away for some reason, I'll still be with you in my heart and mind."

"I know, Mitch. I know," she said, kissing him again.

Sean and Cynthia were already in the garden when the couple got there.

"There you are," said Sean, smiling. "We thought maybe you'd decided to skip out and go somewhere peaceful."

"How are you feeling, Branda?" Cynthia asked.

"Just fine, thank you. Also, thank you again for this lovely pants suit. I feel so elegant in it . . . plus the jewelry."

"What? No diamonds tonight?" asked Cynthia.

Mitch chimed in, "No. She didn't want to look like she was showing off. Modest woman, isn't she?"

"Well, I reckon so, I sure reckon so," Cynthia replied. "Most women I know would be so proud they would wear them if they were alone and naked."

Neither Mitch nor Branda dared look at one another.

Mitch quickly spoke up. "Let me show you where we're sitting so you can stake out your claim. Some of Branda's friends will also be sitting with us. There will be one spare chair. Probably Judge Limson will sit there. Then join us at the gate if you care to and help us greet guests."

"Thanks," Sean said. "I will after I go get a cocktail. How about you, Cynthia?"

"Yes, count me in as a greeter. And get me a drink too. Knob Creek Bourbon and water . . . over ice. And by the way, everything looks lovely."

"Wait until it gets darker and we see the lights," said Branda. "Since a lot of that part had to be done at almost the last minute, I haven't seen it either but can hardly wait. Mitch did a wonderful job planning a lot of it . . . especially the dolphin and flowers in the pool. He told me how it is supposed to look."

Before heading for the open bar, Sean asked, "Is your speech all ready, Mitch?"

"Yep. I read it to Branda. She approves."

During a brief lull during Mitch introducing her to a lot of people coming through the gate, she turned to him and said, "Good heavens. Now I know how the Queen of England feels standing in those receiving lines greeting long lines of people. I'm glad I read somewhere once how she keeps from having her hand get worn out from all the shaking and not to wear rings on that hand. She is right."

"You look like you are thoroughly enjoying yourself, Branda," said Mitch. "Don't let yourself get too tired though."

"I am having a great time meeting all of these wonderful people. Sean and Cynthia are enjoying themselves too. I've had no time to visit with them here since they've been so busy introducing themselves to those they don't know and chatting a bit with everybody. I am going to sit more often for a few moments though so I don't get tired."

When Mary Ann, Linda, Mathilda, Reverend Cummings, and his wife, Martha, came through the gate, Branda stood up and gave all of them a big hug, including the Reverend.

"I am so happy to see all of you! So very happy," she exclaimed.

Speaking all at once, the group told her they were also very happy to see her again and wanted to know how she was feeling and so on. It was like old home week.

Branda introduced all of them to Mitch. She could tell Mary Ann, Linda, and Mathilda were a bit awestruck by his good looks.

Finally realizing the line was being held up, Branda said, "See that table over there with the reserved sign on it? Go stake out your claim there then mingle or whatever, go get a drink at the bar . . . there are soft drinks too, Reverend Cummings, Martha . . . and enjoy yourselves. We'll join you later at that table. And we'll work in a good gab session somehow tonight."

When Annie the librarian and her husband, Bill, showed up, Branda also greeted them with special warmth then directed them to the table next to where she and Mitch would be sitting. She would have liked them to sit at the reserved table, but there just wasn't room. She didn't think it would be fair to ask the caterers to squeeze in one more chair. Annie and Bill understood and did not mind.

Another round of special greetings were in order during the arrivals of the house cleaning staff and lawn crew plus their spouses, Johnny the pool man, Arthur the intercom repairman and their wives.

After taking more periodic breaks to sit down in her "high chair" as she called it, Branda turned to Mitch and said, "How are you holding up? Would you like to sit in my chair awhile?"

"Thanks, but I'm okay. Most of the people are here now anyway. The line has slowed to a trickle. A few late doctors, but that's par for the course. They may have had emergencies or other unknown happenings that are routine in a doctor's life."

"Mitch," Branda said softly for his ears only, "I don't know if you've noticed or not, but every once in awhile, I notice Cynthia looking at me in that strange psychic way of hers. She immediately glances away."

"No, I can't say that I have, but that's more of a woman thang as you say. But I'll start paying more attention," he said.

As darkness approached and the lights came on, guests oohed and ahhed in unison; especially when the special effects lit up the dolphin and floating flowers in the pool. With drinks and hors d'oeuvres in hand, people stood watching and admiring.

"You did a bang up job, Mitch," said Sean.

"Lovely, just lovely!!!" Cynthia exclaimed.

"I had a lot of expert help," said Mitch.

"Whatever," said Sean. "It's first class. Cynthia, let's go take a closer look before we sit down."

"Okay," Cynthia said, taking Sean's hand as they walked away toward the display.

"Oh Mitch," said Branda. "It's looks like . . . well, I don't really know the words. It is just simply beautiful! I'll get a closer look later on. I think you were right though not to play music since it's too hard to talk above it if it's too loud and in a group this size if it is played softly, you can't hear it when they're all talking."

"My thinking exactly. I may turn some on later if it gets quiet enough. And I'm glad you like the special effects. Now, Branda, since there doesn't seem to be anymore guests arriving, why don't you go sit down at our table and start visiting with your friends? I'm going to be making my speech very shortly after I mingle a bit then check with the caterers. I'd like for you to stand beside me as we planned. Okay?"

"Okay," she answered. "Later on, I would also like to go visit at all of the tables."

"Good idea. Meanwhile, let's switch on our communicators, vibrator mode."

Smiling at his use of her coined word communicators, she said. "Done."

Mary Ann and the rest were at the table having a drink of their choice and some hors d'oeuvres when she got there. Annie and Bill had scooted their chairs closer so they could visit too but not lose their place.

Nearly in unison, Mary Ann, Linda, and Mathilda said, "Oh Branda. Your new husband is handsome as a movie star."

"And he's also a nice person," Branda said.

Mary Ann said, "Someday when you feel up to it we've got to have lunch so you can tell us all about everything."

"Are you doing okay healthwise?" asked Linda.

Mary Ann, Mathilda, the Cummings', Annie and Bill also indicated their concern on that score.

"Well, I'll tell you. Mitch is getting ready to make a speech before we eat and then you'll know all about everything. You'll understand more after he talks. Mitch has been in charge of things and has done what he thought best for everyone." After a pause, she added, "Please understand I love all of you very much."

Mitch finally came to the table, asking if everyone was comfortable, had drinks and snacks.

"If there's anything you need, please don't hesitate to ask," he told them.

All said they were fine.

"Then please excuse Branda and me for a few minutes while I make an explanatory speech."

They went to stand hand in hand in front of the buffet table that had been temporarily screened off with movable white latticework panels.

After getting everyone's attention with the help of a microphone he had had set up, Mitch began.

"First, let us welcome all of you to our dinner party. We are very happy to see you. If there is anything we can do to make your time here more enjoyable, please let us know.

"The main reason for this gathering tonight, besides just getting together for some relaxation, is to tell you two pieces of news. One is sad, the other joyful.

"Medical people and a few others here already know the sad part because their professions, or a daily ongoing close proximity to Branda, made it necessary for them to know; especially when she was considered to be possibly contagious until the 26th. We now know she is not contagious so please don't worry about being here. We would never have put you in jeopardy.

"Others of you have been long time close friends to Branda and me. Before now, and after much thought, we decided it might be best for all concerned in this group to only tell a partial truth about her problem. We didn't know what was wrong when we told you and we honestly still don't know what is causing the episodes. Frankly, we were hoping to find a cure or at least a cause before now but, so far, we haven't despite doing lots of research reading and searching the Internet. We will continue doing reading, researching, and now have various tests performed. We had to postpone some tests pending a special report since we weren't sure some of them would be safe.

"Anyway, that's why we told you she was having a foot problem . . . which is the truth . . . and may be ill from having a possible form of rare cancer. That is not the truth.

"We also mentioned the condition might not be cancer but could be contagious. That was an unknown factor at the time. As I said a moment ago, we have determined it is not contagious.

"This is the real truth. You may want to take a sip of your drink before hearing this and please be advised there are plenty of doctors here should you feel faint and need one.

"Parts of Branda's feet are sporadically disappearing. It began May 10th with the small toe on her left foot, has taken all of her toes on both feet, and has progressed to the sections just behind where the toes use to be. We have no idea when, if, or where these disappearances will stop. The warning signs that this phenomenon is about to occur are for Branda to feel warm and weak or to just faint. Only the affected part, not the whole foot, starts glowing, turns pale yellow, goes to light green, then to red, and the part disappears leaving a faint acrid odor. Sometimes this happens during her sleep and she doesn't know about it until the next morning. That's what happened the first time in her apartment. She woke up and the small toe on her left foot was gone."

Mitch waited for the gasps and other vocalizations he expected would occur. He didn't notice anyone needing immediate medical help. He squeezed Branda's hand and turned to ask her if she would like to sit down.

"No, I'm fine," she whispered. "Actually, it's good to get this over with. How are you doing?"

"Fine."

Waiting a moment for the crowd's expressions of shock to subside, he continued. "And now I would like to ask all of you to help. I have set up a special telephone tip line. If any of you know of a cure, or read or hear of anything that resembles this problem, please call. The servers will be putting stacks of cards with the tip line number on them on each table in a moment. Please take one for each person in your party, plus extras if you can think of someone else who might be of help. Even if Branda and I are off traveling trying to find a cure, I will still be able to access that phone line and review any tips given. We thank you very much for any help you can give us in trying to solve this mystery.

"I would like to stress that we are trying very hard to keep Branda's condition as private as possible, but we understand as time goes on, privacy may not be possible. We are just taking everything a day at a time.

"And now for the good news! Branda is going to have our baby . . . sometime in late January or early February. A blood pregnancy test conducted by Dr. Richard Cline has confirmed it." Smiling, he added, "Mother Nature saw to it that our marriage of convenience so I could take constant care of Branda took a sudden turn. So now you can understand why we urgently need more than ever to find a cure for her condition. Thank you for any help you can give."

Everybody laughed and cheered. Branda blushed. Mitch put one arm around her shoulders, gave her a slight hug, then leaned to kiss her cheek.

Smiling, Branda quickly spoke into the microphone, "Yes, Mother Nature has been kind to us." She added, more seriously, "Also God. And, again, thank all of you for any information you might find and share with us about this strange ailment."

The servers quickly began putting tip line cards on the tables. One removed the microphone setup. Bonnie and Chad waited a moment for the uproar to die down, removed the white lattice panels, and announced the buffet was ready. Branda and Mitch turned to look at the food.

"That's the most gorgeous buffet I ever saw," she said, moving closer, taking a long moment to look at the array.

"Yes, I'd say it turned out to be extraordinary," Mitch agreed, also looking it over.

Both offered a special thanks to Bonnie, Chad, and the rest of the catering staff standing by.

As Branda and Mitch walked toward their reserved table where Sean and Cynthia were now seated with the others, Mitch softly said to her,

"You're right, Cynthia is wearing her psychic face when she looks at you. I've noticed her giving you that special look and smile more than once."

"Me too," said Branda. "I wonder why?"

"I'm sure we'll find out soon."

Judge Limson, knowing the sad truth beforehand, again told Branda and Mitch how sorry he was about her condition, but was overjoyed about the baby. Then he went to check out the buffet.

As Branda and Mitch sat, Mary Ann, Linda, Mathilda, Rev. Cummings and Martha, teary eyed from both shock and joy, expressed themselves with words meant to comfort then congratulate. Annie and Bill got up to come over and join in.

Annie said, "Now I understand why you checked out that odd assortment of books last time you came in. Bless your heart. I'll keep my eyes open for any books I think might be of help."

"Thank you," said Branda.

Everyone attending the party began coming to the table two or more at a time to express their sorrow and joy one way or another then drifted off toward the buffet.

The friends that had been with Mitch's family for years helping with the house, yard, pool, and other maintenance requirements, expressed their sadness over Branda's sickness and joy about the baby. There were hugs and tears all around.

Mitch and Branda finally advised Mary Ann, and the rest to go eat.

Leaning close to Branda's ear, Cynthia asked, "All right, but may we bring you something since it looks like you two are going to be here for a long while?"

"Thanks, Cynthia," Branda answered. "But we had some snacks beforehand so we can wait. It would be hard to eat under these circumstances anyway."

Mitch agreed. "Thank you very much though for the kind thought." he said. "We'll go later."

Before leaving, Sean rested a hand on Mitch's shoulder. "See you later, pal," he said.

"Save some for us," Mitch said, smiling up at his friend.

Finally, the flow of people stopped and the couple had a chance to catch their breaths. Mitch spoke to Branda, "I think that all went pretty well, don't you? No one fainted and everybody seems to be dealing realistically with the sad part."

"I agree," she said. "And they sure are happy about the baby."

"Not half as happy as I am, Honey. Now let's feed the little one and the big ones too. Would you like to sit here and have me bring you a plate?"

"No thanks, I'm hungry now and can't wait to get up there and take at least a tiny helping of everything there is. And I sure hope the baby likes lobster because that is one of my favorite foods."

"Oh Lord, I've married a glutton," Mitch said with a smile.

As they stood up, getting ready to head for the food, their table mates began returning from the buffet exclaiming about the fantastic array.

"Never saw anything like it in my life," said Mary Ann.

"I didn't know what to choose. I'll have to go back I know," Linda declared.

"Me too," Mathilda chimed in. "Oh . . . those desserts. I want to try them all."

Sean, Cynthia, and Judge Limson declared the buffet to be one of the best ever put together.

"Dr. Andrews, Branda, this is truly a feast !" exclaimed Rev. Cummings.

Martha totally agreed. "Thank you so much for inviting us," she said.

"You are most welcome and we are happy all of you are enjoying yourselves," Branda said. Mitch concurred, asking them to please just call him Mitch.

Suddenly, something in the air above the pool caught Branda's attention. She tried not to let on. It was a vision, a large one with the old Indian chief holding a cradle board facing him so she could not tell if a papoose was inside or not. The Indian woman was there holding Michele, Branda's mother held Josh and her father had Jason in his arms. Another couple stood nearby. Branda had seen them somewhere before but just now she could not place who they were. She had seen too many faces tonight. All of the vision people were smiling.

Noticing that Branda was staring at the sky in a strange way, Mary Ann asked, "Is something wrong?"

The others also asked.

Snapping back to reality, Branda said, "No. Oh no, I just thought I saw a falling star. I was making a wish." Looking at Mitch, who was also looking upwards in awe, she asked, "Did you see the star too?"

Looking at Branda in a meaningful way, he answered, "Yes, I thought I saw it too. Maybe it's a meteor shower although I don't remember hearing about one going on tonight."

Everybody else at the table looked at the sky for a moment but said they saw nothing. Branda and Mitch continued watching for a moment until the vision faded into its usual silvery mist. They wondered how long the vision had been there.

Slipping a hand in one of Branda's, Mitch smiled and spoke to Mary Ann and the others, "Please excuse us while we go get a bite to eat. It's time to feed the baby and its parents."

Everyone laughed.

As Branda and Mitch walked away, Branda said, "Thanks Mitch. That helped lighten the mood a bit. I gather you saw the vision. Who was that other couple? They looked familiar but I just couldn't place them."

"Those were my parents."

"Of course! I've seen their pictures in the study. Seeing them out of context, I didn't make the connection. Jumpin' George, I wonder what is going on? That was quite a crowd."

"I don't know, but I have a feeling something is definitely going on," he said.

"Yes, between that vision where everybody seems to be expressing something and Cynthia's psychic look, I get that same feeling."

After filling their plates, Branda and Mitch started back to their seats. On the way, they ran into everybody from their table except Sean, Cynthia and Judge Limson. He was off doing the meeting and greeting thing most officials enjoy doing. Sean and Cynthia were back looking at the dolphin and floating flowers and chatting with people.

Stopping the group for a moment Branda asked, "Can all of you stay a bit after the others leave? If you would care to, I would like for you to see the inside of the house and we can talk a bit."

Reverend Cummings and Martha said they had to leave shortly.

"I have to do some more work on my sermon for tomorrow," the Reverend said.

"But we'll take a rain check," said Martha."

"Of course, you may have a rain check," said Mitch. "We'll work something out soon."

The others said they could stay and looked forward to seeing the house.

While Mitch was putting his plate, and the one he carried for Branda, on the table, Branda went to ask Annie and Bill if they could also stay.

"I wish we could," Annie said, but we promised the boys we'd take them to Six Flags tomorrow. We'll need lots of rest for that adventure."

"I imagine so," agreed Branda and Mitch.

Branda managed to have a nice talk with Reverend Cummings and Martha. Branda assured them she hoped to get back to going to church, but couldn't make any promises under the circumstances. They understood. Shortly afterward, the couple said their good byes and thanks then left. Annie and Bill moved over to the departing couple's chairs, visited a bit longer, then also left.

After Branda ate, she excused herself and went to briefly visit the group at each table. Mitch stayed to talk to Branda's friends. He did go into the house for a moment to turn on some big band music, keeping the volume low enough for people to talk over.

Mitch stayed outside with the guests, some of whom were starting to dance to the music along with Sean and Cynthia. Branda took her friends inside to show them the house.

Knowing how busy it probably still was in the kitchen, she took them through the master bedroom door. After completing the tour, they did manage to squeeze through the kitchen and ended up in the den. Branda sat on her favorite couch with Mary Ann. The other two moved a couple of occasional chairs over to face them.

Mary Ann spoke. "Branda, for a woman who hated men and grew up in the country, I'd say you have made some wonderful changes. Mitch is so good looking and seems so nice. And this house is just gorgeous. I'm so happy for you and hope you find a cure. I can't tell you how sad and scared your illness makes me feel. I hope everything works out all right. Having that baby is just wonderful."

"Thank you," said Branda.

Linda and Mathilda basically repeated what Mary Ann had said. They were genuinely happy for her, wished her the best, and would pray a cure could be found.

"And now," said Linda. "Since we couldn't be with you on your birthday, we brought some cards and small gifts for you. We've had them stuffed inside our purses all evening."

"Oh jumpin' George," said Branda.

"Boy, we haven't heard that in a while. We've missed that . . . and you," said Mathilda.

"I've missed you too. A lot! You know what? I don't think I say jumpin' George as much as I used to. I don't know why though. I just realized that. Anyway, thank you for keeping track of me through Sean and Cynthia. I really appreciated that. I hope they told you."

"They did," said Linda. "Mathilda even got to know them. We introduced her."

Branda got a kick out of the funny cards and thanked them for the nicely wrapped gifts.

Mary Ann gave her a small bottle of her favorite Caroline Herrera perfume. Mathilda added a small bottle of her other favorite, Estee Lauder's Beautiful. Linda gave her a small book, Anne Morrow Lindbergh's *Gift From The Sea*.

"I once noticed your other copy was getting all tattered and worn looking."

"You're right, it was. How thoughtful," said Branda. "You know that is one of my favorite books. Thank all of you so much for the cards, gifts and for being my friends. I have been sort of overwhelmed so didn't call you like I had planned to do. But I thought about you often."

Branda gave each one a long hug and thanked them again for their thoughtful gifts.

"Even if I don't get to talk to you often or see you, you will always be in my heart."

"We know," said, Mary Ann. To lighten the mood, she added, "Now, girl, 'fess up and tell us how your marriage of convenience got side tracked. You know how we always tell all . . . well, almost all."

Branda blushed so much they all laughed and didn't press the issue.

Linda smiled and said, "With a man as handsome as Mitch around, that isn't hard to figure out."

"Actually, it was an accident," Branda said bravely.

The women laughed so hard they almost fell on the floor.

When she could speak again, Mathilda said, "Accidental sex. Now that's a new one."

They all went off into gales of laughter again until tears ran down their cheeks.

"Oh, jumpin' George you three," said Branda, finally giving in and laughing too.

Mitch's voice broke in. "Well, I may keep you girls around all the time. I haven't heard Branda laugh that hard since I met her. Can you let me in on the joke or whatever?"

The women laughed even harder.

"Guess not," said Mitch, starting to chuckle himself since their merriment was so contagious. "Anyway, I hate to break this up, but people are starting to leave and I thought maybe Branda would like to come back out and tell them good bye."

The women were still trying to suppress laughs as they walked outside with Mitch.

"Is my mascara running?" Branda asked Linda.

"No, you're fine. How about the rest of us?"

After close inspections, everybody was declared okay. Mitch stood in wonderment at the ways of women.

When everyone, including the caterers, had gone, Mitch and Branda stood side by side with arms around each other's waists watching the dolphin show for a while. After he turned out the lights, secured the house, and they performed their nighttime rituals, they went to bed; tired, but happy.

Sometime toward dawn each had an identical dream-driven vision. Both awakened at the same moment, sat up, looked at each other, saying at the same time: "We're going to have twins! A boy and a girl!"

CHAPTER SEVENTEEN

"OH MITCH!" EXCLAIMED BRANDA, STILL sitting up in bed. "What happened? We must have had the same dream vision."

"Yes. Evidently. What was yours like?" asked Mitch, looking stunned.

"It was the very same group over the pool last night. Only this time, the Indians introduced themselves. The gentleman is Chief War Eagle my great-great-great-grandfather and the woman is his wife, Light Moon, my great-great-great-grandmother. Even though they spoke their Cherokee language, I could understand them perfectly."

"So could I," said Mitch. "Absolutely like I have known it all my life. They are very impressive people. And besides being a chief, War Eagle is also a medicine man and said he will help us understand what is happening when the time is right."

"Yes, I heard that too," said Branda. "And he said at a later time, we will be able to converse with them in their Cherokee language."

"Right, and what else did you hear and see?" asked Mitch.

"After the introductions, my great-great-great-grandfather Chief War Eagle turned the cradle board around showing me a baby was inside. He gently laid the board on the ground and lifted out a boy. Holding the baby to face me, he said this boy was Mitchell and he was our son; meaning yours and mine. Then great-great-great-grandmother Light Moon stepped forward holding the same little girl I saw before; Michele. Your mother and father were standing there smiling from ear to ear. Chief War Eagle handed Mitchell to your dad, and Light Moon placed Michele in your mother's arms. Then

Light Moon explained there had been other visions when we were asleep. In one, she was holding a cradle board facing her with Michele in it and had an empty one propped against her legs belonging to Mitchell."

"That is exactly what I dreamed," Mitch said. "After that your mother and father came closer; your father holding Josh, your mother, Jason."

"Exactly," said Branda. "Did you hear what my dad had to say about why he was only dimly visible in the last few visions; holding something or someone?"

"Yes. He was holding Mitchell but it wasn't time for us to know about our son yet. Evidently, timing is very important in their world."

"Oh Mitch. Mitchell is such a handsome baby and Michele so beautiful. I pray I can stay well and bring those two into this world." Continuing, with tears in her eyes, "And it is so good to see Josh and Jason again in these visions. I did love them very much and still miss them; my parents too."

Putting his arms around her, Mitch said, "Of course you do. Of course you do. And if what we are taught in church is true, you will be together again with them someday and with everybody else you loved here on earth."

"Why Mitch," said Branda, drying her tears. "You are a spiritual soul aren't you?"

"Yes, I guess I am. I'm spiritual, but not religious if you get my meaning. Organized religions leave me cold. In fact, I think more terrible things have been done in the name of religion than from just about any other source. I'm not referring to religion as I believe Jesus meant it to be, full of love, peace, joy, and so on, but about the sort mankind has managed to devise and corrupt; just like it has most everything else on earth. It seems to me rituals and too many money-related activities have replaced the vital heart and soul of what I think God intended His church to be."

"Well, I'll have to give that some thought since it sort of chills my Baptist soul to hear talk like that. Like Scarlett, I'll think about that tomorrow. Meanwhile, what's our next step? Satisfy your medical curiosity and have Dr. Cline verify we are having twins, start figuring out where we are going to put two babies instead of one, and . . . what else? Oh yes, check with Cynthia and see if she was glancing at me oddly from time to time last night because she was already on the twin trail?"

"Frankly, I've learned to believe in those visions and feel in my heart and soul we really are having twins. But I suspect Dr. Cline is going to wonder as time goes on and you begin showing some of the signs you may be carrying more than one papoose. He will no doubt want to do an ultrasound to absolutely verify. Did you have that done with Josh and Jason?"

"Yes. Early in my second trimester," said Branda."It can be done sooner, but when it is done too early I have heard of cases where one twin is hiding the other. It's usually best to wait. I guess we'll leave that up to Dr. Cline."

"Okay with me. But what about Cynthia?"

"We'll just play that scenario by ear," Mitch said. "As for remodeling to make room for the second child, how about this idea? We'll put Michele in the bedroom nearest this one as we had planned, I'll clear out one of the downstairs apartments and move your furniture in there, take your larger vacated area and remodel it into being my study, and put Mitchell in the ex-study which was my former bedroom. Or we could just build a new house."

"Whoa daddy whoa! Jumpin' George. You're moving so fast I can't keep up. But from what my brain was able to compute, that sounds like a good plan to me. I don't think a new house is in order though because it would be great for your son to have your former room and wonderful for both children to grow up in the same home you did. But won't that be quite an undertaking to move all of those things in the study? You won't want to be disconnected from all of those phone lines for any period of time; especially the tip line and those connected to computers."

"Yes, the logistics may get a bit tricky, but I'm sure it can all be done with a minimum of interruption. Actually, I've been wanting to modernize and switch to DSL capability for the computers. Anyway, let's discuss it some more before we start tearing down walls."

"Good idea," she agreed. "On another subject, did you ever read a book called "The Prophet" by Kahlil Gibran?"

"Yes indeed. Another one of my favorites."

"Do you remember his piece about children where he writes, ' . . . Your children are not your children. They are the sons and daughters of Life's longing for itself. They come through you but not from you, And though they are with you yet they belong not to you.' and so on?"

"In all honesty,' said Mitch "I don't remember that one as well as the one on marriage, but I will certainly read it now. There's a copy in the living room that Mom and Dad used to read over and over. They loved his work too."

"And I've never really looked at the one on marriage; I guess because before this, I didn't think much of the institution."

"Tell you what," said Mitch. "Why don't we go eat some breakfast and on the way I'll pick up the book. We can read and discuss the passages on children and marriage while we eat? I can't believe I'm hungry after eating all that food last night, but I really am."

"Good idea. Do you suppose there's any of that lobster left in the fridge from last night?" asked Branda.

"Oh, Lord, don't tell me you're going to crave lobster for the next nine months," Mitch said, smiling. "I can just see me getting up at 3 a.m. trying to find that for you."

She gently tossed a pillow at him and they wound up laughing, ending the fun with a sweet kiss.

As they sat in the kitchen eating and reading Gibran's words on marriage and children, plus other passages, Branda had an episode with her left foot. This time the affected part was behind where middle toes use to be. Mitch's checkup showed her vital signs to be as usual.

Afterwards, he carried her to the den and placed her on her favorite couch. As she lay there, he sat on the floor reaching to touch and comfort her. For a long moment, they remained quiet as she watched the sun making rainbows on the Waterford dish.

Finally, she said, "Oh Mitch. I am so scared. Not for me especially, but for Michele and Mitchell. I'll just have to have faith though. As God wills."

"I'll have a harder time doing that, but for your sake, I'll try. You do make me want to try."

"You'll do fine."

Trying to change the mood, Mitch asked, "How would you like to drive down to Cape and Morley today, maybe stop in Ste. Genevieve for a bite to eat? Or are you too tired? We could spend the night down there someplace if you don't feel up to the drive home."

Hesitating for a moment, she finally said, "You know what? I think that would be a nice thing to do. And if you wouldn't mind, I'd like to go to the cemeteries in Morley and Cape where my parents and boys are buried. Should we invite Sean and Cynthia to go along?"

"We certainly can if you like but, frankly Honey, I would rather just be alone with you. Besides, we couldn't spend the night somewhere because they would have to get back for work tomorrow. This way, we can take our time, stop and rest often . . . do what we want. We'll do something with them later on."

"I see your point. We'd better call them though and I need to call my friends to let them know what we're doing. I don't want anyone to worry," she said. "Say, I know what, how about we invite that group over for a leftovers meal tomorrow night? There aren't many leftovers, but Chad and Bonnie put some in the freezer we could thaw and serve. That plus the other unfrozen goodies that are still good would be enough I'm sure."

"Good idea unless you think you'll be too tired from the trip."

"I'll make sure I'm rested."

The calls were made, all wished Branda and Mitch a good safe trip, and happily accepted the leftovers meal invitation for 6:30 p.m. Monday night.

Branda thoroughly enjoyed the drive down I-55 looking at the long stretches of gorgeous wooded areas with gigantic old pin oaks, maples, and other varieties waving their branches toward God up above as if greeting Him.

From time to time, Mitch used his cell phone to access the tip line. There had been no calls. There were no calls on his other lines either. Being Sunday, he didn't really expect any.

Having gotten a fairly early start, they reached Morley about 1:30 p.m. Bypassing Cape Girardeau for now, she had directed him on how to turn off the interstate at the Benton exit, go a few miles to the town, turn left and go five miles along highway 61 toward Morley. She had him veer left at the curved split that could also take you to Oran, then a short distance later turn left onto the spur leading into Morley.

As they drove along the spur, he asked, "Whose house is that big white one off to the right with the big oak trees around it?"

"That was built by Dr. Clarence D. Harris for his bride, Mary Howle. I've heard it said he was considered a wealthy man but during the depression he gave away a lot of his fortune to help others. His plans were to recoup some of his money via his extensive medical practice but the strain of those years were too much. He had a heart attack and died July 4, 1933."

"You seem to know a lot about him."

"He and his wife were notable citizens and I heard the older people talk about them. In fact, there have been a lot of people from this small town who went on to make names for themselves . . . either locally or elsewhere. There was a good school system and it had teachers that knew how to teach. That helped produce some fine people. I imagine that is still true."

"No doubt," said Mitch.

As they passed another fairly large house on the right, Branda said, "A man from the family that lived there ended up being a Hollywood script writer. His name was Phil Leslie. He wrote for a radio show called Fibber McGee and Molly for years, and later wrote for television sitcoms and movies. Among other siblings, he had a sister, Nancy, who was very pretty I understand. I think she became a top-notch secretary and lived in Washington D.C. for a time."

Arriving at the town's main intersection, she pointed out the large brick building on one corner that used to be the Morley Bank. It had also been a drug store at one time and perhaps other things of which she had no knowledge.

She noticed the Morley Cafe was still on another corner of the intersecting streets catty-cornered from the bank.

"They used to have very good home cooked food in there. I don't know how it is now. It was the kind of place where people liked to meet and visit while they could sometimes eat things like Cotton Pickin' Cake when it was on the day's menu. People who had not been back to Morley for years might run into each other in there during their trips. Returning hometown folks generally made room in their plans to go to the Morley Cafe at least once to eat and visit."

As they continued their tour she pointed out where a cotton gin use to operate many years ago and where the Baptist Church sat at the edge of a park-like area.

"I've heard it said there use to be magnificent old oak trees in this park area and some young man liked to swing around in their branches playing Tarzan, giving that ape man yell. One elderly man told me everybody thought the town Tarzan was going to break his neck but he never did. He did tell me this story about when the Baptists would be in full swing during a revival meeting. If, during the meeting, Tarzan would let out some bloodcurdling yells, the preacher said record numbers of people would flock to the church front answering the invitation to come and be saved. The preacher said Tarzan's call did more to save the sinners in his church than his own sermons ever did. He guessed the yells reminded folks of hell's torments."

Mitch was laughing so hard he could barely say, "You're making that up."

"No I'm not. I swear I'm not. You should hear some of the stories about the old days in Morley. They would fill a book . . . and they're true. And they're humorous because they are true. Luckily, I had the sense to listen when they were told either to me or to my parents."

Finally, she directed him past the Morley Cafe and the row of past and present business buildings.

As they drove by, she said, "That last brick building was Dr. Harris's medical office. I've always wondered what this town was like when it was first founded and was in full swing."

"We can look it up on the Internet," he said.

"Good idea. I understand there was a General Nathaniel Watkins who was instrumental in founding or running the town. He and his wife had a plantation called Beechwood or Beechland just off the road to Benton. It's the Watkins cemetery now. The General's tombstone is quite impressive as I recall. I was up there once. Now I believe it's designated as a Missouri Conservation Area. Statesman Henry Clay was a half-brother to General Watkins; same mother, different fathers."

"Well, I must say, Branda. You have made me want to learn more about this small place on the map. I will definitely look it up on the Internet. You really and truly do have a thirst for all kinds of knowledge."

After continuing a short distance, Mitch noticed a cemetery on the left.

"Is this where your parents are buried?" he asked.

"Yes. Also my brother, Billy, who died two years before I was born."

She found the plots quickly, standing silently for a long time letting tears make their way down her cheeks. Putting an arm around her waist, Mitch stood quietly holding her giving her comfort.

Finally, she dried her eyes, turned to him and said, "Thank you Mitch. Let's go now."

"Are you sure? We can stay longer if you wish."

"No, but thank you. This is enough. Maybe someday we can come back."

"Of course, whenever we can," he assured her. "I'm impressed at all the beautiful big old trees out here and how nicely the grounds are kept."

"Yes, the setting is lovely and the people in charge do a good job keeping it groomed."

He gently kissed away her remaining tears. The tender look she gave him in thanks was followed by the equally gentle hug she gave him.

They drove back to Cape on the old road as Branda called that stretch of highway 61. Leaving flat countryside after going up Benton Hill, it flowed into scenery showing off rolling hills and neat homes dotting farmland here and there.

Mitch said, "I haven't been down in this area for a long time. I'd forgotten how beautiful it is." Nearing Kelso, he added, "Here's more beautiful countryside and there are certainly some very nice homes in and around this area. Amazing how it has grown."

Upon arriving at Cape, they made a rest stop at the Holiday Inn and had a quick sandwich in the restaurant.

"Good idea, Mitch," said Branda. "Even having lobster for breakfast doesn't last all day; although it certainly lasted quite a while. I still don't feel very hungry but the kids may be. I wish I had thought and we had driven over to Wib's in Jackson. They have very good barbecue sandwiches. Of course, there's the Pilot House and Port Cape Girardeau too. Then for some other types of cuisine, there's the Royal N'Orleans on Broadway across from the Southeast Missourian newspaper office, Celebrations, '36', Faithfully Fed, Grecian Steak House and Mollie's plus many, many other places. I've heard at one point Cape had some 130 restaurants."

"We'll have to make a special trip down here just to eat," said Mitch, laughing.

Afterwards, they did a short sightseeing trip then went to see the Mississippi River and watch a barge make its way downriver to New Orleans. As they were preparing to leave, they began hearing a sound that stopped them in their tracks.

"What the he . . . heck is that," asked Mitch.

Branda laughed and said, "Well, we're in luck Dr. Andrews. That's the calliope being played aboard the Delta Queen. That announces it will be arriving pretty soon. Care to stay and watch?"

"You bet, if you do."

"Wouldn't miss it. There's an empty bench over here where we can sit. Did you know they took the important parts out of the Delta King that is permanently docked at Sacramento, California and put them in the Delta Queen so she could still run?"

"No, I can't say that I ever knew that," said Mitch. "Thanks though for informing me."

"But I don't know if she still has those parts or more modern ones," Branda said.

As the Queen finally came huffing along, red paddlewheel churning up muddy river water as she approached, Mitch and Branda watched in awe as the boat captain maneuvered the lady into dock.

"Now that is something I have always wanted to do," said Branda.

"What? Dock the Delta Queen?" he asked, chuckling.

"No, you tease, I've always wanted to ride her from at least St. Louis clear down to New Orleans."

"Well you never know," said Mitch. "You never know."

Deciding they had better go, Branda said, "I once watched while the Queen left. The captain edged her out into the middle of the river, the calliope was blasting Camptown Races as I recall, then he swung the boat around and headed for New Orleans. Quite a spectacle."

"Without a doubt. Once, during the river front celebration in St. Louis on July 4th, I saw the end of the annual race between the Delta Queen and the Mississippi Queen. The Mississippi Queen won. Actress Helen Hayes was on board I understand."

"Well I'd sure like to see that sometime too."

"Maybe we can do that," said Mitch.

"For another bit of trivia, I heard that years ago one of Cape's own musicians played the calliope aboard a steamboat. Legend has it he had to wear a raincoat and hat to keep from being hit by the flying cinders in those days. He also allegedly reported he had to nearly stand on the keys to get them to go down due to the heavy pressure required to operate them."

"What was his name?" asked Mitch.

"Jess Stacy. He eventually left Cape and finally ended up playing piano with Benny Goodman's swing band. My school teacher Kathleen Phinney told me about him."

"I've heard of Jess Stacy too. My mom and dad were acquainted with his piano playing," said Mitch.

After a quick tour around the university grounds, Branda directed Mitch to the New Lorimier cemetery.

Standing with head bowed and hands clasped in prayer she stood in front of the two small graves. Sensing she needed to be alone for now, Mitch gave her space. He stayed a short distance away, watching her closely.

After a time she turned slightly, looking for him, holding out an arm in his direction. Going to her immediately, taking her hand, he stood quietly waiting for her to break the silence she seemed to prefer at the moment. Her tears had already dried.

Finally, she said, "Their graves look so very, very tiny. The babies were so sweet and little and . . . I don't understand why . . . Oh I guess God wanted them for angels. I never know what to think. I just have to remember that saying by Tagori, the Bengali poet. 'Death is not extinguishing the light. It is putting out the lamp because the dawn has come.'"

"That is a wonderful thought," Mitch said. "A truly wonderful thought. I don't recall hearing it before. But I'll remember it now."

After one last look at the small graves and a quick prayer, they went to the car. While she had been saying that last prayer she noticed out of the corner of her eye that Mitch was making the sign of the cross.

As they started driving out of Cape, Mitch said, "This really is a lovely town. I had forgotten just how picturesque it is. And thank you for showing me the Catholic churches; St. Mary's Cathedral and old St. Vincent's. The restoration work in the latter is wonderful. And it has quite a history. There is another Catholic church called St. Vincent de Paul plus many Protestant churches of all kinds of denominations."

"In Mark Twain's book 'Life on the Mississippi,' there is a reference to Cape Girardeau being the Athens of Missouri."

"He's one of my favorite writers," said Mitch.

"Mine too," she said, adjusting the seat so she was practically lying down.

"Are you getting tired? Or not feeling well?" he asked.

"No. I feel fine and I'm really not over tired. I just never rode in a car that had so many buttons to push to adjust the seat. I just wanted to see what it was like."

"Would you rather go on home tonight or stop in Ste. Genevieve?"

"You're the driver. That's up to you."

"Well, the drive isn't that long but I think it would be nice if we spent the night in that historic town. Something different. I know there's a fine restaurant or two there."

After locating and checking into a lovely old B&B, they went to eat at the recommended restaurant. Lobster was on the menu but Branda passed that up for homemade chicken and dumplings.

"You do have a wide variety of tastes," said Mitch, lightheartedly.

"And you're pretty much like all men. Meat and potatoes. Right?"

"Right," he answered.

They took a brief drive around town admiring the historical atmosphere then went back to the B&B. She liked it especially because each room had its own bath. Also, the rooms were tastefully decorated and weren't all frilly and lacy.

Upon reaching the room, Mitch said, "You go first and get ready for bed. I'll bet the kids are ready to rest."

Laughing, she said, "You are something else Dr. Andrews. You are something else and I love you very much."

"The feeling is mutual Mrs. Dr. Andrews. I love you very much."

After both were in bed, she said, "Thank you for a very special day."

"You are very welcome. I have enjoyed it too."

Turning toward each other for a good night kiss, both soon realized passion was waiting for them.

Husky voiced, Mitch whispered, "I have a feeling it's also going to be a special night."

"Me too," said Branda. "I've heard motel or other different bedrooms are a turn on. Now I understand that theory."

Theory became reality as desire's white-hot heat melted and melded them until they finally fell asleep with every cell in their bodies completely sexually satisfied.

Evidently, next morning, the glow from their satisfaction still hung like an aura around the lovers because everybody seeing the couple at breakfast smiled pleasantly and knowingly. Shyly, the lovers smiled back.

When they got home, there was a message from Cynthia on the answering machine.

She said, "Would it be all right if Sean and I came an hour early tonight? There's something important I need to tell you."

Mitch called her at work and told her it was fine to come early. She wouldn't even give him a hint what it was all about.

"I'll bet I know," said Branda. "She's going to tell us we're having twins."

"I'll bet you're right."

"Well, then I think it's time we let her in on our visions and dreams, don't you?"

"Yes I do. Actually, as psychic as she is, I'm surprised she didn't see the one over the pool," Mitch said.

Branda went to their bedroom to rest. Mitch unpacked then went to the study to work.

When Sean and Cynthia arrived, the foursome sat in the living room. Cynthia was looking very serious.

Branda asked, "Does this have anything to do with the way you kept glancing at me at the party?"

Looking a bit startled, Cynthia said, "Was I doing that? I'm sorry, but yes, that's what this is all about. I strongly sense you are having twins."

"Yes, we know," said Branda. "But I'm glad to hear you say it too and thank you very much. It verifies what we dreamed. We're having a girl, Michele, and a boy, Mitchell."

With that, Branda and Mitch explained about the visions and dreams, who was in them, what they said and did.

"Well, I'll be da . . . doggoned," said Sean. "So my Cynthia isn't the only one with a special power."

"That's right but a different kind," said Mitch. "But mine just started the other night. It's more than an awesome experience. Cynthia, did you see anything at all strange above the pool at the party . . . I mean besides the lights flickering around on the dolphin?"

"To tell you the truth, at one point I thought I saw a sort of silvery cloud for a moment but I figured it had something to do with the special effects," Cynthia said.

"I think you were seeing a bit of the vision," said Branda.

"Well, anyway, I just thought I should tell you about my feeling you're having twins in case it would help you prepare in any way," said Cynthia.

"We're so glad you did," Mitch and Branda said, echoing each other.

"And I hope some day I can fully see one of those visions. That has to be an incredible experience . . . and in color. Wonderful!" Cynthia exclaimed.

"Me too," echoed Sean. "That sounds cool as the youngsters say."

Branda told Sean and Cynthia about the first blood pregnancy test exploding and scaring the technician to pieces.

"Poor thing," said Cynthia.

"I checked on her and she's okay now," said Mitch. "I had Dr. Cline explain the situation to her."

"I've been meaning to ask you two if Erin, Sharon and the boys know the truth about my condition and about my pregnancy?" asked Branda.

Cynthia answered, "They know about both things; sadder than they can say about the one, happy beyond belief about the baby. Wait until I tell them there are twins."

"They will be absolutely delighted about that, or should we wait until you have an ultrasound to truly verify?" Sean asked.

"Maybe you could tell them we think we might be, but won't know for sure until the ultrasound is performed," said Branda. "Are they in to your psychic abilities Cynthia? How would they react to vision prophecies?"

"Oh they're used to my 'ways' as they put it, but I really don't know about visions. I'll check that out sometime," said Cynthia. "I suppose it would be better to have the medical test to back up our announcement."

Mitch asked Sean about the Dallas people and what they wanted.

"Oh just poking around deciding whether or not to do some store and restaurant remodeling," said Sean.

"I hope they're not thinking of doing any major personnel changes that would affect you adversely, like a transfer to another city," Mitch said.

"No. Nothing like that was mentioned and, believe me, they talked a lot," Sean said.

"I honestly think they just wanted to come to St. Louis for a little vacation, eat some of Kreis' prime rib and do some riverboat gambling."

After Mary Ann, Linda, and Mathilda arrived, everybody congregated in the kitchen and helped put the leftover meal together, everybody chatting away. Branda and Mitch told them about their short trip, how they enjoyed it; especially seeing the Delta Queen. Branda didn't mention visiting the grave sites.

All declared the food to be as super good as it was at the party. Branda noticed her three friends were more relaxed around Mitch this time. When he asked if they had finally gotten their giggle boxes under control Saturday night they got tickled all over again.

"Yes, we recovered," said Mary Ann, between laughs. "But it was hard."

Branda was grateful they didn't tell him why.

To steer them away from the subject, Branda asked, "What would you say if I told you I might be carrying twins?"

"Twins!" exclaimed Linda.

"Are you?" asked Mary Ann.

"Isn't it too early to tell?" Mathilda asked.

"Yes. We won't really know until the ultrasound is done in a few weeks, but Cynthia believes I am."

"Did she do one of those tests over your wrist with a pencil hanging on a thread?" asked Linda.

"No," Cynthia said, smiling. "I am sometimes psychic about things and I just get the feeling Branda is going to have twins."

"Well, that would really be something," Mathilda said. "Guess I'd better buy extra yarn so I can knit four booties instead of two. Should I get pink or blue yarn or some of each, Cynthia?"

"An ultrasound at about 20 weeks will have to provide that information," answered Cynthia, smiling.

She didn't want to get into the dream vision information unless Branda or Mitch engineered it. They didn't. Neither had any idea how the three women would accept that sort of subject. Maybe they would tell them some other time.

Branda had noticed the three were carefully avoiding the subject of her illness. She knew all cared a great deal but they were trying to keep things cheerful tonight. She appreciated that very much. They had let her know after Mitch's speech how sad they were about her predicament and offered to help her in any way they could.

Since the guests had worked today and had to work tomorrow, they prepared to leave at a reasonable hour.

Standing at the front door, Sean asked, "Have you had any information come over that tip line yet?"

"None so far," said Mitch.

Mary Ann, Linda, and Mathilda wished them the very best and said they would keep their ears open for any information.

"What are your next plans, Mitch?" asked Sean.

"It's full steam ahead," he answered.

But three days later, Mitch slowed down the momentum. He put a serious strain on his relationship with Branda by withdrawing from her for a day and night; only available to her in case of an emergency.

On that stressful day he was not beside her when she awakened. There was no note as usual on the pillow to say where he was and she could not get any response over the communicator. She wondered if he had fallen, was hurt and couldn't contact her or answer.

Walking as fast as she could, looking in rooms as she went, she called his name over and over. No response. At last she found him. He was sitting on the floor in the downstairs apartment looking through a box of Helen's pictures, looking sadder than she had ever seen him. She wasn't sure but she thought she saw traces of tears on his face.

At first she was angry, but something clicked in her mind that saved her from saying anything hurtful. She remembered it was the date of his and Helen's wedding anniversary and also of the day she died.

Branda was beginning to sense the glimmer of a feeling there was more to Mitch's sadness about his relationship with Helen than anyone knew;

something deep, deep down still haunting him. During the relative short time she had known this man, she had learned he had great strength. But his equally strong sensitivity often became his Achilles heel that at times could weaken and drag him to depths of despair.

Remaining silent, she sat beside him on the floor, laying her head on his shoulder hoping to comfort him.

Finally speaking, she said, "It is so hard to relive the pain, isn't it?"

As if coming out of a trance, Mitch looked at her and quietly said, "Yes. Oh, yes. I'm glad you understand. I thought these memories were more deeply buried but when I saw today's date on the calendar, they all got jarred loose again. I'm sorry."

"No need to be, Mitch. I was just worried when I couldn't find you."

"I'm sorry about that too. I could vaguely hear your voice and figured you were all right since you weren't asking for help. I just . . . oh, I don't know. It's like I've been off in another world. Would you mind terribly, Branda, if I went through this alone? I know we once said we would always help each other with our ghosts, but for some reason I need my space right now. But if you get in stress of some kind, please call and tell me so."

Since he requested they leave their communicators in vibrator mode, she had heard no sounds from him the rest of the day except when he briefly checked in with her from time to time to make sure she was all right. She felt somewhat hurt but tried to understand.

During one of his checkup calls, she offered to fix him something to eat and bring it downstairs. He thanked her but said no; that he would come up and get something if he felt hungry or find something in the bar refrigerator.

She spent the time reading for both research and pleasure, resting, eating light snacks, and calling Mary Ann, Linda, and Mathilda when she knew they were home from work. She didn't mention what was going on. She hoped neither Sean nor Cynthia would call because she didn't want them to figure out something was wrong. Luckily, they did not call.

When Mitch finally came to bed late that night, he did not move close and hold her as usual. She was turned on her side facing away from him, still awake, but remained silent. His distance left her feeling lonesome. Tears welled in her eyes.

"This too shall pass," she said, looking toward Betty whose blank stare looked back in the dim visibility from the night-light.

Sometime toward dawn, Mitch tentatively reached for her, whispering, "Branda, are you awake?"

His welcome touch roused her from a light sleep.

"Yes, Mitch. I'm awake," she answered, turning toward him.

"Please forgive me, Branda. I apologize from the bottom of my heart. I was not prepared in any way for my reaction to those two anniversary memories. Thanks for understanding. If you would like to talk about it later, I'm ready."

"If you want to discuss it that's fine with me," she said. "If not, that's all right too. I've thought about it all and am trying hard to see where you are coming from. But I must admit my feelings got hurt a bit too. Mitch, is there more to this sadness bout Helen than you're telling?"

Looking at her searchingly, he asked, "What makes you ask that?"

"I really don't know. It's just a feeling I got this time watching you grieve. Oh, let's just drop it. I don't mean to pry. You need your space to grieve in your way as I often do in mine. Anyway, I missed you so much and was afraid you might leave me . . . or have me leave."

Holding her closely, he said, "Oh Honey, no. Oh no. I wouldn't leave or have you go either. I love you very much. I just hit a rough patch. And again, I apologize. Forgive me?"

"Of course," she said, thinking to herself he looked relieved she had not pressed the issue of there being more to his grieving than he let on.

Patting her abdomen, he added, smiling, "Do you two forgive me too?"

The lovemaking that followed was like a renewal of wedding vows; both determined never to allow another rift to come between them. But one did several months later, bringing to light the secret Branda suspected.

CHAPTER EIGHTEEN

DAYS LINKED INTO WEEKS, FORGING into Branda's fourth month of pregnancy. During that time the couple had stepped up the pace searching for a cause and cure for her illness. The pressure was building. They joined a battery of tests to their ongoing research reading and consultations with other doctors.

Mitch carefully screened out any he thought might even possibly be harmful to her and the babies. X-rays, or anything remotely connected to radiation, were not allowed. As desperate as they were to find a cure, he would also cancel and reschedule any appointments if she seemed overtired or was upset in any way. Neither tests, reading, consultations nor tip line produced any valid information. There were a few more procedures he wanted to try before going to his next plan.

Now both of her feet were gone as well as the lower part of her legs two inches above the anklebones. The only way she could get around was to crawl, have Mitch carry her, or use the customized Gel-cell battery powered wheelchair Mitch had ordered built for her. It was Wedgwood blue since she said black ones looked depressing. That shade of blue was one of her favorite colors. Also, since he knew a rainbow was one of her favorite things, he had a small one painted on top of the control box.

He bought a navy blue van outfitted with a special ramp allowing her to more easily enter and exit from a side door. The ramp could be extended and retracted, lowered and raised. Once inside the van, her chair could be locked in place to keep it from being rolled about during travel. He kept the car too.

Wherever possible and needed, he had grip bars and other safety devices installed.

He hired a personal trainer to develop a special exercise program for Branda. Her name was Mrs. Maudie Finley, a very pretty brunette in her thirties with an angelic personality. She came on Thursdays.

Among other things, learning to strengthen her arm muscles was a big help to Branda; especially when it came to swimming. Mitch had instructed Johnny to keep the pool heated. If it became necessary for helping Branda, Mitch said he would have the pool enclosed.

He was so very good to her it was hard to believe she even considered the thought she was losing him last June. By mutual agreement, they had not spoken of that traumatic day and night since. She sensed that although what she called his flip-flop personality was still there, he always tried hard not to let that edgy side surface.

Since she rarely ever requested anything, he honored her wish to hire a daytime nurse to come one day a week; sometimes two.

"You need to get out by yourself once in a while," she had told him. "Staying home with an invalid 24/7 is not good for you."

"Are you trying to get rid of me?" he had asked, jokingly.

"You know better than that. This is just Mrs. Doctor Andrew's orders. I worry about you." She learned later he mostly went to the main library to do research reading on his "day off" as he humorously called it. Or he made luncheon dates with other doctors to discuss her problem. Rarely did he go horseback riding or play golf. Whenever they were apart he always left on his cell phone and the communicator in vibrator mode and made sure she did the same. Recently, she had started calling the communicator the gadget.

The daytime nurse was Mrs. Lois Watson. She was a nice looking red head in her early forties and very pleasant to have around. She came on Tuesdays.

As Mitch and Branda lay in bed this last Saturday morning in September, Branda commented, "Have you noticed dream visions and the other kind haven't been coming very often?"

"Yes," answered Mitch. "And when they have, the main information we get is to have faith; everything happening is part of the larger whole design."

"So I guess that's just what we'll have to do. At least in the visions we get to see all of the babies as well as the grownups," she said. "And it was so wonderful during the ultrasound last week to see the little ones all snug and cozy inside me. Now I can sort of guess which one is squirming around and giving me a good kick or poke now and then. Of course they both do their share of gymnastics. I was glad when Dr. Cline wanted to check for twins after noticing I was getting slightly larger than normal for a single birth. Of course, we were getting ready to ask him to do it anyway. I'm not sure he would understand visions and dreams. I'm glad he understands we allegedly want to be surprised about the sexes so won't want the ultrasound performed at 20 weeks."

"Right," said Mitch. "And Michele and Mitchell certainly did look content inside you. Babies truly are a miracle. I know you enjoyed those pictures I showed you on the Internet about fetal development."

"Oh yes! They personalized the phenomenon for me."

"On another subject, remember a while back when Chief War Eagle said we would be able to converse with him and the others someday? I wonder when that will be?" Mitch asked. "I'm looking forward to that. There's so much I want to ask him about his knowledge of medicines . . . plus talk to my parents, yours, and Light Moon."

"Since timing is a key factor in their world, I suppose that will happen when it's time," Branda said. "And speaking of time, I'm getting more and more frightened about my race against it. What is going to win . . . my continued and more serious loss of body parts . . . or the babies' births? I do count my blessings that disappearances are not further along than they are. Oh Mitch. How do you stand looking at my disfigurement? I hate seeing it."

"It's all going to be just fine Honey. I do have faith in that," said Mitch, smoothing her hair. "And you must remember that as a doctor I am used to seeing all sorts of things. But of course I hate seeing you upset by it all. That bothers me more than anything."

Suddenly the babies began moving around interrupting all conversation. Branda pulled up her nightgown exposing her naked belly.

Mitch leaned to kiss Branda's abdomen, then said, chuckling, "Hey you two. Go easy on your mother. She's pregnant you know."

Placing a hand over the active babies, he felt and watched the phenomenon in awe. Ever since a couple of weeks ago when Branda had called his attention to the first "baby show" as she called it, he was fascinated. She also put her hand near his to feel the activity.

Mitch said, "I never get use to feeling and seeing my son and daughter do that."

"I know," said Branda, smiling happily.

"Maybe they're hungry," Mitch said. "What would you like to feed them this morning my lady? Lobster?

"Thermidor or Newburg?" she asked, laughing..

"Whatever I can persuade Red Lobster to deliver. Your choice," he said, keeping the banter going.

"Well," she said with pretend huffiness. "If you're not going to charter a jet and go to Maine and get me one freshly caught, I guess I'll just settle for your special scrambled eggs, some Esicar bacon, orange juice, and whole wheat toast."

"Picky, picky, picky," he said leaning to kiss her lips. "Do you want me to bring you breakfast in bed, or would you rather have me put you in your wheelchair and come to the kitchen?"

"If the weather is nice enough, I would like to eat at a poolside table. Lately, I've noticed some leaves are starting to show off their autumn colors. I think I also caught a glimpse of some chrysanthemums in bloom in the patio garden. I'd like to see them."

"I'll check it out. Would you like to take a swim later and get some exercise?"

"I'll think about that. I know for the twin's sake, I need to exercise no matter what even though they seem to be doing pretty well on their own. Now git! I'm starving," she said, smiling.

Giving her tummy one last look, he patted it and said with a smile, "Your mother is getting bossy. Branda, do you need anything before I go?" he asked.

"No thanks, Mitch. And even though I don't usually like to dine in my nightclothes, I'll shower and dress after I eat. I'm hungry . . . or the kids are. I have the gadget on if I need you. And thanks again for helping me get to the bathroom and back in bed awhile ago. Even though I can do a lot of things for myself, it's easier with assistance. I appreciate everything you always do to help me. I hope you know that."

"I do and you're welcome."

After he left she lay looking toward Betty, silently reminiscing to her doll about what had been going on in her life these past few months. The babies had calmed down. Betty stared blankly at the few tears Branda allowed to come down her cheeks.

Quickly brushing them away, Branda said, "Oh Betty. I need God's strength more than I ever have in my life. I know it will come as needed. Sometimes I just feel overwhelmed."

Eventually, Mitch came to help her into the wheelchair parked close to her bedside. Reaching toward the foot of the bed to get them, she had already put on her favorite lightweight powder-blue flannel robe and a pair of the tube-like white cotton leg coverings Mitch had ordered made for her. They came to her knees.

He opened the bedroom door leading to the patio garden, holding it open as she drove her wheelchair through.

"I'm getting better all the time guiding this chair," she said. "At least I don't crash into door frames like I used to."

"You do just fine," he said, walking behind her, glad she could not see the sadness and tension registering on his face.

Despite their efforts to use a light hearted, bantering, approach at times, both knew that was just a way of putting a temporary gloss over the seriousness of the situation.

As they sat poolside eating the delicious breakfast they chatted and reminisced.

Noticing he was wearing the wristwatch she had given him on his 46th birthday July 22, she said, "What is the time in Dublin, Ireland?"

After punching some small buttons, he said, "Five p.m."

"Pretty nifty, eh? Out of all the ones Sean sneaked in here for me to look over, I liked this one the best."

"You know how I like it since I wear it everyday. And I still thank you for throwing that surprise party for me at Sean and Cynthia's house. My doctor and nurse friends, advisors and lawyers had a great time. I think your friends did too."

"They did. You really were surprised weren't you?" asked Branda.

"Yep. I thought we were just going to have dinner at Sean and Cynthia's house . . . just the four of us."

"Well I enjoyed meeting your friends so much at the May 31st party, I decided it would be nice seeing them again. That was nice of Sean and Cynthia to furnish the party place. Of course they wanted to do something for your birthday just like they have for years. But they did let me help with expenses. Since I rarely got out to spend any of that too generous allowance you give me, I had more than enough. And I still have my own savings. As you know, I sometimes send some of that to the people tending the graves of my parents and sons and am going to set up a fund to have that done as long as the money holds out. And I want to leave what I can to Michele and Mitchell even though I know you can provide for them more than quite well. My small investments even pay me dividends once in a while."

"Yes, I think if you put your mind to it you could become quite a financier."

"Well, I don't know about that," she said. "While we're on the subject of money, I feel really bad about my health insurance people canceling me out as soon as they learned the change in my marital status came with an outrageous amount of money attached."

"Well, you can't really blame them," Mitch said.

"I know. But I had hoped to at least pay something," she said.

"No one could ever accuse you of being a free loader or a spendthrift," he said, reaching to give her hand a slight squeeze. Continuing, he added, "And Branda, I will add to your grave-care fund,"

"I don't expect you to do that, Mitch."

"I know. But I want to."

"Well, thank you from the bottom of my heart. You really are something else Mr. Dr. Andrews."

"You are most welcome, Mrs. Dr. Andrews. Now, getting back to the subject of parties, you really enjoyed the wingding Sean and Cynthia's kids had for their parents 25th wedding anniversary June 11th didn't you?"

"Boy, I'll say," she answered. "The country club was the ideal place to have the party, two weeks in Hawaii staying at the Royal Hawaiian Hotel the ideal gift, and having family and friends attend made it very special. It was so good to see Erin, Sharon and the boys again. We had some nice talks while they were home for the event. Since Cynthia had not mentioned our visions to them, I didn't either. As I already mentioned to you, she called them after the ultrasound to tell them about the twins and they were elated. They even liked the idea we supposedly don't want to know the sex of the babies."

"Yes, I imagine the girls are already knitting unisex color booties," Mitch said. "The boys will probably either come up with model trains or a Barbie doll. Little do they know, both would be fitting."

"It was nice Sean and Cynthia chose the two weeks in August that included their birthdays on the fifth and ninth to take their Hawaiian trip. For a belated birthday dinner, we at least got to take them to Kreis's for prime rib after they returned. Do they mind celebrating their birthdays on the same day?" Branda asked.

"Cynthia use to balk a bit at doing that, but I don't think it bothers her anymore. It never was a really serious issue."

"Just a woman thang, I suppose," said Branda. "Anyway, it was a nice summer and I know Reverend Cummings, Martha, Mary Ann, Linda, and Mathilda enjoyed coming often for a meal or just to visit."

"Yes, and we'll have to keep on getting them over here. I enjoy their company too. I was afraid the Reverend would be stuffy but he really isn't. We have had some good discussions. We're on a first name basis now; Charles and Mitchell."

"That's nice. I still can't bring myself to addressing him in anyway but Reverend Cummings. Just an old time hangup. That reminds me Mitch. I know your church believes in early baptism. Do you want Michele and Mitchell baptized that way?"

"I haven't really thought about that. Would you mind?" he asked.

"Not really."

"What about Charles . . . Reverend Cummings?" asked Mitch.

"I think he's more liberal than most but we'll check it out. Anyway, I think it's our decision in the long run. I wouldn't want to be disrespectful though."

Mitch reached to hold her hand and ask, "How are you feeling after that gourmet breakfast?"

"Fine. It really was gourmet to me. And it is so nice to relax out here and sort of have the weekend off from all the necessary commotion made by the remodeling job that has been going on downstairs for months. How are they coming along? I haven't wanted to go down in case it would bother the workmen. Sometimes I think they worked day and night."

"Would you like to go see now?"

"Yes I would," she answered.

"Before we go, there's something I want to ask you. How do you feel about flying . . . traveling long distances?"

"You mean like to Hawaii like Sean and Cynthia did?"

"Yes. Something like that," he said.

"Well, Mitch, I'm kind of embarrassed to admit it in this day and age, but I have never flown anywhere. I never had anywhere to go that required it. I've never even seen the inside of an airplane except in magazines, movies, and on television."

"Well, that is a bit rare these days, but nothing wrong about it. How do you think you would like it? Would you be afraid to fly?"

"No, I don't think so. As long as it wouldn't harm the babies. Why do you ask? Are we going somewhere?"

"One never knows," he said, smiling. "But for now, let's get these dishes to the kitchen, into the dishwasher, and go see the basement makeover."

She didn't say anything but, for some reason, she thought his smile had a sly pleased look to it, like the proverbial cat lapping the proverbial cream.

Mitch helped her maneuver the wheelchair into the elevator.

After getting downstairs, she exclaimed, "Why Mitch! It looks to me like they are the same as finished. It looks great!"

"Yes they have done a wonderful job," he said.

"And pretty fast considering all there was to do."

"Steven Greer, the foreman who is studying to be an architect, said they expect to be through at the end of this coming week," said Mitch.

As he gave her a guided tour, she was amazed at both new and updated equipment in the study and rather surprised to find her furniture in one of the apartments.

"What did you do with the things that were in here?" she asked.

"One of the workmen had just gotten married, offered to buy it, and I just gave it to him as a wedding present," said Mitch.

"You're too much," she said, smiling in admiration. "You know you could have gotten rid of most of my stuff. The only things I'm sentimental about are the pieces that belonged to my parents."

"I know, but . . . well, I still think you might want your space sometime and be surrounded by these things."

"Thanks, Mitch, but you know I feel perfectly at home in your house now and love it."

Leaning to kiss her cheek, he said, "Thank you, Branda. That means a lot to me. And it's our house you know."

"Thank you. And I have also learned to love Ella, Jane, Pete, Joe the yard crew, Johnny . . . well just everybody that works here. The women watch over me like mother hens; the men too in their way."

"Well, in case you don't know it, they really love you too. That's easy to do as I have learned," he said.

Back upstairs, heading for their bedroom, they stopped first at Mitchell's room then Michele's.

Branda said, "The decorators really did a beautiful job with the twin's rooms. I'm glad you left Our Lady's niche in Mitchell's. She's like a guardian angel."

"I must say, Branda. You are more liberal minded than you used to be about Catholic things."

"Oh, I've begun to realize we're all on the same track, just on different trains."

"You do have a way of hitting the nail on the head," he said, laughing heartily. "And now, after you shower and dress, what would you like to do the rest of the day?"

"If you can get a golf game arranged, I would enjoy riding along in the cart. Getting out in the fresh air sounds good to me. Or if that doesn't work out, maybe we could go to Shaw's Garden and look at the flowers outside then go into the Climatron and see what's displayed inside . . . have a late lunch in the restaurant there."

They ended up going to Shaw's Garden on Saturday, and Mitch and Sean playing golf Sunday morning. Cynthia stayed in the cart with Branda. Branda was pretty sure Mitch had arranged that so she wouldn't be alone in case an emergency arose. After the golf game, the foursome had lunch in the clubhouse. After ordering, Mitch excused himself to go make a business call.

"He really does stay on top of things, doesn't he?" Branda asked Sean and Cynthia.

"Yep," answered Sean. "Always has, always will. He has to in order to manage that huge fortune."

Later, as they got into Mitch's car to leave, Mitch asked, "Are all of you up to a drive out to Lambert Airport before we go to our homes?"

All agreed that would be fine with them. Cynthia and Branda sat in the backseat watching the twins do some stretching exercises.

"They often do that after I eat a meal," Branda said. "I guess they're trying to work off my calories."

Sean turned around to see the baby show that was fairly visible even covered by Branda's maternity top. Cynthia put a hand on Branda's abdomen to feel the activity.

"Wow!" said Cynthia. "They really are wiggling around in there. Erin and Sharon use to do the same thing. I swore they were having a fight. I asked them about it after they were grown, but, of course, they didn't remember that far back. Maybe I should have them hypnotized to see if that would cause a recall. That reminds me, Branda. Don't you have a hypnotherapy session coming up soon to get rid of that nightmare and maybe somehow shed some light on your illness?"

"Yes. It's scheduled for tomorrow at 1 p.m. I have had a couple of those nightmares fairly recently and sure would like to get rid of them. I hear the husband and wife doctors who will be treating me are top notch."

"And that would be Fred and Cathy Thompson I suspect," said Cynthia.

"That's right," Branda said.

The twins had calmed down and Branda's attention was drawn to the fact Mitch appeared to be driving into some part of the airport besides the usual way. Cynthia was leaning up to get a better view of their route.

Sean asked, "What's going on Mitch? Isn't this the area where executives park their planes?"

"Yes. It sure is. And there's Branda's and mine just up ahead."

All eyes looked toward a DC-10, it's silvery paint glistening in the afternoon sun, Wedgewood blue detailing enhancing its overall beauty.

Branda and Cynthia were speechless.

Sean gasped then uttered, "Good Lord, Mitch. What are you going to do with that marvelous airplane?"

"I'm taking Branda anywhere in the world that might even remotely have a cure."

"Three jumpin' Georges!" exclaimed Branda.

"So this is the major event I've been sensing," Cynthia said, looking stunned.

CHAPTER NINETEEN

RANDA'S HYPNOTHERAPY SESSIONS DURING THE next two weeks turned out to be successful as far as getting rid of nightmares about Connor assaulting her. But nothing even faintly resembling a clue to her illness came forth.

During the first session at one o'clock September 29th, Dr. Fred Thompson worked with her. In later sessions, either he or his doctor wife, Cathy, or both would see her. They often worked in tandem thinking a patient might be more receptive at times to one sex or another. They said she should call anytime from anywhere if she had any recurring problems.

"It is so good not to have those awful nightmares anymore," Branda said.

"Yes. Thank God for that," said Mitch.

Between those sessions, Mitch set up another kind of routine. He didn't want to finalize trip plans and leave until he found out something else. He was also working on a couple of surprises for Branda regarding the plane and the trip. He was hoping to leave November 1st. Ella and all other employee friends said they would hold down the fort while he and Branda were gone. He also alerted the police and security alarm people about his trip. Everybody who had a need to know was told how to reach him no matter where he was and vice versa.

Right now his top priority was to make sure Branda would enjoy flying. To check this out, Mitch arranged with a friend of his from Parks College of Engineering and Aviation to take Branda for her first airplane ride. The pilot's name was Elwood Higgins, better known as Woody. Another pilot friend,

Joe Choppesky, came along for this ride and ended up coming on subsequent ones. They would fly out of the St. Louis Downtown Airport in Cahokia; operated by Bi-State Development Agency and located near the beautiful old former Parks Air College Campus.

Mitch had explained to her this flight in a small plane would be a whole lot different than being in a large jetliner where you felt like you were in your own living room.

After getting her wheelchair as close as possible to the plane, Mitch had carried her on board, took her chair back to where the van was parked, then returned to join her. "The jet will be more wheelchair friendly," he said.

During that first take off, she exclaimed, "Jumpin' George! This is wonderful."

Once aloft, she ooohed and ahhhed like a kid at a circus. The landing didn't bother her one bit. She was attracted to flying like steel to a magnet.

"What a feeling of freedom," she said. "Isn't there a special poem somewhere about flying? Something about slipping the surly bonds of earth . . . oh I don't remember the words, but now I understand that feeling."

"I'm so happy you like to fly and are comfortable with it," said Mitch. "If you had not been, I would have canceled the trip, sold the jet, and had doctors and people I want you to see flown here."

"You are something else, Mitch. Something good else, that is."

"Besides looking for a cure worldwide, I also want you to see some of this planet."

"Fire up that jet. When do we leave?" she asked.

"As soon as I complete arrangements. Also, Branda, there is a vast difference in power levels between the jet and this small plane. We'll take a short trip in this plane just to make certain you won't get airsick and the kids like it too. Then we'll take a longer one in the jet just to make sure."

Just before her next ride a few days later, Woody gave her a framed copy of the famous "High Flight" poem by John Gillespie Magee, an RCAF WWII pilot killed in a training flight at age nineteen.

After reading the short piece, she motioned for Woody to lean down and gave him a hug.

"Thank you very much Woody. This expresses it all so well. I'm going to memorize it."

During the next ride, Joe and Woody began showing her how to handle the controls while in flight and let her hold the yoke for a bit. Knowing she had no feet to work rudder pedals, they did that part from the other seat when necessary.

"Hey, Branda," said Joe. "You're a natural."

"You said it," echoed Woody. "I can tell you are a real fly by the seat of your pants pilot, pardon the expression."

All laughed.

A trip to Memphis proved Branda was as airworthy as the airplane in which they flew. The twins jiggled around sometimes but not unusually so.

During one such gymnastic session, Branda laughed and commented, "Now I know what some of the moves are these two make from time to time. They're making right and left turns."

The others joined their laughter with hers.

After their early morning Memphis flight, Mitch took everybody to eat at nearby Oliver L. Parks Restaurant in the terminal. Branda read some of the memorabilia on the walls about how Mr. Parks had started the original college in 1927 at Lambert Field. He had two airplanes and was the only instructor. In 1928 the college was moved to Cahokia. Parks gave the college to St. Louis University in 1947 and in 1997 the university moved the main campus to Grand Avenue in St. Louis.

"Some alumni from years past still aren't a bit happy about that move," Joe said. "Parks is the nation's oldest certified flight school. I've heard rumors the university may add on to the name again and call it Parks College of Engineering, Aviation and Technology."

"Over the years a lot of notable people like Charles Lindbergh and Amelia Earhart visited the college," said Woody.

After eating, Joe asked, "Would you two like to go see the old campus? It's not far from here."

"Would that be all right with you, Mitch?" asked Branda.

"Yes, I would like to see it again myself. I haven't seen it in years."

"Good," said Joe. "How about you, Woody?"

"Count me in too."

Each took their own vehicles so they could go their separate ways after the tour.

Branda and Mitch thoroughly enjoyed seeing the old campus with it's towering trees shading lush green grass and winding sidewalks. Red brick buildings trimmed in white were spaced around the grounds.

Woody pointed out the campus chapel where weddings as well as church services had been held.

"It is very peaceful here," said Branda. "It has a serene happy feel to it. One can almost hear and see ghosts of past students and teachers. I imagine when students were here, it wasn't quite as peaceful."

After a quick look at the historic Catholic log church across the road the group parted. Thanks and hugs were exchanged between Woody, Joe, and Branda; thanks, bear hugs, and handshakes between the men.

During the jet trip to Denver, Branda said she was ready to pack and leave for wherever.

For the overseas journey Mitch had hired two flight crews, two security guards, and two extra attendants for the first leg only. The pilots and copilots had already flown the plane on test runs. Mitch had asked everyone to come on the Denver run in order to meet Branda, and for those who had not been aboard to familiarize themselves with the plane. All knew they had a secret to keep from Branda until later on.

The pilots were Charles "Sonny" Elkins and Matthew "Doc" Robertson; co-pilots, Patrick O'Hara and Bob Edwards; Flight Attendants, Alan Dobson and Grant Larkin. The two extras were Ted Mumford and Norman Jacklyn. Adrian "Duke" Steele and Kris "Crunch" Rogers were security guards.

Mitch had hired only men since the trip would be long and quarters, though adequate, were not conducive to a mixed sex arrangement. However, if he had to hire a woman along the trail for some reason, something could be worked out with little trouble. He had carefully screened the employees and had security background checks run.

After landing and the plane was being taxied to the gate, Branda told Mitch, "That flight was better than great. The plane is a dream and all the crew members and other personnel are so special."

From the minute Mitch had introduced her to everyone, it was a mutual admiration society from then on.

On the way home in the van, Branda said, "I love takeoffs. They are . . . well . . . the word exciting doesn't begin to cover it. Landings are too but I find myself putting on the brakes sometimes."

"That's a natural reaction. But basically, you have taken to air travel like a skylark," said Mitch. "And the twins seem okay about it too."

"Yes, all three of us are rarin' to go anytime you say. Who wouldn't be with that gorgeous plane to take them? I never knew you could have one customized the way yours is."

"It's yours too."

"Well, thank you but that's hard for me to take in now. Maybe later. You know I have trouble comprehending the amounts of money you deal with. But at least you also give a lot to worthy charities, to the orphanage, and often see that funds go directly to people who need help. Are you going to keep the plane after we get back?" she asked.

"No, unless you want to keep it. I had planned to sell it then both invest and donate most of the money."

"I think that's a good idea. I guess if we wanted to fly somewhere we could charter a plane," Branda said.

"Hey! Now you're getting the hang of having money," Mitch said, smiling.

She smiled rather sheepishly then added, "As long as I'm in the spending mood, could we have an informal dinner party and invite the plane crews, security guards, Sean, Cynthia, Mary Ann, Linda, Mathilda, Reverend Cummings and Martha?"

"Why of course. I had thought about doing that too," he said.

"Since you mentioned you would like to leave November 1st, we could make this a farewell party for our friends and have it October 30th. There might be too many interruptions from trick or treaters on Halloween night. Besides, we need the extra day to help rest up for the trip. I would like to have the plane group as a way of saying thank you in advance for flying us all over the world."

"All are good ideas! Should we call Chad and Bonnie to cater again?"

"Definitely a good idea too," said Branda. "Do they know how to do a good prime rib?"

"Oh yes," said Mitch. "I have a feeling they had a lesson or two from the chefs at Kreis'."

During the days before departure, Mitch engineered all final arrangements including packing, making sure passports and visas were in order, and made countless phone calls.

Branda once told Betty, "I may be imagining it but he sure acts secretive about some of those calls. I guess he's just talking some last minute big business with his advisors. But I know he has that communications center in that special room on the airplane to keep in touch too. Oh well, whatever. He'll hardly let me lift a finger; says all I need to do is rest, exercise, eat well, look beautiful, and enjoy the ride."

She told house cleaning and yard crews good bye promising to send them postcards; also Maudie her personal trainer and Lois the daytime nurse who came once or twice weekly. Maudie had made sure Branda and Mitch understood what needed to be done each day for Branda to stay in shape; especially since she might be spending long hours on the plane.

The dinner party went smooth as silk; the prime rib meeting all expectations.

Afterwards, she asked Mitch, "Did you notice anything odd about the way Sean, Cynthia and the rest acted; not the plane crew particularly, just the others? Especially when I was telling them good bye and said I would miss them."

"Not really," Mitch answered.

"Oh, you're probably right. Maybe Cynthia was having one of her psychic moments and it was contagious. Pregnant women can get funny notions sometimes," she said. "Speaking of notions. Should I take Betty on the trip or not?"

"I really think she would be better off here. I don't foresee any trouble, but I would not want to run the risk of losing her somewhere along the line."

"I hadn't thought of that. You're right. I'll talk to her via mental telepathy," she said, smiling.

Still keyed up from the party, the couple decided to go for a moonlight swim before going to bed. Mitch said it would be okay since there had been ample time since they finished eating.

Branda said, "I would wear my bikini but it isn't exactly a one size fits all garment."

"No, but your birthday suit is," Mitch said.

"Why, doctor. What are your intentions?"

"The best," he said, smiling before giving her a gentle hug and kiss.

Getting some extra-large beach towels to wrap her in on the way to the pool and also pad the wheelchair when she was through swimming, Mitch carried her into the still heated pool.

Primarily using her arms to go through the water she was able to swim for a bit. Mitch stayed right beside her. Later, she hung onto the side of the pool watching him dive a few times; his tan, wet, naked body glistening in the moonlight as he stood atop the board. Surrounding garden lighting enhanced the effect.

She mused, "How lucky can a woman get?"

By the time he came back to carry her out of the pool, she was ready to make love. As he held her close to him in the pool for a moment, his kiss and body let her know he was ready too. As she sat in the wheelchair, he dried her. Wrapping a dry beach towel around her, he left the wheelchair by the pool, carrying her to the hideaway room as they called it. As usual, she reached down from his arms to open the unlocked door.

"We must remember to lock that before we leave," she said.

"Yes," he whispered, voice husky from passion.

Gently placing her on the bed, he stood gazing a moment at her.

"You are so beautiful, more beautiful than ever," he said. "You have that special glow about you that most pregnant women get. It's amazing and so lovely."

"Thank you, Mitch." Smiling up at him she added, "If I have that aura, I have you to thank for it."

Branda knew he was seeing her in a way that overshadowed the fact she was not still as slim and curvaceous as before. She had the good sense to recognize his ability to see beyond the obvious. Therefore she did not blather on about the loss of her former shape. She hoped his special sight lasted throughout the rest of the months.

Then lying beside each other, they kissed unhurriedly for a moment.

The two continued along their road toward passion's peak, touching, feeling, fondling, kissing as they went. He was careful and gentle. Mitch, completely sexually satisfied afterwards, understandably relaxed a shade too heavily against her stomach for a moment and received some swift kicks on his.

Startled as he and Branda were at first, they soon burst into gales of laughter.

Looking at her stomach, which he had now moved well away from, Mitch said, "Sorry you two. Didn't mean to crowd you."

Branda said, "Maybe they thought you were trying to add another resident to their already cramped quarters."

Both heartily laughed again.

"I wish I had a picture of the surprised look on your face," Branda said.

"Yes, I imagine that would be a prize winning candid shot; especially with a caption underneath about 'unborn twins give dad swift kick.' I must admit that tap dance against my belly was unexpected to say the least. I do believe we have some future soccer players in there; ones to equal Pele."

"Either that or they will be champions at kicking field goals," she said.

Mitch reached to lightly pat Branda's belly, and said, "Okay, champs. I got the message."

As soon as he spoke, the two moved and kicked again putting on quite a baby show.

"The champs are restless tonight," said Mitch.

"I guess we woke them up or something," she said.

"Well, go back to sleep kids. Your mom and dad are," he said, reaching to hold Branda close to him as they finally snuggled under the cover for the night.

They chuckled a few more times as they felt the twins wiggling some more then finally settle down.

"Doesn't that hurt when they get too rambunctious?" Mitch asked.

"Mostly it's just very uncomfortable, unless my ribs get in the way. That can smart."

Branda and Mitch slept until dawn.

They spent the morning doing last minute packing, making sure mail delivery was on vacation mode, emptying perishables out of the fridge, seeing that the hideaway was tidy and locked, plus doing other necessary things.

"Thank goodness Ella and the others will be coming to dust, do some special cleaning, and check on things," said Branda. "Even when I used to take a short car trip, I always felt like I was forgetting to do something like lock the door or turn off the stove."

"That's normal. Just a touch of Obsessive Compulsive Disorder," said Mitch, smiling as he placed some shirts in one of his suitcases on the bed.

Reaching for a small pillow, lightly tossing it at him from where she stood nearby, she said, "OCD my uncle. I'm just cautious."

Looking toward her abdomen, he said, "See there. Your mom is getting violent. She knows I can't defend myself since she's pregnant." Turning to go to her, giving her a playful hug and kiss, he added, "But I have my ways of conquering her."

"Yes, and your daddy knows I conquer easily," she said, hugging and kissing him back.

The ringing phone interrupted. After listening, talking a moment, then hanging up, Mitch said, "That was advisor Edward. He was just filling me in on some business activity. He wants me to enter the information on my home computer as long as I'm here. We've made other arrangements for when I'm gone."

Hesitating a moment, he added, "Why don't you come downstairs with me to the study and help me enter the data? You have been so intelligent about learning the methods over the past months, I know you're ready to do this on your own."

"As long as you stand there and make sure I do it right."

"Not a problem," he said.

After she had finished entering the data, Mitch said, "Since you always say you have a hard time comprehending the amounts of money my businesses and investments generate, let's look up the financial report and see where we stand today."

"You'd better punch the buttons for accessing that. I might wipe you out," she said, smiling.

When the report filtered onto the screen, she could hardly believe her eyes.

"Jumpin' George! Is that section right? The one showing what you made yesterday? Four million dollars? Half of it from real estate, the other parts from oil, shipping, and diversified investments."

"That was a relatively slow day," Mitch said, laughing. "It varies from day to day. That's why we keep such close track."

"And that other section shows your overall worth as of today is still in the billionaire range. Have you paid for the airplane yet?" she asked.

"Yep. Sent the final payment off the other day when I knew you could fly like a bird."

"All of this money still doesn't seem real to me. Which reminds me. Thank you again for all of those new maternity clothes you wanted me to buy for the trip. Cynthia and I had a ball shopping . . . mostly at Neiman-Marcus, of course."

"You're welcome," he said. "Now then, how about we go have lunch and rest? We want to be ready for the ghosts and goblins coming to the door tonight."

"Good idea. I am hungry and a bit tired too. After I get up, and they are home from work, I want to call Sean, Cynthia, Mary Ann and the others to tell them good-bye one more time. I know we don't have to be out at the airport until tomorrow afternoon but I think it would be better if I called them early this evening before the neighborhood children come knocking on the door. There might not be time for calling tomorrow."

"Right. Good plan," he said.

After resting, then placing her calls, she told Mitch, "Everybody appreciated my calling but no one seemed to want to talk long."

"Maybe they were just tired from working all day."

"Yes, that could have been it. I sometimes forget how working all day can wear out a person. I really thought Sean and Cynthia might come over but Cynthia said they were really busy getting some things done before the ghosts began showing up."

"I expect so," Mitch said.

Following an early dinner that evening, they enjoyed seeing little kids coming around trick or treating accompanied by one or both parents.

After the last small group left, Branda said, "Those tiny ones are so cute saying twick or tweet."

Suddenly she grew tearful.

"What is it, Branda?"

"I'm sorry. It just sort of hit me that I might not be around to ever see Michele and Mitchell go around on Halloween."

Mitch kneeled down, reaching to comfort her. Knowing there were no words he could say that would really help at this moment, he gently lifted her from the wheelchair and carried her to the living room couch. After turning on softly played guitar music, he sat holding her in his lap, trying to soothe her as he would a small child.

A short time later while getting ready for bed, she said, "Thank you, Mitch. You understand me so well. I really did not feel like talking a while ago and you sensed that."

"I've been that way myself," he said, giving her a hug.

He held her as both fell into a dreamless sleep. Neither knew the vision was watching over them. Nor did they know until morning that small pieces on both her legs had disappeared.

Distressed as they were when they discovered the disappearances, Branda seemed determined to make the best of it and concentrate on the 'Grand Tour' as she called the trip.

Later that afternoon heading for the airport in a stretch limousine, Branda said, "I feel like a princess or movie star."

"You're even better," he said, turning to quickly kiss her as she sat closely beside him.

"You'd better watch out doctor. This seat is awfully roomy," she said, smiling.

Briefly kissing again, the two then sat in companionable silence, holding hands, watching the scenery along I-270 unroll as they sped by and connected to the panorama along I-70 leading closer to what is formally known as Lambert-St. Louis International Airport.

Heading toward the executive parking area, Branda asked, "Don't we have to go through customs before we leave?"

"Yes, but I've arranged for four officials to come out to where the plane is parked. There will be a long folding table set up and as luggage and your new lighter weight wheelchair are unloaded from the limo, they can check all that as well as our passports and visas. You'll be riding in your regular chair, which they will also probably inspect. I may have to lift you out of it momentarily. They're very thorough here. There will be a portable screening device to check us out for illegal devices and so on. I'll have to empty my pockets and they will probably examine your purse contents."

Branda asked, "Then after all of that is over, the luggage goes on board to one place or another, right?"

"Right," answered Mitch. "And baggage handlers or anyone else having a need to go in and out of the plane will be screened."

"And I get on board like I did for the Denver trip using that special lift ramp you had installed in the plane's aft section near our bedroom?"

"Right. I will ride up with you as before."

"By the way, Mitch, you're right about that new chair coming in handy sometimes for 'lighter travel' as you said. Thank you again . . . for it and everything else," she said looking meaningfully at him, knowing he would understand she meant more than the few words she spoke.

"You are most welcome, Branda," he said, returning her look.

As the driver maneuvered the limo closer toward the plane, Branda glanced at the silvery jet in surprise.

She gasped, and exclaimed, "Mitchell Andrews!!! When did you have that done?"

Feigning ignorance, he asked, "Have what done?"

"You know what! Have "J. George" painted on the side underneath the pilot's window!!! And in Wedgewood blue to match the other detailing. Oh Mitch. I don't know what to say. That is such a sweet and special surprise. So typically you. And I'll remember my grandfather every time I look at that since he taught me those words to use instead of ever cussing."

"And when I see or hear you say them, I'll think of how beautiful you looked that first day in my office. Remember, I asked you about those words?"

"I sure do," she said. "I thought you considered me a silly nut for saying them."

"No way. They tickled me, still do. They are so uniquely yours."

After Mitch lifted her out of the limo, helping her into her regular wheelchair, she looked more closely at the new artwork, admiring it.

Reaching for Mitch as a signal for him to lean down, she gave him a hug and kiss he would long remember. Michael the limo driver, customs officials, baggage handlers, and other ramp assistants cheered, whistled, and clapped in a good-natured way.

Though a bit embarrassed, the couple smiled and acknowledged the ovation.

Turning to Michael, Branda said, "Thank you for the safe drive to the airport."

Mitch added, "And for helping handlers unload luggage and wheelchairs."

"You're entirely welcome," said Michael.

After clearing customs and thanking everyone nearby for their assistance, the couple waited a moment longer watching their luggage going up the conveyor belt toward the cargo hold. Three baggage handlers had already taken the couple's inspected carry-on luggage, garment bags, and folded up wheelchair on board placing them in the master bedroom. Mitch kept his black bag handy as usual.

When the time came to get on board, Branda said, "Well I'm starting to get the flutter-butters a little bit. I can't help wondering what's ahead of us."

"One never knows," Mitch said, locking her wheelchair in place on the special lift ramp. "One never knows," he said again as they ascended toward the open side doorway.

Drawing level with the doorway entrance, the next words they heard were, "SURPRISE, BRANDA, SURPRISE!"

All of the friends she had told good-bye were there; Sean, Cynthia, Mary Ann, Linda, Mathilda, Reverend Cummings, and Martha. Then Woody and Joe, the Park's pilots, stuck their heads into view.

Speechless for a moment, she finally was able to ask, "What on earth is going on?"

"We're going as far as Paris with you and stay a week, compliments of your sweet husband," Mary Ann explained.

"Joe and I are just going along for the ride and head right back home tomorrow night. We have to work Monday," said Woody.

"Oh, Mitch, how wonderful," said Branda, tears of happiness coming down her cheeks. "Oh how wonderful!"

CHAPTER TWENTY

TALKING A MILE A MINUTE, the group filled Branda in about some behind the scenes planning that had gone on to protect Mitch's surprise.

"We were put on a deep secret red alert after Mitch took you on that first airplane ride in early October," Cynthia said. "After that flight and the others, it was man your battle stations. He and Judge Limson were a big help though in helping all of us get our passports, visas and so on. Mitch, the judge, and Sean did everything they could to help in anyway needed."

Sean added, "In case you didn't notice during Thursday night's dinner party, some of us were pretty uptight for fear we would spill the beans."

"I did notice," Branda said. "I mentioned to Mitch that most of you seemed . . . different; not the flight crew and guards as much though."

"They were a bit nervous too but just controlled it better," said Mary Ann.

"Annie and Bill were invited on this trip, but just couldn't make it," said Linda. "They send their love and best wishes though."

"I was in the middle of doing last minute packing when you called last evening," said Mathilda.

The rest echoed similar information.

"I thought all of you sounded funny . . . like you didn't want to talk," Branda said.

"We couldn't . . . at least I couldn't," said Mathilda. "Besides getting last minute details taken care of, I was trying to get ready for the trick or treat gang."

"Besides," said Mary Ann. "I think all of us were again afraid we would let something slip about the surprise and tip you off."

"Right," added Reverend Cummings.

Martha said, "For a moment I thought Charles was actually going to go against his Baptist grain and tell a white lie to get off the phone. He was putting the finishing touches on the sermons for his replacement to give while we are gone and I was busy with final packing and getting ready for ghosts and goblins. Although we pretty much knew in plenty of time about going, there's always lots of last minute things to do before leaving on a trip . . . especially one like this."

The group chuckled at the idea of a Baptist minister even thinking about telling a white lie.

"Oh come now, I'm not that rigid. At least I don't think I am," said Reverend Cummings, smiling.

Changing the subject, Woody said to Mitch, "Joe and I have checked out this fancy bird. It sure is a winner . . . especially if it flies as good as it looks inside and out."

"I had experts helping me," Mitch explained.

"Well," Woody continued, "You definitely have adequate accommodations for everybody. That certainly includes those four bedrooms for crew with two wider than usual twin beds in each plus a chair, nightstand between beds, and a closet with drawers, shelves, and rod for hanging clothes. Four showers, four lavatories, and a lot of storage areas also enlarge the overall comfort zone. Your communications center, master bedroom with its king-size bed, two elegant chaise lounges, walk-in closet, and roomy bath are awesome."

Putting in his two cents worth, Joe added, "Those comfortable wider than usual seats that recline for sleeping along one side and couches along the other side are nifty. Each couch looks like it will recline into a double bed. It also looks like seats one, two, five, and six can have the head and foot reversed so a passenger can face forward like the others if they want to watch a movie."

"That's right," said Mitch.

Continuing, Joe said, "I'm glad there are nearby tables included in all seating arrangements. Now if we can just get up some poker games. Oh, sorry Reverend. I guess you don't believe in card playing."

"Please let me put your minds at ease," said Reverend Cummings. "First thing is, call me Charles. As far as cards and so on are concerned, just because I might not enter in I don't want to be a wet blanket. Please enjoy yourselves. That goes for having your usual cocktails and drinks. Mitch assured me he has plenty of sparkling cider, ginger ale, and such on board for his non-drinking passengers. I promise I won't give a temperance sermon. Actually, I used to play a good game of poker years ago before being ordained and a long-neck Pearl beer was my favorite adult beverage of choice."

"Why we even won a jitterbug contest in our younger days," Martha volunteered. "I still use the set of TV trays we won."

Seeing others in the group visibly relax, Branda said, "You two will have to have a talk with Sean and Cynthia. They used to be in dance contests too. In fact, why don't those of you who care to, enjoy yourselves with some dancing now or later . . . anytime. There is a stereo system on board."

"We just might take you up on that," Cynthia said.

As with most mixed-sex groups, it wasn't long until men were clumped together talking about the airplane; women, in another knot, chatting about decorations. Everybody had finally moved a bit forward to the seating area away from the wheelchair entrance, including Branda and Mitch.

"I love the basic decorating theme using pastel shades of sage green, apricot and cream. So restful," Mathilda said.

"Totally," agreed Linda. "Using the same colors in deeper tones and varying designs for the couches and recliner seats is a nice touch. And it sure is a great idea having those ceiling tracks with privacy curtains attached so they can be pulled around to cordon off each separate seating and couch area. I know you didn't pick any of this out, Branda, but it looks like you might have since I know these colors are some of your favorites . . . as well as the Wedgewood blue on the exterior of 'J.George'."

"Mitch really surprised you with having that name painted on the plane, didn't he?" asked Mary Ann. "Being careful so you wouldn't see us, we managed to peek out a window or two when you drove up and first saw it."

"You can say that again," Branda answered. "He has surprised me with a lot lately."

"And some of it was even by accident, wasn't it?" asked Mary Ann, giving Branda, Linda, and Mathilda a playful knowing glance.

The four smiled broadly, managing not to go into gales of laughter as they had the night of the first big dinner party May 31st; the night Branda had told them her marriage of convenience had gotten sidetracked because of having accidental sex.

All conversation was interrupted by the arrival of Chad and Bonnie coming on board announcing they had food to put in the two back to back aft galleys across from the wheelchair entrance.

Branda asked, "Are you two going along too?"

"No," said Bonnie. "Mitch invited us, but we just can't leave right now. It's a bit too close to Thanksgiving . . . one of our busiest times."

"But we do appreciate the offer," said Chad.

"Is that dinner you're bringing?" asked Branda.

"Yes, plus assorted snacks, hors d'oeuvres, and breakfast," Bonnie explained.

"And what are we dining on this evening?" Branda asked.

"You have a choice of filet mignon, steamed whole Maine lobster, and chicken and dumplings. The last one is a special request of Woody. Seems he's nuts about the dish," said Chad. "Side dishes include Caesar salad, fresh asparagus with hollandaise sauce, twice-baked potatoes, and Parker House rolls. Dessert choices are Chocolate Creme Brulee, white layer cake with fresh lemon filling, and assorted flavors of Hagen Daz ice cream." Continuing, Chad asked, "Mitch did the beverages arrive okay?"

"Yes, thanks. They've been on board since this morning. I checked earlier while Branda was getting dressed."

Having seen through the window in the flight attendant's permanent bedroom quarters for two that the catering truck had pulled up, Alan, Grant, Ted, and Norman came out and went to help unload the food; stopping briefly to greet everyone.

Earlier, from a short distance in mid-cabin, they had watched Branda's friends surprise her. Not wanting to interfere with the old home week atmosphere, they had retreated to the bedroom.

Since Ted and Norman were temporary attendants only going as far as Paris to help serve food, drinks, and attend needs of the extra passengers, they would be sleeping in reclining seats numbers five and six during the night. Mitch had paid for the men's return commercial flight.

As soon as food was squared away in the galleys and Chad and Bonnie had given preparation and serving instructions to the attendants, the couple said good bye.

Bonnie explained, "We would love to stay and visit longer but we have to go work a few more hours on a special order for tomorrow . . . a dinner party for fifty."

Mitch and Branda thanked them for the food.

"I know it will be super," said Branda, reaching up to give each a hug and kiss on their cheeks as they leaned down.

"I second that," Mitch said, kissing Bonnie's cheek and shaking Chad's hand.

After they left, Mitch turned to the group and asked, "How about a drink before dinner?"

"How about a couple," kidded Woody.

"You're on," Mitch replied.

Ted and Norman acted as bartenders while Alan and Grant busied themselves with food preparation after bringing out nuts, snack crackers, and hot hors d'oeuvres.

Branda looked up at Mitch from her wheelchair as she sat sipping Just Cranberry juice diluted in water. "Are we going to eat before we take off or after?"

"According to plan, shortly after. Is that all right or are you hungry now?"

"That's fine."

"I know that lobster dinner is calling to you," he said, smiling.

"Well, you know how these kids love it," she quipped.

Sean walked up to them and asked, "Mitch, what do you have in stock for in-flight movies?"

"Well, your favorite of course . . . "Casablanca" and Cynthia's "An Affair to Remember" with Cary Grant and Deborah Kerr plus a couple with airplanes . . . "Strategic Air Command" and that old one about the "Hellcats." I also ordered "Music Man" and "Singing in the Rain" for those liking musicals.

There are others I can't recall now. Anyway, I know there won't be time to watch them all, but at least there is a wide selection. The screen drops from the ceiling in the forward cabin. Headsets for listening to movie, radio, or stereo sound are inside right armrests of seats and right and left armrests in couches. In the left armrests of seats, there are trays that pull up and flip over to use for eating, playing solitaire, or whatever. In couches, trays pull up from an inside slot tucked between each armrest and seat."

"Boy howdy, you thought of everything," said Sean.

"I hope I didn't forget anything . . . or at least anything important," Mitch said.

Branda asked, "Mitch, do you think I might have time to rest a bit before we take off? Everybody is having such a good time talking and visiting, I don't think I'll be missed."

A cheerful voice behind her answered, "Yes, you'll have time to take a rest but you will be missed."

Captain Charles Elkins, better known as Sonny because of his unusually pleasant disposition, came into her view along with Captain Matthew "Doc" Robertson. Co-pilots, Patrick O'Hara and Bob Edwards appeared on the other side of her wheelchair. Sonny and Bob would fly the first leg to Paris. Doc and Patrick would relieve them after eight hours and complete the landing at Orly Airport 14 kilometers south of the city.

Mitch shook hands with all of them. As they leaned to give Branda a kiss on whichever cheek was handy, she gave them one in return. During the Denver flight, they had become friends. All crew members adored her and felt extremely sorry about her affliction.

Sonny said, "We have already stored our gear on board, will go check the weather, do the walk around with security guards Duke and Crunch in tow, go through the check list, wait for clearance, and see if we can't get 'J. George' on the way at 7:30 p.m. as planned."

Branda said, Sounds good to me. And since Duke and Crunch have been outside guarding "J. George" all this time, I imagine they will be glad to finally get settled in their bedroom quarters . . . after they eat that is." Looking at the men standing around her, she asked, "And what are you going to choose tonight for your dining pleasure . . . steak, lobster, or chicken and dumplings?"

"Wow!" exclaimed Patrick. "I may try all three entrees."

After chatting a moment or two more, the men began leaving to go start their routine. Picking up his nearby black bag, Mitch followed Branda as she headed for their bedroom.

Upon opening the door, she exclaimed then asked, "Mitchell Andrews!!! What other surprises do you have?" She was looking at Betty propped up against headboard pillows.

"I thought you might get homesick for each other."

"You really are something else, Mitch. Thank you," said Branda.

"You're welcome," he said, reaching toward the wall above the foot of the bed.

"What's up there?" she asked.

"Watch," he said, pushing one spot until a panel slid open revealing an open space lined with Wedgewood blue velvet. This is Betty's secret hiding place when we're not around. It's large enough for her to lie down. The rest of the time she'll have to be strapped in during flight so she doesn't bounce around or, in the worse case scenario, become a flying object. We can seat belt her to the bed or one of the chaise lounges . . . whatever is not in use."

"Well, jumpin' George. You do think of everything," Branda said, reaching for him to lean down so she could kiss him.

"Excuse me for a moment, Branda. I want to check and see where the baggage handlers stored our luggage, garment bags, and that fold up wheelchair."

Finding them in the walk-in closet just beyond the bathroom, he said, "We'll sort that out a bit later except for the wheelchair. Do you want it or your regular one kept in here?"

"If it's all right with you, I'll keep the folding one in the bedroom. I'll try using it more to save battery power in this one."

"Good idea," Mitch said. "I'll put your regular one in that special wheelchair storage area just outside our bedroom door."

After having Mitch help her get ready for her nap and tucking her in, she fell asleep almost instantly.

The last thing she remembered was seeing Mitch put his black bag on the floor at his side of the bed and having him pat her stomach, saying, "Now calm down you two, your mother needs her rest. You do too."

The next thing she heard was the door being opened and Mitch saying, "Branda, better wake up now and get strapped in . . . either with the bed-belt or the chaise lounge seat belts. We're getting ready to go."

"Oh, I want to sit out front with the others. Do I have time to go to the bathroom and get out there?"

"Yes. I'll call Sonny on this bedroom intercom phone to the cockpit and give him a status report. He asked me to check on you."

"Okay . . . but don't tell him he has to wait until I go to the bathroom," she said laughing.

"Oh I expect he's heard it all before in his time," Mitch said, laughing along with her. "He is also reminding people on board to shut off cell phones, pagers, and other electronic devices that might interfere with navigational equipment. Since we're going to be in close quarters, we might as well deactivate our gadgets as you call them."

"I've had one on for so long, I won't feel natural with it turned off. Will any of the equipment in your communications room on the other side of our bedroom wall interfere if it's turned on?"

"Not at all. And I hope the extra phone in here connecting me to the outside world never rings while you're resting; nor the red light begins flashing if a message is coming into the communications room."

"Are you expecting a lot of calls . . . or flashes?" asked Branda.

"No. I think my advisors, lawyers, and others pretty much cleared up things beforehand. But one never knows."

Once out in the cabin, Mitch lifted Branda onto forward- facing couch four; closest to their bedroom. Sean and Cynthia sat opposite on couch three, a small coffee table in between.

Preferring to keep her legs covered when seated with other people around, she arranged the cream-colored lightweight cashmere lap robe Mitch had given her. She had learned on the Denver flight that airplanes could get chilly inside.

For safety during takeoff, he placed her wheelchair in its storage area with the other one, coming back to sit beside Branda.

Hearing engines revving, she said, "Oh Mitch. It looks like we're really going on this adventure."

Standing just outside the closed cockpit door, attendant Grant Larkin announced over the intercom, "Welcome aboard flight 'J. George.' Please fasten your seat belts and prepare for takeoff."

After instructing everyone how to use oxygen masks should the cabin lose pressure, and giving other instructions per regulations, he added, "If there is anything I or the other attendants can do to make your flight more comfortable, please turn on the call light above your seat."

As the plane began backing away from its gate, Sonny's voice was heard advising flight attendants to "please take your seats."

"How are all three of you doing?" asked Mitch, turning toward Branda.

"All of us are just fine and I'm excited as usual about taking off."

Mitch said, "As you know we'll taxi forever first. Also, if you'll notice, everybody on board will get very quiet until we are well up in the sky."

Finally roaring down the runway, Branda said, "Here we go. We're close to wheels in the well time."

Waiting to hear a slight whining followed by the thump sound as landing gear was going up and getting locked, she added, "And off we go."

"You're beginning to sound like a veteran flyer," Mitch said, giving her a smile.

Smiling back at him then peering out the window, she exclaimed, "Oh Mitch, look. There's the Arch. The fading sunlight shining on it makes it look like a beacon of some sort."

"And how would you describe the Mighty Mississippi Mrs. Poetic?" he asked, jokingly.

"Well, let's see Smarty Pants." After looking at the river for a moment, she continued, "Okay. I would say, as far as the eye can see in either direction the Mississippi is winding its way sinuously along its riverbed."

"Look out Carl Sandburg!"

Both laughed.

"Hey . . . you're right," she said. "Everybody did stay quiet until we began getting higher."

"And now they will get noisy."

Later, she told him he was right about that too.

After reaching cruising altitude, Sonny announced, "You may now loosen your seat belts but please leave them fastened in case of any unexpected turbulence. Enjoy your flight."

Moments later, Grant announced, "We'll be coming to take your dinner and drink orders now."

Mitch stood up, asking, "Charles, would you say a prayer now before we eat?"

"Of course," he answered, standing to say, "Heavenly Father, we thank You for the food we are about to eat and for watching over all of us during this journey. We also pray Mitch and Branda are successful in their search. And God bless both of them for their thoughtfulness and kindness. Amen."

"Thank you, Charles," Mitch said.

"You're welcome," said Charles.

Attendants distributed food and drink while classical music played softly in the background.

Branda said, "I love this dining room in the sky and . . ." Stopping suddenly, she added, speaking quietly, "Do you see what I see out of the window, Mitch?"

Peering around her to look, he whispered, "Well, it looks like we have quite a vision type escort."

Leaning forward, Cynthia said, "I see them too; the whole group."

"Where?" asked Sean quietly so those seated nearby in their assigned places could not overhear. "Where? I want to see them too . . . Oh! Oh! Now I do. Oh my gosh. Now I do. Tell me again who they are."

Cynthia explained.

In a few moments, the vision disappeared in the usual silvery mist.

After the meal that everyone declared better than delicious, the group decided to watch "Casablanca."

Most dozed a bit off and on throughout the movie.

Afterwards, Mitch and Branda told everyone goodnight and went to their bedroom; Mitch carrying her like a bride.

"I'll get your wheelchair after I get you settled," he told her.

"Mitch, would you mind getting out that framed High Flight poem I packed in that small overnight bag? I want to hang it in here. I brought some of those adhesive hangers you just stick on a wall."

"Not a problem," he said, going off to find the poem and hang it for her in a space between windows.

"Thank you. Now I can read the poem and look outside to get the full effect of what it means. Whoa, kids! Boy are they starting to move around."

"Yes, I see they are," said Mitch.

By the time the couple finally got to bed, the twins had calmed down a little bit.

Lying close, Mitch reached to pat Branda's stomach, "You've had a busy day, but it's time to go to sleep now."

Looking out at the sky with stars twinkling and moon shining like heavenly night-lights, the couple moved even closer to each other.

They kissed, touched, and explored, letting passion at last consume them. But even in the white-hot heat of it Mitch was careful to not lie too near her stomach.

After lying happily satisfied afterwards, Branda smiled and said, "I noticed you stayed out of the line of fire."

"Yes, I remembered those gold medal-caliber kicks they gave me the other night," he said, smiling back.

Both laughed softly, kissing gently.

"Mitch" said Branda. "I hope these bedroom walls are soundproof."

He laughed and said, "Actually, I did have extra insulation put in. I told the workers we were extra sensitive to outside noises."

"And I'll bet they knew better," she said, chuckling.

Later, after helping her to the bathroom and both were back in bed, Mitch asked, "Do you know you are now a member of a special club?"

"What are you talking about?" she asked.

"When people make love in an airplane . . . way up in the air, that is, they are considered to be members of the mile high club."

"Oh for heaven's sake, Mitch," she said, smiling. "That almost sounds decadent. But maybe that's why our lovemaking seemed rather special this time. It was the altitude."

"Perhaps, but I'd rather think it was because of my expertise," he quipped.

Gently laughing for a moment, she gave him a sexy kiss, then said, "I think my womanly wiles caused it."

Holding her closer while he kissed her long and tenderly, he finally said, "Maybe it was a bit of both."

They were too satisfied to make love again at the moment, falling asleep lying as close as possible to each other, lips touching.

Awakening a couple of hours later, wordlessly, tenderly, they began making love, once again reaching new levels of ecstasy.

Afterwards, Mitch said, "Oh Branda. You are incredible. I love you so much. I can't seem to get enough of you."

"I feel the same way, Mitch. I feel the exact same way."

After checking the time on the nightstand clock by his side of the bed, he said, "It's three fifteen. We can get in another nap before we have to get up for breakfast and our early morning arrival in Paris."

The ringing phone woke them up just before the alarm went off.

"Hello," Mitch answered. "Yes, we're up and almost ready. Thanks for double checking." Turning to Branda, he said, "That was Doc. Remember . . . there was a crew switch during the night."

As she began moving to sit up, Betty's blank stare met her own. Something about it jiggled loose a hidden thought.

"I wonder if Mitch was already a mile high club member because of Helen? He didn't say anything about this time with me being his initiation. I won't ask though."

After greeting everyone in the cabin, they sat back on couch four waiting for their breakfast. Having marked down what they wanted the night before on a card, Ted brought their food almost immediately.

As they sat eating and chatting with Sean and Cynthia, Branda suddenly stopped and said, "Oh my jumpin' George. I can see dawn coming up way out there just over the horizon. How beautiful!"

"Yes, it is, "Mitch agreed. "And just wait until you see the City of Lights pop up on your window screen."

"I can hardly wait. Look out Paris, here we come."

CHAPTER TWENTY-ONE

Later, seeing Paris spread below in the cleansing radiance of the early morning light, Branda exclaimed, "Oh Mitch! It looks like some vast unbelievably beautiful patchwork quilt!!"

In her excitement, forgetting for a moment she was crippled and seat belted in, she made a move to stand up to get a better view.

"Oh damn," she said for the third time in her life. "Oops, sorry kids."

Mitch laughed and said, "I suspect they will hear more than that when they grow older."

"Yes, probably so, but their mother doesn't need to contribute to their delinquency so early," said Branda, moving her attention back and forth from window scenes to conversation, as were the others.

Sitting opposite them, Sean and Cynthia were also laughing.

"Don't think I ever heard you cuss before," said Sean.

"Me either," Cynthia said.

"I hope Rev. Cummings and Martha didn't hear me."

"I doubt if they did since you didn't say it very loud and they are sitting on their seat, couch number one," Cynthia said. "That's a bit of a distance between our number three couch and your number four. And somehow I don't think they would be seriously shocked."

"Besides, everyone is busy looking out at scenery and talking just like we are," offered Mitch, reaching to give her left hand a comforting pat, continuing to hold it. "And that word is mild compared to others. I really don't think it will send you straight to hell to say it now and again."

"I guess not, but we agreed to watch what we say," Branda said, glancing out the window again. "Oh my J. George!!! Is that the Eiffel Tower way out there?"

"Sure is. At least that's the way it looked when Dad and Mom brought me here and some other places as a high school graduation present," said Mitch. "And when did you decide to abbreviate your favorite expression?"

"I don't know. I guess it just popped out the way it's painted on the plane. I think I like it better than the original. I don't believe my grandfather would mind."

Sean and Cynthia joined in the congenial laughter that followed all of Branda's remarks.

"Have you ever been here?" Branda asked the couple.

"Yes. On our honeymoon," said Cynthia.

"Ah ha, so this can be like a second one for you," said Branda.

"We hope so," Sean said, as he and Cynthia looked at each other in a loving, meaningful way.

Mitch and Branda smiled at the couple's obvious happiness and intent.

Branda motioned for Sean, Cynthia, and Mitch to lean toward her as much as possible, and quietly said, "I don't know if you've noticed but I think there may even be some new romances in the air on this plane."

"What are you talking about?" asked Sean, echoed by Mitch.

"Men!" said Cynthia, gently chiding them. "I've noticed it too, Branda."

"Noticed what you two?" asked Mitch.

"Is this some more of your psychic talent at work, Cynthia?" Sean asked.

"No," she answered. "Branda, you try explaining."

"Well, if I'm not mistaken I think there has been some special attractions between Mary Ann and Alan, Linda and Grant, and Mathilda and Patrick. Ted and Norman are interested too but not as much. Is that what you think, Cynthia?"

"Yep. Right on the money. I even went so far as to check and find out if the men are single since I didn't want the ladies to get hurt. Patrick has been married, but is divorced. The others are single. Of course, Sonny, Doc and Bob are married as are Joe, Woody, Duke, and Crunch."

"My lord," said Sean. "How did you find out all of that?"

"By striking up conversations and asking them . . . in a subtle way of course," Cynthia explained. "Also, the married men showed me pictures of their wives and children and aren't interested in anyone else."

"And here I thought we were just flying along in J. George enjoying the ride," Mitch said. "Must be one of those woman things to figure out all this romance is in the air stuff."

"Hey city slicker, it's thangs not things," Branda joshed, smiling at him and adding, "If you just pay attention you'll see chemistry at work. I know you understand that brand of chemistry . . . don't you?"

His knowing returned smile and light squeeze of her hand was her answer.

Looking toward Cynthia, Mitch said, "Well, if you had asked me I could have saved you some sleuthing trouble and told you which man is and isn't married. That information was included in the reports I received when I was having them checked out. Of course there were no reports on Joe or Woody since I already knew them and they are just along for the ride but I could have told you they are married."

"Oh well . . . my way was more fun," kidded Cynthia.

As those seated across the aisle looked out, their comments rose from murmuring stage to louder decibel levels. None of the women had ever been out of the United States except for Mathilda who had once gone to Mexico City. Nor had Charles and Martha traveled abroad.

"This makes St. Louis look like a small town," Mary Ann said.

"I can't believe what I'm looking at," said Linda.

"Nor I. It is so lovely," added Mathilda. "I can hardly wait to get on the ground and go see all possible during the week."

Charles and Martha spoke up saying they also wanted to see everything they could.

Before doing their last routine cabin check and going to sit down for landing, Mitch did notice Alan and Grant seemed especially attentive to Mary Ann and Linda with Ted and Norman hovering near all the ladies including Mathilda. He wondered if Patrick would be hovering around Mathilda too if he wasn't busy in the cockpit.

Joe and Woody divided their time between looking out the window and paying attention to the plane's performance.

Sonny and Bob were in their bedrooms finishing packing and preparing for landing. Duke and Crunch were also in their bedroom waiting.

Branda had turned all of her attention to looking out at the view . . . oooing and ahhing now and then.

"This is just like getting to go to the circus for the first time as a little kid," she said, radiating excitement, not moving her eyes from the panorama below.

After landing, clearing a special customs check Mitch had arranged, the group split and got into two stretch limos, heading for Le Grand Hotel located next to the ornate Paris Opera Garnier building.

All luggage, plus Branda's regular wheelchair, was put into the SUV type limo that was better configured for holding such items.

Now that he had been given a chemistry lesson by Branda and Cynthia, Mitch understood why Alan, Grant, and Patrick elected to ride along with his group in the regular limo instead of joining the rest of the flight crew, Joe, Woody, Duke, and Crunch in the other vehicle. Of course, Joe and Woody wanted to talk 'airplane' with Sonny, Doc, and Bob.

Mitch had screened and hired extra local rotating security teams to guard the plane for a week so Duke and Crunch could see Paris. He figured there would be other places along the trip where he could not find relief help for them.

Both assured him they still wanted to go out and check on J.George from time to time just to make sure all was okay.

Sitting beside Mitch, Branda asked softly, "Do you think I made the right decision leaving Betty in her special place on the plane?"

"Yes, I think you will worry less about her being there than in the hotel room and we can't carry her around with us very well."

"I know. I'm just being silly," she said.

"No you're not. She has been your friend for a long time."

"I'm glad you understand . . . a grown woman worrying about a doll is a bit odd I guess."

"Not only is she your friend, she is a special connection to your mom and dad."

"Thanks, Mitch."

"You're welcome."

"And what do we do with my fancy diamond jewelry? I can't wear it all the time. If you've noticed, I've tried keeping it as hidden as possible so no one tries tracking us down and stealing it later."

"The hotel safe is the place for it when you don't have it on," he said. "And you are smart not to flash it around."

"I probably should have left it at home."

"Oh no. I gave it to you to wear, not stick in a safe all the time. I have some great memories connected to that jewelry," he said.

Branda tried not to blush but did. She was glad others were too busy talking and sightseeing to overhear her conversation with Mitch or see her blushing.

Along the route, the main words spoken by all in tandem or separately were "Oh my. Would you look at that and I never saw anything like that, did you?"

Alan, Grant, and Patrick had seen it all before but thoroughly enjoyed watching and hearing the newcomer's and second timer's responses.

After checking in, Mitch asked everyone to gather around while he explained some things. The concierge was taking care of the luggage. They found a private spot with chairs and couches.

"Would any of you like a drink . . . some Champagne perhaps?" he asked.

Most agreed the hour was a bit early for the bubbly so ordered orange or tomato juice or a soda. Joe and Woody decided to live it up and had Bloody Mary's.

"After all, we only have one day here," Joe said. "And it is afternoon back home."

Everybody laughed in a congenial way.

While waiting to be served, Mitch said, "I thought it might be a good idea to go over some arrangements I've made and see if you approve. First, I've hired some cars with drivers that are also trained guides and interpreters to take one or all of you anywhere you want to go anytime. They are on 24-hour standby. I'll give you the number to call. If you want a limousine, request it. Whatever you want is fine. If some of you want to go off in pairs, as a group, alone, or whatever . . . that's your decision. This includes all flight crew and guards too. The company I've hired knows all charges are to be made to me . . . including tips.

"Second . . . I am giving each individual $2,000 cash to spend anyway he or she wants to. Joe and Woody will have to hustle to spend theirs before they have to leave tonight on the redeye. Maybe they can find some trinket or other to take their sweet wives. Ted and Norman leave on tomorrow night's redeye so they too will have to hurry up and spend. However . . . if it's any consolation, I won't take it back if you don't spend any," he added, smiling.

"Good grief, Mitch," Sean interjected. "That is more than quite generous."

All certainly agreed and spoke their thanks. All were also dumbfounded.

Continuing, Mitch said, "Well, I appreciate what all of you have contributed in your own ways and this is one way I can thank you. I thank Branda's friends, now mine also, for coming along to Paris to keep her from perhaps becoming homesick thus far . . . and also for sharing their good company with all of us.

"Now, Branda and I have appointments to see doctors on Tuesday, Thursday and Friday afternoons, but other than that we would like to join you in some sightseeing if that would be all right. And maybe we could all have dinner together each night, or at least some nights, unless you have other plans. Please don't hold back from doing anything because of us. I want Branda to stay rested but to also have some enjoyment but we don't want to interfere with any of your plans.

"Also, take jet lag into account. You may want to rest a bit extra today and tomorrow to give your body clock time to catch up. That is, all of you except for Joe and Woody, the two party boys, who have to speed things up since they have to leave tonight on the redeye. I guess that also goes for Ted and Norman who leave on tomorrow night's redeye."

All laughed in a good natured way.

Branda thought, "Besides this cure-search trip itself and bringing along friends on this part to keep me from possibly becoming homesick, I also think Mitch is hoping these things will help keep me distracted from my ongoing losses. All of this may be helping him too. I notice he sometimes looks a bit . . . oh . . . distracted . . . frazzled . . . something . . . from time to time like some kind of sorrowful shadows are still following him and growing more bothersome."

The group sat or stood around mingling, murmuring, sipping their drinks, one by one going to personally thank Mitch for his unheard of generosity.

At one point he excused himself, asking them to please stay where they were, and went to the front desk. After speaking to the manager, he was escorted to a private office. Coming back out for a moment, he motioned for all of them to come join him.

"Please close the door," Mitch said to Woody who was the last to enter.

After introductions were made to the hotel's director, Monsieur Claude Ferchaud, Mitch took a briefcase from the desk, opened it and began handing out envelopes containing $2,000 to each person . . . including Monsieur Ferchaud for arranging to have the bills ready as Mitch had requested days earlier while still in St. Louis.

Before they left his office, Monsieur Ferchaud smiled and said, "I hope all of you left your diets at home and are prepared to enjoy my country's superb cuisine."

Everyone understood exactly what Monsieur Ferchaud meant during Joe and Woody's farewell dinner that night in the hotel's Restaurant Opera. All were seated at a large round table.

Words like fantastic, incredible, wonderful, and never tasted anything like this were spoken more than once.

Mary Ann declared, "I'm not going near my scale for a month."

The rest agreed that was a good idea.

The only thing that outdid the food came near the end of the meal during coffee and dessert. The twins decided to put on a spectacular show.

Seated on one side of Branda, Linda exclaimed, "Good grief! I can see those gymnastics even under your maternity top."

Laughing while placing a hand on her abdomen, Branda said, "You should try it from my side."

"Maybe they're fighting over that sea bass wrapped in parchment you had," offered Mary Ann.

Leaning closer, Mitch asked, "Are you okay, Branda? I know you got some rest this afternoon, but maybe you needed more."

"No, I'm fine. They'll settle down in a minute . . . I hope."

As all eyes began looking at the wiggling babies, Mathilda asked, "Mitch, do twins run in your family?"

"No . . . actually twins don't run in families despite popular belief," he answered. "At least that's what I was taught. Frequent repeats are just coincidence. I must admit though there seems to be a lot of coincidences sometimes."

Being considerate of her feelings, no one who knew about Branda's deceased twins brought up that subject and, for some reason, no one asked about twins on her side of the family. She wondered if the question had come up before when she wasn't around and had been answered. Whatever the reason, she was grateful.

Mathilda continued, "Pardon my curiosity, but I'd like to know more about twins, what makes them identical or fraternal?"

"I'm not sure if that's good dinner conversation," said Mitch, smiling.

"How about after dinner drink at the bar conversation for anyone interested?" asked Cynthia. "And since I know that stuff, being a nurse, why don't I take Branda up to your room, Mitch?"

"Thanks Cynthia, but I'd like to hear about it myself," said Branda. "For some reason I never thought to ask Mitch about some of the details."

After all were comfortably seated and served in the Foyer Bar Opera, Mitch began explaining.

"DNA testing is the only way to make sure if twins are identical or fraternal. Using a swab, a DNA sample is taken from inside the baby's cheek. The father's DNA determines the child's sex. Twins can be same sex or male and female.

"Zygosity is the characteristic of cell union that happens at conception. This determines if twins are fraternal or identical; not how they look.

"Monozygotic refers to one fertilized egg that splits into two genetically identical parts and shares the same DNA. Even though the babies are identical twins, their appearances can differ.

"Dizygotic, or fraternal twins, come from separate fertilized eggs. They may or may not look alike, just like other kinds of siblings do or do not. Twins may share one placenta or there may be two placentas, or two fused into one. There are a lot of variables where twins are concerned. Look on the Internet sometime and you'll get the idea."

"Thanks Mitch," said Mathilda. "I think it's nice you and Branda elected to be surprised about the twin's sex."

"Yep, we're old fashioned about that I guess," Branda said, feeling a twinge of guilt since she and Mitch did know thanks to the visions.

Cynthia asked, "Mitch have you read about that new ultrasound racket where people are lured into having their unborn babies photographed more or less as a fun thing to do?"

"Yes, and too much of the time the personnel are not trained professionals and the mother may be putting her child in harm's way," he said.

"What a world," said Sean.

After seeing Joe and Woody off to the airport to catch the redeye flight back to St. Louis, all went to bed. A repeat performance of dinner and drinks was done the next night for Ted and Norman.

Sunday and Monday, some had managed to do a bit of sightseeing nearby before the farewell dinners. The grandeur of the nearby Opera building drew them inside leaving them gasping in awe at the magnificent decor and furnishings.

When Mitch took Branda to see the Opera interior early Monday afternoon, she gently cried.

Sitting in her wheelchair at the foot of a grand staircase flanked by wonderful statues at the wide base plus two others a bit further up as the stairway narrowed, she said, "It is so incredible. That's why I'm crying. You know how beauty in any form often does this to me. I know Nature is God's artwork, but God created the men, maybe women, who did this so I think that counts as the same thing. And the lovely balustrade and candelabras! Fantastic . . . beyond words!"

Gently kidding her, he smiled and said, "Well we had better start carrying bales of tissues because the beauty in The Louvre alone will have you weeping for hours . . . to say nothing of the many other places crammed to their vaulted ceilings with wondrous eye delights."

Later on, at various times, all together or in pairs, group members swept through Paris in a sightseeing flurry, shooting miles of film, loving every minute, often meeting at night for dinner to discuss their day's treasured moments.

Although the flight crew had been to Paris many times before, they often joined the newcomers and second timers because they enjoyed being along. Of course, Patrick, Alan, and Grant had their own reasons to admire the city one more time.

One of the group's favorite nighttime dining experiences was in Montmartre at La Mere Catherine. Mathilda had surprised all of them when she requested "It Had to be You" from the strolling violin player then sang along in a beautiful alto voice, glancing often at Patrick.

Afterwards, after applause died down, Branda said, "I didn't know you could sing."

"I'm not sure I can, but I like to do it anyway," said Mathilda.

After having some champagne, Duke and Crunch got brave enough to try escargot.

"By golly, these are good," declared Duke.

"It's all the garlic, wine, and butter," Crunch said. "And the champagne," he added, laughing.

All of them had "done" the Bateaux-Mouches trip, nearly unhinging their necks looking from Rive Gauche (Left Bank) to Rive Droite (Right Bank) as the boat glided along showing off the Seine's panorama of historic sites and monuments.

Everybody was a bit surprised when Charles and Martha joined them for a look at Notre-Dame.

Martha said, "Besides just looking at the overall beauty, I also want to see those famous gargoyles."

"And I want to see the flying buttresses and stained-glass windows," Charles said. Smiling, he added, "Even we strict Baptists love beauty found in many different places."

The budding new romances grew and blossomed in the city that smiled so kindly on lovers. No one blinked an eye when one, two, or all three pairs disappeared, going off holding hands for long walks and sight seeing excursions.

After one such disappearance by Mary Ann and Alan, Branda commented to Mitch, "I wonder if Reverend Cummings and Martha know what is going on?"

Laughing, Mitch said, "I have a feeling they recognize lovebirds when they see them. After all they courted and fell in love. And I don't think they got their kids via some osmotic process. Charles may be religious but he's not a celibate monk."

"Oh Mitch, it's hard for me to think about my pastor making love. But, of course, you're right. I suspect he and Martha have succumbed to the love is in the air atmosphere of Paris as we have . . . and the second honeymooners. I've noticed an awful lot of afterglow some mornings."

"Oh Mitch, do you suppose anyone has noticed us?"

Laughing, he said, "I wouldn't be surprised honey. I wouldn't be surprised. Which reminds me, as I've said before, if lovemaking is getting to be too uncomfortable for you, please let me know."

"I will but so far so good. I'd say we're managing okay," she said.

"I'd say better than okay; especially now that I've got my twin dodging technique perfected."

Both laughed.

Mitch had been right about The Louvre affecting her tearful sense of beauty.

Sometimes she exclaimed excitedly about what she saw; at other times she remained studiously silent, absorbing what she saw, teardrops overflowing.

"Everything in here is my favorite," she said after touring all her endurance would allow in one day. "Of course the Mona Lisa is as special as they say, but the scope of The Coronation of Napoleon I at Notre Dame overwhelmed me. I know we can't see everything but the Oriental, Egyptian, Greek, and Roman antiquities . . . well just everything would be great. And seeing the real painting of The Gleaners was special. We had a print of that in our eighth grade room in Morley. And for me to see original paintings by Rembrandt, Rubens, Goya, Gainsborough, Leonardo da Vinci and so on is unreal. The laces, shimmering silks . . . how did they accomplish that? One of the horses looked so real I thought any moment it would twitch and shake a bothersome fly off its rump."

"I think you liked the statues too and other sculptures," Mitch said.

"Oh my yes. How could anyone make hard marble look so lifelike?"

"Wait until you see The Pieta at St. Peter's in Rome."

"I look forward to that. By the way I hope the nude paintings and statues in here didn't shock Reverend Cummings and Martha."

"I have a feeling they understand fine art very well. If not before, they may now," said Mitch.

A group tour through Versailles had everyone totally awed by the profusion of grandeur and opulent elegance. As in the Louvre, there was neither time nor endurance to see everything.

"But even a smattering is a feast for mind, eye, and soul," commented Branda. "And, Mitch, I'm glad we brought this motorized wheelchair so you don't have to wear yourself out pushing me around this fancy acreage."

"I must admit, I may have put on a new set of muscles pushing you in that fold-up model," he said, with a smile.

Before the week was over, those who wanted to had seen the Eiffel Tower, The Vendome Column with le petit Caporal Napoleon atop, The church of Saint-Germain-des-Pres; the oldest in Paris, The Arc de Triomphe on the Champs-Elysees, the Tuileries, the statue of Joan of Arc at Place des Pyramides, Luxembourg Palace and Gardens, Sorbonne Church, the flower market at Quai aux Fleurs, Place des Vosges; the oldest monumental square in Paris, Sacre' Coeur Basilica and what seemed like a myriad of other glorious Parisian offerings.

Close to a ream of postcards had been written and sent to folks back home. Branda and Mitch mailed several to Ella and the others taking care of the house, yard, and pool.

Mitch and Branda's doctor's appointments had stayed tucked in between excursions. No cure was found. The loss of a piece of her left leg in front of the second doctor was an unnerving experience for the doctor, Branda, and Mitch. After all three doctors had a consultation, they concluded the condition was some "autoimmune system aberration for which there is no known cure."

After leaving the three doctors after their verdict, Mitch told Branda, "That's double talk for they don't know. I'm sorry Honey."

After getting into the limo, Mitch turned her so she could lie back in his arms as she wept. He had raised the tinted glass privacy panel between them and the chauffeur.

Stroking her hair, he said, "We still have a long way to go. Someone will know something."

Feeling the babies suddenly begin squirming, she said, "I hope so. Oh how I hope so."

Looking up at Mitch, she saw tears in his eyes also. Feeling the need to say a prayer, Branda began reciting the 23rd Psalm.

"The Lord is my shepherd. I shall not want. He maketh me to lie down in green pastures. He leadeth me beside the still waters. He restoreth my soul. He leadeth me in paths of righteousness for His name's sake. Yea though I walk through the valley of the shadow of death, I will fear no evil; for thou art with me, thy rod and thy staff they comfort me. Thou preparest a table before me in the presence of mine enemies; thou anointest my head with oil. My cup runneth over. Surely goodness and mercy shall follow me all the days of my life; and I will dwell in the house of the Lord forever."

CHAPTER TWENTY-TWO

ALTHOUGH DOWNHEARTED ABOUT THE DOCTORS' negative verdict, the couple did their best to hide their feelings from the rest when they met for dinner that Friday evening.

After asking about and hearing the story, their friends expressed their sympathies then spent the remainder of the evening also trying to keep the atmosphere light and happy.

In an effort to ease the tension, Branda said, "And after all, this isn't exactly our first disappointment. Having already had my DNA, bone marrow and blood tested, been poked, prodded, stuck with needles, hooked up to monitors, acupressured, acupunctured, MRIed, hypnotized, undergone vitamin mineral therapy, learned some Yoga mind control techniques and so on back home . . . well . . . that is how it's gone so far with no breakthroughs. We're still hopeful though."

Later, after Mitch and Branda got into bed they watched the twins do some nighttime gymnastics.

"Oh Mitch," Branda said. "We just have to find a cure before it's . . . too late."

"I know honey, I know," he said, placing a hand on her abdomen then tenderly kissing her lips. Their lovemaking that night took on a deeper meaning than ever before.

The next day, Saturday, Mitch and Branda mostly rested and packed since Sunday was departure day for them as well as the others. They did go down to have lunch at La Terrasse just outside the hotel, watching people stroll by.

Their friends scattered to do their own thing. All met again that night for a farewell dinner, discussing some of their day's activities.

"I almost went to see if I could buy a five hundred dollar designer handkerchief," Mary Ann joked. "But Alan and I decided to just walk, talk, sit and look at scenery since this is our last day together . . . at least in Paris," she added, smiling.

Smiling back at her, Alan said, "That's right. We hope to see more of each other in days to come."

"We're hoping to do the same," said Grant, squeezing Linda's hand as he looked lovingly into her eyes.

"Ditto for us," echoed Patrick, leaning to kiss Mathilda's cheek.

"Well, well, well, so Paris really is the city for love," said Cynthia, giving Sean a special meaningful look.

Had anyone been watching under the table, they would have seen Charles and Martha holding hands; also exchanging a quick loving glance.

Sonny, Doc, Bob, Crunch, and Duke looked at all the lovebirds and smiled wistfully.

Sunday dawned bright and clear. When Mitch saw Branda was awake, he asked, "Honey, how would you feel about going to a Mass at Notre Dame? I checked and there is one in about an hour."

"Why, of course, if you would like. We have time before meeting the others in the lobby before all of us leave for our airports?"

"You bet."

Later, she was glad they had gone. The beauty of the building inside combined with what she later called the "theater" of the service, brought tears to her eyes.

She thought, "I have never seen Mitch look so reverent."

Afterwards, he said, "I offered up the Mass for a cure and thanks to God for both you and the twins."

She was overwhelmed.

Following the bustle of checking out, thanking Mitch for everything, saying good-byes, offering good luck wishes, and lots of hugging and kissing, the group parted, heading for their airports.

The St. Louis bunch was flying out of Charles de Gaulle Airport that afternoon; Mitch, Branda, the flight crew, and guards were going out of Orly aboard "J.George" continuing their cure quest.

After boarding "J. George", Branda checked on Betty in her cubbyhole.

"She's had a long nap and looks fine. I guess I'd better leave her here or strap her back on one of the chaise lounges like we did coming over."

"Good idea," said Mitch. "After all, at home she mostly sits in her chair."

Both laughed over their concern about the doll's well being.

Mitch and Branda sat seat belted on couch four waiting for take off.

Putting an arm around her shoulders, Mitch used his other hand to turn her face to his, kissing her tenderly for a long moment, then said, "I have a feeling everything is going to be just fine."

"Let's pray so, Mitch. Let's pray so."

She wished she hadn't noticed contradicting shadows in his eyes. She could not get rid of the feeling some deep-seated problem was bothering him. At times, she sensed he was as edgy and near to an emotional explosion as he was when they first met.

"Oh you're just being silly," she said to herself. "Probably something to do with pregnancy jiggling your hormones around. I wish I had a copy of that inspirational prose poem Desiderata to read. Most everyone would like that poem which is probably online or in a library book."

Both watched the runway blur past as "J.George" gained speed, rotated, and climbed out over Paris, heading for London. They waved good-bye to the Eiffel Tower way off in the distance.

Mitch said, "I wish we had had time to go to the L'Alsace region, taken a peek at Colmar and had a meal or two in Strasbourg at the Maison des Tanneurs. As I recall, that was something really special."

"It must have been to stay in your mind for so long," Branda said, smiling.

Since Sonny and Bob were at the controls, Doc and Patrick had come before takeoff to sit in cabin seats as did Duke and Crunch. Alan and Grant were in the jump seats until after takeoff then came back to see if Branda and Mitch needed anything. Since they didn't, the two attendants also went to sit near the others. Both had said for Branda and Mitch to switch on the light above if they needed anything.

When the men were out of earshot, Branda leaned toward Mitch saying quietly, "I sure felt sorry for those two and Patrick during the good-byes in the hotel lobby."

"Yes, watching lovers part is always sad. But it's nice they plan on seeing each other again. We'll have to make sure they get to talk to their girls when we call home."

"Great idea. By the way, Mitch, I want to thank you for this beautiful long light-wool skirt you bought for me in Paris. Now that I've switched from slacks to long skirts for more comfort and to better hide my disfigurement, this one makes me feel very elegant. This pastel blue color is heavenly."

"I'll try to buy you a skirt everywhere we go."

Before they knew it, Sonny was announcing everyone should buckle up for landing at Heathrow Airport in London.

"Oh, Mitch!" Branda exclaimed. "Look at all of those chimney pots on the house rooftops. Wish I could take a picture."

Again combining sightseeing with tests and consultations for three days, the couple sadly again found no cure but Branda was entranced with the city.

"If I hadn't seen anything but the Tower of London and the Crown Jewels in it, this trip would have been worthwhile," said Branda. "The Imperial State Crown, St. Edward's Crown, the crowns of Queen Elizabeth the Queen Mother and . . . well, the whole array is too elegant for words. The whole town is like touring through a history book."

"I totally agree. And I liked seeing and hearing Big Ben again. I remember it from my trip here as a young man."

A quick trip by train to Bath left both amazed at Bath Abbey and the Roman baths.

Mitch said, "I wish Charles could see that abbey's great East window containing fifty-six scenes from the life of our Lord. I read where it was destroyed in World War II then restored."

"I gather you didn't come here on your Grand Tour after high school?"

"Right. We pretty much stuck to the big cities, not outlying towns," he answered.

"On another subject," said Branda. "Have you noticed there have been no visions since that last one taking off from Lambert back home?"

"Now that you mention it, that's right. Odd isn't it?"

"Maybe we've been on the go too much," offered Branda.

"Or they decided to take a vacation trip too to somewhere heavenly like Cloud Nine."

"Oh Mitch," she said, laughing. "I hope they come back sometime."

"I'm sure they will. We haven't had our talk yet. Also, on another subject, Branda. What do you think of the idea of my hiring a nurse in London to continue with us?"

"I suppose that would be all right. But why?"

"Well, with nurse Cynthia and the rest of the women gone home, I thought you might like to have a female around on this all-male safari; someone you can talk to about woman things . . . oops sorry . . . thangs. She could also help supervise your daily exercises like Cynthia helped me do quite often and just be on hand for other nursing duties if needed."

"That might be a good idea at that," said Branda.

After making inquiries and having the lady checked out, Mitch hired Mary Green, R.N. She was in her mid-fifties, had auburn hair and brown eyes. She had been married but was divorced; no children. She chose couch one area for her "home away from home" as she called it, storing most of her clothing and other gear in the overhead compartment. For hanging clothes, Duke and Crunch shared their closet with her. Mitch would pay her fare back to London when the others headed for St. Louis.

Branda told Mitch, "Even though she is much younger, there is a special sweet, caring quality about Mary that reminds me of my mother."

"Yes, she seems like an unusually kind person."

The ongoing trip turned into a geographical kaleidoscope.

Again, between tests, having Mitch give her checkups, and Mary's exercise routines, sightseeing was also part of their lives. Mitch often called Dr. Cline to give him a report about Branda. Above all, he did not want her becoming fatigued.

Mitch also made business calls. He and Branda talked to Ella and the others on most Wednesdays, called Sean and Cynthia a lot, and had Alan, Grant, and Patrick talk to their ladies when he and Branda called Mary Ann, Linda, and Mathilda. He and Branda left the communications room during those calls so the men could take turns and have privacy. The other men also called home frequently. Everyone sent home postcards and letters quite often.

"You don't need to worry about me getting worn out," Branda told Mitch. "In case you haven't noticed, I'm like a kid in a candy story seeing all of these wonderful places. I couldn't choose which is my favorite if I had to. I want to grab all the scenery in sight. And the thrill of adventure, as they say, keeps me from becoming overtired. Besides, you and Mary watch over me like two mother hens . . . or a rooster in your case . . . making me rest a lot. And I thank you both."

Ashford Castle in Cong, County Mayo, Ireland was such an elegant place it drew Branda's beauty-sensitive tears.

Mitch had told her, "The castle is situated on the shores of Lough Corrib, the second largest lake in Ireland."

"Well, I never thought I'd be spending the night in a castle," Mary said. "It's a bit overwhelming and I love it."

All, including the other men, had dinner in the formal dining room. Afterwards, they went down to the dungeon and listened to a marvelous Irish tenor.

Before going to dinner, Mitch had surprised Branda with a white Irish wool long skirt and matching blouse; lightweight and soft as down.

"Thank you, Mitch. Very much," she said, having him lean down so she could kiss him. "Now just how did you manage to get this exquisite ensemble?" she asked.

"I have my ways, woman. I have my ways."

"This calls for diamond jewelry," she told him.

"You're right," he said, smiling, hoping the evening would dull the negative report given earlier by the Dublin doctor they had come to see. The doctor's test and research had not offered any hope.

The couple agreed making love that night in a castle while she wore her diamonds was a definite memory producer.

Branda was further entranced by peat bogs, thatched roofed cottages and the general loveliness of Ireland.

"They aren't kidding about it being the greenest and loveliest shades of green ever," she said.

She was also stunned by the beautifully illuminated manuscripts of the Book of Kells in the Trinity College library in Dublin.

The warmth, comfort and charm of the Renvyle House Hotel in Connemara was also special. Seeing a big dog resting on an entranceway rug made her feel like she was coming home. His name was Jaimie and he wagged his tail in greeting as she reached from her wheelchair to pet his head.

The rest of the trip telescoped into a blur. No one saw the Loch Ness Monster in Scotland, a special mineral mud-bath in Sweden produced no cure, nor were there any positive results in Germany.

"But I sure did enjoy seeing that Glockenspiel in Munich plus all of the other city wonders," said Branda. "And getting to see the magnificent Lipizzaner horses perform at The Spanish Riding School of Vienna was absolutely soul-touching."

"Also in Vienna, The State Opera House in Ringstrasse was also a wonder to behold," said Mary. "And the city of Innsbruck, Austria with that fantastic snowcapped mountainous background looks like a picture postcard."

"Totally," agreed Mitch. "And the Castle of Hohen Salzburg sitting high above the beautiful city was another wonder to behold."

"Yes, and I loved that winged altar by Michael Pacher," said Branda. "As they say, so much to see, so little time."

The well traveled plane crew, and Duke and Crunch, particularly enjoyed Lucerne, Switzerland's covered bridges.

"The artwork inside them makes them so unusual," said Duke. Crunch agreed.

Having flown over the Alps many times before, the pilots and copilots had great respect for their beauty as well as their height.

Although seeing the beautiful setting of Lourdes was quite special, the curative waters did nothing for her that she could tell.

Since Branda loved Spanish guitar music, they made a jaunt to Madrid.

The group dined al fresco with a full moon shining above while listening to a concert-quality guitarist play many haunting melodies. Two of Branda's favorites, Malaguena and Cielito Lindo were included.

Knowing how such music stirred Branda's blood, Mitch leaned close to her whispering, "I have a feeling this night will be one I will remember in a special way."

Squeezing his hand under the table, she whispered back, "Yes. Me too."

Sensing romance in the air, the others said good night and drifted off to their respective rooms leaving the couple alone.

Branda and Mitch sat a while longer feeling sorry for those who had to sleep alone this night.

Just as they were getting ready to leave their table, an old woman dressed like a gypsy came to them.

Pointing to Branda, she said, "You will have your boy and girl then leave for other realms and maybe or maybe not return. You have the disappearing disease. There is no cure."

Mitch was livid. Branda came close to fainting. The guitar player ran the old lady off, apologizing and telling them not to believe her.

"She is always saying things to be dramatic," he said. "I didn't see her coming or I would not have let her near you. It's her way. Sometimes, she suddenly appears as if from a mist."

Mitch generously tipped the musical artist who tried to refuse because of the incident, but Mitch insisted.

"What is your name?" Mitch asked.

"Roberto Olivas."

"Thank you for your wonderful music," Branda managed to say.

"My pleasure."

Although their former mood was shattered, the couple held each other close, comforting one another. Towards dawn, they made love with a sense of desperation; as if their moments for doing so were becoming more and more limited. Even the twins seemed to sense some haunting change because they remained quite still.

Adding to their sense of desperation was the fact Branda had been gradually losing more and more small pieces of her legs as they traveled. The parts loss now came to almost mid-calf on both legs. She counted herself lucky though that none of the losses had occurred in front of anyone except Mitch and Mary. And usually they occurred during her sleep.

Mary had observed a couple of episodes while helping Branda with her physical therapy exercises. Though shocked, she maintained her composure for her patient's sake.

Later, Mary told Mitch privately, "I have never seen or heard of such a thing. Now I understand what you two are going through. And to be expecting twins besides. God bless you both."

Although Branda rarely balked at proposed tests, she did draw the line when it came to doing things with sheep urine and animal, fish, or fowl body parts.

"I just can't see those things doing any good," she told Mitch and Mary. "I think some of those doctors may be using me for a kind of guinea pig."

They agreed.

Branda described Rome as, "Another walk through a history book . . . with an additional very special religious one."

She enjoyed seeing St. Peter's Square and going to Mass in the Basilica of St. Peter with Mitch.

After entering, Mitch had her steer her wheelchair off to the right.

"Why?" she asked.

"The Pieta by Michelangelo is there. Remember I mentioned that a while back?"

Upon seeing it, she gasped, "Oh Mitch. I want to get on my knees and thank God for such beauty."

"I understand how you feel, Honey, but I don't think that's such a good idea, realistically speaking."

"I know. That's just what I feel like doing."

All through Mass, she looked in awe at the surrounding beauty.

The idea of the Catacombs fascinated her but she opted not to try going down for a tour.

"Those passageways do not look wheelchair friendly and, besides, there is something so sad about them," she said. "I'll read about them later."

Mary and the rest had gone off to see other things, agreeing to meet them in the Sistine Chapel to view the picture cycle painted by Michelangelo.

As they entered the chapel, Mitch automatically handed Branda some tissues that did come in handy.

Speechless at the time, and remaining so while viewing the art, Branda later said after leaving, "If I hadn't already been sitting in my wheelchair, I think I would have sat on the floor in astonishment at the glory of that masterpiece."

Those who had not had the opportunity of seeing ancient Roman Forum and other ruins, arches, the Colosseum, Sacred Way, palaces, squares, fountains; especially the Trevi Fountain, monuments, and Via Vittorio Veneto, were amazed to say the least.

"There's more things to see and do here, and everywhere we've been, than it's possible to take in during a lifetime," Branda commented. "Museums alone would take several lifetimes. That one in, I think it was Salzburg, that had that painting of Christ standing with St. Thomas kneeling to feel a wound haunts me still. I didn't realize it at first, but the way Christ is standing, only one of his eyes is showing . . . but that one eye expresses such pathos it is incredible. I'm glad you bought me a print of that, Mitch. Thank you again."

"You're welcome, and I agree that is a very special painting. I tried to buy the original, but the museum director would not sell. I guess I really can understand why. In a museum, a lot of people can enjoy the painting. But you admired it so much I wanted you to have it."

"Thanks for the thought anyway," she said.

"You're welcome."

Athens was as wonderful as Branda expected it to be, but Cyprus was a pleasant surprise because she didn't know what to expect.

After flying into the Larnaca International Airport, getting settled in their hotel and resting, Mitch chartered two helicopters to ferry their group of 11 plus the copter crew to what is considered New Paphos.

"I think all of you will enjoy seeing The Villa of the Mosaics, also known as The House of Dionysus," Mitch said.

Later, Branda said, "You have to see this to believe it. It's so ancient, the mosaic pictures so spectacular, and the heavenly view from atop this hill looking out over the blue, blue Mediterranean Sea will stay forever etched in my memory."

Mitch said, "There are a lot of other sights to see on this island of Cyprus . . . monasteries, churches; including the Church of St. Lazarus, castles, museums and so on . . . just like most places we've been. We just haven't time to do it all."

Skipping unsettled Middle East countries, the group headed for a stop in Egypt to see pyramids. Mitch did consult with a doctor he had contacted there before the trip to see if he had located any cure. No luck.

Calling a networking contact in South Africa, rather than going there, Mitch learned nothing positive had turned up there or in surrounding territories either.

Trying to lighten the mood, Branda said, "I thought for sure some lost tribe would have some sort of potion or lotion . . . maybe an eye of newt or special dance type of cure."

"Actually, I was hoping to hear about some unknown alternative medicinal cure in that part of the world plus some others. There's a lot going on that western medicine folks haven't got a clue about. Oriental medicine has centuries old practices that work but we are often afraid to try. Of course, some alternatives are a lot of bunk too. Separating the wheat from the chaff is the trick," Mitch said. "Even some of our Native American Indians are extremely knowledgeable about cures and have been for centuries."

Although Branda never complained about her increasing girth which had to be making her more and more uncomfortable, Mitch was becoming concerned about her overall health and well being.

Asking her if she was ready to go home, she said, "No. I want to see every place I can. I wouldn't be any more comfortable at home."

"All right," said Mitch. "But the minute you want to stop traveling, say so. Dr. Cline says we should stop before long."

"Okay," she said.

Even with her okay to keep traveling, Mitch kept on calling contacts in places like Moscow, India, Japan, China, Australia, South America, Canada and Old Mexico rather than run the risk of overdoing it by trying to fly there. From the beginning, he had realistic doubts about covering all the territory he once considered doing. None of his calls produced any positive input; not even a maybe.

Since Branda expressed a wish to see Bangkok, he did agree to that.

After getting settled in their suite at the Oriental Hotel, she said, "Oh my word, Mitch. I never saw such service. I mean those young boys dressed in their gray silk uniforms with the matching pillbox hats opening the front doors and the girl pressing the elevator button for us . . . well, a person really doesn't have to lift a finger here. Incredible!"

Mitch bought her a lovely deep blue Thai-silk skirt with matching blouse. The skirt bottom had an intricate wide gold band round it.

"Thank you. That will be another one of my favorites," she told him, giving him a kiss.

"You're welcome. I only give them to you so you will kiss me," he joked.

She and the others ooohed and ahhed their way all through the sight seeing trips; especially during the tour of the Grand Palace with all the ornate adjoining buildings, halls, and chapels.

"Those colorful pagoda-like buildings with spires and towers in the Dusit and Cakri groups, the Emerald Buddha . . . well . . . everything is spectacular and overwhelming.

"Magnificent!" Branda exclaimed. "Mitch, could we please go to Singapore and Hong Kong?"

"I suppose we could take a quick look."

But they never made it to either . . . at least physically.

That night, after the couple had slept several hours, the vision people paid Branda and Mitch a major visit in the hotel suite; first in a dream with War Eagle asking them to wake up.

When they did, War Eagle spoke, "Now it is time we talk. Let us please go sit in your living room."

Mitch's dad was holding baby Mitchell; his mother, Michele. Branda's dad held Josh; her mother, Jason. Light Moon stood beside War Eagle.

Branda asked, "May we hug you before we all sit?"

"Yes, but you will only feel our love . . . nothing solid. When you hold the babies you will physically feel them more since they are so new here in this place of deep time . . . two yet unborn."

After their parents had placed the babies on the soft floor rug, Branda and Mitch enjoyed hugging their own mother and father plus each other's and the two Indians, feeling their love and a great sense of peace.

The two Native Americans spoke Cherokee which Branda and Mitch again understood and could now also use for conversing. It seemed as though everyone understood everyone else no matter what language was spoken.

War Eagle said, "It is now time for you to go home. You will find no cure on earth. The Holy Great God Spirit allowed this journey so Branda could see some of this world before going to another realm."

Branda asked, bravely, "By another realm you mean where I will go after I die?"

"Yes, the realm we are in is where you might come to after your soul passes. But that will not be until after the babies come through you from this place to yours on earth," answered War Eagle.

"How long will I have with my babies?"

"That I do not know," said War Eagle. "That is something only the Holy Great God Spirit determines. His Plans and Laws have times and reasons we know nothing about until we are told. And His Time is not like the kind you know."

"But won't I be able to see all of this world and the Universe from your realm or another? Why did I need this trip?" Branda asked.

"Yes, you may see all you want to see later, but this trip somehow fits into the Master Plan . . . of which we know nothing until advised as I mentioned. We only gladly obey the Master's Will with love in our hearts."

Then the others picked up the babies from the rug placing them one by one in Branda and Mitch's arms.

"Oh, my but it feels so good to hold these little ones," said Branda. "Josh and Jason seem to remember me."

"Of course they do," said her mother and father.

When she held Mitchell and Michele in turn, their counterparts inside her began squirming like never before.

Even the vision people laughed at the show.

"They are getting anxious to be born," said Light Moon.

Never having seen Mitch hold a baby before, Branda was amazed at his reactions; especially when holding first Mitchell then Michele. He seemed disconcerted rather than happy.

War Eagle spoke, "It will be all right this time, Mitch. Do not worry."

"What does he mean?" she asked Mitch.

"It means nothing except to Mitch," said War Eagle. "It will be made known to you later, Branda."

The parents took the babies once again and everyone sat down.

War Eagle said, "Now I will explain Branda's illness. She has a form of Spontaneous Human Combustion, a subject she has felt drawn to for some time since the Holy Great God Spirit put the thought into her mind."

"But I thought SHC happened all at once," said Mitch.

"Not in this case. She has a slow burning type that is one form of purification ritual to prepare a very special soul for a higher plane . . . or realm. She will become whole again there," explained War Eagle. "It may seem cruel to you but it is not considered so where her Eternal Life is concerned. Some of your religious call it a Cross to Bear."

"Are there other people who have or have had this?" ask Mitch.

"Yes, but not very many and it wasn't in the Plan for you to find out any sooner," said War Eagle. "No one afflicted ever finds a cure on Earth because of being selected for this special rite of passage. Death is the only cure."

War Eagle explained further. "The oil of the body acts as fuel. Even if kept under water or a wet compress is used, the body will still smolder from inside. The affected part may try to glow and follow the sequence from yellow to green to red, and leave that acrid odor of burning flesh, but the water tends to abort that. But sooner or later the part will disappear. I was allowed to give you some knowledge about that the night you were in the small water you call a hot tub."

"Is there any chance Branda could go through a reversal and return to earth whole?" Mitch asked.

"That I do not know. Only the Holy Great God Spirit knows that."

For a long time, Mitch and War Eagle sat on one couch discussing medicines and cures for other illnesses.

The rest went to a nearby area and talked, Branda playing with the babies until they fell asleep on the soft rug. Mitch and War Eagle finally rejoined the group.

Towards dawn, War Eagle said, "Branda I know you wished to visit Singapore and Hong Kong. Since you need to start home tomorrow, I will now take you and Mitch on a virtual tour. Just sit back in your chairs and watch."

As Singapore came into view like a movie of which she and Mitch were a part, she said, "I have never seen such a clean city. Spotless! Why can't all cities take a lesson from their example?"

"Amen," said Mitch.

Finding themselves inside the famous Raffles Hotel they went into the Long Bar so Mitch could have a Singapore Gin Sling.

"Word has it this drink originated here in 1915."

After being served one and taking a sip, he added, "And I'm certainly glad it did. Superb!"

Branda sipped fresh pineapple juice, enjoying it as she glanced from time to time at the unique ceiling fans lazily moving round. The blades resembled heart shaped palm fronds.

Next they saw the Shangri-La Hotel showing off cascades of red flowers from large special containers covering entire outside walls . . . top to bottom.

"Incredible," she said.

Finally, Hong Kong came into view.

"I cannot believe the hustle and bustle," said Branda.

"It's a major economic center," Mitch explained.

After touring the Peninsula Hotel, watching the sampans out in the harbor, taking the tram up to Victoria's Peak, and seeing all sorts of new and wondrous sights, the couple was finally ready to call it quits.

Finding themselves back in their Oriental Hotel suite, they visited a bit longer with the vision people.

Finally, War Eagle spoke, "And now we must go. Try not to fear what is happening and going to happen to you. It will be hard at times and you both may falter, but know that you are surrounded by total love at all times."

Hugs were again exchanged all round, babies held and kissed, and too soon the group faded into their usual silvery mist.

After going back to bed, Branda and Mitch held each other close, silently pondering all they had seen and heard.

Finally Branda said, "I guess we just have to have faith."

"It would seem so. I hope I am strong enough. War Eagle said I would be."

"We'll be strong together," Branda said before the two fell asleep again for a short time.

After the couple dressed and ate breakfast served in their suite, Mitch called the pilots and informed them of the new flight plan saying Branda was feeling the need to go home. All understood as did Mary and the guards when they were told soon after.

Rather than have Mary go through any hassle with a commercial flight, he chartered a private jet to fly her back to London.

Since everyone had grown to like Mary very much there were a lot of goodbye hugs. Since she and Branda had formed a special bond, there were goodbye kisses as well as hugs plus promises to keep in touch.

"Now I wish you were going back to Missouri with us," Branda told Mary.

"I would, love, but when I talked to my mother the other day, she says she is very homesick for me. I also think she isn't feeling too well although she would never say so outright."

"I understand," said Branda. "I'll call you now and then."

During the flight home, Branda said, "Mitch I had almost forgotten Christmas is in a couple of days. How could I forget that?"

"Too much going on," he explained.

When "J. George" finally rolled to a stop at Lambert Field on Tuesday December 23rd, and the group cleared special customs, Sean, Cynthia, Mary Ann, Linda, Mathilda, Charles, and Martha were there to greet them. Wives of the long absent flight crew and guards were also there. Mitch had called ahead to notify them of the arrival of "J. George".

Right away, Branda noticed expressions among the group were a mix of happiness with undertones of anger.

After initial warm greetings and hugs and kisses among new and older lovebirds, Sean handed Mitch a front page from the past Sunday's edition of the St. Louis Post-Dispatch.

The main top of the fold headline, followed by a descriptive article, declared:

BILLIONAIRE DOCTOR SEEKING CURE
FOR WIFE WITH STRANGE DISEASE!!!

CHAPTER TWENTY-THREE

NO ONE IN THE GROUP had ever seen Mitch so angry.

"Who's the son of a bitch responsible for this article?" he asked Sean in a tone of voice so quietly controlled it carried more intensity than if he'd been shouting.

"If you mean who wrote it, it is a 'bitchette' as you can tell by the Melanie Hendrix byline," answered Sean. "If you mean who gave Hendrix the information, we don't know and she won't divulge her source or sources. Besides Cynthia and me, your advisors and lawyers have gotten into the act too. Your other friends are also mad about it. By the way, Joe and Woody said to tell you they are sorry they couldn't be here to meet you. Something came up at the last minute but they will be in touch."

Regaining her composure after the initial shock of also seeing the headlines, Branda spoke up, "Well, I guess it was bound to happen sooner or later, Mitch. It makes me furious too, but let's not let it spoil our day . . . or Christmas."

Calming down somewhat for her sake, Mitch said, "You're right, but if it's the last thing I do I am going to sue that bit . . . sorry, woman, and the paper for an invasion of privacy."

"I don't know if that's possible," said Sean. "Your lawyers are looking into it."

"That wouldn't really solve anything though, Mitch," said Branda.

"No, dammit to hell, but it might make them think twice before trying anything like that again. After all, I don't think medically related information falls into some sort of public domain category. I know it doesn't if there is a doctor-patient relationship involved here."

She could tell he was smothering a whole crop of other cuss words he knew and would have liked to let loose. She hoped the twins were asleep, not hearing. They were being quiet at the moment anyway.

As if remembering the group around him, Mitch finally said, "I'm sorry for blowing my top and for cussing in front of you," giving a special glance toward Charles and Martha. "But . . ."

"Say no more, Mitch," interrupted Charles. "I almost feel like letting go with a few words myself."

The others expressed similar sentiments.

After agreeing to keep in touch, more hugs and kisses, and wishing each other a happy holiday season, most of the group disbanded, heading for their homes.

Mitch and Branda had already expressed their special thanks to the flight crew and guards. Branda and Mitch figured sometime later on they would try to have a party and get them, their wives, and everybody else back together.

Sonny and Doc joined Mitch and Branda in staying around to make sure "J. George" was being taken care of and stored properly in a hangar. Doc's wife, Rachel, took a picture of all four with the plane's name in the background.

Sonny's wife, Alice, asked Mitch, "Are you going to keep the plane?"

"For a while at least," he answered.

"You might say "J. George" is like a friend," said Branda.

Michael, the same limo driver who had originally brought them to the airport, drove the couple towards their home.

He said, "I'm sure sorry about all that media blitz. Those people can be so darn nosy."

"Thanks," said Mitch.

"We'll be okay though," said Branda. "But thanks for your concern. I suppose being nosy is part of their jobs. The nose for news sort of thing."

"I'm also sorry about your illness," Michael said.

"Thank you," said Branda.

Driving along with mid-afternoon sunlight filtering through mostly leafless tree branches stripped bare by winter winds, Branda said, "You know.

Although I thank you from the bottom of my heart, Mitch, for that wonderful trip, it's good to be home. I wish Sean and Cynthia had accepted our invitation to join us this evening for pot luck dinner though."

"As she said, Cynthia thinks you need to rest and so do I. We'll see them tomorrow night, Christmas Eve, at their house for dinner."

"Thank goodness we thought to do some Christmas shopping at Harrods in London and have their gifts and others all wrapped and everything. What a grand store," Branda said. "But I guess we won't have time or energy to decorate our house. We'll just pretend."

As Michael started to turn onto their street, he stopped abruptly.

"Look way ahead there Dr. Andrews. It looks like half the TV panel trucks and most of the town's newspaper reporters are in front of your house. What do you want me to do?"

"Back up slowly so you don't call attention to us, and go park on the next street over in some spot where we can still partly see our house. I want to make a phone call."

Using his cell phone, Mitch called a friend of his on the police force.

Fifteen minutes later, Mitch, Branda, and Michael heard sirens. Moments later, they saw all of the media people being escorted out of the neighborhood.

Mitch's cell phone rang. "Yes," he said, answering. "Thanks Mike. I owe you one. And can you arrange for some beefed up security patrols to stay around my house twenty-four hours seven days a week until this thing blows over? Thanks again. Can they start tonight?" Listening a moment, Mitch continued, "Thanks a lot Mike. Fax me the list of names asap. Have the ones for tonight ring the front door bell, three short rings, so Branda and I can introduce ourselves."

Hanging up, Mitch turned to Branda, adding, "Mike will have some people here within the hour. There will be a patrol car and two officers on duty at all times. I'll make a good donation to the police force for this special accommodation plus give these guys a bonus."

Mitch also gave Michael an extra bonus for spotting the media and saving them a lot of hassle.

After Mitch unlocked the front door and shut off the alarm, he and Branda entered the foyer and looked in amazement. As far as they could see there were Christmas decorations, including a beautiful tall tree. Even Michael stood awed, with suitcases in hand he had carried from the limo.

"I'll bet Ella and the rest did all this," Branda said.

"No doubt."

"You sure know a lot of wonderful people," said Michael.

While Mitch and Michael finished unloading the limo, Branda guided her wheelchair throughout the house admiring the lovely decorations.

After thanking Michael and telling him good bye, the couple sat in the kitchen eating sandwiches.

"Evidently, after you called Cynthia and Sean to let them know we were headed home, they brought in this good ham and roast beef so we'd have something to eat. It's good they have a house key and know the alarm code."

"Yes indeed," agreed Mitch, between healthy bites.

"But they couldn't have decorated the house by themselves in that short a time."

"Oh, I expect they had a few elves come in to do that," said Mitch.

"You mean elves named Ella, Jane, Pete, and Joe?"

"Could be. We'll find out tomorrow since it's Wednesday and their day to come."

"I don't know about you, Mitch, but I'm about ready to turn in. Unpacking and putting stuff away can wait until whenever. I guess we should try to get the presents under the tree though; especially those for Ella and the rest."

"I'll take care of that after I help you get ready for bed. I also want to go down to the study and check the FAX machine and see what else I need to do down there."

Hearing the doorbell ring three times, the couple went to answer it. After meeting the security patrolmen and discussing procedures, the couple headed for their bedroom.

Branda was nearly asleep before her head hit the pillow. After taking care of the presents and checking the study, Mitch joined her. Neither knew a thing until the next morning.

"Jet lagged as we are, we had better get up," said Branda. "We don't want to still be in bed when Ella and the rest arrive."

Mitch agreed.

It was old home week when the house-cleaning group arrived bearing presents to put under the tree.

"We'll just have to have early Christmas this afternoon," said Branda.

"Sounds like a good plan to me," Mitch said. "And are you some of the elves that put up all these decorations?"

Smiling, Jane said, "Yes we are. Cynthia called us after you called her and we all came over to get the job done before your arrival."

"Well, we certainly do thank you," said Branda. "It was so nice to come in and see all of this beauty."

Since the house didn't really need much cleaning, the group spent most of the day visiting; including the yard crew and Johnny who had stopped by to welcome them home. The employees expressed their distress about the media leak.

After presents were distributed; everyone saying that's just what they wanted, the workers left.

"We still have time for a rest before going to Sean and Cynthia's," said Mitch. "But first, I want to show you this list of names of security people and to tell you I ripped out that tip line downstairs. It was flooded with some of the goofiest messages you ever heard. Evidently there was a leak to the wrong people about that line too. Our message machine was also so jammed it wouldn't take anymore. I deleted them all. My God but people are crazy. I may have to change our phone number or double the guard . . . or something."

"Well, let's go rest, go to the party, and think about that tomorrow," said Branda.

The next day, after attending Mass at The Priory, the couple exchanged presents.

When she saw the larger size Waterford Crystal piece like the one in the den, she was overwhelmed and wept because of its beauty.

"Oh Mitch, you do find the most wonderful things for me."

"Take off the lid," he said.

More tears flowed when she saw the exquisite diamond necklace inside. Many hugs, kisses, and thank you's later she excused herself.

"Wait here now. I'll be right back."

Returning later with a very large flat package resting on what was left of her lap, she asked him to take and open it.

"Where did this come from?" he asked.

"I too have my ways, Sir."

As he peeled off the beautiful Christmas wrapping, removing the final deep blue velvet covering, he remained totally speechless as he stared in admiration at the lovely full-length portrait of Branda. She was dressed in a pale yellow silk evening gown he had gotten her many months back as a 'just because I love you' present. She had on her diamonds.

"Oh my dear God, Branda. This is so beautiful it belongs in the Louvre, but I will never part with it," he said, kneeling to kiss her tenderly. "How did you manage to get this done?"

"If you recall, you took this picture of me. I gave the negative to Cynthia and Sean a long time ago and they took care of having an artist turn it into a portrait. They brought the package to the house while we were gone and hid it where I ask them to in our closet."

Mitch immediately took down a picture in the living room that had hung there for years, and put her portrait in its place.

Although their life never got back to the even keel it was before the media leak, the couple managed to weather the storm.

Mitch and Branda had arranged a private meeting with the newspaper reporter who had leaked their story.

Afterwards, Branda said, "She sure is a young scared little thing."

"She's tough too. She won't budge an inch on revealing her source or sources."

"I felt kind of sorry for her. And I think she better understands our position now; especially since she got to witness one of my major episodes and saw the twins kicking around. At least all of the media uproar has gone away. I'm glad we still have the guards though."

Mitch even managed to find time to develop all of the pictures they took during the trip. The couple spent many hours in front of the fireplace looking at them and remembering. They had a big catered party during the holidays, invited everybody they knew and had a great time.

He had an offer to sell "J. George" and Branda agreed that was the best thing to do. But he hung onto it.

"I'll just rent it out from time to time to help pay maintenance costs," he said. "That airplane has too many nice memories for me to part with it just now," he explained.

By New Year's Eve Branda's leg losses had reached to her knees. Sean and Cynthia came over to help Branda and Mitch see in the New Year.

"I'm not up to having a party or going anywhere," Branda had said.

Lois Watson, daytime nurse, and Maudie Finley, personal trainer continued to come and help.

"I am getting so ungainly, Mitch, I wonder if I should just stay in bed."

"I asked Dr. Cline about that, Branda. He says not yet, if at all. He wants you to stay as active as possible to make the delivery easier. We have an appointment to go see him next week on Wednesday, January 7, 11 a.m."

Not wanting to go out much, she and Mitch spent time working jigsaw puzzles, reading, and listening to music They also enjoyed having friends come to see them.

She told Mitch, "What I miss most is our lovemaking."

"Me too, Honey, but it has just become too uncomfortable for you now."

By Monday, January 5th, Branda was getting a touch of cabin fever.

"Mitch, could we go to Steak n' Shake this evening? I'm wanting one of their malted milks . . . plus a double steak burger with all the trimmings."

"Sure, Honey. I think a trip out would do you good. I don't know what Dr. Cline would say about that meal, but what the heck. I need to stop at the drug store and pick up some razor blades too."

After eating and enjoying their meal, Mitch started to put her wheelchair with her sitting in it onto the lift ramp.

"Mitch could you just put me in the front seat and leave the chair in back? I get kind of tired sometimes of riding back there."

"Of course."

After parking in front of Dierbergs, he said, "I'll get my razor blades here instead of the drugstore and pick up some milk and bananas too. Remember to keep your gadget turned on. I guess vibrator mode is okay. Keep the doors locked."

"Will do. I'll listen to the radio while you're inside."

Lulled by the music, she was a bit startled when a young girl holding a baby rapped on the window motioning for her to roll it down. The girl had a red bandanna covering her hair. With lighting only from the store's front and surrounding parking lot, visibility was dimmed.

Turning off the music, Branda said loudly, "I can't. It's a power window and I don't have a key."

"I need help," the girl said, also loudly. "I lost my wallet and need some money to buy milk and food for the baby."

After rummaging in her purse for a moment, Branda pulled out a hundred-dollar bill, opened the door a crack, and reached to hand it to the girl.

After quickly taking the money, the girl ran off. A man yanked the door open wider and grabbed Branda, pulling her from the van before she could yell or activate the gadget.

"Please don't do this," Branda pleaded. "I'm crippled and nearly ready to have twins."

Being parked next to Mitch's van, the man quickly and wordlessly lifted Branda through his own car's open back door and laid her across the seat. Although there were cars parked nearby in the front row slots there were no people in them.

Quickly getting into the driver's seat, he sped away.

Finally speaking, he turned his head part way toward her and said, "I know that Branda."

Looking at him more closely as he removed his billed cap, Branda exclaimed, "Connor! Connor! Oh dear Lord. Please don't do this."

"Oh but I am doing this. I've been keeping track of you for a long time, ever since you married that doctor and your wedding announcement was in the paper. That big headline not long ago made me decide the time was right for kidnapping you. With all those guards around you all the time, I've had to be patient and wait for an opportunity like this. And as you well know, I am not a patient man. You'll pay for this, sweetheart."

Branda said, "Please take me back to the van. I'll see that you get all the money you want."

"Yes I want money," he said, "But I also want you again. You always were the sweetest piece I ever had. I don't care how pregnant you are. Remember?"

Before fainting, Branda was able to press the button to activate the gadget.

Inside the store, Mitch felt the vibration immediately.

Running outside he saw that the van door was hanging open and Branda was missing. He caught a faint glimpse of a dark car speeding around a corner.

"Oh dear God," he muttered, prayerfully. "Don't let this be happening."

A lady came up to him and said, "Mister, I don't know what's going on but I got the license plate number of that speeding car as it went past me hell bent for leather. I was just walking up to the store from the parking lot. Darn fool nearly ran over me. I couldn't tell you if it was a man or woman. People need to slow down. World's full of nuts. What happened?"

"Someone has kidnapped my pregnant wife. She's also crippled. Please give me that number."

Writing it down, he called the police while the lady waited.

After completing the call he turned to her saying, "Thank you ma'am. By being so observant, you may have saved my wife's life tonight and our twins she is carrying. If you'll give me your name and address, I'll see that you are rewarded."

"That's not necessary. I'm just glad to have been of help."

Reaching into his billfold, Mitch pulled out several hundred-dollar bills insisting she take them. "Here's my card too. If you change your mind about a reward, contact me, please."

After glancing at the card, she said, "Oh my. You're the doctor whose wife has that terrible illness. Dr. Andrews, I thank you but I really don't need this money and I would do this for nothing. I just hope you can catch that person. My name is Josephine O'Brien."

"Thank you," said Mitch. "Give the money to charity if you prefer."

"All right. I'll do that," she said. "I'm sorry I didn't see more. I wasn't close enough and it all happened so fast. I suppose I'd better stay around until the police come."

"Yes, I'm sure they will want to talk to you," said Mitch.

Opening her eyes after regaining consciousness, Branda saw she was lying naked on a king-size bed. Connor was on his right side next to her with one arm and hand propping up his head. He was also naked, staring at her. A large nightstand lamp provided the only light.

He said, "I must say, you don't look quite the same with most of your legs missing and all swollen up with that doctor's brats inside you but you're still a sexy broad to me. And you still have that beautiful hair and face."

Reaching to fondle one of her breasts, she hit him in the face with all she could muster. He hit her back.

"Still the spitfire, eh?" he asked. "Well, if you remember, I don't put up with that crap. Just for that, I'll give you a taste of what I used to give you on a regular basis."

As he began mounting her, Branda pleaded, "Oh please, Connor. Please leave me alone."

"No way, sweetheart. No way. And quit fighting me or I'll get my rope and tie you up like I have to do my wife sometimes. I've waited too long for this. And although I was tempted to give it to you while you were still asleep, I did at least wait until you woke up. Give me credit for something."

As he raped her, Branda lay still, praying he wouldn't harm the twins as he hurt her again and again. She was thankful they remained quiet. She wanted to scream but didn't dare. She remembered that only made him wilder.

She thought, "He's absolutely and totally crazy."

When he was finished, she threw up all over him, herself, and the bed.

He started yelling at the top of his lungs, "GLORIA, goddamn you, get your sorry ass in here . . . NOW! GLORIA!"

The bedroom door opened a crack and a young girl looked in. She was the same one with the baby who had begged money from Branda in front of Dierberg's. She had long light blonde hair, blue eyes, and, though frail looking, had a good figure. She was not much over five feet tall.

"What do you want, Connor?" she asked. "You told me not to bother you."

"You silly bitch. Can't you see what I want? I want you to get this mess cleaned up. I'll get the lady and me into the shower, but you better have this bed cleaned up and back together with fresh bedding by the time we're through."

Branda was near to fainting again as he carried her to the bathroom and placed her on a built-in seat in the shower. The cleansing water revived her.

"I can bathe myself, Connor," she said.

"Oh no. You might miss a spot. I'll wash you all over," he said. "Then you can do me all over."

Steeling herself as he washed her hair and body, she tried pretending it was Mitch. At least it was good to feel the soapy water cleaning her even though his raping made her still feel dirty.

When Connor held one of her hands forcing her to wash him she closed her eyes trying again to pretend it was Mitch.

"Open those big beautiful brown eyes, Branda and look at me. I've tried to keep my body in good shape so it really isn't hard to look at is it?"

"There's more to a person than the appearance that meets the eye, Connor. It's the heart, soul, and mind that really counts."

"Oh. So you're still full of that philosophical crap are you? You seem to forget it was sex that got us together in the first place. You sure admired my looks then."

"That was a long time ago and I've grown up, Connor," she said. "A lot."

After helping her use the bathroom, he carried her back to the bed. Somehow, Gloria had managed to do all Connor requested. The room smelled of Lysol.

"Well, whaddaya know," said Connor. "That dizzy bitch got it right."

"Who is she?" asked Branda. "And the baby?"

"My wife and son, Connor, Junior. She's sixteen and the baby is nine months old. I knocked her up and we had to get married too just like you and me. Her old man actually came after me with a shotgun. They live in another part of town."

"Where are we now, Connor? In Ladue?"

"Not quite. My parents finally kicked me out and sold the house. They said the neighbors were tired of my behavior and so were they. They are dead now. And you don't need to know where you are. I'll tell you you're still near St. Louis though."

"Connor, where are my clothes? I'm cold." Besides wanting to hide her nakedness, she also wanted to check to see if the gadget was still on.

She thought, "Maybe if the batteries haven't run down, I could switch it to voice mode and try to give Mitch some information."

"Oh they are somewhere safe. You aren't going to need them here. I'll give them back when I deliver you back to that fancy society doctor husband of yours, after he pays me the ten million dollars ransom I called and asked him for. And I'll keep you warm, and even cover you up with a sheet and blanket tonight while we sleep. But as long as I'm awake to look at you, you'll not be wearing any clothes, sweetheart, or me either. And if you have any ideas about using that pager gadget to let the good doctor know where you are, forget it. I smashed that with a hammer earlier tonight after we got here. Are you hungry after tossing your cookies?"

"Perhaps some beef broth and crackers . . . something light." Her heart sank upon hearing about the destroyed gadget.

"GLORIA!" he hollered.

After appearing, he told her to bring them some soup and crackers. His being naked did not seem to bother her.

Gloria soon reappeared with the food. Coming closer to serve Connor and her, Branda was able to see in the lamplight that the area around Gloria's right eye was starting to turn black. The girl's bare arms and neck had old and new bruises plus what she suspected were rope burns. She also had a slight limp.

"That he-devil," Branda thought. "God knows what other damage he has done to her."

Between sipping soup and nibbling a cracker, Branda asked Gloria, "Where's the baby? He looked very sweet when I saw him through the van window."

Looking fearful about speaking to Branda until Connor gave her a verbal okay, she said, "He's asleep. When is yours due?"

"It's twins and they are due in February," answered Branda.

"Boy. One's enough for me. I wouldn't know how to handle two," said Gloria. "Do you know if they're boys or girls or one of each?"

"No, we decided to just wait and see."

"Kind of like getting a surprise," said Gloria.

"Exactly," Branda said.

Looking somber for a moment, Connor said, "Branda did a great job with our twin boys, Josh and Jason. I wish they hadn't gotten sick and died. I go visit their graves now and then. I miss them."

Neither woman said anything.

Connor broke the silence. "Well that's all over and done with. I can't do anything about that."

Suddenly Branda gasped, feeling warm and weak.

"What the hell's wrong with you, Branda?" asked Connor.

"More of my right leg is getting ready to disappear."

Connor and Gloria watched in awe as Branda's entire right knee began to glow, turned pale yellow then light green, then red, and disappeared.

"What is that smell?" Connor asked as the usual acrid odor filled the air.

"My burning flesh," answered Branda.

"God in heaven!" Connor exclaimed, absentmindedly reaching to put his soup bowl on the nightstand alongside Branda's. He missed and the dish fell to the dark blue rug.

Gloria fainted, slumping across the end of the bed.

Exhausted, Branda pulled the sheet and blanket up over herself before lying back against the pillows. Still stunned, Connor made no objection. She fell asleep.

Waking the next morning, she awkwardly managed to get out of bed and to the bathroom and back; sometimes crawling, sometimes scooting. If Gloria had still been there she would have asked her to help. Luckily, there were handrails for people with handicaps in the bathroom.

"I wonder why those are in there?" she asked herself. "They sure came in handy for pulling myself up to the potty. I wonder why Connor didn't wake up. He used to be a light sleeper."

After getting back in bed and getting a good whiff of him, she knew why. "He's been drinking," she mused. "Oh dear Lord. That's when he's meanest. If he stays asleep, after I rest, I'm going to try and find my clothes and get out of here. Maybe Gloria will help me."

When Connor roused, she knew her luck had run out.

"Oh I gotta call that husband of yours this morning and see if he has the money and tell him where to drop it off," he mumbled.

Giggling insanely and reaching to touch her bare breast under the sheet, he continued, "Maybe I ought to just let him keep his damned money and I'll keep you honey."

"Stop it, Connor. You're drunk."

"Guess I am," he mumbled, jerking the sheet off of her. "Seeing that awful leg thing last night made me thirsty. You're still the sexiest woman I ever knew. Let's have some fun, Branda. I wanna have some fun." Leaning over to kiss her breast, he then yelled, "GLORIA! GLORIA! Get your skinny ass in here. Let's have some fun."

Gloria appeared. "I'm feeding the baby, Connor. What do you want?"

"Put that kid down for a nap and come in here."

"He isn't ready for a nap. I haven't finished feeding him," she said.

Stumbling to his feet, Connor got up, went over and hit Gloria in the face and began beating her.

"I told you never to argue with me," he yelled. "Never, ever argue with me. I'm in control . . . always."

As Gloria cowered, trying to protect her face, Branda yelled, "Connor, leave Gloria alone. Is that all you know how to do, hurt women one way or another?"

Gloria spoke up, "It's okay Mrs. Andrews. I'll do what he says or he'll nearly kill me. Connor, stop. I'll be right back." Her nose was bleeding.

Connor went back to lie down beside Branda.

Coming back after a few moments, Gloria said, "I gave the baby his bottle in bed. He'll be okay for a while. Now what do you want, Connor?" She had cleaned up her bloody nose.

"I want you to watch me make love to a real woman and see how it's done."

"Dear God, Connor," said Branda. "You are sick beyond belief."

Connor slapped her and said, "And you can shut your mouth too Missy."

Suddenly the twins began moving around a lot. Connor watched for a moment and said, "Well now, the little brats are awake too."

Gloria stood transfixed at the activity. "That must hurt," she said to Branda.

"Yes, it gets uncomfortable."

"Well I'll calm them down," said Connor, starting to climb on top of Branda. "I'll calm the little bastards down. Get over here and watch, Gloria."

For a split second, since Connor could not see Gloria's face or Branda's while changing his position, the two made eye contact. In that instant, each knew they were women with a common bond and would help each other. They both hated Connor Carson with a passion.

Connor stopped a moment, turned his head and commanded Gloria to step closer where she could watch him. As she approached, he grabbed her arm, pulling her down on the bed.

Starting to rip off Gloria's dress, he said, "I think I'll just have a taste of the two of you. That'll be fun. You first, Branda. You watch, Gloria. I told you we're gonna have some fun."

"I gotta go to the bathroom first, Connor," pleaded Gloria.

"Oh you always gotta go to the bathroom. Well hurry. I'll just play with Branda a little until you get back," he said moving back onto the bed lying on his side.

Branda and Gloria managed to exchange another glance. Branda understood she must get Connor's full attention to distract him from his wife.

Pretending he was arousing her, she held one of his hands to a breast, kissing him passionately.

"Hey, honey, that's more like it. Just like old times," he said. "I'll bet your old doctor can't do it to you like I do."

Branda kept thinking, "Please hurry Gloria, oh please hurry before I throw up again."

From his position, he didn't see Gloria, a few moments later, coming toward his back giving Branda the thumbs up sign. She was carrying some rope and making signs she had made a phone call.

As fully aroused as he could get being full of liquor, he began trying to climb back on top of Branda to enter her. With all her strength, and gagging, Branda grabbed his penis, yanking and twisting as hard as she could, shoving him away from her at the same time. After letting him go, she tried kicking him in the groin with the one knee she had left. The twins began kicking too as if trying to help her.

Even through his haze of liquor, Connor screamed in pain, writhing in agony on the bed. He finally fainted.

"You tie his legs together, Gloria, while I hold his arms," said Branda. "We'll have this sadistic maniac tied up before he knows what happened. Who did you call?"

"Your husband. He said the police were with him; had been all night."

"Thank God. Lets hope they get here soon. Stuff something in Connor's mouth too," said Branda. "I don't want to hear anymore of his foul language when he comes to . . . or have my twins or your son hear it."

After they got Connor tied up, throwing a blanket over his naked body, Gloria said, "I don't know how you did all that other stuff."

"If you mean because of my big belly now, I don't either," said Branda. "I guess I had some help from heaven above, adrenaline, pure old Missouri stubbornness or all three. Could you please get me two washcloths; one with soap and one for rinsing? After touching that animal I want to wash my hands."

"Sure," said Gloria, going to do so and returning quickly.

"Thanks. Do you know where he put my clothes?" asked Branda.

"No. He hid them and wouldn't tell me. I think he suspected I might be on your side. I'll go look though."

"Thanks again Gloria for all you've done. Where are we anyway? Will it take long for Mitch and the police to get here?

"I'm glad to help you Mrs. Andrews. I didn't want to have anything to do with your kidnapping. We're out in the country and it might take a while for them to get here. Of course the police can drive faster so maybe it will be soon."

"Please call me Branda. After all we've been through I think we belong on a first name basis."

"Well okay, if you're sure," said Gloria.

"I'm very sure. I feel like we're friends now," said Branda. "We certainly have a common bond."

"Why thank you. I feel the same way."

Branda tried to rest while Gloria went to check on the baby and look for her clothing.

Returning empty handed, Gloria said, "The baby fell asleep and I can't find your clothes. If Connor comes to, I'll make him tell me. But I did see him put your hundred-dollar bill in his pants pocket after he took it away from me. I looked and it was still there. Here it is."

Looking at the bill in Gloria's extended hand, Branda said, "You keep that. You have more than earned it."

"Oh, I couldn't do that. That's like blood money or something," said Gloria. "Besides, he touched it."

"Well, you have a point there. I mean about him touching it. Kind of makes it dirty, doesn't it? Tell you what, we'll wash it and give it to charity. Some place like a home for battered women."

"That's a good idea. I'll go wash it off with Lysol and put it in an envelope. I guess it wouldn't be a good idea to mail a bill so I'll look up an address for such a place and take it to them," said Gloria, going off to do the job then returning. She put the envelope in her nearby purse.

Exhausted, both women quietly waited, Branda lying in bed, Gloria sitting in an armchair.

Connor, now semi-conscious, was still squirming in pain when the women heard what sounded like a door being broken down. Gloria tried to pull her torn dress to cover herself while Branda used a sheet for covering.

The next voice Branda heard was Mitch's saying, "Where's the son of a bitch. I'll kill him with my bare hands."

Gloria opened the bedroom door, and said, "The son of a bitch is in here. Take him to an insane asylum where he belongs."

CHAPTER TWENTY-FOUR

GUESSING BRANDA WAS NAKED UNDER the sheet and seeing her eye beginning to blacken, Mitch grabbed Connor by the throat strangling him barehanded as he said he would. It took three policemen to pull him off.

"That's not the way, Dr. Andrews," said an officer. "We don't blame you, but this nutcase has to be taken care of lawfully. I hope the judge sends him somewhere for life."

Mitch went to sit on the bed's edge beside Branda who had moved to a more upright position; holding and consoling her as she wept a moment with relief. When she quietly told him about her knee disappearing, he briefly lifted the sheet to look then held her more closely. He also noticed her bruised cheek.

After reading Connor his rights as he lay at the foot of the king size bed, the officer and his partner untied Connor, wrapped him in the blanket and started hauling him away handcuffed. Mitch had a great urge to go kick the daylights out of him.

"Where's my clothes?" Connor mumbled, still somewhat drunk. "I want some clothes."

An officer said, "Don't worry, after we get you cleaned up, you'll get a new orange suit."

Gloria interrupted, "Connor, where did you hide Branda's clothes?"

Staring at her blankly, he said, "That's for me to know and for you to find out bitch."

"Tell the lady," another officer said firmly.

"Oh yeah, I must obey the law," said Connor. "Look in the car trunk. That's where they are I think. Just wrap 'er in any old thing. She'd still look beautiful." He began crying as the lawmen carried him to the squad car. "She'd look beautiful in any . . ." he continued, still crying, his voice trailing off.

"My God," said Mitch, getting up to stand by the bed. "The s.o.b. still loves you, Branda. No offense, Gloria."

"I know," she said. "I don't think he ever did get over her. Sometimes when he was drunk he'd said my blond hair reminded him of Branda. I never was jealous though. I didn't love him enough to be that. I was just foolish, not in love."

"You are wise beyond your years," said Branda.

Two remaining officers took statements from the women. Gloria also made charges against Connor for his repeated beatings and raping during her seven months of marriage to him.

"He also threatened both me and the baby with bodily harm if I didn't help him kidnap Branda," Gloria said.

The officers took pictures of the visible bruises and marks Gloria could decently show them. They cautioned her that the others she described might also have to be photographed at some point.

"Please don't leave town and if you change addresses, let us know," said one officer.

"Well, since I don't have anywhere else to go, I guess I'll be right here. That is until the guy that owns the place comes back from his vacation. He loaned it to Connor for a month and that's about up."

The policeman also took pictures of Branda's black eye and bruised cheek.

Mitch was so enraged about what he had heard the two women say, he said to an officer, "Just give me some time alone with that animal. Where are they taking him?"

"Never mind, Dr. Andrews. Let the law deal with him. Your wife is going to need you with her, not sitting in jail for beating up that louse."

"He's right," Branda said. "The twins need you, I need you, and Gloria needs you."

As if coming to his senses, Mitch looked at the two abused women, and said, "Of course. Of course. I'm sorry. I'm just so mad. I must get you to Dr. Cline to be examined."

Gloria started to say something but hearing the baby cry, she left.

After making sure Mitch had calmed down and all was okay, the officers said good bye.

"Someone will be in touch," said one. "Do you want some help getting Mrs. Andrew's wheelchair out of your van or her clothes out of that car trunk?"

"Thanks but I can manage. The van has a lift and ramp for the wheelchair and I brought some clean clothing for her. I doubt if she wants those old clothes. Right Branda?"

"Oh thank you Mitch. I definitely do not want those clothes in the trunk. If the police need them for evidence or anything, have them take everything."

"That's good to know," said an officer. "We'll be impounding the car so will just leave your belongings inside. He left the car keys in the ignition. Did you have a purse?"

"Yes, but for some reason, he brought that in. It's here on the nightstand and nothing is missing. I checked earlier. He told me he smashed my pager gadget with a hammer. It had been attached to my jacket pocket when he kidnapped me. I don't know where it is now."

"We'll look for it," the officer said.

"Thanks again for all of your help," Mitch said as the policemen started leaving. "I'll see that the door we knocked down gets fixed."

As soon as the officers drove away, Mitch phoned Dr. Cline about getting the women in for an examination as soon as possible today.

"Whenever you get them here, I'll be ready," said Dr. Cline. "I always try to leave room for an emergency. In this case, I would declare one anyway because it is. I hope they hang that s.o.b. by his balls."

"I'd help," said Mitch.

Measuring the busted door with a metal tape he kept in the van, and writing down a description, Mitch then phoned a repairman he knew, explaining the urgency of the situation. He was told a new door would be delivered within the hour.

"Bring a new lock too," he advised the repairman. "We pretty well wrecked this one. You know where to send the bill."

While getting the tape from the van, Mitch had also gotten the clean clothes for Branda. After finishing his phone call, he brought them to her.

Branda said, patting her abdomen, "Mitch, we probably owe Gloria our lives. We must do something for her besides getting her examined. She told me Connor seduced her just like he did me, only at a younger age. She's only sixteen. She isn't as lucky as I was though with her parents. Her father and mother won't have anything to do with her although she thinks her mother would if the father would let her. At least mine, though shamed, kept on loving and seeing me. Also, Gloria is an only child and her parents adored her."

"I totally agree we are going to help Gloria. I can never repay her for what she did. I sure don't think she needs to stay alone here. We'll take her to our house until we can figure out something. Even though the police had pretty well gotten a fix on this location, Gloria's call saved us a lot of time trying to find the actual house. Getting that license plate number last night from that witness and being able to see surveillance videotape from Dierberg's parking lot and the front area was also a big help. We knew right off it was Connor. At least he wasn't driving a stolen car which was a break. The matter of tracing his latest whereabouts and address got to be a bit more complicated."

"You look so tired, Mitch. Did you get any sleep last night?" Branda asked.

"Not a wink. I'm going on nerves and adrenaline now. How about you, Branda. Did you get any sleep?"

"Yes. Gloria fainted from shock when my knee disappeared, and Connor was so stunned he let me fall into an exhausted sleep without bothering me all night. Sometime though he got up and began drinking. And, believe me, he's a mean drunk. At least the liquor kept him from being able to rape me again."

She saw Mitch's scar turning lighter as it often did when he was under stress.

Returning with the baby in one arm, and pulling a lightweight portable playpen behind her with the other, Gloria said, "Sorry I was so long. He needed a bath and some food. Bless his heart. Now maybe I can take care of him the way I want to instead of doing it when and how Connor told me to. Branda, would you feel like holding the baby a moment while I set up his playpen?"

"Oh I would love to," answered Branda.

Leaving for a moment then returning with toys and a bottle of milk to place in the playpen she had put up, Gloria got the baby settled peacefully. He sat there grinning and jabbering at everyone for a moment before he began drinking the milk.

"See what we're in for?" Branda asked Mitch.

"Yes I do," he said.

Branda noticed a shadow in his eyes she had seen before when he was around the vision babies.

"Just my nerves and imagination," she mused.

Hesitating a moment, Gloria said, "Dr. Andrews, before I went to take care of the baby I was going to tell you I don't have any money to get examined by that Dr. Cline you were talking about. Is that Branda's obstetrician and gynecologist? I'll be all right. I heal fast."

"Yes," said Mitch. "Dr. Cline is Branda's obstetrician and gynecologist. And you are not going to have to pay for that or anything else you need."

"Oh, but Dr. Andrews. I can't take charity."

Taking her gently by her arms, looking into her young face, Mitch said, "Gloria, please call me Mitch. I want to be your friend, just like I know you and Branda are now. And as your friend, I want to help you. Branda and I both do. You would not be taking charity. You would be letting us repay you for an extreme kindness and for possibly saving her life and the twins . . . and quite possibly yours too. What you did was an act of Christian charity. Connor is a madman. No telling what he might have taken it in his head to do. Even though I would have gladly given him the ten million or whatever sum he wanted, he is insane, as you well know. No, Gloria. Our helping you would not be charity. Please do us the honor of letting us repay you in whatever way is best for you. Let's start by you letting us take you home with us tonight, after the examination. We'll take it a day at a time until we come up with a plan. For now, you may stay with us as long as you need to."

As tears of gratitude came down her cheeks, Gloria said, "Those are the nicest things anybody ever said to me Dr. Andrews. They remind me of the nice things my daddy and mama used to say before I shamed them and daddy got so mad. Do you mean I did something like the Good Samaritan we learned about in Sunday school?"

"Exactly. And please call me Mitch."

"That will take me a while. My folks told me to always show respect for doctors, the clergy and so on by using their titles."

"All right. Whatever makes you comfortable. Whenever you're ready, you call me Mitch. Deal?"

Drying her eyes, she smiled slightly and answered, "Deal. And I accept your kind offer to see that doctor and stay with you until I can figure out what to do. Thank you very much."

Branda sat smiling at the two. They reminded her of father and daughter.

Gloria left the room for a moment to go get a blanket for the baby who showed signs of falling asleep.

Mitch asked Branda, "Is it my imagination or is she walking with a slight limp . . . not always, but sometimes like a pain hits her? I didn't want to embarrass her and pry."

"Yes, I have noticed that too. I really do think she is damaged internally and in pain."

"I'll be sure to mention that to Dr. Cline."

As Gloria came back into the room, Branda said, "Mitch, I would like to take a shower before we leave. Could you help me?"

"Sure but we'd better wait until the repairman gets here. He should be here shortly. Will we need a chair in there?"

"No, actually there is a seat and handicapped bars everywhere in the bathroom."

Gloria spoke, "That's because the owner broke his leg and needed them temporarily. He says he'll just leave them there for his old age. If it's okay with you two, while you're waiting for the repair guy and the baby is asleep, I would like to take a bath too. I don't want to go to that doctor without cleaning up. I'll use the other bathroom where there's a tub. I like to soak when I get a chance. That almost makes me feel clean after all Conn . . . It makes me feel better."

"You go ahead," Branda said. "We'll be glad to watch the baby."

After everything had gotten done, the van was packed, and the group was nearly ready to go, Gloria called the owner explaining what had happened and about the new front door. She told him where the new keys were hidden.

"He said he had heard about the kidnapping on the news in his vacation cabin at Lake of the Ozarks," Gloria told Branda and Mitch. "He wasn't too surprised. He's known Connor since high school and says he always was a wild one. The only reason he let Connor have this place was because he felt sorry for the baby and me. He said I could stay here as long as I needed to and I thanked him but explained I was going to be with you two for the time being."

After completing his examinations of the two women, Dr. Cline told Mitch, "The twins are all right, but Branda has a slight tear. All in all I think she was lucky to have gotten by with so little damage from that idiot. I hope you file charges to the limit of the law."

"We definitely are," said Mitch.

"I've prescribed some topical ointment and a broad spectrum antibiotic to be taken for a few days," he told Mitch. "Make sure she takes some lactobacillus acidophilus to keep down her chances of getting diarrhea from the antibiotic. Have her keep up the lacto tablets well after she's finished the pills. Her bruises will heal on their own. She's basically a healthy woman despite her affliction. Good genes. I want her to rest, eat well, and, oh, you know the routine Mitch as well as I do."

"How about Gloria? What causes that limp from time to time?"

"My God, Mitch. I've never seen anything like it. She has some internal bleeding and has to wear a pad most of the time. She says it stops now and then. I don't even want to think about what that child went through. What she described to me amounts to physical abuse beyond belief. Makes me sick to think about it. Anyway, she limps because she has two broken toes that are healing but tender plus because of the extensive tearing and wounding inside her. I really don't know how she is even able to move much less take care of a baby. I want her to go to the hospital from here for immediate repair surgery that I will do but she's worried about the baby. Then after a few days, she'll need a lot of in-home care."

"You do what you need to do, Richard. I'll hire round the clock private nurses to take care of her in the hospital, and round the clock nursemaids to take care of the baby at our house. I don't want Gloria worrying one second. And she's to come to our house when it's okay for her to be released. I'll hire the best nurses to take care of her there too. May I see her?"

"Of course. She may be a little woozy from the mild sedation I had to give her just to examine her. There's even some bladder damage. I'm not a cussing man, Mitch, but when I saw what that man did to her, I felt like letting go with a bunch. Frankly, I hope I never lay eyes on the . . ."

"I know, Richard. I know."

"By the way, Mitch. My office girls are having a ball in the lunchroom playing with that cute baby boy of Gloria's. They take turns."

"I know. I went to check on him a couple of times to make sure the girls had enough diapers, milk bottles, and all that stuff a baby seems to need. I do believe moving a battalion of troops is easier than hauling a baby around. Just figuring out those car seat things is something else."

"And soon you'll be doing double duty."

"I think I'll hire a squad of people to help," Mitch said, smiling.

"Mitch, you look exhausted. When you get home, go to bed as soon as possible."

"Not a problem there," said Mitch. "I did manage to catch a few winks on your couch while I was waiting in your private office. Hope you don't mind."

"Not at all."

"I also managed to cancel Branda's appointment for tomorrow. When should we reschedule?"

"Let's wait a couple of weeks," said Dr. Cline. "Now, I'm going to go see my last patient for the day then head for the hospital. I've already called ahead to make arrangements. I'll meet you there. Or do you want me to get an ambulance to take Gloria and you and Branda go home with the baby and rest?"

"I think you know the answer to that," said Mitch. "My back van seats can be fixed to give Gloria a comfortable ride without interfering with Branda's wheelchair or the baby's car seat. I would like for her to be wheeled out to the van on a gurney and handled with kid gloves though."

"Not a problem. See you at St. John's Hospital."

After getting Branda and the baby, Mitch took them to Gloria's room. He carried the little boy.

Still somewhat out of it from sedation, Gloria did light up when she saw the baby.

"Oh hi sweetie. Are you being a good boy?"

The baby smiled, holding out his arms for his mother to take him.

"I can't now, sweetheart. Mommy has to go get fixed at the hospital."

The baby whimpered a little, but Mitch managed to soothe him.

Branda asked, "Gloria, would it be all right if I called your parents and let them know what is going on?"

"Sure Branda. If you think that's the right thing to do. They live on Rustic View Drive in Ballwin. They're in the phone book under Adam Flynn. They won't care though. They don't like me anymore," said Gloria, still woozy voiced, tears welling in her eyes.

"Of course they do," said Mitch. "Of course they do."

"They don't even like my baby Adam even though I chose that name because it's my daddy's. I used to call the baby that when Connor wasn't around. Now that's what I'm always going to call him. Connor at least let me use that for a middle name. My mother's name is Mary. I want to divorce Connor now and change the baby's legal name to Adam Flynn. Flynn is my maiden name and I want to take it back again too for mine. Can I do that, Dr. Andrews? Can I do all of that?" she asked.

"I'll check with a friend of mine and see about it," said Mitch. "I'm almost sure you can."

Branda spoke up, "And Gloria, I'd bet a billion dollars your parents really do like, in fact, love your son just as they really still love you."

"Maybe you're right, Branda. Maybe you're right. I hope so," Gloria said.

As two male nurses came in with a gurney, Mitch explained, "Gloria, we're taking you to the hospital in my van. Branda and I will take the baby, Adam, home with us tonight and later get a nursemaid or two to help us if necessary. You are not to worry about one thing except about getting well. After you're released, you're to come to our house too."

"You two are angels. Absolutely two angels," said Gloria, drifting back to sleep as the men carefully lifted her onto the gurney. Even in her sleep, she winced in pain as she was moved.

"It takes one to know one," said Mitch as Branda used her cell phone to get information and the Flynn's phone number. On the way to the van, she called explaining what was happening to their daughter.

After hanging up, she told Mitch, "They had already heard about the kidnapping story on last night's TV news. They have been frantic with worry since they didn't know where to find Gloria. They're coming to the hospital as fast as they can get there. They also want to take Adam home with them tonight and keep and take care of him as long as Gloria needs them to. They also want Gloria to come back home when she gets out of the hospital."

After meeting the Flynns, transferring Adam's paraphernalia to their car, visiting while Gloria was still in the operating room, and waiting to hear she was all right, Branda and Mitch started for home.

Mitch had told the Flynns, "Please tell Gloria we'll be back to see her tomorrow afternoon."

"We will," said Adam. "And thank you again for all you've done."

"You're welcome," said Branda. "But we're the thankful ones. Your daughter is very special."

Driving home, Branda said, "I would like to see the reunion after Gloria comes to, but that's a private thing. Too bad Mary and Adam couldn't make it before Gloria went to surgery."

"I like happy endings," said Mitch. "And this certainly is one. Adam seemed comfortable with his grandma and grandpa even though I understand this was only one of a very few meetings."

"Yes. He really is a good baby. I think he inherited Gloria's genes. Let's pray to God he has," Branda said.

"That was nice of you Branda to tell them about your youthful experiences with Connor. I think that especially helped Adam."

"Well, I'd do anything for Gloria. Which reminds me. The Flynns told me Gloria once told them she would like to finish high school and go on to nursing school."

"Maybe we can help out with that. Hire some tutors and pay her tuition, or at least help out with it. Adam is a proud man I can tell. I had to do some

M. S. SANGER

talking to get him to let me pay Gloria's medical bills. I finally convinced him this is our way of repaying Gloria for calling me and saving you and the twins from anymore of Connor's abuse, possibly even saving your lives."

As they drove toward the garage, Branda said, "Thanks Mitch for keeping those private security guards around all the time. Makes me feel safer to see two of them here day and night. I'm sure the police force is glad to get their patrolmen back after you made the switch. Sure was nice of them to help us out though."

Too tired to cook, the couple made sandwiches, ate hurriedly, and fell into bed.

Neither moved until noon Wednesday, the next day. Ella and everyone remained as quiet as possible as they went through the house and yard doing their jobs. After waking up and visiting with their employee friends, then going to see Gloria for a while, the couple came back home, ate, and went back to bed. Mitch had only taken some time to check the study to see what was going on in his business world.

"After all, Dr. Cline said you are supposed to stay in bed, Branda. And I'm still tired too."

"I know, Mitch. But I just have to go see Gloria at least once a day. I'll take my pills and rest all of the other hours. And I'm glad you are getting some rest too."

As the days and weeks moved forward, Branda began having nightmares again.

"This time the hypnotherapy sessions will have to be done here," said Mitch. "I've already set up some appointments."

"You are right. I'm getting too big to go anywhere."

Friends came to visit, the hypnotherapy sessions were once again successful, Dr. Cline had declared Branda healed, Gloria was out of the hospital and she and Adam were back home with her parents. They all came to visit from time to time. Gloria was being tutored at home for her GED test since she didn't feel like facing anyone in a regular classroom situation.

During one of the visits from Gloria and the baby, she said, "Dr. Andrews, your friend Judge Limson called me yesterday and said the name changes I applied for are now legal. Under the circumstances, he was able to expedite a lot of the procedures."

"So now you're Gloria Flynn again and the baby is Adam," said Mitch.

"Not exactly."

"What do you mean?" asked Branda.

"I'm Gloria Flynn again but I have a surprise for you. If you don't like it, I will ask Judge Limson to change it," said Gloria.

"What's the surprise?" asked Branda.

Holding the baby up in front of her as if introducing him, Gloria said, "Please meet Adam Andrew Flynn. The Andrew is a variation of Andrews, your last name. I hope you two don't mind. As I said, I can change it if you do."

Laughing right out loud from happiness, Mitch said, "Why thank you very much Gloria, I consider that an honor."

"Well, so do I," said Branda, also laughing.

Together, the couple looked toward the baby and said, "How do you do Mr. Adam Andrew Flynn. We're very happy to meet you."

The baby grinned and squealed as if accepting their greeting. All laughed.

"I was going to call him Adam Mitchell Brandon Flynn but the judge thought that was a bit awkward. I thought the Brandon would be a good male substitute for Branda. The judge was right of course. The Andrew fits better. At least you know I was thinking about you."

Adam held out his arms for Mitch to take him. Only Branda noticed the split second of hesitation and shadow- flicker in his eyes before he did so.

"He didn't used to act that way," she mused. "He was beside himself with joy when he found out I was pregnant. Then when the twins first started moving around he used to love watching and talking to them. In some subtle way, something has changed. I wonder why?"

Later, in bed, she almost asked him about it but decided against it.

Instead, she asked, "I wonder what has happened to our vision family? They haven't been around in ages unless they come at night when we are asleep."

"I've wondered myself but, as War Eagle told us, their Time is not like ours and we must be patient until the timing is right for something to happen or not happen."

"I really looked for them during my kidnapping ordeal," said Branda. "But now that I think of it, Connor did briefly mention that second morning that he had dreamed of ghosts who were very angry at him. I thought he was just hallucinating from the liquor. Perhaps not. I guess I'll learn about all that when I'm supposed to, if ever."

"I suppose," said Mitch.

"One more thing," said Branda. "I'm sure glad you set up those trust funds for Gloria and Adam. She can go to nursing school and Adam can go to college if he wants to. And now, let's get some sleep."

But at three a.m., the twins decided otherwise. Branda was going into labor. It was February 8, 2004.

Mitch called for an ambulance, silent run in the neighborhood. He alerted the security guards before throwing on some clothes and grabbing the suitcase he and Branda had packed a long time ago.

Waiting for the ambulance, Branda said, "We simply must remember that we are not supposed to know we are having a boy and a girl. We have to act surprised."

"We may have to remind each other in some way during the heat of battle as it were," Mitch said. "How about we say 'you're doing great' if we think one of us is about to slip up?"

"Okay, 'you're doing great' is the key phrase," she agreed, wincing in pain. The twins were letting it be known they were getting ready to start marching in their birth parade.

CHAPTER TWENTY-FIVE

H OLDING HER HAND IN THE ambulance, Mitch asked, "Branda do you still want to do the Lamaze technique we practiced? I still think you might want some other kind of help."

"I'll let you know. Let's try it. I wasn't able to do that the other time. Anyway, I suspect we're a long, long way from delivery. As you know this is just the beginning."

"I know, but Richard Cline said to get you to the hospital the minute you felt anything. He doesn't want to take any chances; especially since you have the other problem and the fact you have given birth before which often allows for an earlier delivery time."

"I certainly hope so. The word labor is the most descriptive word in any language. Just ask any mother."

When Branda was finally taken to the delivery room nine hours later, she and Mitch noticed their vision family hovering above, smiling and offering prayers. Branda's mother was holding Josh; her father, Jason.

Light Moon came closer, whispering, although no one else in the room could either see or hear them, "Michele and Mitchell are no longer with us. They have begun their journey from here to Earth through you."

Dr. Cline spoke, "You're doing fine, Branda. Mitch, would you like to have a nurse take over your coaching job and you take over mine; if that's all right with Branda? I believe someone is about ready to be born."

Branda managed to say, "Oh yes, Mitch. That would be wonderful for you to deliver our children."

Silently, she mused, "I wonder if he will seem disconcerted when he holds our babies this time like he was at the Oriental Hotel in Bangkok with the vision family? Or if that shadow-flicker will appear in his eyes like it did when he held Gloria's boy?" But she was too busy concentrating on giving birth to dwell on it.

After scrubbing his hands at a nearby sink, Mitch put on necessary garb and took over delivery procedures. Dr. Cline stood to one side watching in case he was needed.

One of the twins was finally beginning to enter the world.

As the baby crowned, Mitch exclaimed, "Branda, can you see in that overhead mirror? Look at that head of black hair."

"Yes, Mitch, I see. By the way, you're doing great."

Then Mitch became so quiet Branda asked, "Is everything all right? Why are you not talking? MITCH is something wrong?!"

"Oh no. I'm sorry. I'm just overwhelmed. I just can't believe this. We're all together! We made it! This one is really here! And this little face is so sweet."

Branda vaguely thought, "I wonder what he meant saying we're all together, we made it?"

When the baby finally came all the way out of its mother, Mitch briefly held it up for Branda to see and said, "May I present our daughter, Michele Anne Marie Andrews." He then introduced her to others in the room.

The baby gave a lusty cry as her way of saying hello.

"Oh she is so beautiful," said Branda, tears coming, noticing there were no disconcerted or shadow-flicker looks anywhere near Mitch.

"Yes, beautiful, like you," said Mitch, who then began holding the baby close to him for a moment, not minding the mess, and not aware tears of joy were coming down his cheeks.

He whispered in the baby's tiny ear, "Hello, my little daughter, hello. You're here safe, your mother is safe, so there's nothing to worry about this time. At least for now."

After performing cord cutting procedures and letting a nurse clean Michele up a bit, Mitch said, "Ordinarily, Branda, I put a baby on the mother's abdomen if she wants that, but with another one still inside you who might kick her off I'll just put her in the crook of one of your arms. Can you watch Branda for a moment, Richard, until I get back? All seems quiet for now."

"Fine," answered Richard.

Tired as she was, Branda picked up on Mitch's reference to being 'kicked off' by the remaining baby. The couple glanced at each other knowingly and smiled.

Wrapping Michele in a lightweight blanket a nurse had handed him, Mitch placed the baby beside Branda.

As they admired their daughter, Mitch said, "You know what? Every other baby I have ever delivered or seen is usually all wrinkled and funny looking. Michele isn't. She is gorgeous."

He vaguely heard Dr. Cline and the nurses laughing softly in the background.

Branda said, "Mitch, I believe your viewpoint falls into the category of beauty is in the eyes of the beholder. But I agree, she really is a beautiful baby."

As they were examining Michele, counting her fingers and toes and so on, Branda began having contractions.

A nurse took Michele away to finish cleaning her up.

"Be sure to keep her warm," said Mitch.

"I will doctor, I will," said the nurse, smiling.

As the nurse coach came back to help Branda through the next delivery, Mitch went to welcome the other child.

When the baby finally labored and squirmed its way into the world, Mitch again did the introductions; his wife first.

"Branda, meet our son, Mitchell Thomas Mark Andrews."

Young Mitchell also cried his greeting but quieted when his father held him close for a moment whispering, "Hello my son. Like I told your sister, we're all safe, at least for now."

Richard Cline once again took over performing post-delivery procedures as Mitch went to place the baby at Branda's side.

"He has all of his fingers and toes too, Mitch," said Branda. "And he is so handsome, like his father."

Too choked up with emotion from having delivered his children, Mitch could not say anything for a moment. He could only look into his wife's eyes, finally murmur, "Thank you," and ask, "May I kiss you? I love you so much."

"Of course. I thank you too for these children and I love you very much too."

The tender moment and lingering kiss brought some tears to several nurse's eyes.

One commented quietly to another, "You don't see that very often. Usually, after going through labor, the woman is yelling at the man never to touch her again."

The other one said, "From what I've heard, that is one very brave lady."

Dr. Don Eto, pediatrician, came into the room saying cheerfully, "Hi Mitch, hello Richard. I hear there's two new arrivals in here for me to check over."

"You're right and thanks for coming," said Mitch. "Our son is over here, a nurse has our daughter."

After meeting Branda and picking up the baby, Dr. Eto said, "Well, he is one fine looking boy I must say. You two did nice work. And now, I'll go perform some official and medical duties. Ya' know we gotta get that paperwork started right from the get go."

As Dr. Eto walked away, the couple could hear him talking to Mitchell. He was telling the baby it wouldn't hurt a bit to get weighed, have his foot and hand prints made, and he'd go easy with other exams.

Mitch smiled at Branda and said, "Mitchell is looking toward Eto like he understands every word."

Mitch stayed with Branda, sponging her face and arms.

"You are truly amazing, Branda," he said. "You have been through so much and yet you manage to keep cheerful; even through childbirth."

"To be honest, deep inside I often feel like screaming . . . just a blob of quivering jelly. You are my anchor that keeps me grounded. I really almost lost it a few times during these deliveries. If you hadn't been here I think I would have."

When Dr. Eto returned, he told the couple, "Both kids are just fine. Healthy as two Olympic champs. Michele weighs in at six pounds, two ounces and is 20 inches long. Her birth time, day, and date were recorded at

1:15 p.m., Sunday, February 8, 2004. Mitchell is a hefty eight pounds, ten ounces and is 22 inches long. He was recorded born at 1:45 p.m.; same day and date. And I wish they would loan me some of all that black hair they have. My bald spot could use it. Bring them around to my office in a couple of weeks. I took a DNA sample from inside their mouths so we can find out if they are identical twins or not. I should have the results by then, maybe sooner. If so, I'll call you. By the way, Branda, will you be nursing them or bottle feeding?"

"I'm going to nurse as long as I'm able."

"Good, that's the best way," said Dr. Eto. "Do you know about keeping Bag Balm salve on your nipples between feedings to keep them from getting sore?"

"Oh yes," said Branda. "I grew up in the country so know all about that wonderful veterinary medicine that's also good for cold sores, cuts, burns and a lot of other things besides its original intended use on sore cow udders."

"Just be sure you wipe it off good before feedings," said Eto. "One lady I knew didn't do that and could not understand why her baby didn't want to nurse. Even though the salve's odor is bland and probably wouldn't taste too bad it's not a good idea to dine on it. Anyway, it's good you want to nurse but don't let yourself get worn out; especially since I understand you also have a major health problem."

Mitch spoke up. "I've already hired some nursemaids to help us with all of the other baby care. There will be two on duty all the time and a backup if required. They will be working 12-hour shifts."

"Good. Good," said Dr. Eto. "That will help a lot. But feeding two newborns a la Mother Nature is no picnic . . . pardon the semi-pun. Dr. Cline and I want Branda to rest as much as possible and I know you do too, Mitch, since you also fully understand the problems involved. You have my numbers. Call me day or night if anything worrisome to you crops up."

"Thanks, Don. I will. And thanks again for coming today at my request."

"No problem. By the way, you two. You'd better start planning how to run the boys off when that little girl gets older. She's already a charmer. A real sweetheart."

"Mitchell will protect her," said Branda. "That's what brothers are for."

Dr. Cline kept Branda and the babies in the hospital a few days longer than normal.

"I don't always hold with this modern notion, based on health insurance rules and regulations, to practically send the mother home from the delivery room," he said. "No matter how natural some people think the process is, I happen to be old fashioned and think giving birth is not such an easy thing to do."

Later, Mitch told Branda, "I've heard that Richard has been known to lower his fees and/or help a couple or single mom out financially if he thinks a new mother needs extra days in the hospital."

When the couple and their newborns finally did get home about noon the day after Valentine's Day, they were totally amazed at all the presents placed around the living room.

Mitch said, "Cynthia called me to say she and Sean have been over collecting our mail everyday and putting it inside, but I didn't expect this. I thought she was just talking about some bills and business mail."

"Good grief! It looks like the entire Famous-Barr baby department is here. Oh, look Mitch. The cradle- boards are in there. Light Moon once told me they would bring them."

Picking up one child, then the other, Mitch showed them the display of packages.

"See what nice friends we have," he said, after putting them back in their little portable seats.

Branda said, "You couldn't see their faces when they were looking at all that array, and maybe I'm crazy, but Mitch, I swear when they saw those cradle boards they looked at them with some sort of special recognition."

"Like remembering them from Visionland?" he asked.

"Yes."

"Well, then we're both nuts. I sensed that too."

As the couple was taking a closer look at the gifts and reading some of the tags, the two daytime and two nighttime nursemaids arrived along with the backup woman. Mitch had met and interviewed all of them while Branda was still in the hospital and fully explained Branda's illness to them. All were in their forties.

Branda said, "It is very nice to meet all of you. I'm sorry I couldn't see you before now, but I wasn't allowed visitors in the hospital. Rules and regulations you know. Anyway, we thought it would be a good idea for you to come here today so we can all get better acquainted and you can learn your way around the house. We want you to feel at home. After all, we're going to be like one big family in a way. And since we are, if it's all right with you, may we call you by your first names and you do the same with us? Also, if it's still all right with you as I understand Mitch mentioned earlier, we would like for you two daytime ladies to begin today."

The two daytime nursemaids were Marian Emerson and Peggy Norman. Eleanor Mims and Ann Wills had night duty with Tanya Chavez slated for relief when necessary. All agreed a first name basis all around was fine although they said it might be hard to call a doctor by his first name.

After the others left, Marian and Peggy started their jobs, staying on to help the family get settled.

Besides the usual baby furniture in the two nurseries, including a comfortable rocking chair, each also had a double bed and chest of drawers for the night nursemaids. The day ladies were also welcome to take a nap there when not busy with the little ones.

"And now Branda, I believe it's time you went to get some rest," said Mitch. "Sean and Cynthia are coming over later to meet the new additions, bring food for us and the nursemaids, and help us open presents if you feel up to it . . . at least some of them. That pile may take days."

"Okay. You're the doctor," she said, smiling.

As Marian picked up Michele, and Peggy got Mitchell to take them to their rooms, Branda said, "If they get hungry, please bring them to me. I'm feeding them on demand, not a schedule, at least for now if that works out. I may have to express some milk into bottles later on. We're just sort of playing all this by ear at the moment. Just call me on the intercom if you need to find me."

Mitch and Branda looked at some more gift boxes, trying to guess the contents. A few moments later on the way to the master bedroom, they stopped off at the two nurseries to see the twins in their cribs. The couple reached to hug, kiss, and say welcome to each child. Mitch took pictures of the babies with and without Branda, their nursemaids, and had Branda take one of him by each baby's bed.

"I think that just about completes this roll," he said.

Branda smiled, "I would imagine so since you have been taking pictures from day one."

Afterwards, continuing to their bedroom, Branda said,

"Now those two little empty beds look much, much better."

"You'll never know how much better," said Mitch.

Branda was pondering that statement when the couple entered the bedroom.

Spying Betty sitting in her regular chair, Branda said, "How nice to see you again. I hope you'll like the new additions to our family. When she gets older, I have a feeling our little girl will like playing with you like I used to."

Branda got to rest for an hour before being awakened by Marian's voice.

"I'm sorry to disturb you, but Michele is hungry."

"Okay. Please bring her to the master bedroom."

Mitch's voice broke in. "I've been down in the study doing some catch up work, but I'll be right up. I'll bring the baby back to you after she's finished, although we may keep her with us for a while."

"Okay, Dr. Andrews," said Marian.

"I'm Mitch, remember?"

"That's sort of hard for me but okay, Mitch."

When the couple was alone with Michele contentedly nursing, Mitch turned down the sending volume on the intercom so they could have privacy.

"Well, what do you think of the ladies, Branda?"

"Like I told you before, I trust your selection judgment and their references. They seem just fine to me. If something changes, I'll let you know."

A half-hour later, Peggy reported, "Mr. Mitchell Andrews is ready to dine. Is his reservation ready?"

Turning the sending volume back on, Mitch said, "Yes, we now have a vacancy."

"At table two, in the master bedroom," Branda interjected.

All laughed.

Automatically, for privacy's sake, Mitch turned down the sending volume again as he or Branda would continue to do from then on when they wanted privacy.

Since Michele had fallen asleep, Mitch carefully removed her from her mother's breast, holding his daughter in his arms.

When Mitchell began nursing at her other breast, Branda said, "I never get tired of watching these two eat. I can't begin to tell you the pleasure it gives a woman to know she is nurturing her children in this special way."

"I can only imagine," said Mitch. "I get pleasure in just watching them. They also tickle me the way they make those little slurping, gulping noises, sometimes almost a squeaking noise, when they are really sucking hard and being satisfied. And those little hands and fingers that sometimes knead your breast, I guess to make milk flow faster, or just to take comfort from touching you. Anyway, it's a wondrous thing. It certainly gives me a whole new perspective on what breasts are really made for, not just for man's viewing and touching pleasure. Although I guess the one thing eventually leads to the other."

"Well, I never thought of it that way, but I suppose you're right," she said, smiling. "Mitch, may I ask you a personal question? If you don't want to answer, please don't."

"What is it, Branda?"

"I noticed it seemed to disturb you when you held the visions of Michele and Mitchell that time at the Oriental Hotel, and also when you first held Gloria's baby? Am I right or wrong? Was I imagining that? And that remark you just now made about 'you'll never know how much better' seemed to have a double meaning related to the babies finally being in their beds."

Hesitating a long moment, he answered, "No, you weren't imagining any of that. Branda, the reason behind my actions and what I just said, is such a secret not even Sean or Cynthia know about it. Absolutely no one else ever knew, except Helen. My reluctance to hold the babies the times you mentioned, and the reason for what I just said, goes back to my last days with Helen."

"Oh, I'm sorry, you don't need to tell me if it hurts you so much."

"No, I think it's better now to get it out in the open. You have a right to know. First, let me ask if you have ever had the kind of stray thoughts pop into your mind that you neither want nor that have your consent?"

"Of course. I suppose everybody has those at one time or another. Is that what happened to you?" Branda asked.

"Yes. I feel really rotten for even letting such an idea creep into my thinking and am thankful I have finally come to grips with it. I understand the emotions and psychology behind my troubling central thought, but not why I let it almost consume me to the point of possibly destroying our marriage."

"What!" she exclaimed, moving abruptly in a way that caused Mitchell to lose her nipple and whimper for a moment before she helped him find it again. "Mitch, please explain more."

"I panicked and considered running away and hiding from my responsibilities."

"You mean you almost left me and the babies?"

"I'm deeply ashamed the thought was ever there, Branda, but deep down I know I never would have really done that. I love you too much and wanted so much to see my children. You see, you are my anchor too. I just panicked at the thought of the same thing happening twice and had trouble dealing with the idea."

"What thing, Mitch? What thing?"

"Two weeks before Helen died, we found out she was pregnant; after all those years of wanting her to be."

"Oh, dear God, Mitch. And when I became pregnant then began having more episodes, you got so you couldn't handle the thought of going through the same thing you did with Helen . . . me dying before your children could be born."

"That's it exactly," he said. "I reached the point where I didn't want to run the risk of ever bonding with any child for fear of somehow losing them. I never even knew if my other child or children were boys or girls. Thank God, I'm over that, thanks to you and my son and daughter."

"But you were so excited when you learned I was pregnant."

"Yes, at first. I sure was. Then when your leg loss episodes increased beginning back in late September, I began to have my unwanted thoughts.

They hit me full force Halloween night when you got so upset about maybe not being around to see our children go trick or treating and you had small pieces of both legs disappear during the night. I grew more afraid. I never wanted Sean or Cynthia to know or Sean would have knocked me silly and maybe dumped me as a friend. I never told them about Helen's pregnancy because I couldn't stand to talk about it. That, and her death, made me crazy. As you know, I had a lot of hang-ups about her dying. Anyway, can you ever forgive me?"

"Well, of course, Mitch. I can't pretend it isn't upsetting for me to know you even faintly considered going away, but I do understand where you were coming from. But, I hope you know, truthfully, neither of us knows if I will be here or not next Halloween."

"I know, Branda, I know. But I at least have a part of you if the worst happens; Michele and Mitchell."

"That's true. Now I think I understand why you said what you did when Michele had pretty much entered this world. You said, 'We're all together. We made it!' I wondered at the time."

"You're right, Branda. I was so happy."

"Then we'll take each day as it comes for as long as they last," she said, reaching with one hand to touch his face. "By the way, Mitch, I don't think Sean would ever dump you as a friend, no matter what. He would understand and forgive as I have. So would Cynthia."

"I hope so. Branda, sometimes when I think of having those terrible thoughts, I feel like I'm as bad as Connor. If I had been fool enough to carry them out I would have hurt you as badly, in a different way perhaps, but still hurtful."

"Jumpin' George, Mitchell Andrews! Don't you ever say or even think that. No way. There is absolutely no comparison. Besides, you would have been hurting too I think."

"Yes that's true."

"Well, anyway, all that is over and thank you for sharing the secret with me. I'll never tell a soul. This is the secret War Eagle was referring to that time at the Oriental Hotel when he said, 'It will be all right this time, Mitch. Do not worry.'"

"Exactly, but being human I still worried," Mitch said.

"Well, I'm glad I understand all of that now. On another subject, have you heard anything about Connor's whereabouts?"

"Judge Limson says he's pretty sure Connor will be put away somewhere with the criminally insane with no chance of parole."

"The sooner the better so he doesn't hurt anyone else ever."

"Branda, please excuse Michele and me for a moment, I think this young lady needs some clean britches."

"You can call Marian to come do that if you want although you certainly proved yourself worthy of diaper duty in the hospital room. I'm still so glad they let us keep the babies in the room in those little hospital bassinet things."

"They may not have done that if I hadn't hired those special day and night nurses to help out," said Mitch.

Taking the baby over to the fancy bassinet near the bedside, Mitch talked to Michele the whole time he was changing her. Afterwards, he put the nearby diaper pail to good use. A table of baby supplies was also near the bassinet.

As Mitch was carrying her back toward the bed, Branda noticed something dangling from the baby's arm.

"Oh Mitch, you simply must stop buying these kids so many things. You'll spoil them to pieces! What on earth?"

"Happy Belated Valentine's Day my love! Show your mother her present, Michele," said Mitch, holding the baby's arm out as if she was presenting the gift.

Putting Michele on the bed, Mitch removed the diamond necklace from her arm and put it around Branda's neck. Kissing her, he said, "I love you. Will you be my sweetheart?"

"Always, my love, always. And thank you so much. This necklace is absolutely gorgeous. Oh Mitch, you even put one with a pretty diamond around Michele's neck."

"She's my sweetheart too. I hope you're not jealous."

Laughing, Branda said, "No, I just hope you can handle the two of us. We're pretty high-powered women. What did you get Mitchell for Valentine's Day?"

Reaching into his pocket Mitch pulled out the smallest pair of cowboy boots, Branda had ever seen. They were dark-red hand-tooled leather with small diamond stars for decorations.

"These," said Mitch.

Their laughter woke up Mitchell who had fallen asleep nursing, and made Michele slightly jump.

"Oops, sorry kids, didn't mean to set off your startle reflexes," said Mitch.

After Mitch changed Mitchell, and put away the diamond jewelry and boots, Branda called for Marian and Peggy to come get the twins.

Branda got in a couple more long naps between feeding the twins some more.

She was awake when Sean and Cynthia came about 5:15 bringing food for everyone, including Marian and Peggy.

After Sean and Cynthia saw the babies, ooing and ahhing at how beautiful and handsome they were, Cynthia put on the food in the kitchen. The twins stayed blissfully asleep.

"This good roast beef dinner, which is Mitch's favorite as you well know, really hits the spot. It is also a definite favorite of mine," said Branda, sitting on soft cushions in her blue wheelchair. "This fresh fruit salad also hits the spot."

Mitch said, "You know what? If I hadn't already hired a couple of cooks, one of whom will begin tomorrow, I'd hire you, Cynthia."

At six o'clock, Eleanor and Ann came to take over with the babies. Having already eaten, they went to see about the twins, coming back with them to join the others. Now awake in their carry seats, Michele and Mitchell became the center of attention.

After thanking Cynthia and Sean again for the delicious meal, Marian and Peggy told everyone good-bye.

From then on, days blended into routines heavily revolving around needs of the twins. Adult activities were tucked around the edges.

All of the gifts had finally been opened and stored, listed in the beautiful baby books given by Sean and Cynthia, and thank you notes written and mailed. Mitch, Branda, and anyone having a spare moment pitched in with addressing envelopes. Ella and other former employees met the new ones.

The baptisms in The Priory on Sunday afternoon, March 14, went without a hitch with proud godparents, Sean and Cynthia, fulfilling their roles in the ceremony. Though out of the ordinary, Reverend Cummings assisted. Martha watched along with many other friends. Michele's baptismal name was Teresa; Mitchell's was Anthony.

Later, during the christening party at the house, Branda said, "Mitch, it is so nice having all of our friends here. Those who haven't been here to visit before now really seemed to enjoy getting to meet the twins."

"Yes, there wasn't much opportunity during the church ceremony."

"I think everybody understood a moment ago when the kids got cranky and I had to excuse myself to go feed them. I'm glad Marian, Peggy, Eleanor and Ann are taking turns now staying with them making sure they stay asleep. With this crowd here, we may not be able to hear anything over the intercom."

"If the weather was a bit warmer, we could have had this outside instead of in the living room and dining room, with some overflow in the den," said Mitch.

"That would have been nice, especially since you had that beautiful white wrought iron enclosure put around the pool to keep people from falling in accidentally; especially the twins when they get older. But I think we were right to have the baptisms now instead of waiting any longer. And the caterers don't seem to mind the indoor crowd. Chad and Bonnie are great as usual."

Seeing Gloria coming toward them carrying Adam, Branda said, "Oh how wonderful to see you. How is everything going?"

"Just fine thanks to you two."

"And Adam has grown so much," said Mitch, taking the little boy to hold. "Gloria, we want to apologize to you for not including your name somehow with the twins, but we had chosen our parents first names ages ago plus the others."

"Oh but you did include mine in Michele's," Gloria said, with a smile. "I never told you before, but my middle name is Marie just like one of hers."

All laughed.

Branda said, "Well, we're sure happy about that coincidence."

"For sure," said Mitch, handing Adam back to his mother.

"Michele is so beautiful and Mitchell is so handsome," Gloria said. "Just like their parents. My folks think so too. They are standing over there talking to some of your friends. It was nice of you to invite them."

"Well thank you for the compliment," Branda said. "We want to go chat with them in a moment. I see they're talking with Dr. Eto now."

"Oh, that's the twin's pediatrician isn't it?" Gloria asked.

"Yes," said Mitch.

"That was so cute the way he made the announcement a while ago that the twins are identical, saying they are sort of like two peas in a pod. Maybe so, but I noticed Michele already has a kind of outgoing cheerful little personality . . . a real charmer. Mitchell, though also definitely a charmer, has a quieter way about him."

"Since day one," said Branda.

Later, after everyone had left, the twins had been fed, and Branda and Mitch were in bed, Branda said, "Dr. Cline says I am doing well and we can start having sex again next week."

"How do you feel about that?"

"I'm wanting you very much, but I guess we'd better do what he says. Anyway, I don't know about you, but I am pretty well worn out from today's activities and am ready to sleep as long as the twins will let me. They do seem to be sleeping longer at night, thank goodness. At that last feeding an hour ago, they nursed longer than usual so maybe that will hold them awhile."

"I desire you too very, very much, but you're right to follow Dr. Cline's directions. And I too am weary tonight and ready for a good sleep," Mitch said.

Their rest lasted until the earthquake hit at six a.m., jolting them awake. There were no sounds coming over the intercom but they could still faintly hear the twins crying and nighttime nursemaids, Eleanor and Ann, calling for help.

CHAPTER TWENTY-SIX

"OH HURRY, MITCH, GO SEE about all of them," Branda said.
Reaching the door leading out to the hallway he turned the knob.

"Oh, dear Lord, it's jammed shut." Hoping Eleanor and Ann would hear him, he yelled, "I hear you but I can't open our door." Listening a moment, he added, "Branda, I don't think they heard me above their voices and the twin's crying. I still hear all of them. I'll try the door leading to the garden."

It too was jammed.

Adrenaline fueled, Mitch hurriedly began jerking off the bed's top sheet, picking up Betty off the floor, tossing her onto the bed, grabbing the chair the doll had been shaken out of, covering it with the sheet, and heading back toward the glass-paneled door leading to the garden.

Understanding his idea, Branda yelled, "Mitch STOP! Put on your house shoes," watching as he did so.

Raising the blinds covering the glass, Mitch swung the chair will all his strength. Glass shattered but the sheet screened most of it from hitting him.

Turning a moment, he asked, "Will you be all right Branda? I'm going to try getting an ax out of the tool shed or find something to break down our hallway door and theirs. Thank God it's daylight so I can see what I'm doing."

"I'll be fine. The blanket and comforter will keep me warm. Thank goodness the weather isn't freezing cold."

"Okay," he said. "Later I'll stuff something in that hole I made."

Returning a moment later with an ax, Mitch started chopping a sizable hole in the hallway door.

"There. That's done," he said, finally. "Now I'll go get the others."

While waiting, Branda laboriously managed to get out of bed, into her blue wheelchair kept right up next to the bedside, and went to the bathroom and back.

"Thank goodness for all the ongoing physical training sessions," she thought. "My strong arms do come in handy sometimes."

Being successful, Mitch was soon returning with two squalling babies and their frightened nursemaids.

"Poor little babes," Branda said, awkwardly managing to hold one to each breast with help from some creative pillow propping. "I'm sorry you had to cry so long. We just couldn't get to you. Eleanor, Ann, please stay in here if you like. We know you're frightened and there may be aftershocks. It might be best if we all stayed together."

The women needed no coaxing. Everyone was too unnerved to be embarrassed that all were still wearing pajamas or nightgowns. Mitch went to find robes for everybody. He also went to bring orange juice and sweet rolls.

Returning, he said, "I'm afraid the power is out so I couldn't cook us anything since the stove is electric. I'd better find some candles and get out flashlights; also the battery operated radio so we can get some news. We'll have to keep the fridge closed as much as possible to save the food inside."

"When that New Madrid fault cuts loose, it really lets a person know it," said Eleanor.

They had heard on the radio the quake registered 5.9 on the Richter Scale.

Later that day, power was restored and Mitch was able to get workmen to come replace the glass panel he had broken. They were also able to do repair work and replace the doors he had chopped down.

"Thank goodness for having power and new doors. Now everyone can have privacy again," Branda said.

But it was two days before Mitch could get the house inspected for major structural damage. Luckily, there was none despite the first tremor on March 15th and following aftershocks the next couple of days.

The night of March 17th, Branda had her first leg-loss episode since losing her right knee in front of Gloria and Connor on January 6th.

As the couple was getting settled in bed, she said, "Oh no! I'm feeling warm and weak and my left knee is starting to glow."

Holding one arm around her shoulders, using his other hand to hold hers, they watched the now too familiar sight of slowly burning flesh going from pale yellow to light green to red, then disappear leaving the acrid odor in its wake.

Tearfully, she said, "I keep hoping these episodes will stop until the twins get much older."

Still holding her, giving her comfort, Mitch said, "I wish they would stop altogether."

"Me too, but we both know what the vision family said."

Both managed to fall asleep despite their fears, but were awakened by Eleanor's voice on the intercom at four a.m.

"It's time for Michele's dining pleasure," Mitch said, getting up to go get her as a way of helping Eleanor.

"We might as well stay up now for Mitchell," Branda said as she finished nursing the baby girl. "He seems to always follow his sister in about 30 minutes." She was right.

Having learned the hard way not to play with the twins in the middle of the night or early morning hours, Mitch returned each child after it finished and was drowsy from eating.

When he came back to the bedroom, Branda said, "I'm glad you learned that lesson. You used to get them so wound up, they wouldn't go back to sleep for hours."

"Live and learn as they say," he admitted, leaning to give her a quick good night kiss.

But the kiss lingered, releasing sudden waves of long repressed desire that engulfed the couple.

"Are you sure, Branda?" he asked. "I don't want to rush you."

"Yes. I'm sure."

Their lovemaking took on a desperation that had never been present before. Though neither mentioned it both sensed it was because they were feeling the pressure of her latest leg loss the night before added to the knowledge of what was in their future regarding other losses.

"Oh Branda, it feels so good to hold and touch you again. I love you very much," he said. "I've missed you."

"Mitch, I love you more than I can say. And your body feels wonderful under my hands. Please don't wait any longer. I need you now," she said.

The rest of their lives also slowly went back to being as normal as possible. As minutes, hours, days, and weeks silently melded into months, routines had become niched in their proper places. Branda's main duty was nursing the twins.

Friends came to visit, the couple went to visit friends, they took some drives to Cape and Morley and enjoyed seeing the vision family from time to time.

Personal trainer, Maudie Finley, and day nurse, Lois Watson had kept up their duties even though Mitch did not often want to go anywhere when Lois came; which was the original reason for hiring her.

"I would much rather be with my family," he would say, smiling.

Friends and employees were amazed at his constant devotion to his family; especially where the twins were concerned.

Sean told Cynthia, "Mitch has taken to fatherhood like the proverbial duck to water which is great."

Smiling, she commented, "I'm not even sure the nursemaids have much to do since he's always ready and willing to walk Michele and Mitchell, change their diapers, play with them; do everything but feed them. And I think he'd do that if he could."

Very small pieces of Branda's thighs began disappearing in April. Mitch became more and more committed to relieving her anxiety as well as his.

One night at dinner, he said, "Pack up your diamonds, Honey. We're going on a cruise to celebrate our first wedding anniversary and your second 39th birthday. That would be May 17th and May 19th respectively. See, men don't always forget important dates. This cruise is my special gift to you for both occasions, if that's all right. The nursemaids and some other friends will be joining us. But I insisted they bring no gifts; their presence will be their gift to us. Right?"

"Absolutely! Oh Mitch, that sounds wonderful. And of course a cruise gift for both occasions is just great. Good heavens. Who could ask for more? What ship are we going on and where?"

"The Delta Queen from St. Louis to New Orleans. I've chartered the entire steamboat just for our group. There will be Sean and Cynthia, Gloria, her parents, Adam, Mary Ann, Linda, Mathilda, Charles, Martha, Joe, Woody, the "J. George" crew, and anybody else we know that can wangle time off from whatever. Most can't make the whole trip of course because of other commitments. I've hired a Dixieland Jazz band, a Swing band, and a special surprise for you."

"Jumpin' George, you do come up with the most wonderful ideas. Thank you," she said, giving him a long kiss.

"And I thank you for that delicious kiss. I thought about doing this trip a long time ago. We'll be returning though on a chartered jet. "J. George" is rented out just now so we can't use him. And in case you want to know what I want in the way of a wedding gift, you've already given it to me."

"What do you mean? I haven't given you anything."

"Yes, you have. You have given me yourself, Michele, and Mitchell. That's more than I ever expected to have."

Afterwards in bed, he added their special lovemaking that night to his list of already received gifts. Although she no longer wore the Chantilly lace gown, she did put on some of the diamonds for him and made sure she gave him extra pleasure.

The trip was all Mitch and Branda hoped for and expected.

While peacefully floating along enjoying the scenery from her wheelchair viewpoint and his deck chair, Mitch often read aloud passages from "Life on the Mississippi" by Mark Twain.

"I imagine parts of the river he described have long since changed course or just disappeared," Mitch said.

"I still enjoy hearing you read the book," Branda said. "It gives this wonderful trip an extra flavor of steamboatin' days. And I must say the twins seem to be enjoying themselves. Have you noticed how they look around, smile more than usual, and are eating up all the extra attention they are getting from all our friends? Sean and Cynthia play peek-a-boo and pat-a-cake with them a lot. That is, when you aren't doing it," she said, smiling. "You really are a good father, Mitch."

The nursemaids took turns attending the combination parties celebrating the wedding anniversary and Branda's birthday.

Branda said, "I don't think those tender little ears would appreciate that Jazz and Swing music even though it is absolutely some of the best I've ever listened to."

Of course everybody ignored the no gift request. But they had conferred with each other and came up with one special gift from all. Each person contributed a picture or pictures that held a special meaning for Branda and Mitch and put them into one big album. Included were pictures from the "J. George" trip, some from Sean and Cynthia that went back to Sean and Mitch's boyhood together; all sorts of memorable photos. Those who had none to contribute, like the nursemaids, signed their names below congratulatory inscriptions.

"Thank you very much," Mitch said, "This is truly a wonderful book."

"I totally agree," said Branda.

After the parties, Branda and Mitch stopped at the rooms the babies were in with their nursemaids. Branda fed each baby in turn.

Later, in their room, Branda told Mitch, "Thank goodness they are sleeping all night now. I think it helped to add those small amounts of organic baby food you have specially prepared for them."

"Dr. Cline said to try it out anyway. At least you are getting more rest now which is important. I get so tickled at them when they are nursing or you are just holding them. They love to touch your beautiful hair, just like I do," Mitch said.

"Yes, it does seem to fascinate them but then so do a lot of other objects now."

"Well, in case I haven't told you lately, you are a fascinating woman," Mitch said.

"Why thank you, kind sir. You know what? Every night we've been on the Delta Queen, I feel just like Scarlett O'Hara on her honeymoon with Rhett Butler; especially after we get in this bed."

"Well, I don't know how Rhett Butler made love to Scarlett, but I know how much I enjoy making love to you."

"Prove it," she said.

After reaching their usual heights of passion and ecstasy, Branda began crying afterwards.

"Oh Mitch. How can you stand to be near this disfigured body of mine? How can you stand it? Even if you are a doctor, you are still a man first."

Holding and comforting her, he said, "Shhhh, now. None of that. Branda, you are still more woman than I deserve and your heart and soul are more beautiful than ever. If our roles were reversed, how would you feel?"

Thinking a moment, she said, "It would not matter to me. I would love you as always."

"It is the same with me."

As May headed for July, small pieces of Branda's thighs gradually disappeared. She began having more spells of depression.

"Mitch, could we take another trip on "J. George" before you sell the plane?" she asked.

"Well, you must be as psychic as Cynthia. I have a surprise for you. It's time to pack up your diamonds again."

"Oh good. Where this time?" she asked.

"Hawaii. Now that the twins are weaned at the suggestion of Dr. Cline and Dr. Eto because they thought the heavy-duty nursing was becoming too much of a drain on your strength, I think this would be a nice trip to take. Besides, that's where I would like to celebrate my birthday. In Hawaii at the Royal Hawaiian Hotel."

"How wonderful! I have heard so much about Hawaii and that hotel."

"The suites are booked as we speak."

"Are friends also invited?"

Mitch said, "Of course, but I'm afraid since we're staying about a month no one is able to get off work for that long this time except Sean and Cynthia. Of course the nursemaids will be along."

"Yes, Michele and Mitchell are getting so active now, we need all the help we can get," said Branda.

The trip over was like old home week. Again the pilots were Sonny and Matthew, co-pilots, Patrick and Bob plus Alan and Grant as stewards.

Upon seeing the hotel as the limo approached, Branda exclaimed, "Oh what a grand and lovely pink palace. I understand some people wanted it torn down once. Thank God that didn't happen to this historic landmark."

The twins enjoyed playing in the Pacific Ocean surf with help from Mitch and the nursemaids. Sean and Cynthia often joined in. One or the other always stayed with Branda as she watched from her beach chair Mitch placed her in.

"Please make sure I'm covered so I don't offend anyone, she would say."

Wordlessly, Mitch would do as she requested, noting her increasing bouts of depression.

The group did sightseeing on Oahu that included going to the Pearl Harbor Memorial.

Branda noted, "Oh how sad to see those bubbles still rising from the sunken Arizona."

Mitch chartered a smaller plane so the group could visit other islands. Even the twins grew quiet in the eerie Volcano National Park on Hawaii. The silvery solidified lava flows were left contorted into an otherworldly landscape.

Cynthia said, "Legend has it that if you pick up rocks here and take them off the island, that offends the goddess Pele and you will have bad luck."

Sean added, "I heard someone say people who do remove the rocks often mail them back to this island park."

One night after a luau, Branda said, "That buried pig was one of the most delicious things I ever ate."

"And the hula girls were certainly interesting to watch," ventured Sean.

"Personally, I thought the dances the men did were just as good," said Cynthia. "Half-naked and flinging lighted torches around certainly got my attention."

"The twins seemed to enjoy looking at it all," said Mitch. "They appear to like Hawaii very much. I know they loved that small taste of pineapple they had the other day up at the Dole fields."

Branda said, "I never knew pineapple could taste like that. It's like candy. What we get in the states doesn't even compare."

On the evening of his birthday, July 22nd, Mitch reserved a private dining room in the Royal Hawaiian.

"I have a special treat for you tonight everybody," he said. "Especially for Branda."

"But Mitch," she said. "This is your birthday. You are the one that deserves special treats. And maybe you'll just get one you're not expecting."

Cynthia and Sean came into the room carrying a very large package, presenting it to Mitch.

Tears came to his eyes after opening the gift. The card was signed 'With all our love, Branda, Michele, and Mitchell.'

"Oh my," he said. "Oh my. What a treasure of a portrait. You and the twins all dressed up."

"Well, I could not think of one other thing you would like as well, and once again, Sean and Cynthia helped me out. Of course, it was painted from one of your camera shots you took on my birthday aboard the Delta Queen. That artist is not only good, but fast when necessary."

Propping up the picture, coming to kiss her, he said, "You are right. Nothing else would have pleased me more. How on earth did you get it over here?"

"With lots of help from Sonny and crew who sneaked it into the cargo hold."

Sean and Cynthia gave Mitch a small, solid gold trophy with the inscription, "Father of the Century" engraved on it.

"Hold still now, Mitch, while I take your picture with it," directed Sean.

"And now for your present from the flight crew and Ann, Eleanor, Marian, and Peggy. But first a little fanfare. Ta-da-ta-da-ta-da!"

At that signal, a beautiful Hawaiian girl in a hula costume came in to hand Mitch the gift. First she presented him with a gorgeous ginger lei, putting it around his neck and kissing him gently on the lips."

"And now I will dance just for you," she said. "My name is Eva. Music please."

As the strains of Lovely Hula Hands filled the air, Eva performed her graceful island ballet.

"Now I understand what the hula is really all about," Branda whispered to Cynthia. "It really is a story told with those wonderful hand movements. Eva is a true dance artist. Mitch is mesmerized and I don't blame him."

The packaged gift turned out to be a complete Hawaiian looking outfit: beautiful floral patterned silk shirt, and cream colored trousers.

Cynthia said, "When you wear that great looking outfit, Mitch, you'll need to put a red hibiscus behind one ear. Or is that the women who do that to let guys know if they're married or not?"

"No, Cynthia, I don't think I'll be wearing a flower behind my ear. But I really like this outfit. Thank all of you very much. And now for my surprise. Close your eyes, Branda."

Hearing familiar flamenco guitar music, she opened her eyes, saying, "Oh Mitch. Hello Roberto . . . Olivas, isn't it, from Madrid?"

"Si, Senora," Roberto said, not missing a beat of Malaguena.

"Thank you Mitch," Branda said. "What a delightful surprise."

"And from now on you can listen to Roberto whenever you want to and there's a CD player handy. I arranged for him to make an album and he has brought you one."

After he stopped playing, Branda said, "Thank you very much Roberto for coming all this way and for bringing me this CD. I treasure both gestures."

"It is I who thanks you and Dr. Andrews. Since you enjoy my music so much, he arranged for my flight and stay here and for producing my CD. I am eternally grateful for all."

Since there was a CD player in their room, Mitch and Branda listened to flamenco music while lying in their bed.

"I programmed the Malaguena track to play again twice since I know how you like it," he said.

"And you know it makes me very passionate too," she said, smiling at him sensuously.

When Malaguena began, the couple's passion rose along with the music's tempo.

Mitch began stroking and feeling her silky blonde hair.

"I'm glad you let your beautiful hair grow a little longer. You know how I've always loved its color and shimmer."

"And I love your jet-black hair. It makes me desire you sometimes just looking at it, especially when there are strands of it falling over your forehead." Reaching to touch his scar, she added, "Even that scar looks sexy to me. In fact, everything about you turns me on," she said, reaching to feel his body all over. "You feel so good. So good. I love you more than I know how to say, Mitch. More than I could ever find words to say."

Caressing and kissing her breasts, feeling her body, he murmured, "And I love you more and more, Branda. I thank heaven every day for bringing you into my life."

As the crescendo of the music continued to rise, so did the fervor of their lovemaking. Kissing passionately, feeling, fondling, bringing each other to the point where neither could wait any longer.

By the time he entered her they were both ready to climax. After a few thrusts, their cries from reaching orgasm blended with the final climax of the music.

Before falling into an erotically exhausted sleep, he said, "Again, Branda. I love you so much. I treasure you."

Reaching to take his face in her hands, she said, "And I you. You are truly the only man I have ever loved, or could love."

Those were the last words he heard from her until after they got back to the mainland. She was unconscious the next morning and could not be roused by anyone, including the Hawaiian hospital doctors.

CHAPTER TWENTY-SEVEN

BRANDA'S HEART AND RESPIRATION RATES remained normal during the flight back to St. Louis.

"But I can't get her out of the coma," Mitch told the flight crew, nursemaids, Sean and Cynthia. "I'm very glad you're all with me. And I'm glad you're a nurse, Cynthia."

"I thought hearing the twins cry would make her think it was time to get up and nurse," said Cynthia. "I know they are weaned, but it seemed like they wanted her or something. Strange," said Cynthia.

"I've heard babies can sense things grownups can't," said Mitch. "Maybe this is one of those times."

After reaching St. Louis, Mitch admitted Branda to St. John's Hospital. Every specialist he could think of was called but after several days there was no change in Branda's condition.

During one of Sean and Cynthia's hospital visits to see Branda, Mitch said, "She looks like she's just sleeping. She is so beautiful."

"Do you remember once telling me if she ever got really bad you might have to drop her case and have me get her another doctor?" asked Sean. "Have you ever actually thought about doing that?"

"Early on I did, but not now. I love her too much and could never leave her no matter what happens," Mitch said.

Cynthia spoke, "You two are amazing. She hated men and swore she would never again have anything to do with them, and you were an emotional wreck from Helen's death. Now look at the two of you. Head over heels in love and the parents of twins. Life does take some amazing twists and turns. Even with my psychic abilities I don't think I could have foreseen this turn of events. Of course you know what they say about people in comas; even though they can't communicate, they can still hear."

"Yes, that is the general opinion," said Mitch.

"Have the vision people ever told you anything about her final outcome?" Cynthia asked.

"Yes," said Mitch, explaining what the vision family had said to him and Branda at the Oriental Hotel. Sean and Cynthia remained sadly silent.

Mitch continued, "I didn't tell you before, because . . ."

"We understand," said Sean. "You keep hoping things will change."

"Yes."

While eating dinner at home the next night, he told Eleanor and Ann, "I'll help you tuck the kids into bed then I'm going to spend the night as usual at the hospital. The security guards are outside but if you need me, call me on my cell phone. Tomorrow I'll come take you and the twins to see Branda for a while as I've done every day. I keep hoping the presence of all of you will trigger something to awaken her."

Eleanor said, "I can't get over how quiet the kids are when they are there. They just sit on the bed smiling and making those soft little baby sounds at her like they're talking, then reaching to pat her hair often."

"Yes, a person has to see that to believe it," said Ann.

Another hospital bed had been put in Branda's room for Mitch to sleep in since, from the beginning, he had insisted on staying overnight.

It was now August 14th. Just before dawn, the vision people awakened Mitch.

"What is it, War Eagle?" Mitch asked.

"It's time to take Branda back to your house. She will be waking up here very soon."

"But why did she go into this coma?"

"She needed rest from her kidnapping ordeal, giving birth, and her ongoing affliction episodes, but mostly it was done to prepare her strength for the months ahead which will be very hard on her and you. Be brave, my son. Be brave. Remember this is the Plan of the Great Holy Spirit and we will be with you even when you can't see us."

War Eagle, Light Moon, Mitch's parents and Branda's all agreed Michele and Mitchell were growing quickly and were beautiful children. After Mitch finished hugging all of the vision family and holding Josh and Jason for a moment, they faded into the usual silvery mist.

Before going, his mother had said, "Do not worry, Son. All will be well."

Shortly afterwards, Branda woke up, saying, "Mitch, where am I? What is going on? Did I faint or something?"

"Yes, you did something. You have been in a coma for weeks. It's August 14th."

"Oh dear, I missed Sean and Cynthia's birthdays."

He had to laugh, then said, "Leave it to you to worry about something like that. You are unbelievably thoughtful."

On the way home, he filled her in on what had happened.

"I'm sorry to give everybody such a scare. I'm also glad the vision family came and explained it all to you. I do feel strangely rested. And by the way, I could hear you and other people talking sometimes."

When the twins saw her coming through the door they would have run to her if they could. Instead they cooed and babbled as if saying "Hi Mom, welcome home." When Marian and Peggy stood the twins by the sides of Branda's wheelchair, each pulled up and held on to the arms.

"Well, would you look at that," Branda said. "They'll be crawling and walking before you know it."

After getting Branda to bed, Mitch put the twins up on it with her. "Oh how I wish I was still nursing them," she said. "I really miss that closeness and nurturing them that way. But I guess the doctors were right. It was sort of wearing me down."

"And you can still hold and cuddle them. Before long you can read them stories," Mitch said.

"By the way, how was the ride home in 'J. George'? I'm sorry I had to miss that. And thank you for that wonderful trip by the way. I really enjoyed it; especially your birthday party and the part just before I passed out."

"Same here and after you recover a bit, we'll do a repeat performance of the last celebration."

"I can hardly wait."

"Branda, I think you should know I sold 'J. George.'"

"I know you have talked about it, but it makes me sad to think about him being gone. Who bought it?"

"A Texas oil billionaire. It was a wedding gift for his new bride. The plane's new name is Lily Jane," said Mitch.

"Well, I hope they get as much enjoyment out of flying in it as we did."

"Miz Lily Jane commented on how comfy' the bed looked so I have a feeling they will," Mitch said.

As time eased on day after day finally reaching October's Halloween date, Branda got her wish to see the twins wear costumes and go trick or treating.

She said, "Michele looks so sweet all dolled up in her little evening gown and Mitchell in his tuxedo. They look like they're going to the Veiled Prophet Ball. And you've taken enough pictures to fill an album."

"Well they are good looking kids if I do say so myself," he said. "Now I'll put them in this double barreled stroller as I call it, and we'll go wow everybody in the neighborhood."

Branda asked, "Have you noticed how Michele's hair is starting to turn blonde?"

"Yes, and I'll bet one day it will be as beautiful as her mother's."

"Mitchell's seems to be staying black like yours and I hope it does," she said. "And I'm glad they are saying mama and dada now and babbling in a way that sounds like they're talking."

"I've heard twins often develop a language they use just between themselves," Mitch said.

"I've heard that too. We'll be on the lookout for that," she said.

Branda, Eleanor, and Ann handed out treats to the kids coming to the house.

"Of course Michele and Mitchell are still dressed the cutest," Ann said. "Naturally," Eleanor and Branda agreed, laughing.

Later, after getting in bed, Branda said, "Mitch, I am so thankful for still being around to see our kids tonight. Remember last year, I said I hoped I would be?"

"Yes, I do."

"I have a feeling I won't be so lucky again. Hold me close."

"I would enjoy doing more than that if you feel up to it," Mitch said.

"Of course I do, but I still don't know how you can desire this disfigured body."

"As I've told you before, I don't just make love to your body, I also think of your heart and soul which are still very whole and complete."

While their kisses, touches, and caresses turned their bodies into physical fire, their lovemaking that night took on an added dimension.

Afterwards, Branda whispered breathlessly, "Oh Mitch. Now I really understand what it means about the two shall become as one."

"That's in the Bible isn't it?" he asked.

"Yes. At one point I felt like I was you."

"I felt that too; like we were blended."

"I've felt that before, but never like this," she said.

"Me too," he said, kissing and holding her tenderly.

That was the last time the two made love. The next day was the beginning of what Mitch eventually called Branda's trial by fire.

The gradual loss of her main body parts began during the night on November 1st. The usual warm weak feeling was strong enough to awaken her.

Realizing what was happening, she called out, "Mitch! Mitch! Hold me. Help me."

Both watched in horror as a small medium size piece of her lower body glowed, changed colors, disappeared, and left the acrid odor.

Suddenly the vision family appeared overhead.

"And now the end is beginning, Branda," said War Eagle. "But remember we will always be with you whether you see us or not. Have faith." Then the silvery mist took them away from view.

By Thanksgiving nearly all of her lower body was gone. Sean and Cynthia had brought over the traditional meal and everybody went through the motions of enjoying that holiday.

Branda had told Mitch, "Thank you for having that small customized bed on wheels made so you can take me to other rooms and out into the garden now and then. I enjoy the change of scenery. It was nice going to the dining room to eat the Thanksgiving meal and see all of the pretty china and crystal table setting again. Also thanks for having those special coverings made that the twins can't pull off. I do not want anyone, especially them, to see what is happening to me. I think the kids wonder sometimes though why I am encased in a sort of fancy loose sack with armholes. I like the idea of having everyday ones as well as fancy; some made from different weights of wool or flannel, some from heavy silk."

"You are welcome for those things. Anything I can do to help you I will do," he said. "And, yes, the kids do seem curious about your new blanket."

She told Mitch, "It's strange that I am even still hungry since my body parts necessary for excretory functions are missing. I hope you are keeping a diary of all of this for medical journals."

"That has been an on again off again project. I kept records at first, but after a while it became too close and personal. I had a hard time writing it down. But during my first conversation with War Eagle at the Oriental Hotel, he advised me to continue. He pointed out that others who develop the same problem might or might not have a vision family to tell them what is happening."

"And perhaps someday, our children might be interested in reading it," Branda said. "And another thing Mitch, now that I am bedridden, please give my wheelchairs to someone who can't afford to buy any."

"All right. There are a couple of children at the orphanage who can use them," he said.

"Perfect."

By Christmas, her abdominal area had disappeared. In January, the fingers on her left hand were gone followed by her right hand fingers in February. All through the holidays and up until the twins first birthday on February 8th, friends came by to visit.

After the birthday celebration, she said, "Mitch, I think you broke even your record for picture taking plus you made a video."

"Well I just can't seem to help it. Our son and daughter are so wonderful."

"I can't argue with that. And you know what has made these last few holiday months even more special?" Branda asked.

"What?"

"Having such a lot of great friends which certainly includes Ella and the other people who help take care of this place. And who else but Cynthia would quit her job and help take care of me? And Lois, the daytime nurse comes more often than Tuesdays when necessary."

"Yes, indeed," said Mitch. "And it is nice of Gloria to come help out too. Now that she has passed her GED test and is in nursing school she really doesn't have much time but she comes here anyway.

"Well, she and Cynthia discuss nursing subjects which Gloria appreciates and says it helps her with her studies; especially when exams are coming up," Branda said. "I'm glad she brings Adam often. My how he's grown. Thank goodness he looks more like Gloria and her family."

"Michele and Mitchell sure enjoy playing with Adam and vice versa," said Mitch.

"I'm also very glad Sean comes to take you somewhere often and is standing by you like the special friend he is."

"Yes, and as you know, Sean has always been more like a brother than a friend," he said.

As one month flowed into another, the developing twins were a constant source of pleasure to Branda and Mitch despite her ongoing losses. The vision family visited often and Michele and Mitchell let it be known they could see them too.

Since she wouldn't allow Mitch to pick up what was left of her and put her on the wheeled bed, she stayed in their regular bed.

"And if you want to move me downstairs, that is fine," she said. "I will understand."

"Never," he said. "I want you here."

"Could you do me a favor?" she asked.

"Anything I can."

"Please bring my favorite Waterford crystal dish that's on the den coffee table and put it here on my nightstand where the sun can hit it and make rainbows. I want to see that again. Bring the larger one you gave me too. Maybe it will make even bigger rainbows."

"Of course I'll get them. And did I ever tell you the twins love those dishes too? They are one of their favorite things. They love touching the dishes and looking at the 'pretty colors' in the sunlight. I put the large one next to the original. And don't worry about the kids breaking the crystal. I've noticed they are very careful as if they know those are special pieces."

"That makes me feel good to know they appreciate beauty," she said.

The last week of June, Branda said, "Mitch, please don't let anyone see me anymore; not even Cynthia, Sean, and Gloria. I don't know what to do about the twins. With only part of my head left now, it is just too grotesque."

"I have already explained to everyone and they understand. But Sean, Cynthia, and Gloria said they will still come in to see you if you need them. They said they will also still come to the house to keep me company."

"They are so kind. Please thank them," she said.

"As for the twins, I've been explaining to them all along that you are sick and don't always feel well. Somehow, I think they understand. The other day, Michele said 'Mama has a big hurt.' That's the term she and Mitchell use for scratches, cuts and the like they get from time to time as all kids do. I told them that you did have a big hurt. Mitchell said he would kiss it and make it well."

"So that's why he was in here the other day, kissing my cheek a lot . . . what's left of one."

"Yes, I imagine so," Mitch said.

"And they also seem more interested in stroking and patting what's left of my hair more than usual lately. I wonder why?"

"I don't know except they have always liked your beautiful hair . . . as I have too." Leaning to kiss her lips which were still intact, he added. "I still love you so much, Branda. Thank you for being my wife, friend, and mother of our children. You have made my life complete."

"As you have made mine, Mitch. I love you more than I can say. And please always remember the thoughts presented in one of my favorite prayers. "Let nothing disturb you, let nothing frighten you, all things are passing, God alone is changeless. He who has patience wants for nothing, he who has God has all things. God alone suffices."

Branda died a few days later on July 2nd. When Mitch awakened that morning she was gone. The only part remaining was one strand of her beautiful blond hair. It rested on the pillow beside him like a token.

Picking it up, he cried out, "Oh God! Oh no! Please not now. I can't live without her."

As his tears flowed, a sunbeam burst through the window hitting the smaller Waterford dish making a brilliant rainbow.

"Oh Branda! You're here. I feel your presence all around me."

Removing the dish lid, he placed her strand of hair inside.

"I'll keep you here in this favorite place of yours."

Noticing a sheet of paper on the floor, he picked it up, reading a part, "Oh I Have Slipped the Surly Bonds of Earth . . . Put Out My Hand And Touched the Face of God."

Too distraught to read the full High Flier creed, he sat on the edge of the bed and cried with his head resting in his hands. Finally looking up, he saw Betty looking back at him. One lonely tear was coming down one of her cheeks. Picking her up, he held Betty for a long moment, comforting her, before tenderly placing the doll back in her chair.

The vision family appeared but Branda was not with them.

Speaking to War Eagle, Mitch asked, "Where is she? I thought she would be with you."

"Not yet. She may have to pass through other places before joining us."

"Will she ever return to the children and me?"

"I do not know that either at this time," War Eagle said. "But for now, I want to give you this urn to bury her in."

"But I have nothing left to bury," Mitch said.

"This is what you are to do," said War Eagle. "You are to take this urn to your garden, and put these things inside; a handful of earth, a handful of water from your pool, and several petals from the roses and other flowers. Seal the urn in a small steel box. Then you may have a funeral service, inviting all of the many friends."

"Is there any special place I should bury the box?"

"In the same place your parents are buried. You are to lovingly open the skin of Mother Earth making a place large enough for the boxed urn."

Mitch did all War Eagle told him to do. Then the following days settled into a routine revolving around the children.

The vision family returned from time to time but Branda was still not with them.

"We do not understand why she is so long coming to join us or where her journey is taking her," War Eagle told Mitch. "The delay must be part of a Grand Plan and it is not time for us to know it."

"I will keep hoping to see her with you one day," he said. "And thank you for coming to see me."

Often he would tell the children, "Thank God I have you." They had accepted his explanation that their mother had gone to heaven but everyone would be back together someday.

Early one September morning, the twins came in to see if he was awake.

Michele and Mitchell hopped up on the bed, hugging and kissing him, saying, "Good morning Daddy."

After playing a bit, the twins got off the bed so they could do their morning inspection of the small Waterford crystal dish as the sun hit it.

"Pretty rainbow," said Michele.

Mitchell had more to say after lifting the lid.

"Mama is coming back," he said, happily.

Stunned at the child's words, Mitch looked inside the dish.

Instead of one, there were now eleven strands of Branda's beautiful blond hair.

ABOUT THE AUTHOR

M S. SANGER HAS WORKED AS an office clerk, magazine and newspaper columnist, newspaper reporter, feature writer, executive secretary, Braille transcriber, and has published a cookbook. She belongs to a local writers' guild and loves to read. She has been married for 61 years, has two sons, two grandsons, one of whom is married, a granddaughter, two great-grandsons, and one great-granddaughter. Sanger is 92 years old.